Striding Forth

Written by Marie Daley

Dedication

To My Dearest Friends without whom I would find my life lacking! You are My Family from My Heart! You know who you are, both before and after FB: Jux, Bob and Jeanine, Dan and Heather, Seth and Evon, TJ and Barry, Tammie and Bruce, Jim T, Ron B, Michael and Kelly, Timar, Kat and AJ, James C, Paul, Wendy and Tim, Yvonne and David, Cat and Mick, Chuck U, John and Beth, Lilia and Glenn, Lorell, Desi and Mike, Diane S, Gwen, Rim, Katrina, Marc, Clay, Dennis, Sean S, Mike T, Tom L, Lou and Elisa, Marna and Tom, Crystal S, Monica, Katherine, Jennifer F, Lisa S, Rose Mary, Andrea D, Charlene, Michele C, Greg, Ken L, Susan G, Caroline and Doug, Andrew M, Jewel L, Kathy R, Ken B, Mary L, Cristi P, Christi B, Susan H, Heather S, Patty, Tamara S, Stephen, Mark, Erika S, and Kiva the Spectacular.

Special Thanks to:

Tiffany for her assist from her warm heart.

The Adventures of Ryes and Garth

Tayna's Dawn

Winterhaven

Winds of Change

Striding Forth

Table of Contents

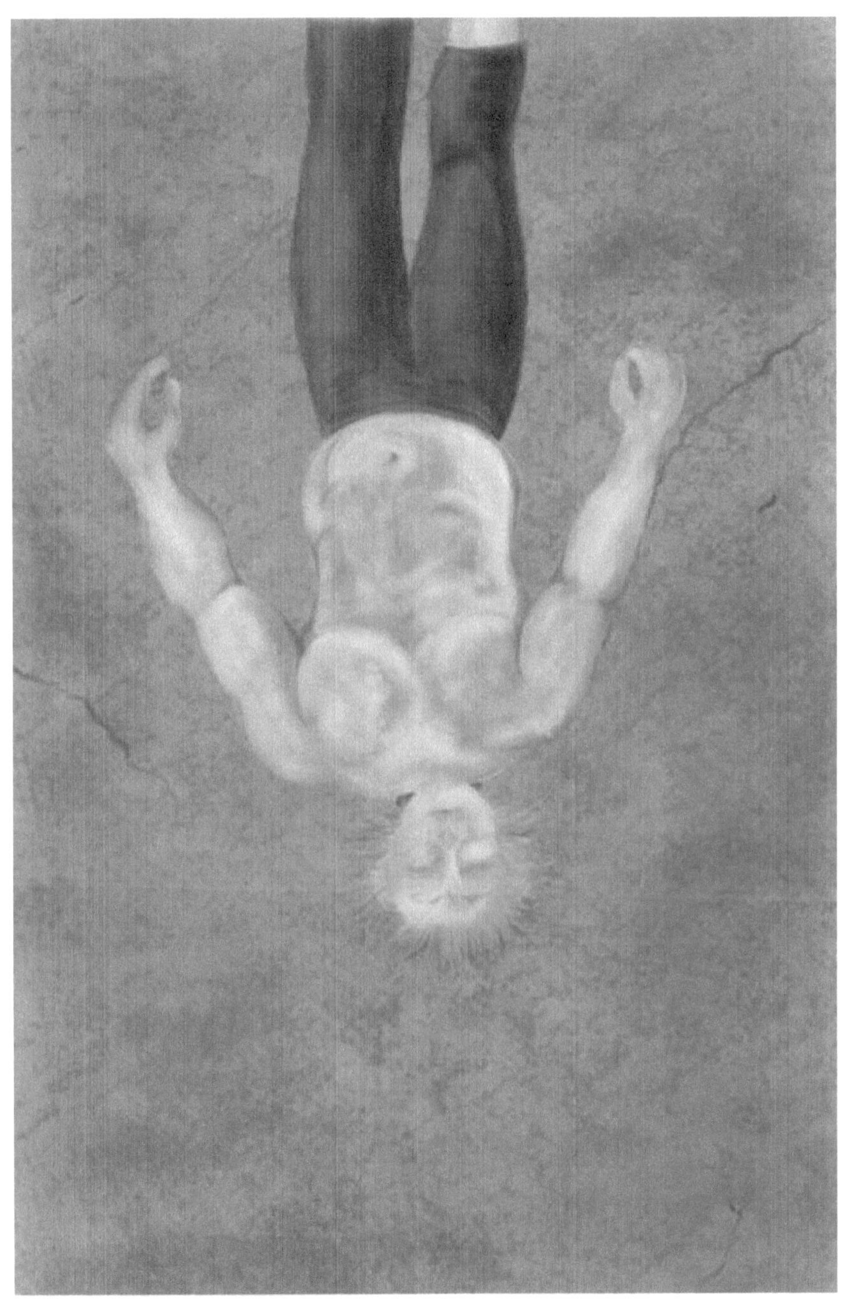

Korman's Punishment original artwork by KM Morgan

Prelude

Messenger

"What is that?" the watch commander demanded of the lowly man, working the scanner board. He fidgeted nervously, not liking such direct attention, especially for something as insignificant as this situation.

"Sir, it's nothing more than a very old piece of their probing equipment, returning to their homeworld. It's moving slowly and probably just bringing them the news of our presence from one of their colony worlds," Kreln replied, sitting back upon his haunches and earnestly meeting the officer's eyes, stalk-to-stalk. "In the briefing last month, it was recommended these be ignored, for they seem to add further confusion to the entrenched enemy, as they sometimes believe that they must launch small rescue missions, which are then considered target practice for our fighters. This then adds to their demoralization," he explained, hoping he wouldn't be demoted for speaking to an officer in such a manner. It was his duty to remind a duty officer of the standing orders in various situations, but sometimes the watch officers took such things as an affront to their rank.

"Very well, monitor it to see that it follows the path it's supposed to. If there are any deviations, let me know. Be sure to pass the situation down, so we can keep a watch for the rescue mission." He then returned to his own post, sitting down upon the dark, carpeted square and digging in with his claws. At least this situation promised more sport later. He made his log entry, feeling very satisfied.

"Sir, there it is," the ensign pointed out the trace upon his screen to the watch commander, as it finally appeared once more. The lieutenant stood at his side to confirm it, too.

"Humph. Okay, dispatch a patrol to check it out and bring it in, if it's something we should take note of," he ordered his lieutenant, then turned to handle more important matters.

"Yes Sir," Lieutenant Patton replied to his back, smiling to himself, relieved. At least it wasn't another wave of enemy fighters making a pass at their defenses. The Darkens, as they were generally called now, were getting more clever with their feints and it was rumored they might break through before much longer. What was left of the Earth fleet was a sorry sight. There was some hope in the newer prototypes being built now; that they could find a way to drive them away from the Sol system for all time. But who knew how long it would be until they'd be ready for combat?

"Ensign Feldman, have it brought in immediately," he ordered, knowing it'd be done with alacrity. Funny the way this thing slipped by their outer patrols... and the Darken patrols, too. He'd have to see to it, personally.

"It really is," a crewman informed him as he stood waiting for scanner confirmations. "An old TX-127 Stinger. It may be almost a hundred years old, but it does have a primitive tesseract unit."

"Did the scans detect any lifeforms, anything dangerous aboard it?" the lieutenant asked.

"No, Sir, it's clean. Almost factory clean," he got in response. He smiled, relieved.

"Is the data cartridge intact?" Lieutenant Patton questioned, looking down at the display, to see it for himself.

"Yes Sir. And from what I can determine from the date stamps, this was only launched three months ago. There's no coordinate information, just locational names and identifications. Looks like someone might be wary of the Darkens, too," the scan tech commented. Patton looked down at him and gave him a nod of his head; it sure looked that way to him, too.

"Consult history files about the proper procedures for data retrieval from this unit, and have it piped directly to my queue," he ordered, then turned to leave.

"Sir?" the crewman stood up, calling out to his back. Patton turned back with a look of tolerance in his eyes.

"Yes?" he asked. The tech looked calm and accepting of his attitude.

"What do we do with the Stinger, itself, Sir?"

"Stow it. We might use it to send a reply back to the colony it came from," he decided.

"Yes Sir." The crewman gave him a salute in response. He returned the salute, and then left for his office. He wanted to see what mysteries this ancient message drone held. He hoped it wasn't merely some colonists whining about their lack of supplies, or weapons. Most of the colonies got the idea real quick that if they cut off all long distance communications and interstellar travel, they were left alone by the Darkens. There was a rumor that some of the stronger, more remote colonies were planning upon striking at the Darkens from their flank, as they sat holding Sol system in siege. He smiled to himself at this, knowing there weren't ANY strong colonies left out there. Earth and her handful of inner colonies were alone, by themselves in this war. But perhaps someone will divert their attention for a short while and grant them some relief.

"Sir, it's a report from one of those old Amitell research stations. It says that they were recently retrieved from orbit and revived by some members of the indigenous population and are the known lone survivors of The Star Quest. I verified all given information and Dr. Cruthers' identification; everything checks out."

"Amitell doesn't exist anymore. Are there any next of kin of the survivors to pass on the information to? Does it contain any information of interest for us?" Captain French asked.

"Your uncle is one of those listed; a Lieutenant Paul Everett French. He was a member of the military support group for the site, Sir," Lieutenant Patton informed him. There was shock in his eyes as he sat back in his chair at this news. "But, at this time he's now younger than you, Sir, since they were in suspension tubes for about eighty years, Earth time."

"Eighty years," he breathed. "He was my dad's youngest brother. Are there any vid shots of the survivors?" The lieutenant anticipated this and immediately handed over a chip. The Captain activated it and studied the image intently. The family resemblance was remarkable. "Copy me all the files and reports. I'll review it and kick this up to Fleet. Thank you, lieutenant, your efforts are appreciated. Dismissed," he ordered, returning the young officer's salute, before he left his office. He turned to his comp unit. He had a few calls to make back home.

Kreln saw the exact same, ancient probe unit returning along the exact same course. He scratched his ear, puzzled. The scans reported no sign of armament, nor anything to grant it any note at all. Since he'd already been reprimanded on this shift for disturbing the watch officer on another trifling matter, he decided to tag it as a piece of space junk to be ignored by the patrols. It was better than have to explain why it was let to pass through their patrols, earlier. He didn't think he would survive another reprimand!

Spring!

Early last spring seven Matlowe villagers set out for the great ruins of Hailys because Sabin was banished for six months for killing a cub-killer; it gave the elders time to collect evidence of the man's guild – one way or the other. It also allowed them to escape Maren's father, Korman, who'd been known to kill others in challenges; Garth wasn't going to ever let him get his claws on Ryes and she didn't want him to get his claws on Garth! During their journey they found the Temple of Doran and her evil plans, but Ryes bested her in a Talent battle. They discovered Hailys and the treasures that could be gleaned from their past. Garth beat Korman in a challenge in Hailys, when he followed them there. After leaving Hailys, they found a deserted human research facility which they named Winterhaven. Later, while Garth and Sabin were away to settle a peace treaty, Ryes called down a derelict, human, colony transport ship, the Star Quest, and she and Maren saved what few humans remained onboard in suspension tubes. Since then the two peoples, both starmen and humans, discovered they could meld; being of one heart in truth. Now they wanted to build a secure future for them all!

"The frost's finally off the ground!" Mitt declared to Garth, as they sat to breakfast in the dining hall. He smiled as he lifted his mug of the human's favorite beverage, coffee, to his lips and took a sip. He found, the last few weeks, he liked it, himself. Wynne grew some of the plants in a special section of her underground garden, for which he was especially grateful. Still, it wasn't a plentiful supply.

"I know, but the wind's still chilly. We were just talking with Darman last night about the plans for his people. It's going to be hard to see most of them leave, if only until late in the fall," he told her. Ryes smiled at this as she put Shaysa back into her tabletop carrier, atop the table they added in next to theirs. It formed a T-shape, but was their best way for her to enjoy some time with the rest of the community at mealtimes.

"This morning we're putting up the frames for the walls of the first apartment building. Weren't you and Axel planning a quick aerial survey? When you finish with that, you can come see where we are in the project," Ryes offered, knowing that with the arrival of spring, they were all going to be busy with the projects they planned out during the long winter months. There were lots of things in the works, and it didn't seem as if they had enough hours in the day to get it all done!

"When's Darman leaving?" Mitt demanded in return, as a frown flitted across her brow. "I forgot the departure of the caravaners was imminent!" She and Minn had finally settled down together, but her adopted son, Sernn, had formed some solid friendships with two of the caravaner cubs and he'd be lonely and probably difficult for a while, with their departure.

"In two days' time," Darman told her, chuckling as he joined them with his breakfast tray in hand. He sat down across from Ryes. "But, the spring gather's not too far off and we'll see you there, as well as the Great Spring Gather. You could get there quickly! You and your flying machines, Mitt! There're times when I envy you," he admitted with a sigh. Rinna laughed and nodded her agreement, having gotten a few chances to fly with her, too. Mitt blushed, not quite comfortable with teasing an elder in return, much less the chief of all the caravaners!

"Well, next year you'll be the envy of all the other peoples when you roll into the towns and villages with your new vehicles," she finally dared. There was laughter and nods of agreement from the others near her.

"Which is why your survey is so important this morning," he returned. "You have to help us find the correct kind of metals in Hailys, for us to salvage for making those fine new rovers. That's why we're not leaving for two more days. I want to be assured that a large enough reservoir exists for all our purposes."

"I'll do the best I can," she promised as Minn and Sernn joined her at the table.

"What're you plotting, now?" he questioned; a warm smile in his eyes. He'd become thoroughly attached to this young woman, whom he now called his wife, in spite of their not formally mating, yet. She wasn't due for her first season until sometime toward the end of the summer - according to Maren. They couldn't wait, even if they already had an idea of what raising cubs was like with the presence of Sernn.

"Plotting? Me plotting?" she volleyed merrily in return, grinning. "You know me too well! Right now the only thing I've got planned is to finish my breakfast and git." Using Mind Voice she reached out to Minn to share her love from within directly, as he shared his in return. Then she included Sernn in their union, once again enjoying the closeness they cherished, then gently let go. "Best way to start the day," she murmured.

"We're going to get those new foundations finished this week," Sabin told Garth, as he paused beside their table. "The computer's unhappy with having the main tower relocated, but we can't box it in with our new construction. It'll ruin our view and defensive capabilities." Garth nodded his head at this.

"Neil's already got it as settled about the project, as much as possible. That's the problem when a system like that gets as complex as it has. It wants to get its plans aired, too," he returned with a chuckle. "Weren't we just setting out from Matlowe about this time, last year?" he questioned. "We haven't even planned on any kind of spring hunt, yet. We're all too busy now to be hunters." This shocked the rest of the starmen around him as they realized he was right! When had they gone from simple villagers to planners and builders of a new city of their own? It wasn't that hunting wasn't important anymore, just that it could safely wait with what they still had stored in the freezers and in dry goods. The spring planting was going to be starting this morning, too, which had Wynne, Shadd, Brenda and Teris all excited.

"No time for hunting? When did that happen?" Sabin returned with a laugh.

"We'll have to make time in a few weeks. Our stores can hold out for a while, but it's always best to have some fresh foods available too," Ryes told him. "I'll look at the schedules and send out some possible dates. We may even get some of the humans to join us. After all, they can't be any worse than the lot of you, when I took you out with me the first time last year," she teased, smiling impishly. This got surprised laughter out of the rest of the former villagers.

"Hey we weren't THAT bad!" Garth protested, looking at her in surprise. The others voiced their agreement with him too.

"You should've heard the way she complained about all the noise the rest of you were making," Rowan put in, as he sat down next to Darman, who was enjoying their banter.

"You never told us," Mitt protested, grinning.

"I didn't know anyone well enough to just speak up. I tried my best to compensate for the racket, instead," she admitted, a merry look in her eyes. "There was a lot of improvement, by the time we found Winterhaven."

"Then maybe we ought to just equip you with recording devices and let you show us how you really go out on a hunt?" Garth challenged his wife, followed by a laugh. She looked surprised at this, then frowned, wondering.

"It'd give you a view and maybe an idea, but I haven't been on a hunt since last year!" she protested. She and Wynne planned an outing to gather some plants tomorrow. Maybe she should get back into the practice a little more, at the same time?

"It's a great idea, even so," Mitt added in support. "Your pupils await your wisdom," she teased outright.

"It won't be the same," she told them, "but, I'll give it a try later this week, after our trip to Matlowe. I'm only happy you decided to let me come along for this one," she told Garth, nudging him in the ribs. He grinned, but Mitt saw a look in his eyes which said he was still very unhappy with the idea. Sabin noted it, too, but since Ardis and Katas had appeared, he gave him a nod of his head and sat down at his table, next to theirs, on the other side of the T. His two small cubs were back to back with Ryes and Garth's, in their carriers, also. Rinna, Sayer and Raby sat down on Darman's other side, grinning.

"I just wish we could come along to help with the cubs," Sayer spoke up, still hoping. Ryes smiled as she shook her head.

"My gosh, you two are around them far more than you need to be. Not that I don't appreciate it, but you should be learning new things and having some fun every now and then, too," she said. "How about if you come out with me on a hunt, after the Matlowe trip and we'll leave Garth with the cubs to mind, for a change."

"Wait a minute, I have to coordinate and run this whole place now. And you want me to baby-sit, too?" he questioned, a smile of mischief in his eyes.

"I seem to recall warning you about this, some time ago," she returned merrily, knowing he was being ornery. "And I think I'm due a sanity break more than ever, with the duties you've handed down to me too." Rinna nodded her head in accord, glad she'd never had to deal with so many little ones at one time, herself.

"That you are, my dear," Dr. Ethan Cruthers spoke up in agreement; sitting down on Rowan's other side. "Why don't the both of you take a break together, later this week?" he suggested. His jovial smile lighting up as he thought they both could truly use one.

The last few weeks had been intense with the work progressing on the repair of the shuttles, preparations for the spring planting, final agreement upon the construction schedule, the continued stripping of the Star Quest, the organization of the investigative teams for both Hailys and Matlowe, the readiness for the departure of the caravaners and the base personnel and equipment which would be accompanying them this year, and the thousand other, normal problems which occurred in an operation this large, and growing. The many young children born by now were a delightful addition to see, in Ethan's mind. His own assistant's pregnancy had him feeling like a grandfather, for the first time in his life. He was so excited and found he could hardly wait for her son to be born!

"Good morning, Doctor," Ryes greeted him, smiling. "I think you're right. Garth and I should go out on the hunt together. Sabin, Torr and Neil can handle things around here for a day. But, we're also taking Sayer and Raby along. So, first I'll have to hunt up some baby-sitters." Rowan chuckled at this.

"Five is more than I can handle all by myself," he admitted.

"I've got to go!" Mitt declared, standing up. Minn pulled her back down, gave her a kiss and let her loose. She leaned down again and gave him a more passionate kiss, teasing him, then winked as she took her tray and headed for the belt to receive it. She was quickly out the door with a sigh. She knew she should volunteer to help with the cubs, but had too many other things to get finished this week. Maybe next time? She hurried to the pad and her waiting chopper. She saw Axel's out and ready too, but he and Kerry hadn't been to breakfast yet. She shrugged to herself, already having her flight plan set, so boarded her machine and began her preflight check. They liked to sleep in some mornings, for which she couldn't blame them.

"I'll let you handle this one," Maren told Tennan, then returned to his studies. He felt, since he was serving as the Chief Medical Officer for Winterhaven, he'd better understand anatomy more as the humans understood it. He found such knowledge actually helped him focus more, when he was applying his Healing Talent.

Tennan stood in the doorway to her brother's office for several long seconds, seeing he was thoroughly immersed in his studies. She blamed the humans for this sudden, in-depth fascination he had for their bodies and the way they worked within. He had an extremely strong Healing Talent, yet thought he should now know medicine and healing as the humans practiced it. What a waste! She finally turned and strode down the corridor to the treatment room where Teris sat awaiting mending.

"Hi Tennan, sorry to bother you today. I can't believe on our first day of planting, I had to go and drop that heavy drum and tear up my leg and foot," he explained, realizing he was nervous and mindlessly chattering like a bird.

Ted had just left the room, telling him Maren said she'd be taking care of him today. It had to be Tennan, of all people. He almost preferred the humans! Medical care was now divided into three levels of treatment. Small matters, like scratches and stomach aches were handled by the human staff. In between things were taken care of by Tennan. And traumas, or deeper concerns, were seen by Maren, who was assisted by his humans. The system worked well, while affording the humans plenty of time and exposure to the starmen, so they could complete their studies of their physiology.

"Sorry to keep you waiting so long," she apologized. "Let me wash my hands, then get a look at that leg of yours." His shoes were off, pants leg cut up to his knee, and the wound areas cleaned with his leg resting atop a sterile pad, awaiting treatment. She stepped over to the sink, still feeling silly about this strict requirement Maren put upon her now. Other than the strange pictures he showed her, she still had no idea what bacteria were, or why she had to do such things to stop their spreading to others. It seemed so childish. She was a Talent, after all!

"Not a problem," he assured her, watching her closely. He knew her, as he felt no one else ever could. He tried to start conversations with her before, but found himself frozen within, in utter fright. He knew Korman held no power here, but his menacing voice still whispered in his nightmares, late into the night. Tennan quickly washed her hands, then dried them on the disposable towel, tossing it into the waste chute.

"Let's see now," she said smiling, as she stepped over and gently placed her hands upon his leg. She closed her eyes, centering herself within, extended her healing abilities, mending the deep gashes and shattered bone. Still, it took longer than she thought it should, as something tugged at the corners of her mind, demanding attention. When she finally finished, she stood for a few moments, using her Talent to take full measure of her patient's health condition, then withdrew. She opened her eyes, realizing she stood practically nose to nose with Teris, as he sat upon the treatment table. Then, it hit her... HE WAS THE ONE! His scent was unmistakable; she'd know it anywhere! She gasped, as she suddenly stood frozen to the spot in utter shock.

"I..." Teris started, not sure what to say. The look in her eyes said it all, already. She knew!

"Did he truly give you any choice in the matter, at all?" she asked in a low voice, her eyes glued to his as her heart was hammering in her chest.

"No, he didn't. I guessed it was you, but he told me he'd rip my guts out and let me die slowly if I ever breathed a word about it to anyone - especially you! I've wanted to tell you for such a long time," he admitted. Somehow, voicing the threat aloud seemed to melt its power and he felt free for the first time in a very long time. He smiled for her at last.

"How could I ever thank you for fathering such a beautiful daughter?" she teased in return, tears in her eyes. "I know what my father's like and could well understand why you never spoke up before." Suddenly, she threw her arms around him and rested her head against his shoulder. He put an arm around her, then turned upon the table so he could hold her more properly. She wept quietly as he held her, crooning to her in a soothing tone.

"Do you mind if I see Tian, sometime?" he asked, as her crying seemed to abate somewhat, after several long minutes. She pulled back, looking up to him with a happy smile and wiping at her eyes.

"Of course you can," she assured him. "She's in my office right now, taking a nap. Come on," she urged. Teris looked surprised, then jumped down off the examination table, grabbed his shoes and followed her out the room. She held onto his hand, as if she'd never let him go. He smiled to himself at this, hoping. She was his mate after all, and the only woman he wanted to be with.

They went into her office and she closed the door to afford them more privacy. She stepped over to the crib and gently pulled down the light blanket, so he could see her all he wanted. Teris leaned down, gently nuzzling his own daughter for the first time, tears coming to his eyes. The only scents he caught from her were hers and Maren's. He craved to hold her, but didn't want to wake her yet. He had so much to talk with Tennan about first.

"Maren tried to restore my body to its proper rhythm. Apparently, our mother had accelerated my development, so I came into my first season far too soon. Now I'm due for my next one in a few months. He thinks my third should be more on track, once more. So, since we already mated once - not by choice for either of us - I was wondering if you wanted to try it again freely? I'll understand if you don't want the `honor,' once more. I can only imagine that you don't hate me for what my father did to you the last time." She practically held her breath. She'd been trying to decide whom to approach, but hadn't settled upon anyone yet. Here, at least, they'd been together before, even if it was blindfolded. He was someone familiar.

"Your father terrified me the last time," he admitted, meeting her eyes. She suddenly looked crestfallen. He stepped closer to her, taking her into his arms, smiling. Tennan looked up to him, surprised. "I'd love to mate you again. You were my first and I don't see any reason to take up with anyone else," he assured her. A bright smile instantly swept across her face, as she threw her arms about him and stretched up to kiss him. Teris returned the kiss passionately. His heart was beating wildly, wanting so much more. She seemed to catch on, as she nodded toward the small couch across the room.

"Let's take a few minutes to make sure everything's working well. I wouldn't want you to have to go back to the fields, without a thorough check," she teased. He chuckled as he nodded his head in agreement, following her lead. Perhaps this "accident" had been fated today? He surely felt it was his lucky day, after all.

"This city was immense," Mitt commented over her radio to Kovin and Phil, as they communicated with her in the new control room. It was expanded with a separate area for computer operations, the regular tower watch station, the regular communications station and now two auxiliary monitoring stations for special projects like theirs. They were looking at the readings the instrumentation on the chopper Mitt was sending them to see.

"And I think I remember ever inch we walked last year," Kovin teased with a laugh. Mitt laughed with him while Phil appeared puzzled.

"Looks like we need a refresher. We didn't cover near enough of it from what I see," she volleyed in return, grinning to herself.

"Only if you're flying us over it, Mitt," Kovin vowed with a sigh, as laughter was lighting up his eyes. "I'm not tackling that on foot again!"

"Really? Ryes is planning a spring hunt. You're sure you want to stay home and just keep an eye on things?" she challenged.

"A hunt?" Phil asked promptly, wanting to be sure he heard it correctly. "A real hunt? For wild animals?"

"How do we get in on it?" Kovin added, avid interest in his eyes now. "I'm sure I'm out of practice!" he added with a groan. Mitt's merry laughter filled their headsets. Darman and Rinna came into the control room, spotted the pair and walked over, noting their mirth.

"Is it good news?" Rinna asked, hope showing in her eyes. Kovin and Phil looked up from their screens and grinned as they gave her a nod.

"There's a plentiful supply to be had," Phil told them, as Darman signed in relief. Both caravaners now had big smiles across their faces.

"The only problem, as we see it, is where to start the extraction. We want to grab the beams and metal plates from a place that won't cause further collapse of the remaining structures inside," Kovin explained, also smiling as he gave them a nod.

"Why would that be a problem?" Rinna asked, wondering. "No one's going to be living there."

"We want to go there to find what we can of our original technologies and who knows, maybe if Winterhaven gets big enough, we'll have to use what's left of Hailys for living space?" Kovin replied, chuckling at his humor. Darman's eyes took on a speculative look, as he thought on it.

"So, did they have lesser villages ringing the larger city?" he asked, wondering. Mitt, who'd been listening to them through the headset, shifted her flight path further north.

"Tell Darman there was nothing like that to the south, nor east sides. I'm headed north to check there," she told them. Her eyes centered on the towers, which were still distant, as curiosity lit up in her heart. Phil repeated what she said for the caravaners. Darman gestured for one of the headsets and Kovin took his off and handed the fragile-looking device to him. He quickly donned it with now-practiced ease, giving him a nod of thanks.

"Mitt, why not look near that space ship landing place Ryes was telling us about last month? Where they were Time Walking to see her aunt?" he asked, hoping. "Wouldn't they have to stop the city's buildings to keep the people safely away from the star travelling ships?"

"That would sound right," she returned, "Give me a few minutes to get over that way." She changed her course again; a little disappointed but promised herself to check out the north towers soon. Since they'd been to the space port before, the location was set into the nav system. After another half hour, she was finally over the area where Hailys did, indeed, end before the starport complex began. It surprised her after a fashion, as she grinned to herself chagrinned.

"What do you think now?" she asked over her mic, having been listening to the others discuss the coming hunt. The caravaners were explaining how a larger hunt should be conducted to the younger men. This reminder that there was something more important that needed their attention brought them all back to the screens. Mitt ran a slow sweep of the area, going further towards the starport in small increments to give the instruments time to get a good reading.

"That is amazing!" Rinna's voice was clearly heard over her headset. Mitt grinned to herself as she wondered if the men even noted that she'd taken over. During the winter months she'd gotten to know and understand how Rinna used power subtly to get what she knew needed to be done, accomplished. She didn't need to be loud and demanding, as her own sister usually behaved. She got things done with a quiet air of command, akin to her brother's demeanor. People listened and obeyed. Mitt imagined she just gestured for Darman to hand over his headset and he did without thinking about it. She smiled as she imagined he was well trained through the years they'd been together.

"This looks like the place we should start," she agreed. "We only have to figure how to get it out of there."

"We do have Ryes and I believe she could use the practice," Rinna wisely counseled. Mitt could hear the teasing smile, in her voice.

"Yes, we do," she responded, her own grin widening. "And yes, she does need the practice," she agreed. She continued her flight out to the middle of the starport area, marveling at how huge this area had been, too. And she noted the scans showed whole starship shapes below. This was something she suddenly wanted, too.

"After the hunt," Darman finally put in, having noticed the screen and the readings before them. As he had taught Ryes many things about life when she was younger, she'd taught him many things about how to deal with the human technologies they lived among now. While he didn't understand all the instrumentation was displaying, the metals he did note and understood.

"It's an amazing treasure trove," Phil commented, as he and Kovin had given their attention back to the displays too.

"Are those starships?" Kovin questioned, not believing his eyes.

"I think so," Mitt returned. "And quite a few seem to be intact."

"We need them," Rinna declared suddenly, as if voicing what was already in Mitt's heart. "Those are our true future!"

"I believe you're right, Grandmother Rinna," she replied, feeling the truth in her words.

"But first, let's start with Tayna and new vans to travel the roads. Then we'll worry about the stars and the good and evils they might contain," Darman insisted.

"And that looks like a warehouse area, probably for the starport," Phil supplied, surprised so much seemed intact. "We need to check them out further!"

"Come on home, Mitt. We have all we need," Kovin advised, grinning. "We have a hunt to plan, first." She laughed at hearing this as she turned for home.

"On the way," she said. She took scans as long as she flew above the ruins, hoping for as much information gathered in one trip as possible. You never knew what true treasures still lurked below.

"Taroom!" Nalin called out as she was reluctant to trespass in his new home, which they were busy building in Matlowe, itself. The walls were up and the roof was up and they were working away on the

inside. The most amazing part of this house was it was two-story!
The first ever in Old Matlowe! It'd been the talk of the Village all
winter long. People from Winterhaven had come over to help with the
building, as well as repair and pour new foundations nearby. People,
who'd come in from Riverward, and now some other hamlets and
villages out of the east, were also helping in turns; learning the new
skills in building sturdy new homes; homes they'd soon be living in,
themselves. Many relished a winter free of the crippling snows and
were finding ways to live their lives anew.

"Nalin," he answered her call, appearing in the doorway, "How
can I help you?" He wiped his hands off on a rag, as a tired smile
graced his lips. She returned the smile, happy to have given him an
excuse to take a break.

"Kort says we're leaving tomorrow and that Axel dropped off
something for you from Rowan. It's a big box that was heavy," she
replied.

"From Rowan? Truly?" he questioned, wonder in his eyes at
this news. He glanced behind him, then back to her. "Give me a
moment and I'll go back with you." She nodded, expecting it. He
turned and walked up the wide stairs to the second level. She heard
him talking to someone up there, then appeared a few moments later,
practically running down the stairs. She giggled at this.

"What?" he asked, grinning widely. "It's a little like an
unexpected Winterfest gift." She nodded and they both walked back
towards the Yuri; sometimes racing each other while laughing. The
old, crumbling walls that had once lined this path were now gone.
The world was opening up around them, again.

Kort was pulling out the last few boxes to load into his van.
They were getting everything ready for the journey's start tomorrow
morning. The fact that only three families would be leaving from
Matlowe for the first time in all caravaner history made it a
memorable start for their annual departure. They were actually
leaving three other families here to stay the whole year in Matlowe!
That was amazing! The rest of the caravaners would be leaving from
Winterhaven. Some would be following them to the east or north,
while others would be headed west, or south. The business of the
land lay before them. It was a lot of work to maintain peace and
order, but it was a life to which they each dedicated themselves fully.
And this year a handful of humans would travel with them to learn a
little of their ways and the peoples of Tayna, as they could. It
promised to be an interesting year!

Rowan, Darman and Rinna's home had been fully stripped of
all their personal possessions. Most of the furnishings had been left
behind and the home now served as a small community gathering
place for this small collection of homes and families. There were new
rugs and paintings supplied by Darman and Rowan, who took their
own ones back to Winterhaven. The bedrooms were now meeting

rooms and Rowan's loom room was now a small library with several bookshelves with books to be shared by all living in their small community. More had been saved from the fires of Riverward than was expected. The loft now served as a classroom so their children could all learn reading and writing. And the great room was the inside meeting room when things needed to be discussed or shared. The kitchen was still the gathering place for the hunters. Having freedom and new responsibilities had finally freed the people from the fire's terrors and sorrows at last. Kort paused and realized he was going to sorely miss both New Matlowe, which they'd all fallen into calling this area now, and Winterhaven. In his heart, they were both his true homes and where he planned to retire, when it was time.

"Kort!" Nalin called out, waving, as they came out of the trees. He laughed as he waved back; glad she'd been quick in her errand. Nahees' sister was always someone he'd found could count upon to help. He set down his box and waited for them to join him.

"Thanks for coming," he told Taroom with a smile and nod.

"What's this about a box sent by one of the flying machines - just for me?" he asked amazed. "It sounds extravagant," he added. Kort laughed and nodded his head in agreement.

"Darman also sent some things for the rest of us, as well as for those who are staying this year. Elders do seem to get what they want done, accomplished," he replied.

"That they do," he agreed. Kort gave him a sweeping bow in jest and both men fell to laughing. Nalin swatted at him playfully.

"I have to make sure all my things have been properly packed!" she declared as she stepped up the porch and into their home.

"In another four years you're going to have your hands full as suitors start seeking her out," Taroom observed. Kort nodded his head, having turned to watch her disappear down a hallway inside, then turned back.

"That I will," he said, then sighed. "Let's get your box, now," he added and gestured Taroom follow him. He had a small storage cabinet built into the one side of his home, as did some of the other caravaners. Right now it was unlocked, so he opened it up and gestured at a large green box. Taroom ran his hand across the top, then down the sides; wonder playing in the depths of his light brown eyes at this curious container.

"It's made of metal?" he asked, unsure. It was finely made!

"In part, and a substance called plastic. The humans have many such and have given a few to us to have, too," he related.

"And this box is mine to keep?" he questioned, wondering. Kort gave him a nod and smile.

"It is," he assured him. A big grin broke out across his face as laughter lit up his eyes in joy. "Let me help you with it. It's pretty heavy." Kort squatted down and lifted up on one end as Taroom hefted the other. They carried it over to a nearby table and set it down carefully. "Well, are you going to open it?" he teased, wondering if he could figure out the clasps that sealed the box, on its front side. It didn't take Taroom long to figure it out as he pulled the latches up, releasing the slender metal loops that held it locked tightly. He pulled the loops free then slowly opened it to peer inside.

On the very top was a beautifully-made green and blue blanket. Taroom laughed as he ran a hand across the weave, noting how soft it felt. It was fine, indeed.

"He's learning to use some of the new fibers the humans have available and loving it. The dyes are amazing too and hold the colors well," Kort explained, tugging on his new shirt which was an amazing shade of blue. Taroom nodded his head.

"This in itself, as well as the box, are great gifts," he said, then Kort pulled back the blanket to reveal the real treasure beneath. Taroom gasped, then gently fingered the tools and books that lay there before him. Tears sprang to his eyes as he picked up a wide leather belt with many tools and a few devices hanging from it. He shook his head amazed. Aylita walked around a corner and saw him holding up the belt. The tools were so new they gleamed in the sunlight, dazzling her eyes. She stepped closer to see them for herself.

"Oh, Taroom, where did you get such a marvel?" she asked breathlessly, wondering.

"From Rowan. He sends us some late Winterfest gifts," he told her. She helped him fasten the belt around his waist and admired it with joy.

"He's an Elder with great wisdom," she commented. "Your name's carved into the tools, too, so no one else can claim ownership!" Taroom handed her the blanket and her eyes misted with tears as she held it and cuddled it in happiness. "This is amazing!"

"And these books," Kort said, seeing what some of them were titled. "Rowan said he found them among his things and wanted them to be yours, most especially, Taroom. He'd forgotten he had them. He said they're for a man with forward-looking vision."

Taroom picked up one that caught his interest immediately. He opened it up to see pictures of the tall buildings of Berrals and illustrations drawn about their structures within. Perfect material for a carpenter! He laughed.

"I think he wants me to remake Old Matlowe to be a great city to challenge the cities in the east," he stated, grinning as he looked at the other books still in the box. There were also more tools.

"I think he wants you to create what you find in your heart with new ideas for how to make it happen," Aylita suggested, grinning.

"He is the wisest Elder I have ever met, as well as the most generous," Taroom finally answered, still awed it was all for him and his family.

"That's the truth," Kort agreed with a laugh. "Let's get this over to your home, now." Taroom gave him a nod and gladly closed the box, locking it again, then lifting his end, using the sturdy handle built into it, as Aylita followed with the blanket in her arms and a big smile alighting her face in joy.

New Possibilities

"You're sure you've got enough backup batteries?" Ryes questioned, worried. It was like sending her own cubs out into the world for the first time.

"Yes, Ma'am," Eric Crandall assured her with a laugh; enjoying her fussing. She was just like his own mother, only much younger! "I'll be sure to call in my reports, regularly," he promised, trying to appear solemn once again.

"And I'll keep a close eye on him, to make sure he doesn't get himself into too much trouble," Rinna promised with a smile. It was hard on Ryes to see them go off into the unknown, as she knew it. She sighed and finally smiled, then threw her arms about Rinna, giving her a hug and kiss. She was her grandmother and always in her heart.

"Thanks, I don't know what I'd do without you," she admitted, as she held onto her. Rinna laughed as she hugged and kissed Ryes, in return. This was the first time in years they weren't crying upon parting from each other! They were both smiling! Next she hugged Eric closely, wishing him well in a soft voice.

"I'll be careful," he promised with a chuckle as he let her go. She gave him a nod then turned for the next of her charges, Paul French, who stood before Damian Hacker, Steven Granada, Wyatt Thurlowe, and Gracie Ortega. These people were finally chosen to journey with the caravaners this year, to officially survey what of Tayna and her peoples they could; to collect information they all needed at Winterhaven. She felt closer to Eric, because he put in so much time serving as her and Neil's aide, but still knew she'd miss the others, just as much. Paul threw up his hands with a merry chuckle and smile.

"I promise to be careful, too," he assured her, then threw his arms about her for a big bear-hug. He was a big guy who was as tall as Torr and well-muscled as Sabin, yet was one of the gentlest men here. Ryes laughed as he released her, giving him a nod of her head.

"You'd better come back in one piece, too," she threatened, teasing him. Then stepped over to Damian, who'd helped watch after the younger cubs, and it was hard to see him leave. He'd been so good at teaching them!

"Be careful, or you'll have all the kids here upset with you," she reminded him, trying to look serious.

"And their mothers, too," he finished, smiling. The children had made a "special book" for him with each of their pictures and a small drawing, story, or poem written especially for him by each of them. Ellen helped them create it and it touched him deeply. Ryes laughed at this in full agreement, as she hugged him too.

"We'll see you at the spring gather," Steven promised, as he was next, suddenly feeling like he was being cut off from all he knew of as "safe" in this world. It was daunting, yet exciting.

"Yes, we'll expect you to be there on time," she teased. Steven was one who usually showed up to their meetings a few minutes late. He was always trying to do so many things at once, he often forgot. He laughed at this, nodding his head in agreement.

"Since Missa will be driving, I think I'll be able to make it," he agreed. There was laughter from the caravaners as they knew him well by now, too.

"Wyatt, don't get so wrapped up in your studies that you forget to report in." Ryes gave him a hug, too. He blushed as he returned it. The community here was small enough that after the long winter, everyone knew each other well by now.

"I'll try not to," he promised, going as far as he felt he could. This was a fascinating world, and now that they knew more about its origins, there was even more to learn. He was excited about this journey. Tayna called to him in a way he could never explain to anyone else. Ryes saw his inner struggle and laughed as she nodded her head.

"At least give it a try," she agreed, knowing the caravaners he'd be travelling with would keep an eye out for him, too. Finally, she stepped over to Gracie. She was so very reluctant to let her venture out with a small group of caravaners alone. She was bound for one of the northeastern routes, heading for Cootain. They wouldn't be at the spring gather, as they had a far distance to go, but would be back for the fall gather. At least, once they had their communications satellite up in orbit, they'd have clear reception for her reports. It should be up well before they reached Cootain.

"Keep on the alert," she advised, "The caravaners may know you, but few others would behave in a civil way around you. That Badge of Passage should help, though. We'll signal you, as soon we have the new system operational," she promised. Gracie gave her a solemn nod of her head, and then threw her arms about her, hugging her tightly. Ryes returned the hug with a heartfelt sigh. With Gracie being a woman, some customs might be slanted against her. It was why she asked Darman to give her a Badge for this journey, which he did gladly with true understanding.

"I'll be very careful," she promised. "I'm going to miss you," she added as she kissed her cheek and pulled back from their embrace. Ryes smiled at last, her stomach still in knots.

"I'll miss you, too," she told her, then looked to the others, "all of you." There were replies mumbled and shouted, and then they started to break up, heading for the vans and families to whom they'd been assigned, getting last minute good-byes from the others, who'd be staying here in Winterhaven. Garth threw an arm over Ryes' shoulder, hugging her to his side.

"They'll be fine," he assured her. She chuckled as she looked up to him.

"I just wish I could go along," she admitted. He laughed at this, knowing her well. Yes, this was what lay in her heart for a very long time.

"You'll just have to content yourself with flying over everyone's heads by helicopter, rather than the longer journeys," he teased with a merry smile in his eyes. "I think our journey here to Winterhaven was the last, old-fashioned way of traveling for you." She sighed, knowing he was right, giving him a nod.

"At least I still get to go out hunting," she ventured. Even if she could feel the death of what she stalked, the forest was still her home and sanctuary.

"For now," he hedged as he waved good-bye to Darman. "I can envision a time when we both might be too busy for such leisurely pursuits." Ryes looked up at him sharply, wondering what he meant. Then realized what he might've implied and sighed. If things kept up the pace they'd taken, they might all be too busy to be simple hunters and gatherers. It saddened her in a way she could never explain.

"Why the long face?" Ardis demanded, seeing Ryes suddenly looking downcast - most unusual for her! "I'm sure they'll all be fine," she assured her with an encouraging nudge and smile.

"Oh, it's not that. Just... all the changes we still have before us," she explained, spreading a hand out, palm up. Garth gave her a nod of his head, agreeing with her phrasing. It said it all.

"We'll talk about it later. We have to check our things for the trip to Matlowe, the day after tomorrow," he ordered. Sabin gave him a nod of his head, seeing there was something more on his mind, as he threw an arm about his wife's waist.

"Come Ardis, let's go check on our cubs," he urged. She gave him a strange look, but allowed herself to be led away. Ryes sighed heavily.

"The humans are having the time of their lives relearning how to create with their hands, once again. And here we are, having the time of our lives, getting to learn to create with their handy machines. We're surely a mixed lot," she commented as she looked up to her husband, mischief in her eyes. "I know a great place where we can catch a few minutes, just for ourselves," she teased in a low voice, smiling.

"Too late, Maren's heading toward us and he doesn't look happy about something. I bet he needs to talk with you," he told her, a sigh of regret following. Not that they didn't get time for each other at night, but it was rare when they could frolic together at any other time. He put his arms about her and kissed her heartily, then released her as Maren stepped up to them.

"I hate to bother you, but could I talk with you a moment, Ryes?" he asked, "cousin to cousin," he added. She gave Garth a wink, then let him go, turning to see the look in Maren's eyes. It was a serious matter indeed.

"Anytime," she assured him, "How about if we take one of the rovers out to gather some plants I didn't get a chance at yesterday?" she suggested. He smiled. It'd give them some time away from interruptions here in the facility, and the chance to get out and unwind from the pressures on them both. He hadn't been outside of Winterhaven since he went to fetch her out of the icy sleet of a powerful storm on Winterfest day last year!

"Sounds like the best idea," he agreed. Garth smiled and gave her a nod of his head in agreement.

"I'll take care of our cubs and see that Sabin, Neil and Ted handle things for you two, so take your time," he told her. She smiled her thanks as she grabbed Maren's arm and headed toward the garage with him in tow.

"Wait, shouldn't I tell someone where we're going?" he laughed out, wondering if they could just take off like this anymore. She laughed, shaking her head.

"The Base Commander just told us to take our time. What do you think? Between Tennan and Ted, I think they'll be able to handle things in the medical department without you for a little while," she informed him. He suddenly realized she was right! He took the lead, now pulling her along.

"Let's get out of here before Jim Dawe decides he has to escort you," he reminded her. "If I can't look out for you all on my own, what good am I?" he added, realizing he meant it. After all, Garth trusted him to take care of her! She laughed as they picked up their pace to a quick trot. They ended up racing to number seven, each opening a door and jumping inside. Ryes kicked the engine to life and pulled out quickly. She saw Bethany waving to her, but merely waved back as they pulled away, up the road heading toward Hailys.

"We made it," she commented, smiling merrily as Maren relaxed back into his seat. Now they both pulled on their restraints, otherwise the computer would bug them about it, nonstop.

"Ah, I've missed this," he told her, as his gaze watched the scenery outside moving quickly past them; he was well past being distressed with her speed.

"I got to go out yesterday, but yes, I've missed running out with only you, cousin. It sure beats having an entourage in tow." He heartily agreed, having seen the way she had to plan each expedition out, making sure she hadn't forgotten anyone, or anything. No more making a quick dash for a rover! He wasn't quite ready to talk with her, suspecting anyone in the control room could tap into their conversation over the rover's radio, so bided his time until they pulled up beside the building where the bubblenut trees stood upon. He smiled as he recognized it.

"It wasn't so long ago, yet it seems like it was a lifetime ago," he told her as they got out of the rover, grabbing a sidearm each and a small water container. Ryes smiled back at him, fully agreeing.

"It was an eternity ago," she agreed with a laugh, securing her door. She walked around to the back and took out a large sack to put bubblenuts in, for everyone back in Winterhaven to try. The first ones should be ripening by now. They climbed to the top of the hidden building in companionable silence, memories of all that passed in this last year fresh in both their minds.

They laughed like cubs as they gathered the fallen nuts; Maren daring enough to climb the biggest tree to shake down more. It was a banner year for this old tree, its branches drooping under the weight of the nuts growing upon them. They finally sat, looking down upon the avenue, where they spent so much time last spring, trying to pry out the secrets these old ruins held fast. They were barely beginning to decipher what the crystal rods held, having finally unlocked and copied the information. They munched happily upon the nuts, talking about the journey they made last year.

"Tennan told me yesterday that Teris is Tian's father and she's looking to mate with him when she next comes into season in a few months," Maren finally told her with a heavy sigh. "It seems she just figured it out."

"You don't sound too surprised," Ryes observed, wondering.

"I followed Korman after he set Tennan up in that old house. I was worried that our father wanted to try mating her, first. So, I saw who he picked and heard how he threatened him. It's no wonder Teris kept quiet. Disembowelment is a foul way to die," he told her, his mouth twisted down in distaste.

"You don't approve of Teris?" she asked, seeing this seemed to go deeper. He was very upset over something.

"Not really, but she won't listen to anyone. So, if I leave her alone about it, she may give up on him and look elsewhere? It seems everyone I suggested is wrong in her eyes." He met Ryes' eyes with the rest of his inner burden begging to be voiced. He just didn't think he could. "When did my sister become like my mother? After I moved out, she really changed! All I did was turn my back for a few moments."

"Look at Rowan! Last year he was ready to curl up and die in a dark corner, now even I can't keep up with him! I have to scold him for running in the halls, as if he were a cub!" Ryes protested, shaking her head. "The only one I know I can blame is myself. After all, if I hadn't taken the lot of you out hunting and somehow gotten enmeshed in your lives, I might've fallen under Doran's clutches, without Garth's life to fight for. And after all that, we find Winterhaven and look where that's led us all." Maren laughed at this, nodding his head in agreement.

"I still don't think you would've fallen under Doran's power, though. But, I do know we saved the lives of most of Matlowe Village when we found our new home. Even if several villagers moved in with us, it still left more food behind for the remainder. They owe you in a way they'd never understand," he scolded her, teasing. She laughed merrily as she shook her head again.

"Tennan has to live her own life now," she finally sobered, reminding him with a sad smile. "I know you're littermates, but she's got her own path to tread. She still doesn't approve of you and Dotti and nothing we've done will ever change her mind. She IS just like your mother!" She saw a pain go through him at the mention of Dotti's name and frowned. Could it be what lay at the heart of his problem? Were they having troubles of some kind?

"Dotti..." he started, not quite sure where to begin. Ryes closed her eyes and grabbed his hand. If he felt this deeply about it, it had to be something serious, for sure. If so, the most direct way was always the best. Maren felt better as he saw what she intended, so closed his eyes too, trying to relax as he centered himself. He reached out to her, still reluctant.

There was the presence of her pool of power, which never dimmed, even when she was unable to tap it from the end of her pregnancy until just a few weeks ago. He knew her frustration with being unable to use her abilities, but now felt her irritation as Ted and the others wanted to conduct a series of tests to see exactly what she could do and try to fathom how. She was not a willing research participant.

He finally opened up and let her see what bothered his mind and heart so deeply. Dotti pined for a child of her own to hold. With Brenda's little one and the large number of cubs recently born, she felt left out of things. It was something Maren knew might happen, but so far everything he tried to distract her with didn't last. He was helpless to know what to do. She vehemently refused to consider an artificial insemination by one of the human men, here in Winterhaven and he was unable to give her what she craved so deeply.

It was true that they had 23 chromosomal pairs, as the humans, and they were closer genetically to them than more than ninety-eight percent of the other animals upon their homeworld, but there was still that one point six eight difference in their genetic coding, which lay as a great gulf between them.

"She wants me to try using my Healing Talent to help fertilize a child within her. A child which would be from both of us. If I do this, it could result in a terribly misshapen thing, which would be better off never being conceived," he admitted. She felt his strong tide of emotions on this issue. He wanted a child as much as she, but thought it would never matter to him if it were fathered by another human, as it does in her mind. Ryes understood Dotti's view, too well. Maren was where her soul and heart rested. No one else's child would ever come to mean the same.

"You have to try," she pressed. "I know what this means to you, especially within, to consciously create something with your Talent which goes against nature, but for the sake of both of you... please try. If you need my help, I'm here" she offered, understanding this was something he could never breathe near his own sister. Her own Healing Talent may be weak next to his, but it existed and she could lend him the strength with her pool of power to tap for such a task. "Could your Talent operate upon such a deep scale, as to make the child `right' from its very inception?" she questioned, wondering with the finite scope required for such a level of healing. Mentally he smiled at her, shaking his head.

"I've no idea. I know that the more I actually know about the body and its functions, the better and faster I can direct my abilities, but I've never tried it on such a scale, before. What happens if I fail and it's mis-formed?" he pressed.

"What did we do with Rhin?" she returned, "Either redirect it to the way it should be, or abort it and be ready to try again, later. She won't give up until you succeed," she reminded him. "You know Dotti, once she sets her heart upon something."

"So, you two come all the way out here to pig out on bubblenuts and have a chat, which you could just have easily have had back home?" Mitt demanded merrily, having joined in, in their inner conversation.

"Mitt!" Maren replied, exasperated, "Can't we have any peace, anywhere?"

"Not you two," she quipped back. "Jim demanded I bring him out to where you went. He's just polite enough to not barge in on the both of you. You know he has to watch your backs, but was happy to see you were both armed, at least," she told them.

"Mitt, this is serious," Ryes told her. "Dotti truly wants to have Maren's child."

"Then he should help her to do so," she agreed. "It'll all work out, I'm sure. You remember ol' Ryun? I bet she still wants to bear a cub, even if she never will."

"Wait a minute, I did forget about her!" Maren agreed. "I'll make sure she can have her own cubs, since we're going to Matlowe the day after tomorrow, anyway," he told them, happy to see there were others he could still be of service to, which he hadn't thought of before.

"If you can try to help her have cubs, why not your own wife?" Mitt pressed. "Maren, I believe in you and know you can do it!"

"I do, too," Ryes added, giving him her full support. He finally gave in, deciding to try at least. "Do you think you'll need my help?" she asked.

"For this attempt, yes I will," he decided. "I've never attempted a healing upon this level and don't want to fumble this one," he told them.

"I'll bring Rhin along, just in case," she returned. They felt that once he accepted the challenge, he could relax again. They withdrew from the inner commune, opening their eyes to the lush, green world about them.

"How about after dinner?" Maren asked Ryes, smiling.

        "How about as soon as you two get back?" Mitt countered.
"That way you can make sure things are settled, one way or the
other, so she can go with us to Matlowe."
        "That's an idea," Ryes agreed, smiling. "If you can pull her
out of the labs, that is," she teased her cousin. Dotti was helping
Bethany with some computer modeling, which Dr. Cruthers decided he
needed done. Bethany admitted to her that Dotti was much better at
it than she was, so was taking lessons from Dotti.
        "For this, it'll be no problem," he promised, standing up and
giving each of the ladies a hand up.
        "Then let's finish gathering these nuts and head on back,"
Ryes suggested, waving to Jim. He strode over to them, looking
unhappy.
        "You know you're supposed to have an escort at all times," he
scolded her.
        "I did," she quipped back, "Maren." She pointed to her
cousin, standing beside her. Jim frowned at this in disapproval. "Just
give us a few minutes to gather more bubblenuts, then we'll be on the
way back home." He gave her a nod of his head, then stepped closer
to look down upon what was an ancient avenue, below them.
        "Nice place to have lunch," he commented, finally smiling.
He'd keep it in mind the next time he and Bethany had time to sneak
off together.
        "It is," Ryes agreed. "It hasn't quite been a year since we
were last here to eat lunch, but the place hasn't changed much," she
sighed.
        "Yeah, Kovin found your trail up here and when we saw the
group below, we knew we'd found you at last," Mitt told them as they
turned and started picking up more of the fallen bubblenuts. "That
was the day you went Time Walking and Ardis started her season. I'll
never forget that one! I thought I'd lost my brother to you, for sure,"
she admitted. Ryes looked at her surprised, as Maren chuckled in
understanding.
        "You have to understand, Ryes. Garth never paid any
attention to any of the other women in Matlowe and the only one to
really occupy his time was watching over his little sister, Mitt. Karr
had Gann waiting upon her, hand and foot, so Mitt felt secure knowing
her big brother always kept an eye out for her. You come on the
scene and suddenly she's second. It must've stung, at the very
least," Maren explained. Ryes straightened up, blushing darkly at
hearing all this for the first time.
        "I'm sorry, Mitt. I never knew..." she started, not sure how to
apologize for something of this magnitude.
        "It's all right. Now I have the big sister I've always wanted,
and still have my brother's love. But, he's so busy now, he doesn't
have much time for either of us. He's the one I really feel sorry for,"
she assured her, smiling.
        It had been exactly as Maren said. The lump in her throat
betrayed her remembered feelings on that day, so long ago. She

decided to get to know Ryes, to understand this change in Garth, so she could deal with it. She intended to split them up, but when she learned Ryes was pregnant, she knew that idea was on the wing. As she sought to find anchorage once more, she discovered Ryes' inner core of steel gave her the strength to find the center within herself. And somehow through it all, she came to love Ryes, as if she were her own, older sister, knowing she could never be the cold, cruel woman Karr had come to be.

"And our cubs will need him more and more, as they grow older," Ryes added in, sighing. "If we can get things going, the momentum should help carry things onward and free up some of his time for more important pursuits." Jim smiled at this line of conversation as he helped gather the nuts with them.

"I can't wait for my son to be born," he admitted. "Maybe if we can use this coming winter to take a break and bond with our families like we should, next spring might be much happier?" he queried, hoping. Ryes and Mitt laughed as Maren looked thoughtful.

"Yes, we'll give it a try. After all, once our apartments are finished, we'll have far more living space for each family," Ryes agreed, then began to look for more nuts. After a few more minutes, they had almost more than they could carry.

"Raya's going to love these," Mitt declared as they carefully tread down the path, down the grass encrusted building.

"Forget Raya, Shadd will be absolutely delighted," Ryes countered.

"She does love these things," Maren agreed, recalling last year when she decided to try growing her own bubblenut trees, so she'd never have to be without. The little seedlings she started last summer beside their creek had survived well through the cold winter. Given a few more years and they'd have their own trees providing plenty of nuts for everyone. Ryes laughed in agreement as they packed them aboard the helicopter, for Mitt to take straight back to Winterhaven, then boarded the rover as Mitt took off.

After lunch, Ryes was going over some of the plans she wanted in place while she'd be out of the office while over in Matlowe Village. She was waiting for Maren to come and get her to help with Dotti. But, Mitt and Axel came in with anxious looks on their faces. It appeared to be important. Ryes stored her program and stood up, ready for anything, she hoped.

"What happened?" she asked, wanting to be direct. Smiles broke out on their faces and Axel gave her a nod.

"Nothing dire, but we need your help," he replied. Mitt nodded, letting him take the lead. "It's time to get to the shuttle engines and we have an idea, which only you can do, from what we know of your abilities." He, too, could be straight to the point most times. She smiled at this, her eyes lighting up. Mitt chuckled.

"Can you spare some time, so we can at least try?" she requested, looking hopeful.

"Sure," she assured them and stepped around her desk. The three of them headed off down the hallway for the shuttle hangar. When they got there, Stephen Fairfax was there waiting for them.

"I don't know why you need me, Axel. I'm more a pure scientist than star craft technician," he told him.

"You're just the person we do need today," Axel assured him, smiling as he gestured him over to the chairs he and Mitt had arranged earlier this morning.

"Good afternoon, Stephen," Ryes said, smiling merrily, wondering what they did have planned now?

"Good afternoon, Ryes," he replied, giving her a nod and smile. He'd never been in a place where the bosses were so open and friendly with everyone, before. He politely held her chair for her as she giggled in embarrassment, then settled onto the seat.

"So, what is it you need all of us here, today?" she asked, looking to Mitt and Axel as they settled into their places. One chair was empty, still. Raya rushed in, a little breathless, but a happy smile upon her face.

"Just in time," Axel said, appearing delighted.

"I had a couple of little ones who needed mommy," she said as she sat down on the empty seat, seeing they appeared ready now.

"They're certainly more important," he replied as the others were all smiles and nodding their heads in agreement. Then his eyes practically gleamed as he looked over at Ryes. "Mitt and I have an idea for changing the engines on these two ships and need your help, Ryes."

"And how do I fit into this?" Stephen questioned, wondering. He'd heard about her amazing abilities, but never thought he'd be included in any important projects.

"You have a unique understanding of the nature of atoms, their structures and bonds, which is invaluable for this project. You know things on a molecular level," he stated, as Ryes appeared puzzled.

"Let's start and see where it goes," Mitt urged as she reached for Ryes' hand, ready to begin. She still had a big grin, as she gave Ryes a merry wink. "How do you know if you can't do something until you try?" Ryes huffed a laugh and gave her a happy nod in return.

"A new day for new discoveries! Anything for you, Sis," she returned as she gripped her hand, then extended her other hand to Raya. Raya grinned as she gladly took it, wondering what kind of wonders they'll find today?

"Everyone please relax and join hands," Raya requested. Axel knew what was needed and immediately complied, while Stephen paused a few moments with his uncertainty and a touch of fear in his eyes, then he grasped both Axel's and Raya's hand and closed his eyes, too. Raya closed her eyes as both Mitt and Ryes had called up their Talents, ready to being. Raya established the meld of minds and managed to get Stephen calmed down and more relaxed as she assured him they'd only share what thoughts he wanted to project to them. Once he was settled, Axel took over, to direct them.

"Mitt has shown me how dangerous and wrong our shuttle engines are. We want to try to remake them by taking them down to the molecular level and reshaping them the way they need to be, to best do the job we need them to do," he let them know.

"Molecular level?" Stephen questioned, wondering and understanding why he was included now. He'd been a chemist before his enforced cryogenic sleep and could help them with the way the atoms should be behaving and the bonds formed. Somehow this pleased him immensely.

"We need you," Mitt assured him, seeing he now grasped his role in this project. Then she and Ryes reached out to the first shuttle engine and the wrongness screamed to their senses through their Inner Sight Talent. The others could see it clearly now, and were shocked.

"Let's use your Manipulator and Fire Shaper to start breaking them down," Axel instructed as he and Mitt took over her Talents and wielded them as if surgeons. She got a feel for what they wanted after a few minutes and with Stephen to help guide her Talents down to the molecular level, they pulled all the molecules of the engine into a dense cloud of loose matter, ready to be reshaped.

"Now for the hard part," Mitt teased. Slowly and carefully they put together the new engines the way Axle, Mitt and the AI had designed them. When they finished they still had plenty of leftover isotopes.

"Finally, we have the truth of the universe in our hands. Let's pull these dangerous atoms apart and remove the danger," Stephen directed. Ryes redirected the energy and heat released as they slowly reformed the molecules to become harmless materials which were far safer to use for other purposes, dumping the inert materials into some empty nearby bins. They could be used by the replicator to create new, needed things. When all had been done with the engines on the first shuttle, they repeated the process on the second shuttle, which went more quickly, now that they had the process established. Once finished there, Axel then had them remove all danger from the Quest's engines, themselves, as well as the remaining, damaged shuttles which were not going to be any more than extra parts for the two they were keeping. Stephen actually started using Ryes' Talents himself, seeing she'd let him use them during the last few ships; showing them an even faster way to do it, now that he understood.

"That was a lot of work!" Ryes complained, feeling drained but deeply satisfied. "And Stephen, that was amazing! I learned so much from you, that I'm still trying to grasp it all." He grinned from ear to ear, pulling his long dark bangs out of his eyes.

"And you gave me a real vision of how to reshape our world, one molecule at a time. You have fantastic powers, Ryes!" he declared, standing up; feeling as if he'd been jogging for the last hour, now. He helped Raya to her feet. She gave him a grateful smile.

"That was amazing!" she stated, still stunned. "I never knew you could build things so complex in such a way. Now I've seen the universe within is as beautiful as the one without!" Her wonder was still shining in her eyes as she looked to the massive bulk beside them.

"I never imagined doing that before either," Ryes told her, "but now I do know a little more of what I can do and am going to have to practice it more on a far smaller scale." She stepped over and gave Raya a hug, then Stephen and Mitt, with Axel last. "Thank you, Axel!" He chuckled, giving her a nod, letting her go.

"I had better get back," Raya said turning for the door, her wonder still glowing in her eyes.

"Me, too," Stephen agreed, still dancing on the clouds as he trailed after Raya. Mitt pulled her aside, after the other two left.

"Did you feel it? It wasn't just a combination of your Talents working in concert," she said, as Ryes gave her a nod; surprise in her eyes. Axel realized it, too.

"So, what're you going to name your new Talent?" Axel asked, joining the women.

"How about Molecular Manipulator?" she asked, laughing. "I feel astounded, but it's unique and operates apart from all my other Talents. It is a new Talent!"

"So, you're a Talent of Many and amazing," Mitt teased, laughing as they all hugged again.

"Smart observation, Mitt," Axel added, laughing.

Village Visit

"Maren," Ryes prompted, seeing he was talking with Jon and Justin in one of the treatment rooms, "we need to get something finished today, before heading for Matlowe tomorrow." He looked over at her, puzzled for a moment, and then a smile broadened across his face.

"Give me a moment and I'll be right along," he promised. She gave him a nod and went to the waiting room, looking at the new wall displays about personal health, until he rushed out and grabbed her hand.

"Let's go," he urged; his joy was shining in his happy brown eyes.

"I kept waiting for you to come and get me, so I finally thought I'd better get you, myself," she mildly scolded as they walked quickly out of Medical, heading for Dr. Cruthers' office. "Did you get a message out to Dotti?" she thought to ask.

"I didn't want to take the time," he chuckled. She laughed, nodding her head. There were always distractions for him in Medical.

"I'll take the lead on this one, then," she assured him, "You wait out here." She gestured him to stay out in the hall as she finally stepped into Ethan's office.

Ryes saw Bethy was gone from the reception desk, so knocked gently on Ethan's door, hoping he was still around. She heard him give permission to enter, so opened the door and peeked around it, her hair falling in a long, curling cascade of a red-gold veil; having skipped her braids this morning. He chuckled and stood to gesture her to enter. A bright smile lit up her face as she came in. Within were Bethy and Dotti, apparently in a meeting with Ethan.

"Sorry to interrupt," she apologized, "but I was wondering if I could borrow Dotti for a special project I wanted to get completed before we head over to Matlowe Village?" she requested. Ethan appeared curious, but gave her a nod of his head.

"We can manage without her today," he replied, smiling grandly, feeling she was up to something. Dotti was blushing and acted as if she had no idea she'd be needed for any project of hers.

"Thank you so very much," she replied, giving him a nod. She pulled back her hair from her face and saw the curiosity alight in all their faces. Dotti stood uncertainly, but came over to join Ryes by the door.

"I'll be back as soon as I can," she promised, turning back to Dr. Cruthers.

"Keep her as long as you need," Ethan said, looking to Ryes.

"Thank you," she replied, then smiled, giving him a small bow, and urged Dotti out and closed the door gently behind them.

"What's up?" she asked as she urged her out in the corridor. She was surprised as she saw Maren was there, waiting for them.

"Hopefully, something wonderful," he told her, taking her hand. "Let's go get Rhin from the ladies," he urged. This had her puzzled, but willingly fell in with them as they hurried down the corridors, lightly laughing in joyous mirth, as if two school children playing hooky from their classes.

"This is embarrassing," Ryes commented as she sat, holding a sleeping Rhin in her arms, as her cousin and his wife made love. She sat in a chair in their bedroom with her back to them, but still felt so terribly intrusive. Dotti's light laughter sounded in response to her muttered comment.

"For all of us," she told her in agreement. Maren smiled down at her, trying not to chuckle. He was torn between being solemn as such an attempt should be taken, or laughing out in pure joy at the thought of fathering a child of his own. It was something he'd given up when he fell deeply in love with Dotti, well before he ever met her, thinking she was so different, they could never have any cubs. Dotti saw his thoughts reflected in his eyes and giggled merrily as she stretched up to kiss him.

"This should be a time of joy for us," she whispered, smiling as she teasingly nipped at his neck. He finally relaxed, putting Ryes' presence from his mind. This was for them, after all and she was right; it should be a celebration.

Ryes sat and sighed as they focused upon each other and finally forgot her. She had a million things on her mind to worry about, but knew she could never desert her cousin in his time of need. For the both of them, she'd do her absolute best. She looked down at Rhin in her arms. He was so little and so perfect. If the two of them could help correct the "wrongness" they felt within him while he was still in her womb, they could help correct and repair any child he and Dotti conceived. It may take time, but she knew they could do it! He'd saved Sernn too, after all, and he'd been living with his wrongness for eleven years. Suddenly, she felt a gentle touch upon her shoulder, startling her from her inner contemplations.

"Let's try, now," Maren told her in a low voice, not wanting to wake her younger son. They needed total concentration right now. Ryes nodded as she got up from the chair, still cradling Rhin in her arms. He was a Booster and some new unnamed Talent, and even if he was too young to direct his Talents himself, they could still use him to focus their abilities. He was that powerful!

They stepped over to Dotti's side, as she lay naked upon their bed and grinning in anticipation. Ryes blushed and closed her eyes, centering herself within and extended her hand to lay it gently upon Dotti's stomach. Maren centered himself, placed one hand over Ryes', then closed his eyes as he extended his other hand low over Dotti's abdomen and released his Healing Talent, boosted by Ryes' Talent and her power. Rhin's presence sharpened his abilities and he suddenly had a confidence he never knew before, as he delved within, seeking the tiny seeds from which they could forge their child. He felt Dotti's mind join theirs, as she had to be a part of this too, tapping in through Ryes' abilities, having put her hand over Ryes.' After what seemed an eternity, Maren opened his eyes as Ryes and Dotti dropped out of the linkage. He smiled down at his beautiful, human wife and sighed in relief.

"We're going to have a daughter," she breathed; happiness filled her heart as tears filled her eyes. Ryes stepped back as the two lovers wrapped their arms about each other again. She smiled as she quietly let herself out, sealing the metal door behind her once more. She quickly walked down the corridor, heading for her office. She'd get a memo out to Ted and Ethan immediately; telling them Maren and Dotti wouldn't be back the rest of the day. The humans called it a "sanity" day and she felt he and Dotti more than deserved a little time to themselves right now. They had some celebrating to do.

"Okay. I'm reading the control panel for this door is over here, somewhere," Montigue Elbridge insisted, looking puzzled. Ryes frowned as she stepped up next to him to see the scanner's reading for herself.

"Oh!" She suddenly realized, stepping up onto the Elder's platform before the circle and sat down upon Old Metta's chair. He looked like he was about to have a heart attack over this trespass, but didn't dare move toward her. The humans stayed around her, as if protecting her from some imminent danger. Garth looked relaxed, even amused with her actions. "Here," she gestured to Monty to join her on the seat. He appeared puzzled, but complied. Once he sat down, he saw what she saw and surprise was written in his bright blue eyes.

"That's got to be it!" he agreed, smiling. He quickly ran his scan again, trying to see how the mechanism might work, which was situated under a gray ten-inch square plate, beneath their feet. Ryes looked up to Garth, smiling her triumph.

"Underfoot all this time," she teased, being careful to not meet Matlowe's Chief Elder's brown eyes. She leaned over and looked at the readout on the device Monty held in his hands, then grinned, seeing the solution before he did. She got down on her knees and depressed both left and right sides, about the middle of each edge, at the same time. The metal plate popped open to reveal a panel beneath. It looked like one of their computer controlled panels, where you entered a sequence upon a numerical keypad. The whole thing looked to be made of a shiny gold metal, which hadn't aged in all the years it sat hidden.

"Just get away from that!" Metta ordered, stepping up to them with anger in his eyes. Ryes straightened up and looked at him levelly, feeling her own anger rise to the surface; startling him as he saw it clearly.

"How DARE you," she scolded in a low voice. "You knew about this and never told anyone about it. This isn't something just for you to own! It belongs to all the people of both Matlowe and Tayna! You're as self-involved as your youngest brother!"

"Do you happen to know the combination?" Monty pressed as a distraction, wondering about the anger in Ryes' voice. It was something new to his ears. She never lost it like this back in Winterhaven! He wondered at her history with these people.

"It was lost when my grandfather died suddenly of a fever, when I was a young man. He never awoke, so never told my father what it was," Metta admitted, still feeling the sting of this cub's words. If something of import lay below, did it truly belong to all of Tayna, or just Matlowe? It was something he never considered before. And where had her timidity fled? She was fierce and confident now; used to ordering others about.

"Many good things are lost, when those we greatly respect die suddenly," Dr. Cruthers comforted the elder, stepping closer and taking his arm, urging him back from Ryes and Monty. "It's why my people developed a consistent form of record keeping," he explained, once he had Metta's full attention.

"They aren't going to break anything, are they?" he pressed, nervous about this creature's nearness, but now that he did see him so closely, he saw his jovial smile and a merry light in his eyes. He found himself liking and trusting this human, to some degree, in spite of himself. He walked back toward the stone seats at the far side of the village center with him.

"No, no, they'll be very careful," Ethan assured him, as Rowan smiled. He stepped over to join them; sitting on Metta's other side.

"You wouldn't believe the miracles these young ones can pull off," he told him, clasping his shoulder companionably. Metta nodded his head, giving in and letting go his frustrations. If there was some kind of treasure here, he'd do his best to see that some of it remained in Matlowe, where it belonged! All he'd had were hazy stories of what lay below from his cubhood.

"Where're you going?" Mitt asked Maren, seeing he threw his satchel over his shoulder and was headed into the village proper.

"Going to pay a visit to Ryun," he assured her, with a wink. "If the people of Matlowe know they truly have a Healer at their call, it might help to promote Winterhaven in their eyes. Dr. Cruthers wants to build a contact center here, so this'll give them a reason to start using it." She looked surprised at this, but gave him a nod to his logic.

"She's the best place to start. I hope you have someone in mind to mate her, once she's back to normal?" she asked, in a low voice, lightly teasing him.

"That's her responsibility," he assured her with a chuckle, blushing. "I have enough going with Dotti right now. I don't think either one of us got any sleep last night!" Mitt smiled a knowing smile at this news.

"You succeeded?" she pressed, meeting his eyes. He gave her a nod of his head. "And I bet you're keeping it a secret for now?"

"Most definitely," he agreed. "Once we're sure our daughter's stable, we'll announce her pregnancy. Until then, keep it to yourself, please?" he requested. She gave him a nod of her head, understanding very well. There were those who'd be incensed over a child created from the two people's bloodlines - on both sides!

"You can count on me!" she assured him. He turned and headed off as planned, still smiling with pride.

"Ryun?" Maren called, as he stepped up to her doorway. He heard her light steps as she crossed the room within, coming to see who was calling. She was genuinely surprised to see him at the door; her brown eyes were filled with curiosity. She kept her light brown hair short and neat and was dressed in a light tan tunic with colorful pants.

"Maren, is there something your mother needs?" she questioned, wondering why he was here. Hadn't he moved out of the village, she puzzled?

"I came to offer to help you, actually," he told her with a smile. "If you have the time, may I come in?" he requested.

"I don't recall needing anything," she replied, but stepped back and bid him enter. He did so with a gracious bow to her, causing her to smile at this. It was so rare that she was offered any courtesy. "Please sit down and I'll bring you some tea," she invited, leaving her door wide open, as if to take in some fresh air.

"Thank you," he replied, taking a seat near her open window. It looked out upon the south gardens and he saw wildflowers growing near the window; a beautiful sight on a spring morning. He suddenly realized he was feeling a little nervous about this visit. Ryun was a good ten years older than he, but if he'd stayed here in Matlowe, she might've been one he could've taken to wife, as he knew his father had tried to father cubs on her several times - never succeeding; he didn't care who took her now. But, since he'd left with Ryes upon her journey, and she awakened his Talent, then called down the human starship, there was no one who'd ever measure up to his beautiful Dotti! Ryun returned shortly with a mug of tea for him and another for herself.

"So, I thought you'd left Matlowe forever?" she questioned, seeing he was nervous about something.

"As a place to live, yes, I've left Matlowe far behind me for good. But, as a place where I was raised and now that Ryes awoke my Talent, I feel it's my duty to help the people of Matlowe, as I'm able," he told her, then sipped his tea. It was good. He smiled for her in gratitude. It wasn't as good as Ryes', but it was far from the worse he'd tasted. "This is very good," he praised.

"Thank you," she replied, thinking over what he told her. "But, why have you come to see me?" she pressed, appearing truly puzzled.

"My Talent's Healing. I want to see if I can find the cause of your inability to have cubs of your own. If you want to be able to have them, after all," he told her, meeting her amber-colored eyes steadily. Ryun's breath caught in her throat as his words echoed within her mind. Cubs of her own? He had to be making some kind of a sick joke!

"How can you do such a thing?" she demanded. "Does this mean you mean to mate me on the spot, too?" she demanded, furiously. Maren blushed at this accusation.

"I only want to find the cause of your problem. Whom you mate with is entirely up to you. If you want to keep this all as a secret between the two of us, fine. It will be. And if you take a mate when you next season comes, you'll see if I was successful, or not. I've a wife of my own and truly only came today to help out," he replied, setting his mug down before he spilled it all over. How could such a simple offer go so wrong, he wondered? She sat back in her chair, astounded. He meant it! The truth was plain in his eyes! He was in pain over her accusation.

"Alright, I'll let you see if your Healing Talent can overcome my curse," she agreed, feeling she had nothing to lose over this attempt. "As long as you do keep this between the two of us," she added. He gave her a nod of his head in agreement, understanding her too well by now.

"Mitt and Ryes do know, but they'll keep it quiet, if I ask them," he admitted, knowing he had to tell her the whole truth, now.

"What happened to Marla's cub? Is Marla all right? Did the cub die quickly, or was it a lingering death?" she suddenly questioned. The whole village knew she was having a lot of trouble with carrying this last child Garvin fathered. They only hoped she'd live through the ordeal. She was too kind a person to die so young! Maren laughed at this, shaking his head.

"Marla's fine and so's little Myran. I healed her, well before she was born and attended her birth to make sure both mother and cub would be well," he informed her. She looked at him in shock at this news.

"She named her Myran?" she asked. "It was Marla's grandmother's name," she told him with a sigh. "Will I get a chance to see them sometime?"

"Anytime you like, we'll arrange for a trip to Winterhaven for you, if you don't mind traveling very fast by machine," he assured her, smiling. "May I?" he requested, pointing to her abdomen. She finally gave him a nod of her head, then he went down upon his knees and placed his fingers, splayed across her stomach. She tried to relax as he closed his eyes, then felt a strange warmth within as he extended his Talent out to her body. It seemed like it took a long time, but he finally opened his eyes, looking puzzled.

"This will take a few more sessions to finish. Who did this to you?" he suddenly asked; the injuries being very old to his senses. She blushed a dark gold at this question, knowing he had the gift for sure now.

"When I was young, a few years before my first season, Korman caught me down by the river and decided to acquaint me with what it would be like later. He was still coming down off a blood lust from a mating and was very rough. He tore me up a lot. I could feel it at the time and he terrified me, but there was little I could do. I was so young and my parents had died the winter before, so was alone in my pain and agony," she related to him, tears blinding her eyes as she finished her tale. Here was one of Korman's sons, but there was only sadness and compassion in his eyes for her.

"If I could pay him back for all the pain and misery he's given others," he growled out, low in his throat. Ryun put a hand to his shoulder, suddenly.

"Let it go. I did long ago. He'll pay for all he's done, in good time. He's getting old and doesn't even try at challenges anymore. Garth broke his spirit last year, when he defeated him. He lives with Tanns and stays out of sight for the most part," she told him, wanting him to let go his anger, before it hurt him too. She suddenly wondered what it must've been like for him to live in that house, with Korman's cruelty about him each and every day? It must've been like surviving all seven hells, themselves. No wonder he was so bitter.

"I'll do my best," he promised, then sighed. "Would you like to come back with us to Winterhaven, until I've finished your treatments, or would you prefer I return here, until we've set you back to right?" he asked, finding a smile, once more. "I have to warn you, the humans live with us, as if we're all one people in Winterhaven. In fact, my own wife is a human," he explained, feeling it needed to be said up front. He shifted back from her a little, then returned to his chair. Ryun sat and looked out her window for a few minutes, contemplating her answer, while he waited quietly.

"I'll come with you," she finally responded, looking back to him and smiling with genuine warmth in her eyes. "My newest batch of cheeses need to age and that takes months. I don't think I'll be missed much and I do want to see Marla's newest daughter." He laughed at this as he stood up.

"I'll be back shortly with some friends to help you pack," he offered. "Is there anyone else here who might need healing?" he asked, still wanting to be of service.

"Actually, there is. Your mother's having trouble carrying this newest one. If anything happens to her, the gods only know what

Korman'd do to the rest of your siblings," she related, hating to be the bearer of bad news. His face went ashen as he thought on it, himself. He gave her a nod of thanks, as he snatched up his bag.

"I'd better get right over there," he agreed, then turned quickly for the open door. He didn't need to imagine what his father would do - he knew already! He began to trot down the path, heading for what he used to call home.

"Maren?" Tanns questioned, suddenly finding her older son in her kitchen. His face looked grim. "What're you doing home? If your father finds you here, he'll kill you," she warned, her heart suddenly hammering in panic. "Korman made that threat, as soon as he recovered from the injuries Garth inflicted upon him.”

"I'm here to see how you and the cub you're carrying are doing," he told her. He immediately closed his eyes and centered himself. He extended his hand and his healing abilities to her very swollen stomach, hoping his father wouldn't return to find him doing this. It was the one time he was truly vulnerable!

Suddenly, he realized she was wrong and he knew it was due to Korman's violence. Had he actually beat his mother up after he recovered from the challenge with Garth, he wondered? Raya had revealed to him what she'd seen in Ryes' mind of what happened when he once caught Rein and Tobin down by the river. What he'd done to Rein had been monstrous and unforgivable. That he'd finally turned upon his own treasured mate was astounding, and he suddenly feared for her life. He did the best he could for his mother and tiny sister, then withdrew and opened his eyes.

“You’re a true Healer!” she breathed, astounded and suddenly so proud, feeling so much better and pain-free.

"Ryes found my Talent and opened it up, and Rowan thinks I’m even stronger than Grandmother Jana,” he told her, seeing how happy this made her. “I truly need to tend my tiny sister more, but I don't think you'll come back with us to Winterhaven, will you?" he asked.

"I need you to do a big favor for me," Tanns suddenly began, nervous about having to ask such a thing. He met her eyes, quietly waiting. "I want you to take Tars, Karis, and Rowis back with you. I know they'll be a burden, but I'll breathe easier knowing they're with you and Tennan," she pleaded. He sighed, pain for her suffering in his eyes.

"Of course I will. I want to take you back with us too, but since you're not going, perhaps I can get Ryes to help me finish healing this tiny sister of mine, before we leave. Please, mother? Please come to Winterhaven?" he begged. She unexpectedly threw her arms about him and started crying. He was taken aback. His mother had always been so strong before. He wrapped his arms about her and held her close. For all the small, cruel snipes he'd seen her deploy against others, he knew there was a deeper well of kindness and dedication. Hers was the healing hand when sickness or injury befell others.

"I can't," she finally sobbed out, "Not yet," she told him. "I'm still needed here."

"When we get our contact station built, the villagers can call us any time they need our help. So, will you come live with us, then?" She pulled back, looking up to him, wondering when he'd gotten so much taller?

"I'll consider it," she promised. "Right now, let me gather up some things for your sisters and brother. So you won't have to provide them with EVERYTHING," she told him, smiling at last as she let him go.

"I almost forgot," he said, pulling open his satchel and taking out several plastic-sealed packages. "Ryes sent these for you. She was out gathering plants a few days ago and said you'd need them." Her face held shock at this unexpected generosity. After all the years and trails she sent her upon, this kindhearted niece still thought of her and her needs, when they lived so far apart. She took the packets with unsteady hands, her tears threatening to return.

"Tell her," she started, then sighed, "I'll tell her when I bring your siblings out to you. In the Village Square?" she suddenly asked, meeting his eyes again.

"Yes, in the Village Square," he assured her. "Unless you need help with anything, I'd better get back," he told her. She nodded her head, understanding.

"We'll be out there, shortly," she promised, feeling relieved. At least her children would be safe.

"This new construction is amazing! Even more than Winterhaven's," Sabin commented to Garth, nodding towards the new housing being built beyond the Village Square. He turned to look, seeing it and nodding his head in agreement.

"We've created Winterhaven so it's all new, but Matlowe we've known all our lives! Phil and Kovin's crew did a great job in pulling down almost all the old structures, to open a path for the new construction," he added. A tall, but broad-shouldered starman emerged out of the almost completed house and strode over towards them. Garth realized he'd been introduced to him the last time he was in Matlowe by Rowan, but was unsure of his name now.

"Pleased to see you again," Taroom said, as he stopped before both men, a glad smile alighting his face. His thumbs were proudly hooked into the top of his new tool belt. "I wanted to thank Rowan for these wonderful tools he sent to me and to show you the new house I've almost finished for my family, here in Matlowe," he explained, appearing so very proud.

"You're the carpenter from Riverward," Sabin said as he gave him a nod of his head, smiling too. "Good to meet you. My name's Sabin."

"I'm Taroom," he replied, extending his hand. Garth chuckled as he crossed his palm with his own, as did Sabin.

"If we're not interrupting your work, I'd love to see your new home and compare it to what Kovin and Phil are building for us in Winterhaven," Garth told him. He gave him a nod in understanding.

"Our building techniques are similar and yet different," he replied, still grinning in pride as he gestured towards his own home. They readily followed, curious to see it even more.

"They showed you pictures?" Sabin asked, wondering. Taroom nodded his head again in agreement.

"It was surprising to see moving pictures on the little, thin flat box," he admitted, the wonder was still plain upon his face. "You truly have forgotten treasures in your new home!" Garth chuckled as he gave him a nod.

"They're like what our ancestors had and are far better than doing without," he agreed. "I know I was led by the spirit of Tayna, herself, to find Winterhaven. Something inside of me kept us on that pathway to our new home." Sabin gave a nod of agreement at this.

"I know she guided my steps to this new home, too," Taroom related, as they stopped before his new door. "With all the dangers we were facing, both living outside the protective wall of Riverward, and then on the road coming here, we still made it hale and whole. And we've prospered here, too! In New Matlowe we've helped to grow our own food and the hunters give us meat, spices and plants they gather. The caravaner elder, Eluna, who's staying here this year with her youngest children have been schooling our children and they're learning so much about the world, it's put me to shame for all that I thought I learned when I was young in a far greater town." He laughed at this as he noted they were admiring his craftsmanship used in the making of the door itself.

"This is amazing," Garth breathed out as he fingered the graceful carved and stained image in the door. It was a large bounder amid a flowering bush. The paints used and the stains were eye-catching, and the carving was richly done; filled with exacting detail. "What's this?" he asked pointing to a small door set about eye-level in the door and it puzzled hm.

"That is our peep hole," Taroom explained as both Garth and Sabin were enrapt with only his front door. "It allows us to see who's calling before opening the door to invite them inside."

"That's a good idea! We should make them, too," Sabin agreed, nodding his head. Taroom opened the door and invited them to go inside before him. They did so with enthusiasm, eager to see what treasures lay within. Taroom chuckled, thinking he'd get a few moments to speak with Rowan afterwards.

Standing Firm

Finally, the great circle, itself, rose up into the air as if it'd never been more than a giant portal. It stood poised above them, standing upon one edge for several, long moments, then it slowly folded within itself, as if it was a folding fan, then swung down to lie upon the ground to one side, revealing a wide stairway and gigantic doorway over thirty feet down below. The surface beneath where the circle had set appeared to be a hard, gray stone that looked very smooth. The same kind of stone lined the walls of the stairway down, but were a lighter shade. The door appeared to be a dull-shiny bronze-colored metal with another keypad beside it, which also looked to be made of gold. The dust and fine dirt raised in this operation startled those standing too close, who started coughing and gasping for air.

"Didn't I warn everyone to stand back?" Ryes questioned Monty, who was laughing at the display before them; relieved they finally figured it out.

"That's what I heard," he agreed, merrily. "Of course the warning came almost half an hour ago, when we started trying different combinations on the keypad." An ancient child's rhyme had provided the correct answer and Ryes only tried it, as she'd run out of other ideas.

"A quick reminder would've sufficed," Mitt shouted to them, recovering from the cloud of dust as it settled out of the atmosphere. She saw the mischief in both Ryes and Monty's eyes and knew they hadn't expected to succeed so quickly.

"Keep the villagers back. Let's let the first team remain small. Only myself, Sabin, Jim and Monty," Garth ordered. Something about this strange vault below them caused the hair on the nape of his neck to rise up in reaction. "The rest of you will hold yourselves back from this entrance, until we have it opened." He stepped over to the elders' platform and his wife. "What'd you use to open the circle?" he asked her in a low voice, in English.

"Would you believe the Fisherman's Chant?" she returned likewise, smiling. "The number sequence of the fish he caught during Winterfest week was unique enough and stuck out in my mind," she admitted. He smiled at this as he shook his head.

"You mean you'd run out of other ideas," he volleyed in return, knowing her well. "I want you and the cubs well back from this operation. Something has my nerves on edge," he admitted. The smile melted from her face as she gave him a nod of her head.

"Been spending too much time around Ryes," Maren teased his friend, returning to see a great hole in the ground where the Village Circle had stood, and Ryes and Garth in quiet conversation; speaking in English. Garth turned and smiled, nodding his head.

"Most probably," he admitted. "Just keep an eye on her and make sure she keeps back," he requested. Maren gave him a nod at this, understanding. At least their cubs were safely locked up in the rover, across the other side of the village square.

"I've got a few people returning with us. Ryun and my siblings," he informed them. Ryes smiled in surprise at this, but he threw her a look and she understood it was a matter best kept under wraps, for the time being.

"How's your mother?" she asked.

"She'll need the both of us to help heal the cub she's carrying. I think Korman took out some of his temper on her, afterwards," he said in a low voice. Garth looked grim at hearing this news. He would've never thought Korman would turn on Tanns because he finally lost a challenge. Maren saw the look in his eyes, knowing he felt the same way. Ryes was startled at hearing it, too.

"She won't come with us?" she pressed, worried for her aunt now.

"No, but she wants me to take charge of my younger siblings. I don't know how Dotti's going to take this, but we're going to need a larger apartment, right off," he cracked a smile at this as he imagined the look on Kovin's face when he tells him, too.

"All right. As soon as Tanns shows up, do what the two of you must. Ready, Monty?" Garth asked, seeing he was politely trying not to listen in, but couldn't help overhearing with them discussing things right beside him. He smiled guiltily, then gave Garth a nod of his head in response. All the humans had learned it was what the starmen responded to, more than any voiced acknowledgments. Learning to live together had been an interesting adventure so far.

"Be careful," Ryes cautioned them, both. Garth smiled at this.

"Always," he assured her. Monty nodded his agreement, coming off the platform to stand beside his commander. They walked over toward the pit, and Monty activated his scanner as they drew neigh upon the stairs leading down, joining Sabin and Jim. One of the three drones came down to hover over his shoulder, as he ordered it. Bethy had control over the other two.

"What's the matter?" Dotti asked Maren and Ryes, as they walked over to join them, staying back from the pit, but still with a good enough buffer between them and the growing crowd of villagers.

"Our little family's just increased," he informed her. Bethany looked at him with questions in her eyes, as Dr. Cruthers smiled, his eyes twinkling. He finally took out his pipe from his pocket and placed it in his mouth; not quite ready to light it. He had a very limited supply of tobacco and Brenda and Ryes had yet to find another plant, which would suffice as a substitute. The seeds they salvaged from his present stock were still very tiny seedlings, barely begun. It still comforted him to have it, at any rate.

"Who?" Dotti asked, smiling as she shook her head, amazed. Just as they got things going themselves, they were blessed once more.

"My three youngest siblings, Tars, Karis, and Rowis. My mother doesn't think they'll be safe here with her anymore," he told her. Dotti's smile melted as she nodded her head at this.

"We'll just have to ask Kovin to squeeze us into a larger apartment from the start," she assured him as she wrapped an arm about him, leaning against Maren's side as he put one of his arms about her waist, too. She was smiling again. They would weather it together.

"He's going to have a fit," Mitt commented, laughing lightly, "all of Kovin and Phil's careful planning undergoing another change."

"They'll just have to get used to changes, as Winterhaven is a growing village," Ryes commented, her eyes full of mirth.

"Change is always a part of life," Ethan added, amused as he thought they were only starting, with many more changes still ahead of them.

"So, what's the plan?" Bethany asked, worried for Jim and the others.

"To check out what's below. It might only be a simple storage area, but since it's blocked from our scans, we won't know until they get that door opened," Ryes told her; not knowing what to expect, either. The door was immense! From the look of it, six people could easily enter at the same time and not be crowded waking in. Still, she hoped...

"Ryes used the number sequence from the Fisherman's Chant," Garth admitted to Sabin. "That didn't work, what other old rhyme can you think of which has numbers in it?" For the life of him, Garth couldn't think of any others.

"How about that one about catching squeakers?" he suggested, grinning. "Of all the things, nursery rhymes?"

"Maybe we should ask Old Metta what rhymes his father taught him as a cub?" he returned, agreeing it seemed silly.

"It's one way to pass on important information, which will keep, even if writing is forgotten," Jim pointed out to them. "Some more primitive cultures rely upon rhymes and verses as a way to pass on their history, orally," he explained.

Garth looked thoughtful for a few moments, seeing what he meant. He suddenly got an inspiration and punched in a particular sequence, which did come to mind, from an old story which was passed down through the generations. There was a brief flash of lights on the door itself, then some clicking from within the control panel. He'd done something. They waited, hoping and wondering what lay within.

As they activated the mechanism, Ryes suddenly felt the energy released from within the great portal. She whipped around and faced it, as if facing down a challenge.

"NO!" she shouted, as the explosion began, a great fireball reaching hungrily out to Jim, Monty, Garth and Sabin from around all the sides of the great portal. It froze, as if it were a live thing, in mid-motion, obeying her command due to her Fire Shaper Talent. The four men stood rooted for a couple of heartbeats in utter shock.

"Quick! Move!" Garth ordered, as they scrambled for the stairs, running back up; the drone trailing them.

In her mind, Ryes saw part of the energy was focused upwards, but a greater part focused downwards, to destroy what lay beneath. She diverted the focus of this second force to flow with the first one. As soon as she saw the men clear, she released the forces and directed them skyward. A thunderous sound shook the ground, reverberating through the air; knocking several people off their feet. The great, massive portal was propelled up, high into the air over their heads. Then, as it rapidly descended, she managed to stop it again. She was breathing hard with the strain, but saw others still in danger.

"Hurry, I can't hold it for long!" she yelled. Garth saw her face was a mask, as the strain of this inner fight raged within. He was torn between saving the others and his wife!

"Move!" Sabin ordered the villagers and humans standing under where the portal intended to come down. There were screams and shouts as the people ran, realizing their very real danger. They quickly cleared out of its way. Ryes finally released her hold on the massive, twisted metal and it crashed down into the plaza, causing a huge shallow crater with the energy of its impact and throwing more people off their feet. Garth ran over to Ryes as her legs went out from under her and she crumpled to the ground, as a puppet with its strings cut. He caught her just before she hit it.

"So much excitement," she teased, smiling, "I feel as if I ran all the way here this morning." He smiled down into her eyes, shaking his head, glad she was all right as he stood back up. Her skin was ice-cold.

"Now I know why you insisted upon coming," he told her, shifting to hold her better in his arms.

"The sensors should've picked that up," Jim commented, scratching his head as he looked to Dr. Cruthers, who stood in quiet contemplation of both the thick, massive piece of metal and the petite woman, who managed to stop its fall, even if only momentarily.

"They might've had some kind of jamming feature built into the door itself; to keep out unwanted, alien visitors," he replied. "Ensign Elbridge, could you please scan what lies below with the most sensitive settings? We might've already tripped the only booby trap, but let's be sure before anyone else takes another step down there," he ordered. Monty gave him a nod of his head, already adjusting his scanner unit and sending the drone down to the opening below, as Jim stepped over to check the scan settings with him.

"Are you all right?" Dotti asked, as Maren was checking Ryes his own way, with his eyes closed in concentration.

"Yes. I just feel tired, is all," she assured her and Bethy, who both looked at her in concern. She noted the fear in Old Metta's eyes as he stood behind them, contemplating her, too. Maren opened his eyes, giving them a nod of his head with a smile.

"Just overdid it a little," he agreed with her, "Not that I think anyone here would disagree that it hadn't been called for," he teased his cousin, smiling.

"It's been a long time since I needed to do anything like that," she agreed. "I almost forgot I could."

"I'm glad you don't need to remember how," Sabin commented, stepping closer, giving her a smile of gratitude. "So, are we going to carry her down there with us?" he asked Garth, teasing with humor in his eyes.

"I think she gets to stay up here with Maren, Dr. Cruthers, her grandfather and the ladies, while we go down. Even if there are more traps, I'd feel better knowing she was safely out of the way."

"Wait a minute," Ryes protested, "First off, you can put me down. Secondly, I want to see what's hidden there too. Especially what it is that makes all that destruction worth it!"

"You can see it, after we finish checking the area is safe," Garth ordered, meeting her eyes. She huffed a breath, but knew he wasn't going to tolerate her protests when he felt this strongly about it.

"All right," she gave in, reluctantly. He finally smiled, as he set her back upon her own feet. She realized she felt fine physically, but internally she was winded. It was a strange feeling to be so tired, when she had plenty of energy to draw upon for other things. "You be careful," she warned Garth again, meeting his eyes.

"I will," he promised with a quick kiss and chuckle, then he and Sabin went back over to see what the scanners were displaying. Ryes began to brush off her clothing, realizing she wasn't used to being stared at by so many people. Every villager in the area was now in the square staring at her. Some, like Metta, viewed her in shocked horror, while others were curious. Most just stood waiting to see what else would happen. This had been the most excitement they'd had in over a decade! Dr. Cruthers stepped over to her, smiling and chuckling.

"I seem to recall you once telling me you could stop something, if it were very important to you," he said. "I never knew you could stop something this massive." Rowan nodded his head at this, utterly amazed. He still couldn't believe it was his granddaughter who'd done this great feat!

"The first time it was to save my life," Mitt told him, speaking loudly for the nearby villagers to hear. "I was being run over by a runaway cart. The second time was to help the Star Quest land and save your lives." Then she stepped very close to the small knot of people. "Let's move the rovers closer, so we have some kind of cover. Some of these people are making me nervous. It's like they want to lynch Ryes for a Talent she happened to chance being born with," she suggested in English, in a lower voice.

"Fear of the unknown can be great, indeed," Ethan agreed, than gave a nod to her, in understanding and concurrence. "It may be wise if we have at least one of them available for our purposes. Make it look like we need some of the supplies stored within," he added. Mitt smiled at this, giving a nod to him, then quickly trotted toward the rovers.

"Ignorant… superstitious," Maren commented, under his breath. Ryes smiled at this, shaking her head.

"They are as they've always been," Rowan commented. "You only see things with different eyes."

"I was the outcast here, and now I hold some kind of rank, which even they would note. You've got to admit, it'd gall some of them," she reminded him. They were all staying to the English, now. Mitt started up the rover and drove it over beside them, turning it around so it was directed toward the road outwards, once more. The rover moving toward them surprised the men near the underground entrance, so Ryes gave them a thumbs-up sign, to assure them this was planned. Garth noted the looks from the other villagers and gave her a nod of his head at this, seeing they were using good sense.

"I knew we had some, Dr. Cruthers," Mitt declared with a smile, bringing out some folding chairs from the back.

"Thank you, my child," he returned, chuckling. "Please place them over there," he directed. Whereas the rover partially blocked their view, it still provided them with greater safety. He had the chairs placed so they had quick access to the rover; yet were also close to the underground entrance. She quickly set them up, going back and forth a few times until she had all ten ready; an open invitation for friendly villagers to join them. Dr. Cruthers and Rowan walked over to them, as if they were tired and needing this small bit of comfort. Maren chuckled at this display. Of all those on today's outing, these two were the ones who'd most likely last the longest.

"What're we going to do with that?" Metta questioned, finally coming closer once more, indicating the portal lying nearby. Ethan invited him to sit in one of the chairs, so he accepted and sat down between him and Rowan.

"If you have no need for it, we'll gladly take it off your hands," he offered generously, smiling.

"Please?" he asked, glad they didn't have to figure out how to lift it. It looked very heavy. "Do with it as you see fit."

Ethan chuckled at this, giving him a nod. They could always use the scrap metal and examine it more closely to see how it managed to block out their scanner from detecting the explosives.

Was it something inherent in the metal, itself, or some device activated when they opened the cover above? More riddles to solve...

"It's no problem. We'll put in a call to have it picked up, immediately," he assured him, giving a nod to Lt. Saliman to place the call back to Winterhaven, concerning the matter. She smiled, heading toward the rover's transmitter. She noted Mitt now had a sidearm strapped to her waist, and since some of the villagers were throwing Ryes hostile looks, she decided to do the same. Just in case. And a request for more backup might be appropriate, too.

"There must be something very valuable below, for it to be so well guarded," Rebin commented, stepping over to join the other elders. She found this human elder to be very interesting.

"Or it could be they needed a place to hide with some protection, where anyone trying to dig them out would be hurt, while they'd be safe," Ethan countered, as he gestured her in invitation to use one of the chairs. She sat on his other side.

"Ryes?" Sadie called back from the rover, "I think there's a couple of little ones who need mommy right now," she told her, smiling. Ryes sighed, realizing the explosion probably awoke them.

"Duty calls," she teased the others around her with a smile, then quickly trotted toward the rover. When she climbed in, she noted only Shyla and Rhin were fussing a little. In a few minutes they might drop back off to sleep. "What's up?" she asked Sadie, knowing there had to be more here, which required her input.

"Torr wants to know how many you need sent out in support. He saw what happened and is concerned about the mood of the villagers," she informed her, handing over the mic. Ryes took it with a small sigh, thinking upon the situation. She didn't want to overwhelm the villagers, nor add more uncertainty to the mix, which might goad them to action of some sort, but the thought of backup was appropriate.

"Torr?" she questioned into the mic, having made her decision. "Could you have the AI estimate the mass of the portal? I'd like to see if one of our largest choppers can lift it. If so, I'd like one of them dispatched to retrieve it, and another, smaller one with a few, helpful hands for the operation. I'd rather you, Garvin, or Glyn pilot the smaller craft. Land it right here in the middle of Matlowe," she ordered.

"Just a moment, waiting for the computer's confirmation of the mass," Torr replied, then after a few moments. "It's all right. It falls well within tolerances. We'll be on our way, shortly," he promised, "But, Shadd told me she's piloting. She needs the practice more." He laughed as he spoke. Ryes smiled at this, understanding it too well. She, Shadd, Ardis and Brenda now grabbed every chance they got to get out and take a break from their little ones. Raya was still too busy in the kitchen and had plenty of helpful baby-sitters, for her to feel the need yet. They now had some of the women working as care providers for the cubs too young for school, as a part of their work assignments. They rarely lacked for volunteers.

"Thanks, we appreciate it," she returned, then handed back the mic, so Sadie could hang it upon its bracket. "That should make matters much better for all of us," she told her, smiling. Sadie smiled in return.

"They may think the men of Winterhaven are strong; they have no idea their worst nightmares would come from crossing the women," she teased, fastening on her sidearm securely. Ryes laughed lightly at this, nodding in accord.

"Someone's got to look out for the guys," she agreed, slipping a stunner into her pocket. "Make sure Maren, Dotti and Bethy are either armed, or have stunners, too," she ordered. Sadie gave her a nod of her head, having this idea, too, then slipped back outside. Ryes noted Mitt had left the back door to the rover open, something she never did, but could see she intended to keep as many accesses available, if needed. She now turned back to her infants. Rhin was thoughtfully watching her, as Shyla was now chewing her fist with a determined look in her eyes. She smiled at them. So small, yet their personalities were starting to crystallize, already. She started checking them, to see if they needed changing.

"Maren?" Ryun finally approached the gathering of humans and starmen, her stomach was filled with flutter-wings, but she was determined to finally have cubs of her own to raise. He turned, smiling as he saw her.

"As soon as we're sure there're no more nasty surprises down below, we'll head over to your home and help you pack up," he assured her, gesturing her closer. "I'd like you to meet my wife, Dotti. Dotti, this is Ryun, one of the finest cheese makers to have ever lived in Matlowe. She'll be coming home with us to visit Marla," he explained, feeling it was all that needed to be said. Dotti smiled as she stepped forward and offered her hand, starman style. This surprised Ryun, but she smiled shyly as she crossed her palm with her own, noting their hands were much alike, except this Dotti lacked retractable claws. Her fingernails looked strange, but still usable and were painted prettily.

"It's always nice to be able to take a short vacation every now and then, to see a little of the world," she offered. Ryun looked to be older than Maren, but still many years younger than Marla.

"Yes, a vacation," she agreed, seeing this was the perfect cover. "This will be my first and I'm a little nervous about it," she admitted. "But, we won't need to pack up a lot of things. I've got most of what I'll need already sitting over there," she said as she pointed out the small pile she'd made of what she felt she couldn't leave behind her, even for a few days, across the square. "I've locked up my home and asked Aric and Rami to watch over it for me while I'm gone, so I truly won't need anything else," she explained. She couldn't get over Dotti's bright, blonde tresses. They curled so beautifully! And her ears with their dangling pieces were eye-catching!

"Good, then we'll get you loaded," Mitt assured her, smiling. Dotti nodded agreement, as they went over to Ryun's possessions, directly. She stood for a few moments, undecided. Ryun then spotted Ryes with two, healthy cubs, as she sat on the rover's tailgate, playing with them. Maren noted her interest, then gave her a nod of encouragement.

"Go ahead and say hello, while the rest of the cubs are still napping. Once they wake up, she won't have much time for conversation," he told her, walking back toward Ryes, inviting her to walk beside him.

"How many cubs does she have?" she questioned, shocked.

"Actually, I gave birth to four, but we gained little Shyla, here, when her mother died giving her birth," she told Ryun, herself, smiling and gesturing for her to come closer.

"Oh my goodness! How do you manage them all?" she queried, surprised to be so welcomed by this former outcast. She rarely saw her unless she was helping one of the caravaners in their booths here in Matlowe in the winter, or when Rowan sent her to buy some cheeses from her.

"Only with a lot of help," she informed her, laughing as she spoke. Then she noted Korman trailing Mitt and Dotti back to the rover. The smile melted as she gave a signal to Maren, who turned to look. Mitt and Dotti both saw the sudden anger in his eyes. They glanced back, saw who was behind them, then hurried at a faster pace back to them. Korman kept his pace slow and deliberate, his eyes glued to Ryes and her cubs.

"Bethy," Sadie whispered in warning, seeing Mitt and Dotti hurrying back toward the rover with a strange, large starman following in their wake. Bethany turned from listening to what Metta was telling Dr. Cruthers, to see the stance Maren was taking near Ryes. She recognized Korman from one of Ryes' memories and suddenly understood. She signaled Rowan, then rushed toward the others. This surely looked like trouble of some sort!

"Sorry for the rough handling," Mitt apologized to Ryun, as she and Dotti dropped her things down beneath the tailgate of the rover and turned to deal with Korman. Maren stepped up next to his wife's side, wishing he had more than a stunner in his pocket. He saw Mitt and Dotti had their hands to their pistols and Bethany and Sadie were almost with them, too.

"I wouldn't step any closer, father," Maren called out, deciding to let the women handle things after all. Let him have a taste of justice at the hands of those, so like the ones he abused through the years. He still strode closer, until he was almost two paces from the gathered women. Mitt, Dotti, Sadie and Bethany all had their pistols drawn now, aiming them straight at Korman. Ryun stood rooted in shock, near Ryes, not sure what she should do.

"What are these things the women hold?" he finally asked his son. They looked as if they held something they felt could stop him. There was a grimness to their faces as they stood their ground.

"They're called pistols. They're human-made weapons and a pellet from any one of them can instantly kill you," Maren explained, smiling as he enjoyed seeing him stymied.

"It's against all custom for a woman to bear weapons against a man!" he shouted, getting angry. He wanted to kill the cubs Ryes held in vengeance for his defeat, since Garth was below with Sabin and the two, younger, human men. Their children deserved death!

"It's human law which allows a woman, or man, to defend themselves, or those they care about, with deadly force in self-defense. Since we live with our humans, we've adopted many of their ways and this one law is most reasonable," Maren replied. Ryes stepped up to stand between Mitt and Dotti, her son in her arms.

"Old murderer, the only reason you're here showing your face is you think Garth's too busy to deal with you. I'm far more deadly than my husband and it's only out of respect for his wishes, that I stay my Talent now," she told him, her voice carrying ice.

"Your cubs are small. You're powerless," he retorted, sneering. Now Maren knew he must've known about the vulnerability of a Talent, shortly before and after birthing cubs! He planned his attack upon Tyra, Ryes' mother, on purpose - when she'd be most helpless - so he could do as he wanted. But before he could voice his own threat, Mitt started laughing in Korman's face.

"You'd better look behind you," she boasted, smiling viciously. "That large metal plate was stopped midair by Ryes and her Talent, to keep it from killing those who stood in the path of its fall." Korman ignored her, dismissing her taunt, keeping his focus upon Ryes.

"You can't do anything to me," he stated. She was sorely tempted, but had promised Garth she'd behave. Then she saw him, Sabin and the others approaching Korman from behind.

"I don't have to," she returned.

"What do you want with my wife and cubs?" Garth demanded, standing with his hands upon his hips as he stopped a good two paces behind Korman. He quickly spun around to see the rest of the men and elders standing another two paces back, ready to back him up if needed. He turned back to his son, furious at being so caught with no warning from him!

"No son of mine will ever speak to me the way you have, ever again," he stated, then turned and stalked off. As he passed, Garth noted the cold look of threat in his eyes. He appeared as if he had something else in mind right now, as if he was plotting a new way to get at Ryes.

Maren stood rooted in surprise. His father always said what he meant. He couldn't be mistaken, could he? He wouldn't go that far! Ryes saw a strange look in his eyes and wondered what the problem could be? Korman's last words puzzled her. Suddenly, Mitt gasped as she figured it out.

"Your little brother!" she told Maren, surprising him with her verification. "He means to kill Karis, instead," she pressed, hoping she was possibly wrong.

"You're right!" he returned. He quickly turned to leave, but Mitt put a hand to his arm to stall him a moment, handing over her sidearm and holster. He gave her a smile of thanks, then trotted off, taking a different path from his father's, noting Sadie and Sabin were following. He knew where Karis usually played and hoped he'd still be there with his friends!

"Do you really think he'd take out his frustrations upon Maren's little brother?" Dotti asked, hoping they were wrong.

"Unfortunately, he might," Garth told her, stepping over to the women, glad to see everyone was all right. They were just holstering their weapons, but still looked unsettled with the outcome. Was Mitt correct in her deduction?

"I behaved," Ryes chirped in with a small smile, making an attempt at humor. He finally smiled at this, as he stepped up to her, wrapping her and Rhin up into his arms.

"Yes, you did," he agreed with a sigh. "I don't ever want you to use your Talents to cause others violence," he told her, "They're gifts and should be used to help, or heal."

"I know," she replied, understanding his reasoning.

"That's a very good viewpoint," Ethan added, "but what about self-defense?" he pressed. Garth frowned as he considered his point. It was valid.

"If there were no other alternatives and was truly a desperate situation," he amended, knowing this issue needed to be addressed, too.

"Well, I do have my stunner in my pocket, to make sure there's at least one other choice," Ryes pointed out, smiling at Dr. Cruthers.

"A very good idea to always leave yourself an `out,' my dear," he agreed, "but, still, never be afraid of using whatever means lies at your disposal, if necessary." He realized she was the only one of their "Talents" who might actually be able to kill another person at a distance. He knew why Garth was so strict with her due to her youth and inexperience, but didn't want to see her shackled, if ever faced with a situation she couldn't handle any other way. He didn't want her to pause and cost her own life!

"Ethan's right, cub. Just in case you find yourself cornered, don't hesitate to do as you must," Rowan advised, seeing she looked reluctant, even with their encouragement, in the light of Garth's opinion. He saw Ryun appeared puzzled, as they were all speaking English once again. He chuckled as he gave her a nod of his head. "We sometimes forget ourselves," he apologized to her in Dolbith. "We don't mean to be rude." She smiled at this, blushing, as the rest turned to note her presence among them.

"It's all right, Rowan. You all seem very close. Maren invited me along to visit Marla, if you don't mind," she explained.

"You're more than welcome," Garth assured her, as he released Ryes. Rhin was crying and squirming, wanting to be fed now.

"A never ending job," Ryes commented, "Excuse me while I take care of this tiny, bottomless pit." She set him into his carrier on the tailgate, and climbed back up into the rover. She picked up both cubs and disappeared within. Garth chuckled at this, as his sister gave him a sharp look of reprimand.

"I don't have the equipment to deal with them," he returned, teasing her, gesturing toward his muscular chest.

"Once they're past the nursing stage, you'll have no excuse," she asserted, smiling sweetly in return. He nodded his head, knowing she was right. She turned back to Ryun. "I'll get your things stowed properly, now," she told her as she bent to retrieve them from the ground, under the tailgate. Garth bent down, lending Mitt a hand.

"I hope we didn't break anything," Dotti apologized to her. "We were just worried with Korman here," she said, but Ryun held up her hand to stall her.

"Maren was right in standing back and letting the women handle things. Korman's needed women to stand against him, for a long time now," she assured her. "He's terrorized me for too many years," she finally admitted. "It was good to see that there are some laws written to protect everyone equally. And thank you, Garth, for freeing Matlowe," she added. He smiled with a huff of a breath, as he placed a large bundle up on the tailgate.

"You can thank Ryes for convincing me I could do anything I set my heart to. I would've never tried to stand up to him, if I hadn't decided I never wanted to see her suffer his claws." She saw the clear truth in his eyes and gave him a nod in respect.

"Let's get you up here, out of harm's way," Rowan told her, as he lifted Ryun up onto the tailgate of the rover. She was surprised at his strength and laughed lightly at being treated as if she were a cub again. What happened to the elder she used to know, who used to move as if he carried the weight of the world upon his shoulders?

The Past Revisited

"Karis?" Maren called out upon reaching a particular, old, crumbling house. A small face peered out at him, but it wasn't his brother's, it was Matis. "Do you know where Karis is?" he asked the cub, trying to keep the panic from his voice.

"He and Tars took Reevs and Rowis fishing over at the deep pond," Matis informed him. "I tol' him they'd get into trouble," she added. He smiled at her, shaking his head in understanding.

"I'm trying to keep him out of trouble," he assured her. "Thanks," he offered, then quickly turned for the pond. He knew it well, as well as recalling the times he'd been scolded for trying to fish there himself, when he was a cub.

"You know where they are?" Sadie asked, seeing he had a particular direction in mind.

"It's a local hangout where the cubs like to go, right Sabin?" he asked, recalling the many times they snuck out there when younger. Sabin chuckled at this, smiling at the memories.

"Yes, I recall getting my bottom spanked a few times for being caught out at the pond," he agreed. "Garth, Torr, Maren and I were all little troublemakers," he told Sadie with a big grin, as they trotted toward the forbidden pond.

"And you're all my bosses now?" she volleyed in return, her eyes filled with humor as she laughed aloud.

"See? You've fallen in with the wrong crowd," Maren teased, finally smiling. There was no way Korman could get to him before them! The way narrowed again and he took the lead. He dodged around the thick brush and trees, then rushed over the top of the small knoll. The pond lay below them and they could clearly see there was more than a half dozen cubs all talking loudly and laughing, as they tried to catch their own fish for dinner.

"Karis! Tars! Rowis!" he called out. There was a sudden cessation of movement, as all the cubs realized they'd been caught. "All of you come on," he added, trying not to smile. Reluctantly, they gathered their things and climbed up the hill to join them, looking dejected.

"Get home," Sabin ordered, as they stopped in wonder to gaze at the human woman with them. She smiled, used to the fascination by now. It always took the young ones aback, at first. She was like them, yet not so at the same time. The curiosity danced in their eyes, as uncertainty kept their questions in check.

"We're trying to help mother, Maren. If we can catch some fish for dinner, she'll be happier," Tars protested. Maren knelt down before his siblings, gathering them to him in a hug, tears of relief threatening to blind him.

"Mother's asked me to take you home with me. She's afraid for you. So, we'll give her your fish, as soon as she comes to say good-bye," he promised.

"She doesn't want us, anymore?" Rowis questioned, stricken by the rejection. Sadie knelt down next to the child, seeing her tears welling up from the hurt within.

"She wants you more than anything, but she wants you safe even more than that, honey," she assured her, crooning in a low voice.

"What are you?" Tars asked, sniffing back her own tears.

"I'm what's called a human," she explained with a laugh. "There're lots of us living where you're going," she added. Maren smiled as he picked up Rowis and stood up, drying her tears.

"My wife's a human and we'd better get back to her, or she'll be worried about us," he told her. He took Tars' hand as Sadie took Karis'. They walked a few paces behind the rest of the cubs, everyone heading back into Matlowe, proper.

"He's around here, somewhere," Sabin warned in a low voice, in English. "His scent's on the wind."

"I noticed," Maren agreed, as Sadie kept an eye to the light woods around them. "He shouldn't do anything, as long as we keep the cubs close to us."

"That, and he doesn't know about you, Sadie. You're the unknown element to his mind. He probably thinks humans as barbaric creatures to allow women to use weapons against men," Sabin added. She smiled at this, unsure even so. He was a big, dangerous-looking starman.

"But, if he wants to kill the cubs, what's going to stop him?" she questioned. Now she knew what that stink upon the wind implied! She knew their sense of smell was better, but this was something even she couldn't mistake.

"You've got a point," Maren agreed, with a sigh. He set his youngest sister down and drew his sidearm, making sure the safety was off. Sadie copied him, then extended her backup weapon for Sabin to use. He smiled his thanks and gave her a nod of his head.

"What's that?" Karis asked, seeing they each carried the strange-looking metal things.

"Something deadly," Sadie replied, "Just in case." He looked unsure of this, but since his older brother approved and held one too, it must be allowed. "Let's keep moving," she advised, now that they were more prepared for action. Sabin nodded his head in agreement.

"Over there," Maren spoke in a low voice, in English. Sabin and Sadie saw where he was looking and noted Korman glaring at them with hate-filled eyes. He stood back away from them, not attempting to come any closer. Maren scooped Rowis back up, holding her with one arm, so he could still use the pistol easily; while Sabin likewise picked up Tars. Sadie urged Karis up on her back, with his legs and arms securely wrapped around her torso. They broke into a trot as Korman disappeared, retreating from them. Even the other village cubs were frightened and hurried to keep up with them, feeling the danger too.

"Will he let us alone?" Sadie questioned, hoping they would know one way, or the other.

"I think so," Maren replied, still staying alert. Sabin gave a nod of his head in accord. They hurried back to the rovers.

"He's still fixated upon Ryes," Rowan commented aloud to himself, as they were returning to their chairs beside the stairs down.

"I had hoped by now, he would've seen things differently," Metta replied, his voice full of sorrow. "I tried to talk with him about it, but he refuses to listen. It's not Ryes he's truly after, but Tyra."

Rowan was shocked to hear this from Metta! He found he had to bite back upon the retort he wanted to make about this lack of listening running in his family line, but saw the genuine concern in his old friend's face. His heart went out to him as he suddenly realized how OLD Metta was becoming. He moved as if there was stiffness in his joints and he was constantly out of breath. The changes were alarming!

"I can't believe he'd threaten his own cub! Karis is nothing more than a young innocent," Rowan said, noting Rebin's interest in their conversation. She was Matlowe's youngest elder.

"Perhaps, it'd be best if Maren takes his younger siblings back with him to this place you now live?" Metta suggested, frowning. "I don't want Korman in any more trouble. My son, Sonta, hates him and won't tolerate his temper, as I have in the past."

"You're stepping down?" Rowan questioned, shocked at this news. He must be more sick than he thought!

"It's time," he returned, sitting down upon the chair, heavily. "I can feel it inside." Rowan stood contemplating this stubborn old man, knowing exactly what he meant, recalling it was the way he felt last year, before Maren's healing touch.

"Why don't you come back with us for a visit?" he offered. "You haven't seen anything of Tayna, herself, except this village. You deserve the chance to view the mountains, or see what great Hailys looks like up close," he offered, hoping he'd take him up on this one.

"Mountains?" Rebin breathed, smiling to herself, "I've only imagined what those were like." She was ready to see what lay beyond Matlowe, herself! Her cubs were grown and out of her home, except for her youngest, Riss. "May I and my son come, too?" she asked. Rowan chuckled at this, seeing Metta was still considering his offer.

"Yes you may, my dear," Ethan assured her, smiling as he finally decided to light his pipe after all. The prevailing breeze would pull it away from the people sitting around him. Let them see the savage human smoking!

"How long would I have to stay for this visit?" Metta finally questioned, watching curiously as Ethan packed tobacco from a pouch into the bowl of the strangely carved stick he'd stuck into his mouth earlier.

"As long, or as short, as you'd like," Garth assured him, hearing their conversation, as he stepped over to join them. He'd gone to speak with Ryes for a few moments while waiting for Sabin to return. "We've promised to attend the Caravaner's Spring Gather, then the Great Spring Gather where the mountain dwellers, plainsmen, caravaners and other peoples meet. You're both more than welcome to come with us to these events, or not, as you please," he offered, then saw Maren, Sabin and Sadie returning, having the children with them and a few others, who ran to their own homes. Everyone looked safe and sound, even if each of the adults had drawn weapons in their hands.

"Mitt? Could you please move the other rovers over here, too?" Garth called out in English, feeling they might as well have all three vehicles closer together, now.

"All right," she yelled back, waving. "I'd better make sure to leave plenty of room for the chopper," she told Bethany, smiling to see Maren and the others were safely returned.

"I could imagine Axel yelling at you, if you didn't," she teased. Mitt gave her a nod of her head, laughing at this as she turned to retrieve the rovers.

"He'd have a fit, for sure," she agreed, over her shoulder, then trotted off. Bethany smiled to herself, imagining the scene.

"Where's Ryes?" Maren demanded, still worried for his cousin.

"Busy feeding the horde," Dotti assured him, smiling. He smiled his relief as both he and Sadie holstered their pistols. She crouched down so Karis could get off her back. Sabin returned her backup weapon to her, giving her a nod of his head in thanks.

"I'd better get back to our explorations," he said, grabbing three more lanterns out of an equipment locker, in the back of the rover.

"What's down there?" Bethy asked, wanting to go down with the men, but knew with her pregnant condition, they'd never let her. Sabin's eyes lit up in mischief.

"Many interesting things," he teased, tauntingly, "We're taking scans of everything, so you can all see it later." With this he went to join Garth and the rest of the exploration group as they headed back down.

"I want to see it now," Dotti protested, pouting. Maren chuckled at her behavior.

"So do I," he added, "but, someone's got to keep an eye on things up here." With this he lifted Tars up, to sit upon the tailgate, then turned for his other two siblings, wanting them as safe as possible. He saw one of the other rovers coming toward them, then frowned. "Where's Ryun?" he suddenly wondered.

"In helping Ryes," his wife told him, lightly laughing. "Are you going to introduce us, or not?" she added. He gave her a nod of his head as he put an arm around her waist, pulling her closer to his side.

"Tars, Karis, Rowis, I want you to meet my wife, Dotti, and another good friend of ours, Bethany," he spoke in introduction, gesturing so they'd know who was whom.

"Hello," Tars ventured, shyly. She was the oldest, all of ten years old. The two siblings who were born before her died of a coughing sickness. She saw there were a lot of humans here already, and her older brother was possessive of this one. She was his wife and she was amazed.

"Pleased to meet you," Dotti told them, smiling as she leaned against Maren's side, content. It was probably more than they could comfortably handle, but she'd never refuse this responsibility. She knew Tennan was too wrapped up in Tian and her pending season now. "I can't wait to show you our new home," she added.

"Is it big?" Karis questioned. He was seven years old, but his eyes took in every detail of this human, who looked so strange in his older brother's arms. They looked different, but so very happy. "And do you have some human cubs for us to play with, too?" he added, hoping there'd be a human girl for him, too.

"No on the human cubs right now," Maren laughed, then sighed, "but yes on our house being big," he assured him. "Even our present home is bigger than mother's house and our new apartment will have more room for us, as a family. It should be ready to move into in another month."

"I'm going to park the other large rover closer to the chamber below," Mitt said, as she stepped over to the others, having just parked the small rover next to this one.

"That's a good idea," Bethy agreed. "And let's take a break. I just realized what Brenda and Ryes meant before, I need a quick snack right now," she added, blushing as she put a hand to her stomach.

"You're going to have a cub?" Tars asked her, her eyes round.

"Yes, I'm going to be having a son of my own, soon," she assured her, laughing. "So, when he's bigger, you can all play."

"How do you know your cub will be a boy?" she pressed, frowning as she wondered about it.

"Your older brother told me," she replied, giving a nod of her head toward Maren.

"I think you're right about that break, Bethy. I'll be right back," Mitt promised as she went to get the last vehicle. Sadie chuckled, feeling a little more relaxed. Most of the villagers had either gone back home, or taken seats around the edge of the square, waiting to see what would happen next. No signs of trouble, now.

"How did you know, Maren?" Tars pressed, wanting to understand. He smiled as he looked into her honey-colored eyes.

"I'm a Healer," he told her, "And so is Tennan, but she's not as strong a one as I. Maybe when you're older, you might be one, too? The Talent does run in our family."

"I could be a Healer?" she gasped out, amazed at this news. She understood the significance this held.

"I want to be a Healer, too," Karis piped up, tugging upon Maren's shirt. She was almost five years old and his favorite little sister. He laughed at this, nodding his head in agreement.

"You may all be Healers. We'll only know when you get older," he assured her.

"Here, let me get out some snacks for everyone," Dotti offered. She knew she might as well get used to having to care for these children, now. She had her own in the making and hoped to be an old hand, by the time her baby was born.

"Ah, much better," Jim agreed, switching on his lantern as they reached the bottom of the stairs. Now they could clearly see the writing upon the walls. "What did they mean by this, `To those begotten, so as not to be forgotten?'" he asked. Sabin shrugged as Garth looked thoughtful.

"That this was left for us, those who are descendants of these people, so we wouldn't forget them and all this world had been before," he decided, speaking in a low voice. "I only hope what they stored here was worth that explosion. It must be something valuable, because Ryes told me the greater force was directed downwards, to destroy what lay here. She merely redirected the energy and we all know the result of that, but at least she was strong enough to prevent anyone from being hurt." He activated his own lantern and turned for the passage they were exploring when Rowan came down to get them, earlier. They were quickly at the first intersection with two smaller hallways leading off left and right. The main one continued straight ahead. They kept to the main corridor.

"You mean she can direct the flow of energy?" Monty asked, amazed to hear this spoken so casually.

"Yes, to some extent, for short periods of time," Sabin replied, as Garth frowned at the question, realizing something.

"This is not the time, nor the place," Garth advised in English. "We won't discuss what Ryes can and can't do, while we're still in this village. Once we're home, you can talk with her about it yourself," he ordered. The other three men gave him nods of their heads, as they realized what he was saying. There was still danger here for Ryes, especially with their numbers so small. Who knew who was listening as their voices echoed up and down the wide corridors, conducting through the open portal above?

"Here's that library," Sabin pointed out an open door to one side, after they resumed their explorations in a more somber attitude.

Earlier, they opened and looked into several of the rooms, to get an idea of what was here. The setup reminded them of Winterhaven, to some degree, but they had yet to find the central computer system, or power plant for this site. The light panels embedded at regular intervals into the walls above their heads, close to the ceiling, spoke to them of a system which used energy. "Let's see if we can get one of those readers working," he suggested.

"That's an idea," Jim agreed, smiling. "Maybe they left us some clues, so we can figure out what happened, and who might lie behind Hailys' destruction?"

"Maybe," Garth agreed, as he stepped into the room; the rest of the men right behind him. "This one table seems to hold more importance. It's far larger, there are chairs with higher backs set around it, and one seat looks to have more significance than the others, like this was where their `Base Commander` sat."

"Look here," Jim spoke in a low voice. He indicated a larger crystal rod set within a cloth-lined depression in a finely-crafted, open wooden box, which set upon a distinctive stand. It stood to one side of a desk, near the door. He held his lantern steady as Garth stepped over to look at it more closely. It seemed it was set up to draw attention to its importance. There was a light film of dust upon it, so he blew it off.

"This has to mean something," Monty agreed, speaking barely above a whisper, himself.

"That looks like some kind of reader," Sabin supplied, also in a low voice, his lantern centered on a large reader which was placed in the middle of that larger table. "I hope it still works and can take this thing."

"Let's find out," Garth replied, speaking in a normal tone of voice. If there were any ghosts here to bear witness, he felt they'd be ashamed to see their descendants behaving in such a timid fashion. He smiled to himself as he saw his louder voice startled the others. He picked up the crystal rod and walked over to the table. From the memories Ryes gave him from her trips into Hailys' past, he activated the reader and was relieved to see this one did, indeed, function. It'd be far faster than the tedious methods they were currently using to extract and copy the data the crystal rods contained, using the human's equipment and computers. Eric had done an excellent job in getting things started there, before he left with the caravaners. He cleaned off the crystal with a handkerchief Ryes insisted he always carry. It'd proved handy at times.

"Do you know what you're doing?" Sabin asked, concerned. If it was an important memory rod, could this reading machine damage it, or erase it, if they failed to enter a special code, like the large portal?

"No, do you?" he volleyed in return, smiling crookedly. Sabin sighed as he nodded his head, smiling. "I'm going on the memories Ryes showed me from her trips into the past."

"It's better than nothing," Jim agreed, smiling, "Yes, we risk losing what it contains, but at least we're recording everything, so we'll have some record of it - if we can get the information readout," he reminded them, pointing to the small drone quietly flying over his head.

"That's what I think," Garth replied as he slid the crystal into the reader in the way he recalled from Ryes' memories. There was a wash of light and static, then the wall behind the great chair began to glow and an image was projected, much like the holos of the humans. They stood practically holding their breaths, waiting.

The image suddenly grew distinct and an elder stood before them, who looked almost exactly like Maren. He was a little taller, a little heavier, but the resemblance was remarkable. He looked at them and smiled warmly, then sat down in the taller chair, even if it still sat before them, empty.

"Please, take a seat. I have much to cover and hope you are not in any pressing hurry," he said. Even his voice sounded like Maren's, but his accent was strange, although not hard to understand. Garth smiled as he thought they should send Monty out for Maren to see this, but didn't want to waste the time right now. He'd show him later. They each pulled out a chair and sat down, as he bid them. He could hear the helicopters arriving outside and knew they'd be busy for a while, trying to get that heavy door lifted and out of Matlowe, anyway.

"There's more excitement here than ever was in Riverward," Chel commented as she, Aylita and the children were sitting on a bench Taroom had created last month and set on the village square side of the house for them to use when they wanted. Amarr was in his wooden pen, playing with some soft toys Aylita made for him. Taroom had gone back to New Matlowe, saying he had one more thing to finish before he'd be ready to watch. They'd promised to fill him in on the parts he missed. Siah came from around a corner of their house, looking uncertain.

"Is it safe?" she asked in a low voice. "There was a loud thunder that shook everything over in New Matlowe."

"As safe as it will be," Aylita replied, grinning as she nodded towards where the Village Circle once stood. "They found a way below the Village Circle and a booby-trapped door at the bottom," she explained, pointing to the wreckage of the same door where it rested in a shallow crater. Siah's eyes widened in shock at the sight.

"It was amazing! Ryes, who is wife to Garth, their leader, has a Talent that stopped it from falling and crushing quite a few people. She just stopped it in the middle of the air! My heart's still pounding to have seen it," Chel told her, appearing charged.

"I'm sorry I missed it," Siah replied, smiling as she doubted their tale. Still, she sat down upon the bench to wait and see what would happen next, too. "Why are they so mad that she has Talent?"

she eventually questioned, doubting what she was hearing from the other villagers. Farra, who was standing nearby, turned with surprise written in her eyes at hearing Siah. She stepped closer to the women and children.

"I apologize, as it's sad that someone who never gave any of us grief, and did her best to help the young cubs, should be looked upon in such a way. Ryes having Talent that works like this is a blessing," she told them, blushing. She turned back to look at the anger on some of the faces nearby, "I don't understand why they're so mad at her."

"You're born with Talent and it's what you do with it, once it awakens, that makes it bad or good. I've only seen the good, myself, in Ryes," Aylita replied, smiling for the village elder, who was a teacher for the cubs in Old Matlowe. She nodded her head in agreement.

"I'm going to see what I can do to get some to see reason," she said. Siah immediately stood up.

"I'm going with you, so I can understand them better," she offered. Farra smiled at this, her brown eyes lighting up with humor.

"Your help is most welcome," she replied. The two women started to head for the nearest knot of unhappy villagers, together.

"Siah's finding her place here, finally," Chel commented with a warm smile.

"Finally," Aylita agreed, nodding her head and smiling in turn. She hoped they could help turn them around.

The helicopters arrived over an hour later, kicking up more dust and debris into the air, as the smaller one landed in the village square, near the rovers. The larger one hovered above, stationary over the target piece of metal, lowering a large metal hook, at the end of a sturdy cable. Shadd jumped out the pilot's door, laughing as she hurried over to Mitt, giving her a hug.

"I love flying!" she declared, "You're going to have to let me go up in the choppers more often." Mitt laughed, knowing her friend was shaping up to be a good pilot, now that she could relax more around the machines.

"I'll talk with Axel about it," she promised. She noted Shadd was wearing a sidearm, too. It was good to see that Torr had briefed everyone, before sending them out. "Let's get this hunk of metal secured, first. Things seem pretty quiet, right now," she advised. Shadd gave her a nod of her head, letting her go. Minn was right behind her, smiling down at his petite, determined wife.

"We brought the cable net, but it looks like it's going to be a real job to get it under that thing," he told her, unhappy with the time they could end up wasting here in this mud-hole of a village.

"I'll take care of that; I need the practice," Ryes assured him, speaking English as she approached. "Just get it into position," she ordered. She saw Quinn Mercill and Phil Medina heard her, immediately turning to unload it out of the storage compartment in the back of the smaller chopper. Minn, Kovin and Jon Alvarson rushed to help them spread it out, near the ruined portal. After a few minutes, they were ready for the next step of the operation. Ryes closed her eyes, centering herself within, then deliberately reached out to the massive door and pushed it upwards, just a little bit, away from Tayna's grip, which the humans called gravity. She heard a gasp nearby, but held onto her focus.

"Hurry, get it into position," Mitt directed, seeing the strain upon Ryes' face; after stopping the explosion and then the door as it fell, she could well understand.

Sadie cast a wary eye to the rest of the villagers, as she heard their voices raised in protest of this flaunting display of power. She wondered why they so objected to Ryes here? The shock upon the faces of their own crew was expected at least. Even if they all knew Ryes had special abilities; this one was new. She smiled as she could well imagine the stories which would circulate at tonight's dinner!

"Got it!" Shadd told Ryes, not wanting her to overdo things. If she overtaxed her Talents, she might not be able to react when she needed to, and this crowd looked too restless to relax around here. She couldn't believe she used to call this place home! She saw her own mother and her waving for her to come and join her, but she ignored it. This wasn't a family visit today.

"There," Ryes sighed out, as she gently released it back to Tayna's keeping, in pure relief.

She opened her eyes to see the crew quickly securing the final bolts of the netting, getting it properly gathered and set onto the hook Axel extended down from the helicopter. In a very short time, the larger chopper rose higher into the air, the door suspended below as it turned back for Winterhaven. They all breathed a sigh of relief at this; then as Ryes and the others were turning back for the rovers, a scream shattered the air. Ryes' heart constricted as she realized she left only Bethany and Ryun with her cubs. With Korman still loose nearby, she feared for them all! They all ran - full out - as a group, they were heading for the rovers.

As they rounded the back end of the vehicles, they stopped to see Ryun standing in shock, her hands covering her mouth, as Bethy pointed to the square beyond. Tanns lay upon the ground, blood seeping through her tunic from several long gashes, as she struggled to reach them. Ryes and Maren ran for her, immediately. As they stooped down beside her, Korman charged out at them from the shadow of one of the buildings near them. Furious, Ryes took out her stunner and fired. Korman came to a hard stop as he dropped face down to the ground, unconscious; still half a dozen steps away from them. Sadie was quickly at their side, her pistol drawn; seeing she wasn't needed this time. She stepped over to turn him face up, to see if he was still breathing and smiled as she noted his expression of utter shock. He looked fine, otherwise.

"Let's get her back now!" Maren decided, picking up Tanns and turning for the chopper. He was glad it was Ryes who had reacted first, or he'd have shot his father to death for what he'd done to his mother. "Mitt!" he shouted, "Get it fired up!" Mitt quickly moved to comply, seeing it was a serious emergency. Her heart went out to Maren at seeing Tanns in such a way. Ryes rushed back to jump into the one rover, then emerged with one of her infants in her arms.

"Maren!" she called, as he was about to board the chopper. "Take Rhin with you; he might help," she suggested, feeling torn. She knew Rhin could boost his abilities and could go with them, while she had to stay here for now. He paused long enough to give her a nod of his head.

"Here, I'll take him for you," Rowan offered. He was going to be there to talk some sense into his daughter once and for all time, if Maren could heal her. She had to let go of Korman! "I'll take care of him, until you return." She sighed as she handed him over to his keeping.

"Thanks, grandfather," she replied with a smile. He quickly jumped in, careful of the infant. She stood, watching the chopper lift off, turning for Winterhaven.

"So much excitement for such a friendly visit," Dr. Cruthers commented, stepping up next to her. "I'm sure your aunt will be fine, but you'd best see to helping with your younger cousins. They still don't know Dot at all, and at least you're a familiar face. I can imagine this sight might've terrified them." Ryes looked at him in surprise as she realized he was probably right.

"Oh, yes," she breathed, rushing back to the back of the rover, to see how the younger ones were doing. They were crying as Dotti and Bethy were trying to comfort them; a look of helplessness in their eyes. Ryes stepped closer, her heart going out to them.

"She's going to be all right," she assured them, not sure if they'd want her comfort, after all. Aunt Tanns had never cared for her, would her younger children view her any differently, she wondered? Maren was her one hope...

"Why didn't Maren take us, too?" Tars demanded, wiping at her eyes, looking accusingly at the Huntress, as if it were her fault.

"He needs to give his full concentration to your mother, to heal her properly. He left Dotti behind too, but she's not crying, because she understands," she explained, stepping closer.

"Why did you give him your baby, too? Is he sick?" Karis questioned. He knew Maren left Matlowe to be with her and his friends, so she had to be a person they could trust in his eyes.

"Because Rhin can help him heal your mother," she replied, smiling. Karis let go of Dotti to move over and wrap his arms around her. Ryes smiled in surprise at this, hugging him back as she kissed the top of his head. "Maren's the best Healer ever born. He'll have your mother well, long before we reach home," she assured him, sure of this in her heart.

"She's not going to die?" Rowis asked, looking up to Ryes, still crying as she clutched Dotti's torso tightly.

"No, she won't. Maren won't let her die," Dotti stated, sure on this score.

"How about our father?" Tars accused, looking to see him still lying on the dirt. "Did you kill him?"

"No, I didn't," Ryes assured her, "He's merely stunned; taking a nap. He'll wake up later this evening and be just fine." She seemed to accept this as Rowis scowled.

"Does he know where you live? Will he find us there?" she asked. Her eyes were round with fear playing in their depths.

"It wouldn't matter if he tried. There're too many people there who'll make sure he leaves us all alone. He'll never hurt you cubs, again." Rowis and Tars each released a sigh at hearing this, hoping.

"Ryes, do you need us to do anything?" Shadd asked, feeling a little useless.

"Why don't you and Sadie go pack up some of my cousins' and aunt's things? That way we can set them up with some sense of home, when we get back to Winterhaven," she suggested, thinking this might be the best idea.

"Let's go pack up everything. I don't think Maren will let her return, until Korman's gone for good," Shadd counter suggested in a low voice, seeing Metta walking towards them. What could he want, she wondered? Ryes gave her a nod of her head, thinking she had the right of the matter. Sadie went into the back of the largest rover and pulled out some empty containers, which they loaded into the smallest rover. Shadd gave her a nod and the two of them quickly departed in the small rover with Shadd driving; knowing the way.

Legacy

Metta first checked to make sure his youngest brother was still breathing; not believing they'd outright kill him and leave him lying like this on the ground. Then he came to a decision. If Korman was going to behave like this, it was time he left Matlowe, before he'd be called forth to defend his actions again. The last few months had been a nightmare and it was time Korman stood in the circle by himself to atone for this needless violence! Metta stepped over to the human elder, since Rowan left quite willingly in the flying machine. That had been another astounding thing; that the younger men and women rode in it from out of the air, but Rowan appeared to fully trust the strange, noisy machine which young Mitt seemed to control. It spoke volumes.

"Elder Ethan," he began, not wholly sure of his acceptance with this man. Ethan turned and gave him a nod of his head. "I believe I'd like to come to your village for a visit, after all. What am I allowed to bring?" he asked. Ethan smiled grandly at this; seeing this might be an opportune moment for him to leave Matlowe, with his brother on a rampage, hurting others.

"Only what you feel you need with you. We do have clothing available, if you don't mind our styles," he told him, gesturing down the length of his body. He was dressed in lightweight slacks and a colorful murkin shirt today. He wanted something comfortable, yet providing some protection. The plant fibers of the murkin were very tough and even naturally flame resistant, native to a planet named Celynia, which lay almost between Tayna and Earth. He took a moment to wonder how that colony fared now? "We also have a plentiful supply of food on hand, so you don't have to worry about bringing any of your own. And all our guest rooms already have beds with fresh blankets, pillows and sheets to use."

"Thank you, I'll be back, shortly," he replied with a nod. He didn't think too much of the clothing, nor knew what a sheet was, but felt better about not having to worry about providing his own food. It'd leave more for his grandchildren, at least. Rebin overheard them and stepped closer as Metta left.

"May I and my son, Riss, come today, too?" she asked, hoping. Dr. Cruthers grinned merrily.

"Yes you may, my dear," he assured her. "I believe we'll still have plenty of room."

"I'll be right back," she promised, smiling gratefully, then rushed off to gather her son and their things. Minn stepped closer to the good doctor.

"Looks like we're slowly stripping Matlowe of its citizens," he commented, smiling at the thought.

"They're only coming for a short visit. I'm sure they'll tire of the lot of us, very quickly. We're all too busy to do any proper entertaining," he teased in return, as he turned to face Minn. His eyes were crinkling in merriment. Minn chuckled in response, as did Jon, Phil and Kovin, having overheard their comments.

"Will it be much longer?" Kovin finally asked, in a more somber tone.

"I don't know. You'll have to ask our intrepid explorers," Ethan replied, gesturing toward the hole in the middle of the village square. "I'm sure they wouldn't mind, if you went down to join them to help," he offered. "I think the construction crews back home will be able to carry on with your absence, for a short while," he added, knowing why he looked so anxious. Kovin and Phil were the ones in charge of the building projects and chaffed to be forced to stay here, when they'd rather be back in Winterhaven doing what they enjoyed best.

"Oh, we'll be just fine and will head on down to see things, too," Phil assured Dr. Cruthers as he pulled Kovin back away from him, smiling grandly. Ethan chuckled as he towed Kovin all the way back, on the other side of the rover.

"What?" Kovin asked in a low voice, seeing his friend had something urgent he wanted to say to him. He noted Ryes looked around the vehicle to make sure it was only the two of them, then returned to what she was doing, leaving them in peace.

"If you keep that up, he'll suddenly decide we've been doing nothing but work lately and need a break. He'll then order us to take anywhere from a day, to a week off for our own good, while our work either sits, or is screwed up by everyone else," Phil warned him speaking urgently, also in a low voice, then sighed heavily. "It took me almost a month to get things straightened out from the last time he did that! So, lay low, away from Dr. Cruthers, until we're finished with our bigger projects," he advised. Kovin's eyes widened in surprise, as he gave him a nod of agreement.

"Let's go check things out below. Can you imagine what they've done to build their underground building using the techniques from Hailys? And to keep it secret here in the middle of Matlowe? That has to be amazing," Kovin offered as a distraction. "And it'll keep us away from Dr. Cruthers," he added. A big grin blossomed across Phil's face as his eyes lit up with curiosity.

"You're right, there're some new interesting things to go investigate," he agreed as they both turned for the steps down.

"Oh, Phil, Kovin," Dotti said as she came around the rover, finding them still nearby. "Maren and I will need a larger apartment from the start. We now have his younger brother and sisters added to our family," she explained with a guilty look on her face. Both men stopped and frowned at this, but Kovin gave her a nod of his head, appearing to have an idea.

"You'll have it," he promised. His eyes met Phil's and his friend gave him a nod at this, and then smiled.

"Sure, Dotti, it'll be no problem. We'll give you the one next to Sabin's. It has four bedrooms and is pretty spacious," Phil assured her. Kovin nodded his agreement to this, then took out his minicomp and made a note, just in case. They'd already heard from Shadd that she and Torr wouldn't need it, after all. Dotti smiled in relief, and wondered who originally was supposed to have that one? It couldn't be merely empty; unassigned. The two men headed off before something else was changed again, but Minn was in their path of escape.

"Going below?" he asked, curiosity dancing in his golden eyes. "I'm ready to see it, too!" Phil gave him a nod. A broad smile graced his lips as he nodded back and fell in with them, ready to see what wonders lay below, too.

Ryes leaned against the back of the rover; having been listening in on them and smiling to herself. The idea of vacation time held merit. She'd have to talk with Ethan, as soon as they got back to Winterhaven. Maybe once their larger buildings were finished, they could each take an enforced break separately? They'd been working steadily upon the plans all winter long and now were putting things together with a willing crew under their command. It was going smoothly, overall. And, if they hadn't gotten the people under them trained well enough by then, it'd be only their own fault if things didn't run well while they were away.

Metta set his things down beside the largest, wheeled machine, as he saw Minn, Kovin and a human start down the stairs into the mysterious door below. He thought it was time to see this hidden place for himself. There hadn't been any further explosions, nor shouts, nor sounds of alarm, so it couldn't be too bad.

"Father, what're you doing?" Sonta questioned, stepping up to see his wife had been correct. He had two large bundles of his things sitting next to one of the wheeled machines.

"I've been invited to spend some time in their new village," he explained. "How better to understand them, than to see it for myself?" he questioned; then extended his hand to clasp his son's shoulder, a proud smile upon his lips. "You're taking my office at the next full moon phase of Porr and it'll be easier if I'm not here for everyone to look to, when it comes to any decisions you have to enforce."

"No one's going to do that," Sonta denied. Metta shook his head at this.

"I remember when I first held the post, the whole village looked to my father for verification, or his opinion about my decisions, as if I was still a cub and it was his final say which carried the true determination. It frustrated me as it took years for the village to get used to me being the leader," he related to him, his eyes casting back into the past as he looked toward the chair he'd sat for too many years! Yes, it was about time. He wanted to have a grand adventure before his time came. This seemed the best way to find it and far better than lying in bed waiting for his end!

"I'll miss you," he replied with a heavy sigh. Metta smiled as he turned to look into his eyes. He was so proud of his courage and loved him so much.

"I'll miss you, too," he assured him. "Let's go down and see what's below our feet, which has been hidden for uncounted years?" he pressed. "After all, it belongs to us, too. And as elders, we should be a part of this historic day."

"The human elder remains up here," Sonta observed, smiling in return. He, too, was itching to know about the hidden treasures.

"Yes. Someone has to keep an eye to this unruly bunch of cubs," he replied.

"But, I thought Garth was in charge?"

"He is, but he's probably counting upon Elder Ethan to watch things here, while he's below." Sonta smiled his agreement, gesturing to his father to precede him down the steps. He was sure this was the case, too. They trailed after the ones before. When they reached the bottom, they saw the inscription upon the wall at the entrance.

"Ryes was right; this was meant for all of Tayna!" Metta declared, somehow troubled by this discovery. Sonta nodded his head in agreement.

"Like the maps carved into the walls of Berrals, whatever lies here was meant for all starmen," Sonta agreed with a nod.

There were lights coming from a room, further down the corridor and a loud voice could be heard speaking. Metta steeled his courage and stepped closer to see what they saw; his son walking beside him with far more confidence. The hall was long, dark and echoing, but somehow not too scary. The doorway was open and welcoming as they approached it. They crowded into the huge, dark room behind the younger men to watch this moving, talking image in awe. No one else in this room seemed shocked by this curious visage and its ability to speak. Metta calmed himself and focused upon what was being said for it had to be important to be so saved for so long.

"...in the light of this, we felt to limit the number of laws we pass down, so as to keep them simple and easy for all citizens to follow," the man sitting in a chair said, as he spoke to those gathered in the room. His accent sounded strange, but was easy to understand. Metta stood in shock, again. He looked like an older version of his nephew Maren!

Suddenly, the scene shifted to display a tall, silvery monolith with writing etched deep into its surface, the letters accented with black, to make them stand out all the more. It stood next to the elder's platform, in Matlowe's village square. There was a profusion of plants blooming around the platform, which looked like it was newly built, and cubs could be seen running and playing behind it. Upon the monolith were written twelve laws.

"I've seen this before," Garth muttered, frowning as he read what it displayed. He paused the recording.

"It's not there now," Jim pointed out, wondering.

"It does look familiar," Minn agreed, "I just can't think of where I've seen it. It wasn't out on display," he added, trying to bring it more clearly to mind.

"Aric's workshop, lying against the wall with the other scrapped projects," Metta spoke up, remembering it, having puzzled it out with the young men. Garth turned and saw the others standing near the doorway.

"Have a seat. This is a holo our ancestors left for all of us. I have it paused, right now," he told them, gesturing toward the chairs.

"You're right!" Kovin agreed, smiling at Old Metta and Sonta, wondering how they managed to finally find the courage to join them?

"What's it doing in his workshop, when it belongs out for everyone to see?" Sabin asked as they stepped closer and took seats.

Sabin noted Sonta had curiosity written in his bright eyes. He took a seat next to his father, wondering at this hidden room. It seemed to stretch out into a deep darkness to the left of the door, out of the range of their strange lights.

"Was it in need of repair?" Sabin finished, smiling at their newest explorers, then Garth met his eyes speculatively.

"We'll have to get a look at it. If it's in good shape, we'll put it back into Matlowe's square where it belongs. If it needs to be repaired, we can always copy it from this holo and create a new one, for all the people of Tayna to see," Garth suggested to the elders, feeling it'd be best to get their leave in this matter. Sonta nodded agreement while Metta's eyes were alight with ideas.

"The first law is, `Do not commit murder, nor suffer a murderer's presence,'" Jim stated in comment. He smiled to himself at this, recalling the story of Sabin's banishment from this very village and Garth's description of the sour look on Metta's face when he later rescinded his decree, when there was more than enough evidence to support his claim that the man he killed was a child killer and did, indeed, deserve death. "It's one of our own, oldest laws." Sonta looked surprised at this, but gave him a nod of his head. They were obviously a civilized people.

"Yes, it is," Dr. Cruthers agreed in Dolbith with a soft chuckle, stepping into the room. His eyes quickly assessed the situation, then he crossed the room to take a chair next to Garth. He couldn't wait to see what lay down here any longer. "Your wife has command of the situation upstairs and I believe Maren should be able to handle his mother's healing quite well. He's on the way back to Winterhaven," he informed Garth and the others of what had happened up above in English. Garth's eyes widened in surprise, but he merely gave him a nod of his head in response.

"Maybe I should go give the ladies a hand?" Jim suggested, staying to the English, meeting his commander's eyes.

"Let them handle things. The attacker is stunned and shouldn't be a problem for hours, at least," Ethan assured them. "Let's get on with this delightful display," he invited in Dolbith, gesturing toward the holo of the monolith. Garth relaxed a little at this, then gave him a nod of his head and smiled as he took the reader off of pause. If there was any great need, Ryes would send for him. At least Korman wasn't an issue now!

"As you can note, three of the laws were written especially for our Talents. These ones are as they are on Kahmarr, itself. Since I am the crown prince from Kahmarr, I am sworn to uphold all twelve of these laws and bring justice swiftly and fairly. My children understand their duties and will follow suit, passing on their responsibilities to their children, in turn."

"As you have already discovered, we have passed down the access codes to this archive through children's rhymes. We felt they were our best foil, in case of an invasion. You would have to think like us, to be able to gain entry here. This great library contains all we could salvage out of Hailys, Pygoth and Montas. It is still too dangerous to do any serious excavations. Hopefully in another twenty years the deadly remains of the gases used to exterminate the populations underground will have chemically broken down enough to allow us to salvage even more. We lack the proper reagents in a quantity enough to make Hailys safe again. We truly have so little knowledge left to pass on, considering what lies in only one of our greater libraries back in Resdan, upon Kahmarr."

"As of last report, Kahmarr is fighting for her very existence. My heart grieves for my family and friends. We get our news through very indirect methods, for now. Demia is the only major homeworld of our allies, which is known to still be holding out. All the other homeworlds have fallen and the remaining colonies, like us, have maintained a low profile in hopes of escaping detection by the Snagospin warships."

The image again shifted to display a huge dark starship, bristling with bulbous protrusions which might be their weaponry. It rotated slowly to give the viewers time to see it from all angles, then changed once more, to display one of the murdering aliens. It was obvious it had died violently, but still its body displayed a strange appearance. The legs bent backwards, as if their joints were reversed. There were four arms and four legs, each ending in a heavy claw, with the "hands" having an additional, smaller, opposing claws; four in total. Their eyes were on four stalks, with small mandibles bracketing the mouth; the body was a head, long neck and torso, all covered with a thick dark-wooly fur. The remains of the clothing it once wore were laid out beside it. The colors were bright and clashed and appeared to be a jumpsuit.

"Those are our enemies?" Jim breathed out, startled. Dr. Cruthers was studying the image intently, as Garth froze it for all of them to view it longer; to know their true enemy. Metta gasped, horrified.

"Why do we so threaten them, that they're compelled to wipe out entire planets?" Minn questioned. "We're different-looking, but not beyond being able to live side-by-side, I'm sure."

"They have their own views of what they want to tolerate, or not," Garth responded. "He said they only go after strong civilizations. If we could ever unite enough firepower, maybe we could knock them back to their original colony worlds and get them to leave the rest of us alone?" Sonta nodded at this, wondering how they could succeed, when their ancestors failed?

"That is what we could hope for," Ethan replied, sighing. After seeing the wreckage of the Star Quest, hearing of the genocide campaign they launched against the older civilizations, and their strange silence from Earth, he knew it would eventually come down to either exterminating these Snagospin completely, or restricting them to their own worlds, until they realized they'd only be allowed out to play if they behaved. "Go ahead and resume the recording. We'll discuss them later," he suggested. Garth gave him a nod of his head, glancing around to make sure everyone else had seen enough, then took the reader off pause.

"Their Talents are very strong, but are only tuned to detecting signs of the greater civilizations, such as starships and long distance communications. Interstellar travel is kept very discrete and the handful of brave traders, who try to keep our intersystem communications open, risk everything in each and every voyage. Fewer and fewer ships are left as time passes and I foresee a time when we will be completely cut off."

"I have established a group of Foresters to travel in caravans to conduct trade agreements here upon Tayna, so we will have a regular, ready access to intelligence and can maintain some kind of peace among the peoples. We are letting each group self-govern, to some extent, but these laws will be handed down to each and every surviving town and village. We have revived our shipwright skills and now have a small fleet of trading vessels, to maintain contact with the other continents. We are establishing a group of Foresters to run the caravans on the other, larger ones, too."

"Our only Talent of One was rumored to have disappeared here upon Tayna, several years ago. A search of all Talents still alive has turned up nothing. She may have perished in the attack. I had hoped to breed her, so as to preserve her Talent through her descendants. A Talent of One is only born once in twenty-five thousand years. She might have been the only one to have fought the Snagospin Talents and triumphed. We will never know now."

"All I have to pass onto my descendants is Healing. My true-mate has Booster and Visionaries in her bloodlines, through the Foresters. If I had had the foresight my dear wife possesses, I would have invited quite a few of my friends to Tayna to `party' with us. But, I did not find her until I was here on Tayna, vacationing. At least we would have a greater pool for future generations. You must preserve your Talents, at all costs. They are truly the only chance of victory against the Snagospin, according to my wife."

"She says a great leader of peoples will arise named Garthed?" he asked, looking off to the side, then turned his attention back to his audience. "I apologize, as it is the closest I can come to your name. She advised me to tell you to rule with your head and your heart. You will reunite the surviving planetary colonies and save one of your allies, Dirt, although I believe she said it will be far too late for Kahmarr. I know our small library is not much, but use it for all the Star People upon Tayna, as well as other worlds, as you see best," he offered with a small bow, then the image froze, as if finished. Garth exhaled the breath he hadn't realized he was holding, quietly, his eyes still glued to the holo before them.

"He was talking about you, Garth. You were just saying we need to unite what firepower still exists," Sabin told him, seeing the thoughtful expression in his eyes.

"It's not Dirt, it's Earth and at least Hailys is the correct name for the city of ruins," Monty spoke up in response. "It sure sounds like he's talking about you, Sir," he added, looking to his leader. Even if Garth wasn't human, he had no qualms about following him.

"Could a Visionary see so far ahead?" he asked Sabin, meeting his eyes with doubt clearly in his own. It couldn't be!

"After seeing what your own wife is capable of accomplishing," Dr. Cruthers spoke up, before Sabin could, "Why wouldn't someone as strong as she, who's able to look ahead, not be able to see you and the rest of us? What is a Talent of One?" he questioned, catching Garth's eyes.

"I have no idea," he replied, then suddenly got an idea. "We were thinking of having Ryes and Sabin take one more journey back in time, in Hailys. Perhaps her Aunt might be able to tell us?" he suggested. He checked the reader and noted there was one large, last, encoded message left on the crystal. With the way it was stopped, it meant it might be something only for him, if he was the man he was talking about. How could he reunite the colonies, or save Earth? It was a lot to swallow, for sure. They only wanted to rebuild Tayna, herself, not take on this monumental task! They still had Winterhaven to build, first.

"You just broke your own rule and told the Matlowe Village elders that your wife can Time Walk," Sabin reminded him in English. Garth realized he was right, as he stood to face Metta and his son.

"You and Ryes can walk through time?" Sonta questioned Sabin, as they all stood. Garth deactivated the reader and removed the crystal. He'd check the rest of it out, later. So, Ryes had been right in using the nursery rhymes after all. How to unlock the rest of the message would be their next task.

"Yes, we can," Sabin lied. "Actually, I take her back with me as a safety measure. It's a dangerous Talent and I feel better with having her along. We ran into her great aunt the last time."

"Amazing," he replied, astounded. He wondered what the city looked like, even now, having never had the courage to make the journey.

"Well, O' Great Savior, at least we have some readers which work and a more established facility to utilize for copying the information they stored," Ethan teased Garth, smiling. He chuckled as his friend turned a dark gold color, blushing.

"We'll leave an investigative team here to get it organized and get copies of everything stored on their computer and memory rods, for our library back in Winterhaven. The more copies, the better to preserve it for the future. The important stuff should be copied and distributed by way of the caravaners, to all of Tayna. We still need to find the other, old cities, which might've had underground archives, too," Garth said, listing their priorities. "I want Jim, Monty, Sabin, Phil, Kovin and Minn to finish with our initial survey. I have to radio back to Winterhaven," he ordered. The men gave him nods of their heads, then assembled a few steps away, talking in low voices. In a few moments, they dispersed. Two started exploring deeper into the library, itself, heading down the stairs nearby, as the remaining four went out to check the other doors down the hallway and to head downstairs to the lower levels.

"You've grown, Garth," Sonta commented, stepping around the table. It amazed him; the quiet note of command this young man held already. He'd never considered him outstanding before. By the time he became an elder, he could see him as a great leader of men.

"In the past year, through our travels, I've learned far more than I could ever have imagined," Garth admitted. He suddenly wondered when Sonta started looking so old? He was only about fifteen years older than his own father, and Garvin was so full of energy, he found himself pressed to keep up with him at times!

"Exactly what are your plans for this place, and Matlowe?" he pressed, wanting to know what they could expect. "After all, we've had enough surprises with the immigration of new families and other opportunists from out of the east!"

"Exactly?" Garth returned, taking a more serious demeanor. "We'll copy all the information this facility holds, in hopes that it'll be preserved for future generations. This place was left here not just for Matlowe, nor Tayna, but for all starmen. After we've finished with it, why not leave it open for other scholars from across Tayna, and other worlds, when we reestablish star travel, to come and learn what they can of our science and history?" he suggested. "And maybe add in their knowledge, so it can be a repository for higher learning in the future?"

"Yes, you could charge them for lodging, as they conduct their studies," Dr. Cruthers added, smiling. "You could form your own tourist-based economy. After all, three major caravan roads intersect here, making for easy access." Garth laughed at this, shaking his head. The good doctor would be giving them ideas!

"And Matlowe would become as great a city as Cootain is rumored to be," Garth added, but he saw the sharp interest in Sonta and Metta's eyes. "At least we're the ones to originally discover and open it up. I could have Phil and Kovin meet with the Matlowe elders later, to design an inn for your visitors to use and some temporary housing units we call apartments. You could even build a tavern for evening gatherings and perhaps a small university at some point later, as well as some small, permanent shops for supplies," he said, wanting to make sure they appreciated they had an active a role in this venture, before they decided to start charging them, too! Ethan chuckled, noting it also.

"Yes, this should be made available to all the citizens of Tayna," Metta agreed, smiling. Suddenly, the light panels overhead came on, as well as the air flow system, surprising the villagers. Ethan chuckled.

"It appears they found the main circuitry," he mildly commented.

"I've got to check in with Winterhaven," Garth excused himself, turning for the door, covertly pocketing the large crystal as he exited into the main hallway. He'd see what else it contained, away from the villagers! What he truly wanted to do now was get the full story out of his wife, first. He was sure the women would have Korman well contained by now.

"That did it!" Kovin told Minn, clasping him on the shoulder in pride.

"I think it's working with all those power circuits lately that's helped the most here. Look, there seems to be more than just support for this facility. If I understand this, it might be able to provide power to Matlowe Village, itself," he said, sounding excited as he indicated the way the panels were set up.

"I wonder why they shut that part down?" Phil asked, as he stepped closer. "We'll have to trace out the circuits later, to see if we can figure why." Minn groaned loudly and laughed at hearing him.

"I can guess it means I'll have more work to do here, once again," he told them with a big grin upon his face. "And here I thought I'd left this small village far behind me!"

"At least you're married to the fastest pilot in Winterhaven," Phil teased while Kovin laughed, nodding his head.

"Now wouldn't it be amazing to have simple electricity available to all the villagers? Maybe we can teach them they need to be a part of the future, too?" Minn suggested.

"I'd still call Winterhaven my home. I'm never coming back here to live," Kovin replied, "but it'd be amazing to see this village grow, all the same."

"Let's see what Taroom thinks of this place and our ideas," Phil suggested, "Once we finish what Garth wanted us to get done."

"That sound like a good plan," Sabin said, as he joined the other men. "He seems to have a good, open mind."

"He does," Kovin replied. "Rowan suggested we include him in our planning for the new housing here and he's had great insight. And as a carpenter, he's used to working on building structures. So, this will be easier for him to grasp, overall."

"Let's finish getting a feel for the layout here first, then see what Garth says about including Taroom right off," Sabin said, as he turned to look at the large, nearby door next.

Measured Revenge

"He told them to turn this place into a tourist attraction?" Bethy laughed out, believing Garth. It sounded like something he'd do to make sure the site was preserved. "Next will come the fancy restaurants, hotels and night clubs! Bet he's now offering them training in how to maintain the site and how best to show it off, so nothing's damaged," she added. Ryes shook her head at this, amazed. New discoveries must be pretty common for humans to have it down to a routine progression! Garth laughed and nodded his agreement, then pulled Ryes aside.

"Excuse us," he told the others and headed for the largest rover. She looked puzzled, but waited patiently. Once they were inside and the door sealed, he turned to her.

"What?" she asked, seeing a strange wild look in his eyes.

"I forgot myself and mentioned you and Sabin will be Time Walking over in Hailys in front of Metta and Sonta. Sabin then told them that HE took you along for extra insurance," he informed her. She smiled at this, nodding her head, unsurprised. "It's not too commonly known back in Winterhaven, but I'm warning everyone to keep quiet about your Talents while Metta and Rebin are our guests. But, I'll need you to sit on me, just to be sure." He looked deeply troubled over his lapse.

"I'll do my best to keep an eye on you," she promised with a laugh, hoping her smile would help him break back through. He finally gave her a shallow smile in return, even if his heart wasn't in it.

"I'm going to have Phil run an analysis of their power system and see if we can remove that large reader to Winterhaven. I don't know if it's the only one which will take this memory rod," he said, pulling it out of his pocket to show her, "but it's one I know will play it. It stopped at a certain point, as if it had finished its run, but there's still more than three-quarters of the information un-displayed. I've a feeling it's a private message for me and I'm going to need your help to figure out how to unlock it."

"Why would it be for you, alone?" she asked; it wasn't like him to make assumptions like this without cause.

"He addressed me as Garthed, directly, saying his wife was a strong Visionary and saw me opening this place up," he related to her, smiling to himself in self-doubt of the other claims he'd made. She leaned close to him and gave him a kiss on his cheek.

"I don't see why whomever this was, wouldn't leave you a private message after all," Ryes breathed, smiling. Garth turned and pulled her close, giving her a proper kiss.

"I want you to keep this rod safe for me for now. What else happened while I was down there?" he pressed as he released her, handing the crystal over. She smiled as she put it into the waist-pouch she wore, after wrapping it in a handkerchief to protect it. "Exactly what happened up here?" he demanded, a little anxious now.

"As we were distracted by the operation to lift the portal out, Korman attacked Tanns. She managed to drag herself out into the Square, and as Maren and I were checking her over, he charged. I stunned him and he's still lying where he dropped. Sadie was nice to make sure he was breathing. Maren had Mitt take him and Tanns back to Winterhaven in the chopper, but she lost a lot of blood! Rowan went along and I gave him Rhin, in case Maren needs the extra help to heal his mother. I have Shadd and Sadie packing up Tanns' things, to take back with us. I don't think Maren'll let his mother move back here, without a serious argument."

"I would've never believed he'd ever harm Tanns," Garth declared; "he's deeply obsessed with you! We'll have to take steps to make sure he doesn't get at the team we leave here, when we're so far away," he said, worrying about Korman's sanity.

"Put a limiter collar on him," Ryes suggested, smiling. "We'll set up a perimeter to exclude the Village Square and wherever we set up their living quarters.   And we'll make sure each team member wears a warning-activation device at all times that will turn on automatically; in case he tries to sneak up on someone." He laughed at this, feeling relieved with this idea. It was another interesting device the humans used long ago for their studies on the starmen. It could prove very useful now.

"That's the best I've heard yet. Let me put in a call to Winterhaven and update them on the situation. Then they can send out the limiter and supplies needed to use it effectively and we'll have the whole thing set up before we leave. We have a long drive home and I want to make it back tonight. I'll also need you and Sabin to determine who'll be on the team we're leaving here."

"More work," she teased, grinning merrily. "We'll also take some warning-activation devices out with us, when we go hunting later this week - just in case," she decided. "We're still going hunting, aren't we?"

"If I don't take you hunting, I'll have Ethan upset with me," he admitted. "He's strict in enforcing time off."

"That's nothing compared to what I'll do to you," she threatened, her eyes lighting up mischievously. He chuckled as he nodded his head to her, understanding. "You call home and I'll go see if Shadd and Sadie are finished, yet. Also, the cubs will be up soon, demanding some room for play. I'll see if my little cousins would like to help keep them entertained. It might take their minds off what happened to their mother and the fact that their father's lying on the ground; not moving."

"That's an idea. So, git and we'll get this all finished in a more timely manner," he urged her. She gave him one more kiss, then opened the door and jumped out, slamming it behind her. He shook his head at this, reaching for the vid set this larger vehicle held. He wanted to see how Tanns was doing, first off.

       Later that morning, Phil climbed back up the stairs, got his bearings, then walked over to the small knot of people gathered next to Taroom's new home. They were admiring an ornate rocking chair he'd obviously made. Taroom noticed him and stepped over to see what he might want.

       "Good morning, Taroom," Phil said as he approached. A big smile spread across his friend's face as he gave him a nod.

       "Good morning to you too, Phil. How can I help you?" he asked. Phil chuckled and gave him a nod in return, now well-practiced in starman manners.

       "We have some curiosities below and wanted to show you a few things and get your opinion on some ideas we have about it," he explained. "Can you spare him for a few minutes, Aylita?" he asked, looking over to her and waving. She laughed as she stood up and came to join the men. Siah trailed after her, curious to meet one of these new people for herself.

       "Where're you dragging off my dear husband now, Phil? Did you find some new, interesting toys below?" she teased, laughing. He gave her a nod.

       "We've found some very interesting things that are meant for all starmen on Tayna and beyond," he replied, "But what I want to show Taroom only involves Matlowe Village itself."

       "Sounds like more work ahead," he said with a laugh and shake of his head.

       "Can only Taroom see it?" Siah asked, curious about the tempting opening below, as was everyone else in the Village. Phil smiled at her, but shook his head at this.

       "For right now, only Taroom. Once Garth clears it, there will be small tours of the facility for all the villagers. This treasure is your trust to hold and keep for all upon Tayna. There was some talk of establishing a higher level school for studying what lies below and preserving it for the future, but that is only being discussed and the elders need to make their decisions about it, first." The nearby villagers had gathered around to hear what Phil was telling the others and there were murmurs of surprise being openly expressed. Taroom gave him a nod of understanding and put an arm around Phil's shoulders for a companionable squeeze, then released him.

       "Then let's go see what can be done to help Matlowe, first," he suggested. Phil laughed and nodded and the two of them headed for the stairs down. There was a scattering of happy cheers being voiced in their wake.

"FOUR?" Rami questioned in shock, standing at the edge of the groundcover Ryes had spread out, so her cubs could wiggle and crawl around and make happy, squealy noises with their simple version of play. Her own son was stretching out his arms, wanting to be set down to play, too. Ryes looked up and blushed.

"It's been a very busy winter," she assured her. Aric stepped over to see them for himself. "Actually, I sent Rhin back with Maren. We have five little ones and I usually need a lot of help in managing them."

"All Garth's?" Aric questioned, equally astounded.

"All but Shyla. Her mother died when she was born in Menna's Hold, in the northern mountains. Garth had settled a peace treaty with the plainsmen and was on his way home when he was caught and held captive in the hold. Later, they gave her to him for a stolen windracer. He was the one to bring her home to me, so he may not be her father in truth, but is from the heart," she explained, indicating the cub who looked to be Shaysa's twin.

"She looks just like your own," Rebin commented, smiling to see so many little ones born at the same time.

"She even acts like she was born with the rest. It's a blessing we have Maren; he's a very strong Healer. Otherwise, I don't know if I would've survived their birth," she laughed, recalling that day too well.

"You look like you need a large-sized infant play yard, so you can keep them all in one place," Aric observed with a laugh. "Taroom made one for us and his sister." Ryes laughed and nodded her head.

"It's a good idea," she agreed, "I saw it and thought it'd be good for both at home and away, now that they're older and more active."

"Who's this one?" Tars asked, holding up one of her cubs. She was having fun with so many little ones to play with!

"Her name is Jann, in honor of our grandmother, Jana," she told her, smiling.

"She has pretty green eyes," she said, as she cuddled the infant in her arms. "Grandmother would've liked her." She recalled the stories her mother sometimes told of Jana and how she could Heal others. A rover approached and came to a halt nearby.

"All finished," Shadd said, after jumping out, having pulled it to a stop and shut it down, the quick way she'd learned. "I only left the stuff that looked like it might be his behind," she told Ryes, hooking a thumb over her shoulder, indicating Korman.

"What're you going to do with him?" Sadie asked in English. Ryes frowned at this.

"What do you mean?" she returned in kind, wondering. "He can't do anything to us now."

"To make sure he doesn't forget that you can do things to him, and he's powerless to prevent it, as I've heard he's been to others before," she suggested, "Come on, be creative!" Ryes thought on it as she redirected Gareth back toward the center of the blanket.

She had a feeling Sadie was right and it'd be one way to discourage him from following them back home.

"What language is that you're speaking?" Rebin questioned.

"It's from our homeworld," Bethy replied, smiling. "It's called English. We usually speak a blend of English and Dolbith back in Winterhaven and sometimes forget ourselves, when we're not home," she explained; wondering if Ryes would take Sadie up on her suggestion? Suddenly, Ryes jumped up and signed to Dotti to keep an eye on things for a few minutes. Dotti smiled as she sat down in her place, supervising the cubs' containment.

Ryes went around to the back of the rover and started looking in the storage bins. She just got an incredibly ornery idea! She found what she was looking for and noted Garth just getting out of the larger rover for the second time, heading her way. Sabin and Phil were coming toward them from the underground site. She smiled mischievously as she trotted over toward Phil; sure he'd know!

"Phil," she said as she stopped in front of him and Sabin. "What's the amount of weight this can support, and how long does it take to set up?" she asked, displaying a tube she held in her hands. He took it and checked the symbols.

"It'll support about two hundred pounds per cubic foot and it sets up pretty fast. It's tacky in a few minutes and well hardened in under an hour, but if you can leave it alone for a whole day, it'll cure and hold what you want to glue indefinitely," he told her, puzzled. "Do you need to fix something?" he queried.

"Great, but not quite!" she returned, then trotted back toward the rover, going around it and over toward Korman. She pulled out her beltknife and stood over his still form, looking down.

"Now wait a minute! You're not going to carve him up!" Aric demanded, concerned, as he stepped closer to prevent a tragedy.

"Never!" she assured him with a glint of mischief in her eyes, then bent and carefully slit open Korman's tunic. She then took out a large, permanent marker and wrote "Murderer" across his chest in heavy black ink. She resheathed the knife, smiling in satisfaction. Garth, Sabin and Phil were standing behind her, as well as most of the women. She "lifted" Korman's bulk up with her Talent and turned him over so she had access to his back, as she held him floating in the air. She opened the tube of adhesive and liberally squeezed it out, making a scrolling pattern across the back of his whole body; leaving only his head and hair free of the tacky substance, all the while humming to herself.

"What're you doing?" Garth asked, chuckling as he realized she was finally getting back at Korman a little for all the pain he inflicted upon her, her whole life.

"You'll see," she teased, then floated him over to the wall of one of the remaining abandoned huts and "pasted" him to the wall upside down, holding him there for several long moments gently using her Fire Shaper Talent, making sure he'd stay put with a light warmth.

The rest of their party was laughing merrily. Ryes turned around with a big grin alighting her face.

"You're leaving him like that?" Sabin finally managed to get out, after laughing over it so hard. Other villagers were now gathering around to see for themselves, some laughing at her daring, too.

"Citizens of Matlowe," she shouted, "Feel free to let Korman know what you think of the way he's tried to ruin everyone's lives here through the years!" she invited, indicating his body with her hand. "He won't awake until this evening and will never know who did what!"

"It's truly a small payback for all he's done, but well deserved," Garth commented, still amazed at his wife's daring. "Ethan's never going to believe this." Seeing no one else stepping forward, he did, taking the marker and changing its color then writing "Old Woman" under Ryes' statement. He chuckled as he put the marker on the ground under Korman, and walked away; gathering his wife to his side, as he led her back to their children. "I hope to never get you that mad at me," he teased. She laughed merrily at this, shaking her head.

"Impossible," she assured him, "And if you ever did, I'm sure I could come up with something far more creative." He rolled his eyes at this, but laughed with her, glad he brought her along on today's foray. They still had much to finish before they could head for home.

Sabin noted Aric was in the village square, having just put down the marker on the ground with a mischievous smile upon his lips. Sabin chuckled as he stepped over to this village icon.

"Aric," he started, meeting his eyes with a smile upon his own lips. "I need to ask a favor of you," he added. The metal smith appeared puzzled, then stepped over near him, as Sonta took up the marker next. He appeared to marvel at its color-changing ability for a moment, before using it.

"How can I help you, young Sabin?" he asked. Sabin huffed a laugh, recalling it was his grandfather's name as well, as he gave him a nod. He might have known his grandfather when he was a young child, himself.

"You have something very precious in storage in your workshop which belongs back out here, in the Village Circle," he explained, "and we need to retrieve it to copy it, so we can make it available to all of Tayna."

"What would that be?" he questioned, puzzled; not able to imagine anything of such great importance in his keeping.

"The column with the Twelve Laws inscribed upon it," he told him, wanting to see his reaction. His brows furrowed for a moment, then a look of surprise alit in his eyes as he gave him a nod; the light of understanding appeared written upon his face.

"My father was unable to repair it after it was damaged," he warned Sabin. "I know I've lacked the skill to do anything about it, either."

"We'll figure it out," he assured him. Sonta stepped over, appearing happy and had heard what they were saying.

"They will fix it," he added, as he clasped Aric's shoulder. "Garth needs it and so do we, as well as all Tayna. Come, let's go together and bring it back out into the light," he invited. Aric gave him a smile and nod, then turned to lead them over to his workshop and the precious column. Sabin waved Monty over to join them; sure they'd need the extra hands.

"That was far closer than I thought," Maren sighed, talking to Ted as he just finished doing the deeper healing his mother needed to be able to carry his youngest sister to term. Not wanting to argue with her, he put her into a deep sleep state from which he knew she wouldn't wake from until tomorrow.

"She sure lost a lot of blood," he commented, looking at his scans.

"I know. Korman knew I was a Healer and could keep her from dying, but he cut if far closer than he thought. It's a good thing Ryes sent Rhin along to help focus and boost my Talent. I never thought he'd EVER use her like this!"

"What I don't understand is why he's so obsessed with Ryes?" he returned, frowning as he met Maren's eyes.

"Because he was deeply humiliated when her parents left Matlowe, with her mother shoving him into the village well and getting everyone there to laugh at him," Rowan explained; a squirming, fussing Rhin in his arms. "Ryes is the mirror image of Tyra, her only surviving child, and Korman tried to take her, as a way to finally triumph over her mother."

"But, Garth fought him and defeated him," Maren added, smiling to himself, recalling that day in Hailys. "He doesn't dare do anything when Garth's around to tear him to pieces. So, my father's resorted to pulling cruel stunts like this!"

"He's terrorized Ryes all her life," Rowan added, shifting the infant to his other shoulder. "I only worried when she told me she and Garth spoke true-mate vows."

"Why?" Maren pressed as he held out his hands to take the cub. His grandfather gladly passed him over as he was starting to cry.

"That she'd do such a thing with the first man to take an interest in her. I hoped she wouldn't come to regret such a decision later. But, after seeing them together for months now, I know it is as was meant to be and am content."

"True-mate vows are like marriage vows?" Ted questioned, wanting to make sure he understood it.

"Deeper," Maren returned, smiling. He stepped over to one of the cold supply cabinets and pulled out a small bottle of formula for Rhin, opening it up and shaking it, before uncapping the nipple. "They bind the two souls together for life and beyond," he related, as he offered Rhin the nipple. He took it readily, used to the bottles when being baby-sat by others. "Dotti and I know we're true-mates from another life. She called it soul mates. Even if our life's paths originated far apart, we'll always be together. Did I ever tell you that we each dreamed of each other and fell in love, long before Ryes brought down the Star Quest?" He looked up to see the shock upon Rowan and Ted's faces and grinned. "Guess I didn't."

"MAREN!" Tennan declared in shocked horror from the doorway. "You can't mean it?"

"Yes, I do," he told her with a flash of anger alighting his eyes, "I thought Ryes once showed you how deeply connected Dotti and I truly are?"

"She did, but TRUE-MATE VOWS? She's not a starman!" She recalled Ryes had hinted at this in that rapport, but had dismissed it at the time. After all, it was when she awakened her Talent, and that was a far more important event!

"She's my wife and I expect you to treat her with all due respect," he ordered, then Rowan stepped between them. He knew one was just as stubborn as the other!

"Let's get your mother settled into a regular bed, for now," he ordered them, as a diversion.

"Were they always like this?" Ted asked, relieved some sanity might prevail with Rowan's intervention. The siblings immediately let it go at his insistence.

"Even worse. It's hard to have grandchildren who behave like this, even now that they're adults," Rowan admitted with a smile. "In a way, I was lucky to only have Ryes to raise."

"I'll go get a cart," Tennan volunteered, seeing Maren was still feeding one of Ryes' brats. She felt she needed to get out of that room anyway. Between Maren and his pet human, she felt she couldn't breathe!

"We'll have a little talk about this, later," Rowan promised his grandson. "With Raya's help," he added, letting him know he intended to get to the bottom of this, before the matter would be settled. Maren sighed, giving him a smile and nod of his head. It was only fair, considering the great-granddaughter of his, which Dotti was now carrying.

"Any time, you have the time. And as long as Chuck can spare Raya for a few moments," he promised.

"I'd like to understand this, too," Ted prompted, hoping he could be included. The more he felt he could understand about these starmen, the better. When Maren was first appointed over him and his staff by Dr. Cruthers, he'd been deeply insulted. Not only was he an alien, but still young with no medical training; his amazing Talent aside. Through time, he saw Maren more directed their efforts and strove to keep their problems small, taking blame and responsibility for his crew. He never harshly reprimanded them, merely redirected their viewpoints, trying to use reason and logic to get things ironed out. Through time, Ted came to respect him, offering his support freely, as did the rest of the staff.

"You're more than welcome, if my grandfather doesn't mind," he invited with a nod of his head.

"I'd rather it be the two of us, but do understand, so don't object," Rowan replied, seeing them looking to him for his response. He smiled at Rhin, as Maren put him to his shoulder to burp him. "I've forgotten how active little ones can be. It's been forever since Ryes was this size, and even longer since your mother was so tiny. She and Ronn were a handful, but between Jana and I, we managed them."

"How many children do you have?" Ted asked, wondering.

"Only three. Our youngest died of a terrible fever my wife was unable to cure. She was a Healer, but not as strong as Maren. Jana and I were true-mates and after she drowned in the Yuri, I never felt the inclination to take another wife. She was my life and love. No one could ever replace her," he explained. "So, I raised Ryes myself, instead of turning her over to Tanns. With her deep attachment to Korman, I didn't think she'd survive too long in his home," he said, thinking back to those hectic first days. "The village elders almost came to the point of banishing me, because I stubbornly refused to give Ryes over to Tanns. The short time that I did was only because I had to see Ronn's final resting place. Tanns and Korman had broken up at the time, because he mated both of her best friends. By the time I returned, they were just starting to make up. I took Ryes back and settled down beside the river. Tanns didn't speak to me for years; having little Maren and Tennan to keep her busy soon afterwards." The other two appeared amazed at his short tale.

"Here we go," Tennan said as she returned, pushing the cart into the emergency treatment room. "Let's get mother settled." Maren gave her a nod of his head, handing Rhin back to Rowan.

"He should be a little easier to hold now," he teased, with a merry smile. Rowan chuckled as he took his great-grandson back, seeing he looked like he was ready to drop off once more.

"Thank you," he told him, "It's truly has been a while." Tennan chuckled at this, giving her head a shake. She almost forgot he was her grandfather, besides taking on the responsibility of raising Ryes himself!

Maren and Ted lifted Tanns over to the cart, as Tennan held it steady. They draped her with a sheet, then all four of them escorted her to one of the recovery rooms to put her in a bed for the night. They barely said a word among them, until they had her settled and as comfortable as could be.

"She should be fine until tomorrow," Ted assured Tennan, seeing the uncertain look in her eyes.

"I'm going to check my treatment rooms then get Tian and stay with her for a little while," she returned, not liking this human's closeness to her brother. She left the room.

"I'll be staying, so I can speak to her when she wakes up. There're a few things we've never gotten straight through the years," Rowan stated with a deep sigh, as he settled back into a chair; a sleeping Rhin in his arms.

"Go ahead and call it a day, Ted. I'll take care of things until whoever's next arrives," Maren told him, turning back to his second in command. Ted gave him a smile at this, glad it'd been an otherwise slow day. He had a few things to think about. Their history and events that shaped their past could have bearing on their current behaviors. He never regretted this new future he'd been granted.

"Thanks!" he replied. "Justin will be here shortly, to keep an eye on things," he informed him. Maren gave him a nod, then turned back to Rowan as Ted left.

"If you need anything, just let me know. I have the system set up to alert me if anything happens with mother. I'll be in my office." There was nothing else for him to do. Dotti was still out with the expedition team and he had no idea how long they'd be gone.

"I'll be fine," he assured him with a smile.

"I'm sure Ryes will be along, as soon as she's able to pick up Rhin," Maren told him, "but, if you need me to take him for a while, just bring him to me. I don't mind."

"It's too bad you're true-mated to a human, grandson. You'd make a fine father," Rowan admitted, smiling. There was a strange look in Maren's eyes suddenly, which had him puzzled. Were they planning on having one of the human men impregnate her, so they could have children he wondered?

"I'll talk with you later, grandfather," he replied nervously. He realized he'd need Ryes' help, when it came time to breaking the news to him. She knew Rowan best and would make sure things wouldn't get out of hand! He decided he needed to do another quick review of the human genome research, so thought it could easily occupy the time waiting. He truly needed Dotti right now!

Chances, Changes

"I'm going to check on Maren and Tanns," Ryes told Garth as he drove the rover down the ramp and into the garage. The rest followed to their parking spots.

"And pick up our son?" he added, smiling and glad to be home again. The other four had fallen asleep already. "I'll put the rest to bed," he offered. She grinned merrily at this, giving him a nod of her head.

"They seem to sleep better when you check on them before going to bed, yourself," she said, wondering if he noticed it?

"It does seem like it," he agreed, chuckling merrily. "Good thing we spoke true-mate vows, so you'll keep me around them for a good, long time." She laughed at this as did Bethy and Jim.

"We're going to go grab something to eat and go right to bed, unless you need something done first," Jim offered, being it was already eleven o'clock in the evening.

"You've more than earned your rest," Garth assured him. "Goodnight," he bid them as he began the rover's shutdown. "I'll have Kovin and Minn help with getting the new residents settled and we'll leave the sorting out and putting things away for tomorrow. You best get going, wife," he prompted. She gave him a quick kiss then got out of the vehicle and trotted for the main doors. She was looking forward to getting some rest tonight, too.

Ryes soon came into the medical center, seeing Justin on duty up front. He looked up as she stopped for a moment at his counter.

"Is Maren still here?" she asked. He grinned as he hooked a thumb over his shoulder.

"In his office. I think he's waiting for Dotti," he informed her. "He was studying again. He's determined to be the best healer possible."

"He already is the greatest! Thanks!" she returned, giving him a smile and nod of her head, then headed down med's main corridor. It was funny, she thought, it wasn't that long ago Justin had been incensed with Dotti and Maren's attachment to each other. Either he was finally adjusting, or was hiding his hate better. She realized she'd have to ask Raya if she could do a little serendipitous snooping for her, so there wouldn't be any unexpected surprises at some time in the future.

Ryes paused as she saw Maren with his head down upon his desk. Either he was worn out from healing his mother, or there was something truly weighing his heart. With Dotti's pregnancy, she could bet it had to be what was bothering him. She stepped over to him, to offer him some comfort. She put her hands out to rub his neck for him, but as she touched his shoulders, a Vision opened up to them both...

Ryes and Maren saw she lay in agony at the base of a low hill. On the grass beside her was Dotti, who lay at a strange angle and was still. Fear coursed through her heart as she moved toward her friend and discovering her own leg was broken, the pain causing her to scream out; part rage, part agony, both within and without. In spite of the intense pain, she squirmed over to Dotti's side and straightened her out. She was still breathing, even if her face was very pale. Ryes could hear the sounds of a fight above them, with Maren's voice sounding like he was in absolute fury. Her heart wrenched as she hoped he'd be all right. Then, she pushed everything else away from her mind and heart. Ryes dove within and called up her Healing Talent, extending herself to Dotti and the little one she carried, first.

"RYES!" Maren shouted, jumping out of his chair, swinging around to face her. Then he saw her face. The Vision had taken her totally by surprise, as it had him. All color had drained from her face and she was breathing hard, as if she'd been running for hours.

"That makes our second," she commented as she staggered back to plop down heavily in one of the other chairs in his office; not meeting his eyes in this moment.

"I can't lose both you and Dotti!" he declared, denying the Vision.

"We're not lost, just regrouping," she teased with a smile. "I should be able to take care of both Dotti and myself. You concentrate upon what you need to handle," she implored, fearing for him in truth.

"I only saw the two of you. We rarely go out alone," he observed, frowning.

"Maybe the others are preoccupied, or helping you? I didn't recognize the area, so have no idea what we're even doing there. Don't worry about us! Just make sure to watch your back. If our support has been either killed, or injured..." she sighed heavily, "I don't want you facing off whatever you're fighting alone!" Her sadness and shock still plain on her face.

"I'll go armed from now on," he promised. He looked almost ready to cry. "Dotti's still pregnant. She looked about four or five months along."

"We'll be fine!" she emphasized, "You be careful, please?" she begged, her eyes meeting his. He nodded his surrender as she stood up, feeling more centered again. Maren wrapped his arms around her, doing his best to hold back his tears. She hugged him back. She had only wanted to comfort him, not add to his misery.

"How's your mother?" she asked, as they held onto each other.

"Fine, thanks to your lending me Rhin," he replied, getting a better grip upon himself. Since their last one had come true, then this one should, too. "Why are our Visions shared?" he asked aloud, still wondering about it.

"I don't know," she admitted reluctantly, "Maybe because we're in tune with each other on some level? I'm glad Rhin could help today; I thought he'd be needed," she stated, glad her instincts were correct once more. At least he'd been able to save his mother.

"What's the matter?" Sabin asked, stepping into Maren's office, fearing the worse. It looked like they were comforting each other. "Did Tanns take a turn for the worse?" Garth stood behind him, questions in his eyes.

"Just another Vision," Maren told them, letting go of Ryes and turning to his friends. "We had our second shared peek into the future."

"Show it to me," Sabin ordered. Visionary was his Talent and he wanted to know if it was a real Vision, or not. Maren looked surprised, but gave him a nod of his head and centered himself within. As he extended his hand, Garth stepped over and took Ryes' hand. Their eyes met and she knew he needed to see it, too. She and Maren showed it to both Garth and Sabin, as she enfolded them with her Mind Voice Talent, to be sure it was clear.

"That's not around here," Sabin commented after several long moments. It was more clear and complete than any of his own!

"No, it's not," Garth agreed, opening his eyes. "You, Dotti and Maren are not allowed to go out without an armed escort," he ordered his wife.

"And endanger more lives?" she fired back feeling she couldn't imperil anyone else, but saw the emotions in his honey-colored eyes and knew she had little choice. "All right," she surrendered. "I thought you were going to put our little ones to bed?" she followed, wondering what he was doing here already?

"Raby and Sayer took over and are doing it," he replied, smiling, once more. "We'll both check on all our children, before we go to bed," he promised. She smiled up at him again, liking this idea.

"I can't wait for our apartment to be finished," she stated. She didn't mind living in the comfortable corridors down here, but she wanted a view of the horizon from time-to-time, too. Garth chuckled at this, knowing her heart well.

"How's Tanns?" Sabin asked, seeing the brief, silent contest of wills between his friends and their return to normal once more.

"She'll be fine and is sleeping now. It looked far worse than it was, but she did lose a lot of blood," Maren told them all. There were looks of relief on their faces at this news.

"We packed up her things," Ryes told him, "And will have it waiting to be set up for her tomorrow. Perhaps Tennan could take care of it, so when she's up, she'll feel more at home?" she suggested. Maren smiled relief at hearing this, knowing it was so like his cousin. There were times when he felt he had the wrong sister! He and Ryes were far closer, than he and Tennan.

"And you'd never believe what she did to your father!" Sabin taunted with a chuckle. Ryes blushed as Maren looked puzzled, wondering what she'd done after he left.

"Well?" he pressed, as Garth and Sabin chuckled merrily, practically unable to speak at the moment. This only peaked his curiosity! She sighed heavily.

"I glued him to a wall and invited the citizens of Matlowe to write what they wanted on his body with a permanent marker," she admitted, "It was petty, but I couldn't help myself." Maren threw back his head and laughed heartily at this admission. It was so unlike her, yet perfectly like her! He could just imagine the scene!

"Did Jim, or Monty record it so I can see it, too?" he demanded, catching his breath.

"I did," Sadie bragged as she joined them, mem chip in hand and ready. She thought it might help lighten his day. He quickly snagged the offered chip and activated his computer. He inserted it and saw the whole vid with everyone, but Ryes, laughing at the display. Ryes sighed guiltily, then quietly left the office, heading for the recovery rooms. She knew Rowan would be with Tanns and only wanted to retrieve her small son.

"What're you doing here?" Tennan challenged her, meeting her in the hallway. There were days when they were as close as littermates, and days like this, when she was in a disgruntled mood and nothing Ryes could say, or do, would make her happy.

"Just picking up Rhin," she informed her, as her cousin glared daggers.

"Where're my younger siblings?" she demanded, shifting so as to not quite block her way, but still partly obstructed the access past her.

"In Dotti's care, as Maren left them," she replied. "They're fine and Dotti's getting an appreciation of what it's like to have a whole herd of kids to look after." Tennan stood meeting her eyes; her anger still burning. "Your mother wanted Maren to take them in the first place, before the attack. She knows you have your hands full with Tian and helping out here," she added.

"I'll talk with her when she's awake," she threatened, as if that said it all. Ryes gave her a nod of her head, then stepped around her to go get her son. She wasn't going to start a fight today, after all everyone else had been through. Tennan glared at Ryes' back, but as she finally turned for her own office, she saw Garth in the hallway behind her, watching her quietly. There was a presence about him which made her feel uncomfortable. He was their leader, after all, and Ryes was his wife.

"He used your mother as bait to lure Ryes and Maren away from the humans and their protection. It worked and it was a good thing she merely stunned him. We don't need any further animosity now, so it'll be best if you control your temper. A Healing Talent is a gift, given to help others; don't detract from such a blessing with pointless intolerance," he advised in a low voice. Tennan suddenly blushed darkly, giving him a brief nod of her head; dropping her eyes from his. She felt the sting of his reasonable words more deeply, than when her own brother lectured her. Garth stepped around her and she saw Maren looking at her speculatively, having been behind Garth at the time. Her blush deepened as she pushed past him, Sadie and Sabin, to run to her office with tears in her eyes. It was time for her and Tian to go home, instead. She'd see her mother in the morning. Maren sighed in relief.

"How's she doing?" Ryes asked Rowan, as he held Rhin in his arms, sitting in a chair next to Tanns' bed.

"It looked far worse than it truly was. I don't think Korman meant for her to die; merely look like it was possible." She sat down next to him and sighed. She took Rhin as he passed him over and put him to her breast as he started to fuss. It was well past his bedtime!

"For all that she's done for him through the years," she commented, "it seems poor payment."

"In a lot of ways, they're a lot alike and deserved each other," Rowan insisted with a sadness coloring his voice. "First the loss of her sister and mother, then your mother and father. She pulled away from me, seeking solace with Korman, in spite of his inner drive to take every woman in Matlowe, to prove that he can do it. But, he always came back to her. It was years before she started speaking to me again. As if it was all my fault Jana drowned in the Yuri. And the way she's treated you; as if you're supposed to have died, so your mother could've lived. I never told you that when Korman attacked your mother as she fled with you, he raped her twice. She lost her will to live and sought death as her escape." He watched her closely at this revelation; hoping it wouldn't be too much for her to bear.

Ryes' eyes misted at this, understanding why he'd hold back such information until she was well settled with a family of her own. She would've tried to kill Korman, herself, and probably come to grief over it. Now she only craved to protect her own daughters and friends, whom she loved.

"Someday he will pay for all his crimes," she finally breathed out in response. "Did she tell you this while she was dying?" she asked, wondering.

"She gave me her memories directly, mind-to-mind, before she died. That's how I know with certainty all the events of the time," he assured her, tapping the side of his head. "Perhaps, when things settle a bit, I can show you what she gave me? Korman..." he practically growled out, still seething deep in his heart for what he'd done to others through the years.

"I wonder if Tanns didn't finally figure out a way to make Korman's seed sterile, using her undeveloped Healing Talent, until it was time for her own season?" Ryes conjectured, finding her voice once more, around the tightness in her throat. It was the best distraction she could come up with right now. Yes, she wanted to see her mother's memories, but not yet. She knew she wasn't ready... Rowan looked at her in utter shock.

"It sounds like a possibility. He hasn't fathered any other cubs in Matlowe in years," Garth agreed, speaking in a low voice as he stepped into the room. He heard Rowan tell her about her mother's rape and knew they'd have to discuss it later tonight. It'd been such a long day, with too many surprises!

"But, because of his aggression, few other cubs were sired, unless it was done furtively," Rowan said, agreeing with them, now seeing it as a real possibility.

"So, the population in Matlowe should increase, now that he's been publicly humiliated and bested," Sabin added. "How's she doing?" he asked Rowan.

"Resting," he replied. "Maren put her deeply under, so she won't be up until tomorrow."

"I was going to suggest to Tennan to set up a room for her mother, but after the way she was in the hallway, it'd be better if I did it myself," Ryes stated.

"I'll handle it," Maren volunteered. "Have either of you spoken to Torr in the last two days?" he suddenly asked.

"No. Why?" Garth asked, turning to meet his eyes.

"Something's up," he advised, as well as he could.

"Is that why Ardis was looking after little Tobin last night?" Sabin asked. Ryes looked puzzled. "She said something about Shadd saying she had dried up early."

"There's more to it than that," Maren invited, looking unhappy.

"Then tell us what you know!" Sabin demanded.

"I can't. It's privileged information," he returned, obviously uncomfortable with this demand.

"Sabin, why not go ask Torr, yourself?" Ryes cut in, before he could get Maren any more upset.

"Let's go get things sorted out," Garth suggested, seeing Ryes being defensive of her cousin's stand. She'd never let anyone bully Maren. Maybe the source was best after all? Sabin huffed at this, but gave Garth a nod, following him out of the room. Ryes stood up and leaned down, giving her grandfather a kiss.

"I'll talk with you later," she promised with a smile, "And then we can open up those memories, too, if you want to share them with me." He gave her a nod of his head and smile. He intended to stay at his daughter's side, until she awoke. But now there were a few things he needed to think upon as he waited.

"Want to grab a late snack, since we all missed dinner?" Sadie suggested, smiling.

"That's an idea," Ryes agreed as Maren smiled and gave her a nod of his head, too. "I'll have something sent to you, grandfather," she told him. He gave her a nod of appreciation. The three of them left the clinic area, heading toward the dining hall.

"I caught Shadd and Mason together in one of the shops, last week," Sadie told them in a low voice, once they were finished eating and down to drinking their last mugs of tea. The other people who'd been out to Matlowe today had headed off to bed, with Dotti herding off her new charges for the showers and bed, too. Garth and Sabin had left as soon as they finished eating, so it was an open, companionable feeling now. "They were going at it pretty good, too."

"Mason?" Ryes questioned, shocked. "You've got to be kidding!" she declared, seeing where this was going, now. "Poor Torr."

"Most women aren't like you and Ardis," Maren added, in comment as he looked into his mug of tea. "True-mate vows are extremely rare. How many different husbands did Tara have? You said she was like a mother to you, when you were little."

"Three," Ryes breathed, starting to understand things more clearly. "It's just that Rowan never mated again, and Darman and Rinna have been together as long as I can remember, the same with your mother and Korman. I forget how fleeting most other partnerships are, once the cubs are born."

"You're not going to throw Garth out now, are you?" Sadie questioned, appeared worried. Ryes and Maren both laughed at this.

"Never!" she declared. "We've taken true-mate vows and are now willingly joined together for this life and beyond," she explained.

"Then Sabin and Ardis have taken such vows, too?" she pressed, understanding dawning in her eyes.

"Yes, they did, as soon as Sabin returned a few months ago," she assured her. Sadie looked relieved.

"For we humans, we have marriage vows, which are supposed to stand for the rest of our lives, but not many make it very far and many marriages end in a divorce."

"We starmen only stay together while the cubs are small, usually the first two years. But, if the woman feels like it, she can tell her mate to leave at any time," Maren explained. "Dotti and I have spoken true-mate vows and are now married. But I don't know, with my younger brother and sisters to look after, she may throw all of us out." Ryes and Sadie laughed at this, seeing the grin upon his face. Then Ryes saw Garth, Sabin and Torr coming into the room and the look upon their faces.

"Oh my," she breathed as they came straight over to their table, sitting down opposite them.

"Maren, what happened?" Torr asked.

"There's a code of ethics among healers," Ryes began, without looking at either Garth, nor Maren. "A healer does not discuss what happens between himself and his patient."

"She's right," Sadie agreed in a low voice, granting support.

"Maren's not a human healer," Sabin growled out, starting to get angry.

"It still applies," Ryes retorted sharply.

"It's all right," Maren spoke up, heading Ryes off before she got too upset. "Torr's a part of this and deserves to know. She came to me to dry up her milk and make sure she wouldn't come into season for quite a few years," he admitted. "I only did it because she wouldn't leave otherwise. She said she couldn't handle you, nor Tobin, anymore." Torr met his eyes, seeing the truth, then gave him a nod of his head in understanding.

"It's her choice," he stated, his voice catching. "All her things are gone from our quarters and I wondered what was going on. She hasn't said one word of what she was doing. With what was happening out in Matlowe, I didn't feel it was the time to talk with her about things, either. I only worry about Tobin," he told them with a heavy sigh.

"Ardis has plenty of milk to feed Tobin," Sabin said, clasping Torr's shoulder in sympathy.

"I always thought your first was supposed to be special. But, maybe that's only among humans," Sadie commented. "I still remember Karl. We married young, but our work separated us later, and he's probably long gone by now. I wonder if he ever remarried?" she breathed, looking down into her mug. Maren gave her a hug in comfort. As he released her, she suddenly looked up to him. "Did it take this time?" she demanded, suddenly needing to know right now. He appeared surprised, then chuckled.

"Right now?" he asked, she gave him a nod of her head. So, he closed his eyes and extended his Talent with a hand upon her stomach. After a few seconds, he opened his eyes. "Yes, it did. You're carrying a very healthy son." She sighed in relief, her eyes filling with tears.

"You're pregnant?" Ryes asked, knowing Sadie usually hung out with her or Wren, not with the human men. There was the rumor that she and Gleds were free mating.

"Yes, finally. Karl left me some of his sperm, in case anything ever happened to him, when he left Tayna a lot of years ago. I was happy it'd been left behind in storage in the med labs here and forgotten when we were evacuated. The computer preserved all the genetic material here, while we were on the Star Quest. This was our third attempt and thanks to Scott, Ted and Maren, we succeeded at last."

"That means almost all the human women, except for Grace, Wynne and Dotti are now pregnant," Sabin commented.

"That's amazing," Torr said, surprised. "And many of the
starwomen either have young cubs or are pregnant, too. Is there
something in the air, or water here?" he teased.

"We're just a growing colony," Garth replied with a smile.

"Dotti's pregnant, too," Maren quietly stated, then sipped his
tea, waiting to see their reaction. Ryes smiled and blushed while
shock registered in Garth, Sabin, Sadie and Torr's eyes.

"How?" Torr asked, seeing his cousin speechless.

"Who?" Sabin questioned. Maren sighed as he put down his
mug. He glanced over to Ryes while she gave him a small nod of her
head in agreement and encouragement.

"She's mine. Dotti was feeling left out and I finally gave in
and tried. She didn't want it to be anyone else's, but mine," he told
them, inwardly quaking. He was glad of Ryes' support and more so
that it would be his closest friends to hear of it first. With Sadie to
give him a way to gauge the humans' reaction.

"Amazing! I didn't think such a thing was possible!" Sadie
declared with a big grin, delightfully surprised

"It took a lot of effort. Ryes and Rhin had to help us, but we
managed. Dotti's afraid to let out about it, but I figure we might as
well let everyone get used to the idea, before our daughter's born."

"And you didn't tell me?" Garth asked his wife, taken totally
by surprise.

"I promised Maren and Dotti," she teased, impishly smiling.

"Do you think you could do this for anyone else?" Torr asked.

"I don't know and no one's asked me about it, so it's not an
issue yet. I think I'd want to be sure that the couple has a close
attachment first," Maren told them, feeling this would be the best way
to approach the matter.

"You and Ryes had best tell Dr. Cruthers," Garth suggested,
"and Sadie, keep this quiet for now. We'll see what Ethan advises
first, before letting such news out freely." Sadie gave him a nod of
her head, understanding. She realized she and Gleds needed some
time for a talk about things. Her own present pregnancy and any
future children were on her mind. Did she want a human-starman
mix? Would such a child be accepted anywhere outside of
Winterhaven?

"When's she due?" Garth questioned, thinking on the greater
picture. Something like this could either bond both peoples closer
together, or widen the gulf permanently. He decided to speak with
Dr. Cruthers himself, as soon as they finished.

"We still have to determine that, yet," Maren admitted, "But,
she's about as far along as Sadie's little boy."

"You sure are one to stir things up," Torr teased his friend
with a laugh.

"Runs in the family," he quipped back, winking at Ryes. She
laughed in agreement, waking up Rhin.

"Gleds?" Sadie softly called from his door drape. If he was asleep, she'd wait until tomorrow. She heard him stirring and practically held her breath, waiting.

"I thought you'd stop by tonight," he said, pulling the drape aside. "Come on in," he invited with a teasing smile. He enjoyed the time they spent together; wishing she was more comfortable with him to acknowledge their relationship in front of others. He felt no shame about the deep love he felt for her, but she was still not as sure about things. There were times when he wondered if she loved him, or merely used him for her own sexual satisfaction and emotional comfort?

"Let's go to my room. I need to talk with you," she countered, excitement in her bearing. This was the first time she invited him! "It's important," she added, seeing he looked puzzled. He gave her a nod and stepped out into the hallway. But instead of her walking apart from him, she took his hand, leaning her head against his arm. It shocked Gleds, but he let her hand go and put his arm around her waist, smiling, feeling a little uncomfortable as she wrapped her arm around his too. There was little traffic in the halls this time of night, but she'd never behaved this way before! They reached her room, went inside and she sealed the door behind them, turning to face him as he stood looking around. On a shelf, he saw an old picture of her former husband with herself appearing very young, but next to that was one of the two of them laughing from last Winterfest, as they danced. That put a proud smile upon his face for a moment.

"What do you feel for me?" she asked, meeting his eyes as he fully turned her way, needing to know this right now.

"I love you and wish we could spend more time together," he admitted, "but, I understand with the attitude I've heard expressed about Maren and Dotti, that you'd want to keep things quiet." She stepped right up to him, looking up into his golden eyes.

"Could you stand it if people said such things about us, too?" Sadie asked. He looked down into her green eyes, feeling very serious about this matter.

"If we were together like they are, I don't think anyone else's opinion would matter," he told her, wanting to wrap his arms about her. She sighed heavily at this, relieved somewhat.

"Gleds, I'm pregnant. My former husband left some of his seed in cold storage here, in case I ever decided I wanted a child. Scott, Ted and Maren finally succeeded in impregnating me with his child. I'm going to have a son, and I think the both of us would be better off if you were fully a part of our lives," she told him, her heart pounding in her chest. "I love you too, but do you love me enough to go through all this with me? To raise a child as a son, who'll look nothing like you?" she questioned. His heart hammered as he bent to kiss her.

"Yes, I do. I love you so very much, my Sassy little Sadie," he assured her as their lips parted. She finally smiled as she threw her arms about him, kissing him back passionately.

"What would you say to you and I having our own baby in a couple of years?" she pressed. He chuckled at this, surprised.

"I don't think it's possible, but if such a thing were, and the child could be healthy, I'd be a very proud father all over again," he replied.

"We'll just have to see," she teased as she unzipped his jeans.

"Wait. Is this safe with you being pregnant?" he demanded, not wanting the boy cub hurt by their passions.

"As long as we don't get too wild," she answered him. "My mother and sisters all had lots of healthy kids and I don't think they ever stopped because of a pregnancy."

"We'd better check with Ted or Maren, first," he cautioned. This was serious!

"In the morning," she decided as she started pulling down his jeans. He finally surrendered to her needs, being as gentle as he possibly could, hoping their infant boy would be all right. But his heart was flying and it seemed to them both that at some level their souls were melding into one, as they made love in joyous celebration.

Plans Afoot

"Oh, we have two last minute appointments," Bethany told Dr. Cruthers as they finished going over the day's schedule. "Gleds and Sadie need to talk with you, as well as Maren and Ryes."

"I wonder what they're plotting now?" Ethan chuckled as he nodded his head to his assistant.

"Ryes and Maren, that's anyone's guess. As for Sadie and Gleds, I have a couple of ideas," she admitted.

"So do I," he returned. "Add them in, there's still room on my dance card." She raised an eyebrow at this, but smiled and nodded her head. She got out of her chair, coffee mug in hand.

"Yes Sir," she replied, "And I'll make sure we have some aspirin ready for when after Ryes leaves." Ethan chuckled, giving her a nod of his head as he turned to his comp screen. The door quietly closed behind her.

Gleds and Sadie stepped out of Dr. Cruthers' office as Maren and Ryes entered Bethany's office for their appointment.

"Maren," Sadie said, stepping closer to him. "Is it all right for Gleds and I to have sex? He's uncomfortable about it with my being just barely pregnant," she asked in a low voice. With the music Bethy had playing, she didn't think it would carry too far. Maren looked surprised by this request, but gave her a smile.

"Let me see," he offered. She nodded her head, so he closed his eyes and centered himself, then put a hand to her stomach and extended his Talent. After several minutes, he opened his eyes and looked into hers.

"Well?" she demanded, impatient.

"Yes, but keep it low key, like you're already doing," he advised. She blushed at this, then gave him a hug.

"I told you," she turned to Gleds, telling him in a louder voice. He smiled his relief.

"She insisted," he offered his friend in explanation.

"I understand, only too well," Maren agreed, from his own experiences with Dotti. "Human women always have things their way!" He hadn't known Gleds and Sadie were a couple, but saw Ryes wasn't as surprised about them being together. Gleds chuckled at this, then the two of them left, arm-in-arm. Bethany watched everything with great interest from her desk, trying to be polite; knowing she could always get it out of Ryes, later.

"He's waiting for you," she prompted, seeing both of her friends watching Sadie and Gleds leave.

"Thanks, Bethy," Ryes replied, turning back to her once more, smiling. Maren gestured for her to precede him, then opened the door for her, as she laughed lightly at his gallantry.

"Good morning," Ethan said, gesturing for them to take seats. "How can I help you?" he questioned, knowing if they were here seeking his advice, it must be a weighty matter, indeed.

"Good morning! We need your insight on an important matter," Ryes started as Maren looked uncomfortable. She liked getting right to the point. "What would you think of a child who was a cross between a starman and a human?" she questioned straight out, meeting his eyes. Ethan looked shocked, then sat back in his chair, considering what she asked, as well as left unsaid.

"Then you already have such a child in the making?" he pressed, sure of this from the way Maren was behaving.

"Yes," he responded before Ryes could speak up. "Dotti wanted a child of her own, but wouldn't accept it being anyone else's, but mine. I've tried getting her to choose one of the men here, but she refused. We've been arguing over this for months, so I finally gave in and had Ryes and Rhin help us accomplish it," he explained. Ethan saw this admission cut him deeply, almost as if he were unsure if it could be a misuse of his Talent.

"I take it that the child is healthy?"

"Yes, she's healthy and `feels' right, but I don't want her existence to cause problems here in Winterhaven," he admitted. Ethan chuckled his agreement as he sat back once more for a moment of contemplation.

"The youngest rebel rouser, yet," he finally teased, grinning. Ryes chuckled at this. He saw Maren wasn't up to his jests, so softened his smile. "If you want my opinion, I don't believe your daughter's creation could be construed as a misuse of your Talent, and as long as you can help her to be born healthy and strong, there shouldn't be any problems. Sure, it will take time for people to adjust to the idea, but it might be the final element to bond this community here together, for all time. It's a wonderfully exciting time, to be sure," he offered. Maren thought upon it for a few moments, then gave him a nod of his head.

"I'll do my best," Maren replied, smiling at last, "she's my daughter after all. We're going to have to pick out a name for her!" Ethan chuckled, giving him a nod of agreement. He'd have to add in a few minutes to have a quiet discussion with Dotti, too. She was his assistant and she should've said something to either him, or Bethy, by now!

"How and when do you think we should start letting out the news of her existence?" Ryes asked, serious about the problem once again.

"Wait until she's at least a few months along," he suggested. "That way we can break it to the command staff, first."

"I did break it to most of the command staff, last night," Maren admitted.

"Who exactly knows?" he pressed, wanting to know in case of damage control needs.

"Mitt, Garth, Sabin, Torr and Sadie," Ryes supplied. "Everyone's been cautioned to keep it under wraps for now and I feel confident they will."

"That's why Sadie and Gleds were asking about wedding ceremonies. I suggested they accompany us to the spring gather and have Darman marry them then. I'd rather not stand in his stead as the recognized cleric."

"Sadie's already pregnant with her former husband's child, Karl Saliman," Maren explained. "It's taken Ted, Scott and I three attempts to finally get it accomplished for her, to honor him and what they had hoped before. And now with Gleds in her life..."

"I could understand why they'd want their relationship formally sealed," he replied. "Now, as to how? Why not throw a Founder's Day for Winterhaven on the one year anniversary of when you discovered this site? Then make the announcement at that time, after everyone's had a few drinks and can be relaxed," he suggested.

"Our own Founder's Day!" Ryes declared smiling, delighted with this idea, "Our very own holiday!"

"But shouldn't Founder's Day be when you humans established the site as your base of operations?" Maren pressed, frowning. The when to announce it seemed perfect to him, too.

"We never intended this to be a permanent installation, much less the city we've been planning as a community," Ethan assured him. "No, Winterhaven wasn't a true home until you two and the rest of your small band first set foot here and decided this was where you wanted to stay to live. So, Winterhaven's Founder's Day will be based upon your arrival and establishment of this base as a home." Ryes sighed and gave him a nod, smiling her approval, as Maren finally saw the distinction and gave him a nod too.

"Another thing to add to our calendar," he groaned, looking to his cousin with a raised eyebrow.

"But this promises to be fun!" she merrily teased him, seeing he was being too serious, "We'll just have to come up with some activities which everyone can participate in."

"I'll appoint Bethy to lend you a hand with establishing the planning committee," Ethan teased her, knowing she was busy enough as it was with everyday operations.

"Thank you, so very much," Ryes replied. "I think that about covers it," she declared, standing up quickly.

"What about the rest of that memory rod from yesterday?" Ethan pressed, wondering how much Garth told her about it.

"Garth's already got Monty, Neil and Rein working on it. Once they get the rest of the information unlocked, there'll be a private staff meeting to view and discuss the rest of the message," she told him, knowing Garth wouldn't object. "He doesn't want Rebin and Metta knowing about it, until he chooses to let them know the rest of it, or not."

"Very wise. After all, if his wife was such a strong Visionary, he'd know we'll unlock it and how we'd handle the situation from the start, so the mysterious Prince from the past might have structured it this way, on a purpose."

"That's what Garth felt," she agreed. "I'd best get going," she explained, "I've got little ones to feed now." Ethan laughed, giving her a nod of his head as she stepped over to the door and was quickly out, closing it behind her. He well understood, by now, her need for haste and directness in everything!

"If I'd known Dotti and you were having such problems, I would've spoken to her about it sooner," Ethan apologized, seeing Maren stayed behind. He smiled at this, giving him a nod of his head.

"We did finally settle it, though," he replied with a sigh. "I just didn't want her to think she had to get pregnant because everyone else was. But, she does know how to get her way," he admitted.

"Most women do," he agreed with a chuckle. "I recall my first wife, Shelley," he added, sighing as he remembered her smile.

"So, you were married, at one time?" Maren pressed, smiling at the look in his eyes. "She must've been someone very special."

"Yes, she was very special! And I was married three times, actually. My research usually got in the way, or in Shelley's case, it was her family who decided I wasn't good enough for her. It took them nearly ten years to break us up," he said, his eyes still sad at that remembered pain. "I'd still be married to her, if it'd been my own choice," he admitted.

"Did you ever have any children of your own?" he questioned, surprised he was getting responses to his queries.

"No. We were going to wait until she had her Ph.D., too," he said, chuckling. "She kept getting sidetracked with helping to manage my staff, leaving her own work sitting by the wayside. I wonder what our children would've been like?" he speculated, thinking of the past once again.

"It's too bad you didn't think to leave her some of your sperm, as a parting gift. You might've had great-grandchildren on Earth by now," Maren teased, smiling as he saw the surprise in his eyes.

"Yes, hindsight is the most clear vision," he agreed, "I wish I had." He smiled ruefully and sighed at this, then looked at Maren, once more in the present. "Is there anything else I can help you with, this morning?" he asked more briskly, with a smile.

"No. I think we covered it all," Maren replied, getting to his feet. He gave Dr. Cruthers a small bow, then went to the door. "Talk with you later," he said, and left as Ethan gave him a wave of his hand.

"Finally," Garth teased, seeing Maren leaving Dr. Cruthers' office. He looked surprised to see him here, then gave him a nod of his head.

"Sorry, didn't know you had an appointment with Ethan," he apologized.

"Not an appointment, exactly," Garth admitted; "Just time for a quick chat before his next official appointment." Maren turned for the door out, but Garth put a hand to his shoulder, stopping him. "I'll be by your office in a few minutes, too, if you have the time to spare," he said in a low voice.

"Not a problem," Maren assured him, grinning. It must be about his daughter! "Got to see how my mother's doing," he said, as his friend released him. Garth gave him a nod, then went on into Ethan's office. Maren watched his back for a few seconds, then gave Bethy a wave of his hand, and hurried out the door. It was a busy morning.

"Maren?" Tanns mumbled, opening her eyes and seeing her oldest son at her side. A warm smile lit up his face as he gave her a small nod.

"How're you feeling now?" he asked as a merry light danced in his eyes. She drew in a deep breath and put a hand to her stomach, feeling her tiniest daughter kicking vigorously. A happy smile of surprise lit up her face as she sighed in relief.

"I'm feeling much better, now," she admitted, realizing she actually meant it deep inside. "At least your father didn't get you," she finally breathed, reaching out and grasping his hand. He nodded.

"He meant to kill Ryes, too, but she was faster, as I was busy keeping you from dying," he admitted to her. There was shock in her eyes at this as she guessed what he might have implied, but his chuckle broke through to her and then she appeared puzzled. Maren gave her another nod, then held up a large photo of Korman glued to a wall with colorful writing all over his body.

"He's not dead," he assured her, "and I was told he wasn't happy when he awoke later that night and needed help to get pulled off the wall." She sat up and took the photo from him, put a hand to her mouth in surprise for a few moments, then started to laugh merrily.

"Oh, she's delightfully evil," she finally said with a laugh, "and I love her! I feel free for the first time in my life!" She looked to see the understanding in his eyes. "How're your siblings?" she asked, needing to know.

"They're spending the day with Dotti, while she's introducing them to life in Winterhaven. We wanted to be sure you have as much time of peace, as you feel you want before having to deal with their needs too," he told her. "If you like, we can take them in for as long as you need," he assured her. "Do you feel ready for breakfast?" he added, seeing her emotions playing out in her eyes. She noted his concerned inspection, then smiled for him from the heart.

"You truly were my best child," she breathed out, giving him a nod. "Yes, I think I'm ready for breakfast."

"I had hoped so," he replied, "and if you're ready afterwards, we'll get you over to your new rooms. I tried to get it set up as I thought you might like it, but Tennan decided I didn't know anything and is rearranging it all over again." She laughed merrily.

"You two haven't agreed on anything in years," she stated. "Breakfast first and then I'll go see it and put it the way I truly want." He laughed as he gave her a nod.

"I'll be right back with your breakfast," Maren said, then left the room. She looked at the photo and was amazed anew.

"He's going to be so mad. It's a good thing we're far away from that now," she commented as she still lightly chuckled, admiring her niece's daring.

"Uh, Maren, could you spare a few minutes?" Justin asked, peering into his office from the open door. Maren looked up from his computer screen, then seeing who it was, gave him a smile and gestured for him to enter.

"Not a problem," he assured him. Justin appeared relieved as he stepped in and closed the door behind him. Maren usually kept the door open, as an invitation to any and all to call upon him at need. He only closed the door when there was a private conference being conducted. His staff knew this, so he was now aware Justin had something serious to discuss. "What can I do for you?" he asked, giving him his full attention as he took the seat next to his desk.

"It's kind of embarrassing," Justin began, then pulled up his shirt to reveal a set of long scratches on his side.

"Who did this to you?" he demanded, seeing they weren't deep, but did look painful.

"It wasn't because of any argument, or anything," he replied defensively, blushing, "Sana just got a little overexcited this morning." Maren's eyebrows shot up at this, then gave him a nod of understanding. "From what I heard you and Ted once discussing, I was wondering if she's starting into her season. She's never had a problem controlling her claws before. She sometimes likes to use them to lightly brush my skin to tease me. But normally it's so light, it doesn't scratch."

"Sex is one of the few times a man, or woman, starman does lose some self-control," he admitted smiling, as he extended his Healing Talent and quickly erased all signs of the scratches. Justin sighed in relief. It wasn't that they were all that painful, but that he knew it'd be days before they fully healed.

115

"She didn't mean to do it," he stated. "She couldn't apologize enough. We started out just playing around, then it suddenly turned serious. She just couldn't get enough of me this morning," he admitted, blushing again.

"It sounds like she may be coming into her season," he admitted, puzzled. "I didn't know you and Sana had taken up with seeing each other."

"Well, at first it was just out of curiosity, for the both of us, then we started seeing each other on a regular schedule. Now, we're living together with Fane calling me 'dada' the other day. It's more than just the sex. We really connect deep down and I don't know what I'd do if I couldn't wake up to her sweet face in the morning," he admitted, smiling with the joy in his eyes as he realized this small truth in his life.

"Does she love you as much as you love her?" he asked, recognizing his tumult of emotions from his own life with Dotti.

"She says she loves me, but I don't know if she's still as comfortable with things, yet," he confessed, unsure.

"Does Sabin know about this?" Maren thought to ask, wondering how he'd feel about his sister hooking up with a human?

"I don't know. I'm sure he suspects. I know Sela knows and has accepted it, but I don't know what she'd think, if we wanted to marry." Maren realized it was tearing him up inside. He could well understand. He sat back with a sigh.

"I think if Sana's truly coming into her season, it may be the time to sit down and discuss it. After all, if you were given a choice, would you truly want to marry Sana and live with her for the rest of your lives?"

"When Dotti showed us what you meant to her, I finally understood a lot of things about life in general. That it wasn't the person on the outside, but from the heart inside," he started, looking down at his hands. "I think I finally found a little of that piece of happiness in Sana. I was going to ask Raya if she could spare a few minutes to let Sana and I discuss this on a level where there could be no misunderstandings, but haven't approached her about it, yet." He looked up, meeting Maren's dark-brown eyes, giving him a nod of his head. "Yes, I want to marry her and live with her for the rest of my life. I've tom-catted around before and never really knew what love was, until I started seeing her."

"Good, let's call her and Raya in here and see where this goes," Maren told him, turning to his computer and tying in the messages to be relayed. Justin wasn't sure if he was ready to face up to this, right at this moment, but knew it needed to be settled now if Sana's season had started in truth. He took in a deep breath, letting it out slowly, trying to release his anxiety in the process. Maren smiled at this, giving him a nod of his head.

"I'm here for you," he assured him, reaching out to clasp his shoulder. Justin finally smiled at this, feeling better, knowing he meant it.

"You've been the youngest and most amazing boss I've ever had," he admitted.

"I try my best," Maren replied with a chuckle, sitting back in his chair. "We'll first see if Sana is coming into season, then what she feels deep down for you, then we'll worry about the rest of her family. You do know that even if she loves you deeply, she might want another man to father her cubs," he warned, getting serious about it again.

"I couldn't give her any children, so it'd have to be up to her if she wants another baby," he stated, already having given this matter some thought. Maren nodded his head to this, understanding. "Could you be a surrogate father?" Justin suddenly questioned.

"No. Dotti and I are true-mates. I can't father anyone else's children, even through artificial insemination," he informed him. "A true-mate vow goes deeper than a marriage vow. It ties both souls together on into what lies after life." The door opened as he was explaining this to Justin, and Sana and Raya heard the last of what he said.

"You're considering taking true-mate vows?" she asked Justin, coming on into the room, taking the chair next to him. He smiled for her, as she threw her arms about him, hugging him with tears in her eyes. She whispered something to him as he put his arms about her, too. Raya looked puzzled as Maren shook his head. She "peeked" within his mind and saw he was only explaining to Justin why he couldn't father Sana's future cubs, even on his behalf. She smiled at this, giving her head a shake.

"It sounds like what I do feel for you," he admitted, speaking a little more loudly, so the others could hear him, too. "Maren was just telling me how deeply he and Dotti are connected. I'd never demand anything like that of you, unless you felt you wanted it, too," he explained.

"Exactly," Maren agreed, "Let me give you a quick check first," he requested, looking to Sana. She smiled, letting her love go and gave Maren a nod in agreement. True-mate vows! Justin felt that strongly about her? She recalled the way his face lit up when Fane called him Dada the other day. He'd been so proud, almost as if he was her father in truth! Raya pulled up the last, empty chair and sat down near them. Now she understood why he summoned her here this morning.

"What do you think?" Justin asked as he opened his eyes.

"You're correct in your assumption." He turned to meet Sana's eyes. "Your season is upon you. I asked you and Raya to meet with us here to discuss things on an intimate level, where a clear understanding is possible," he told her. She blushed, surprised. No wonder she practically attacked Justin, as soon as he awoke this morning! She gave him a nod of her head, then smiled courageously for Justin.

"I'm ready," she replied. Justin smiled as he took her hand, giving a nod to Maren.

"Good. I want everyone to relax and close your eyes," Raya spoke up, taking over. This was her Talent, after all. They did as she requested, Maren being an old hand at this. She reached out to all of them, enveloping them in a welcoming warmth as she began to unravel this problem. She and Maren realized that the bonding between Sana and Justin was not quite as deep and strong as his and Dotti's, but it was far more than they'd found in many others. They left them alone to discuss things directly.

"I thought of all the people here, I had better warn you first, so you're not caught off guard if you see it in some of our minds," Maren told Raya, while they waited. "That and since you've been with all of us the longest, I thought you should know first."

"What?" she asked, feeling his hesitation and curious about what could be this important.

"Dotti's pregnant," he finally replied. Justin and Sana had then turned their attention back to Raya and Maren just as he was relating this news to her.

"Dotti's pregnant?" All three returned, astounded. Maren was embarrassed now, not meaning to let out about this to anyone but Raya. They were all excited by this revelation.

"Yes, she is and the child's mine, and we're expecting a daughter," he finally admitted, once they all calmed down. "We're keeping it under wraps until our Founder's Day celebration, when we'll announce it to everyone."

"Could you help us to have a child, too?" Sana and Justin both pressed, hoping and charged with such an idea.

"Maren, do it. It'll mean so much to them. You felt what they share," Raya pressed, feeling his reluctance.

"I'd need Ryes and Rhin to help," he warned them. "Are you sure?" he demanded. They were connected within, after all. "Can you weather the slights, as Dotti and I have for the last few months?" He showed them some of the problems they'd had.

"We'll make it," Sana declared. "We've had our share of looks, too. It's funny, but it's mostly other starmen. Very few of the humans treat us any differently."

"We have each other, the rest should be manageable somehow," Justin assured them. "Please ask Ryes, if she has the time?"

"What about your brother, Sana?" he pressed.

"We'll tell him, as soon as we leave your office," she decided, feeling it'd be the best next move they could make.

"Then I'll see if Ryes is available," Maren surrendered. If it were a done deal, how could Sabin truly object? After all, it's Sana's choice of who father's her cubs! "There is a risk here," he pressed, knowing Justin could well understand this point.

"We understand, but we believe in you, Maren!" Sana assured him, feeling exalted now. Maren dropped out of the link, feeling a little unsettled over what he started here. He quickly typed in an urgent message for Ryes, explaining the basic background, so she

wouldn't think it was an emergency. He immediately got a response
from her and sighed.

"They'll be all right," Raya said, speaking directly to Maren's
mind, so they couldn't hear her. They'd all dropped out of the inner
link and sat waiting. He gave her a nod, hoping she was right. "I'd
better get back," she said aloud, standing up with a smile. "I think
the rest of you have this well in hand."

"Thanks, Raya, for everything," Justin said, standing and
offering her his hand. She took it, giving it a shake, human-style, as
she smiled teasingly.

"It's not a problem!" she agreed. "And I already know, not to
let anyone know about all this until it's officially announced." With
this she opened the door, just as Garth was about to knock on it.
Justin sat back down.

"Am I interrupting something?" he asked curiously, seeing the
remaining three seated.

"Not yet," Maren assured him. "Maybe I'd better stop by your
office later?" he suggested. Garth gave him a nod of his head, then
saw Ryes coming down the hall toward her cousin's office with one of
their cubs in her arms. There was something afoot here and he
wasn't sure if he wanted to know what it was yet.

"As soon as you can." he returned, then stepped back from
the door to let his wife in. She gave him a quick kiss in passing as
she laughed lightly.

"I'll tell you later," she promised, then quickly joined the
others in the room, as he let the door close behind her. Garth was
uncomfortable with where his suspicions were taking him, so decided
to go visit Sabin, before returning to his own office. If his sister was
involved, it might be better if he were there when the news hit him - if
what he suspected they were up to was true.

They decided to return to Sana and Justin's quarters, so as to
make it easier on everyone. Justin told them he'd given up his
bachelor quarters almost two weeks ago, having moved in with Sana
and Fane. Ryes couldn't believe the change in Justin, recalling what
he'd been like when they first rescued him off of the derelict the Star
Quest had become.

"Now I know what you meant," Maren sent through to Ryes,
as they waited for the happy couple to finish their lovemaking. "This is
embarrassing!"

"Yes, it is!" she returned, smiling merrily. They were sitting
with their backs to them, wishing they could wait in another room, at
least, but these quarters didn't have such luxuries. "I'm going to have
to check with Phil and Kovin about their apartment assignment," she
commented, recalling there were a lot of other things they needed to
still take care of today.

"Aren't you and Garth going out hunting, tomorrow?" Maren
asked, trying to distract her. If she got too wound up over things, it'd

be harder for him to tap her pool of power. She sighed, remembering it too.

"It's going to be a nice break," she agreed, "but, I've never hunted with a bow before; only practiced shooting it. He's going to have to teach me," she admitted. Maren almost laughed aloud at this. They'd forgotten she'd been made to stay in Winterhaven the whole summer and fall, since she was carrying Garth's cubs. This was going to be her first chance hunting in almost a year's time!

"I'm sure he'll go easy on you," he assured her, sobering a little.

"You're deluded," she retorted, "Are you sure you've met Garth?" she teased. He quietly chuckled.

"We're ready," Justin said, seeing they were conversing internally. The hope and happiness in his eyes was unmistakable.

"And so are we," Maren assured him, standing up. He'd put Rhin into a light sleep, so he wouldn't distract them while they were working. Once he grew up and could get some practice in using his Talent, they wouldn't need to do such things. Ryes stood and the three of them returned to Sana's side. She was smiling her own inner joy.

"And I'm as ready as I'll be," she assured them.

"And you're sure you both want this?" Ryes asked, wanting no doubts.

"Yes!" the declared in unison. She laughed and Maren closed his eyes, ready and concentrating as he placed his hands lightly upon her abdomen. Ryes closed her eyes and put her hand upon his shoulder, drawing up her own Healing Talent to help Maren, and opening up access to her inner power for him. He also used Rhin's Talent to focus his efforts, as before. After what seemed an eternity, they both opened their eyes and sighed relief.

"Well?" the couple pressed, excited and hoping.

"I accidently went too far," Maren admitted as he blushed, trying not to smile too much. He saw the surprise in their eyes. "You're going to have two sons. I wasn't quite sure of the first one and tried for a second child, but it turned out they're both fine and healthy," he explained. Justin shouted out a laugh, then hugged Sana, kissing her passionately. Ryes laughed at this as she shook her head.

"I'd better go have a quick talk with Garth," she told her cousin.

"I'm going with you. I had a part in this, too," he asserted, putting an arm around her shoulders. "I'll log that you'll be out on leave for the next couple of days," Maren told Justin, when they finally surfaced for air.

"Will free mating be all right?" Sana questioned still feeling a faint stirring of her season, not quite out of her system, but not wanting to harm her sons. Maren smiled and nodded his head.

"As long as the two of you keep it slow and gentle," he warned her.

"We will!" Justin assured him.

"See you later," Ryes promised, turning for the door, Maren beside her. They let themselves out, closing it behind them. "Now for the hard part," she sighed.

"Garth's not going to believe it!" Maren agreed. "I wonder if anyone else will want crossed children, too?"

"As long as it's not frivolous," Ryes stated, wanting a precedence set from the beginning.

"That's exactly how I feel about it!" Maren replied. They turned toward Garth's office, hoping.

"Sana? Sure I know she and Justin have moved in together," Sabin assured his friend, as soon as he wrapped up his meeting with Kovin and Phil and they left. "It's only been two weeks, but I give them another month to start getting concerned. Seena's been ragging on me about them being together for weeks. She thinks it's scandalous, but I figure it's Sana's choice." He suddenly met Garth's eyes, wondering why he asked?

"I was just curious," he told him, seeing the suspicion suddenly appearing in his friend's eyes.

"Don't tell me, you just saw them together for the first time?" he huffed out with a chuckle, smiling. "He's been good to both her and Fane. In fact, Seena almost swallowed her tongue yesterday when Fane called him Dada, right in front of everyone at dinner. I think it surprised Justin and Sana, as much as anyone else. Sela and Keals laughed, while Ardis thought the whole thing was great," he related. "It seemed pretty funny to me, too."

"I wish I could've seen it. One of these days I'll be able to have dinner at a normal time," he admitted, "no more extended meetings! Yes, I just saw them together in Maren's office, discussing something." Sabin swung his chair around.

"Like what?" he pressed, suddenly serious.

"I don't know, but Raya was just leaving and Ryes was coming in to join them," he told him, as much as he knew.

"They wouldn't dare," he almost growled out. Garth chuckled.

"She has a mind and will of her own. If she chooses to mate with Justin, what of it? Remember when we didn't have a choice, back in Menna's Hold?" he reminded him pointedly. It was like a bucket of ice water thrown upon Sabin's budding anger. He did recall it - too well - the way Senah used him, when he'd rather never be near her! Now he understood the women's right to choose their mates freely, more than ever before in his life.

"You've got a point," he agreed, repressing a shudder. "I guess he's still better than Spann, who fathered Fane. Talk about an opportunist! Getting to her while we were out hunting that week.

He's never once tried to show any caring for neither Sana, nor Fane. At least Justin has brains and a heart, even if he's a human."

"Sabin... Ryes and Maren are here to see you and Garth," Wren announced over the desk's small communicator.

"Let them in," he replied, giving Garth a nod of his head, seeing he expected them. They came in, looking unsure of their welcome.

"Now exactly what did you two do?" Garth asked, after the door closed. They each took a seat, Maren looking to Ryes to see if she would speak up first.

"We helped Sana and Justin, so they could have a child of their own," Ryes daringly spoke up, her eyes holding no fear, nor regrets.

"I first made sure it'd be the best we could do for them. I had Raya help me commune directly with them, to know what's in their hearts," Maren admitted. "If it'd been anything but a deep connection and true request, I would've never attempted it."

"And did you succeed?" Sabin demanded, sounding more gruff than he meant to. Sana was his littermate after all. He realized Fane was two years old now. Was Sana about to go into season again? It seemed too soon!

"Yes, she's going to be having Justin's two sons," he replied, meeting his eyes. "She started her season this morning and wanted it so very much. You should've seen how happy the both of them were." Sabin quickly turned and typed in a short message to Ardis, getting her affirmative right away.

"I just asked Ardis to pick up Fane from Seena. The less our mother knows right now, the better. Sela will listen to me, to some extent, but I know she's not going to be happy either," he explained, turning back to his friends. "If this is what she wants, then I can only support her," he said, giving in. "I'll tell everyone that she's in her season and still wanted Justin."

"So, we'll have two pregnancies to announce on Founder's Day," Garth commented smiling and looking relieved.

"Sana usually wears loose clothing, so it shouldn't be too obvious for some time yet," Ryes added, relieved Sabin would support his sister in this.

"And Dotti's usually wearing her lab coat, so hers should be fairly well concealed, too," Maren agreed.

"Let's get down to appointing a committee to oversee the Founder's Day celebration," Garth suggested, smiling to see things working well so far. He knew the headaches wouldn't start until after the announcements.

"And you'd better get things set up for tomorrow," Ryes advised, smiling impishly at her husband.

"Oh, yeah," he agreed, having already forgotten with everything else being more pressing. "Our hunt." The others laughed at the expression on his face, teasing him.

"I'll make sure things don't go completely haywire here," Sabin promised him with a hearty laugh.

The Huntress

"Garth, if you can't let the job go for a day, then what's the use?" Ryes demanded, starting to get angry with him, as he hung back up the mic; having checked on something minor he forgot earlier. "Do you have the right people appointed to the right positions, or not? You have to let it go for a short while! Eventually, I hope we can get things running well enough so we can have more time together as a family. Wasn't that the whole reason we wanted to have cubs in the first place? To have a family to raise together?"

"You're right," he finally gave in, sighing heavily. "We are a family! We haven't had as much time together, as we've both wanted. I merely forgot, with so many other concerns. I'm sorry," he apologized, hoping he sounded sincere. She threw him a warm smile, her eyes lighting up from within, seeing she won, then returned her attention to her driving.

"You three ladies seem pretty calm about leaving the cubs for the whole day," he teased, trying to get some kind of worry out of them too. Ryes laughed merrily at this, winking over her shoulder at Sayer and Raby.

"I only feel sorry for Rowan and Ethan. I can't believe they actually volunteered!" she replied, still smiling. "I can bet that by the time we get back, they'll either be situated with Maren and Dotti, or Bethy and Jim."

"I'm betting on Maren and Dotti," Raby agreed, speaking up from the back seat in the rover.

"I'm betting on Bethy and Jim," Sayer piped up, putting in her vote. Garth laughed at this, finding it interesting the women had no faith in the two elders.

"Then I'm betting Ethan and Rowan will still have them contained, by the time we get back home," he told them with assurance. "After all, Rowan raised you all by himself." Ryes laughed again, as she swerved around two trees which came up in front of their vehicle. She was making her own way through Hailys, looking for a spot Mitt described to her last evening. "So, who're you betting on?"

"On a second thought, I'm betting it'll be someone else entirely, but someone we'd trust," she decided, smiling. She drove down into a depression, then climbed back out, after splashing through the small stream flowing across the bottom.

"Maybe I should be driving?" Garth warned her, thinking she was driving too fast for the terrain. She huffed at this, her eyes lighting up with mischief.

"I know where I'm going," she assured him, then found her last landmark, breaking the vehicle to a quick halt. "See, got us here, safe and sound."

"I don't know about that. I think I left my stomach back there, fifteen minutes ago," he teased. She had an ease around these things, he knew he'd never match! Now, he preferred the choppers to driving the rovers. He couldn't wait to pilot one of the shuttles, when they're ready for launch. Funny, he thought, the shuttle cockpit still wasn't the one he and Sabin saw in his Vision.

"Then next time we'll use a chopper," she volleyed in return, as if guessing his thoughts. He rolled his eyes at that, as he unfastened his seat restraints.

"I won't say it'll be faster, from the way you drive, but it might make me feel safer," he teased with a laugh.

"I don't think you could find your way home from here, driving," she countered in return, daring him with an impish light in her eyes.

"I could home in on our beacon," he retorted with a smirk on his face. She laughed and nodded.

"I could see you doing that," she agreed, "And end up driving us into a deep pit." He sighed, knowing she was right.

"Come on, let's get those scans fitted on you. You threw down a challenge for the rest of us and we're serious about taking you up on it. So, you're going to have to show everyone exactly how you hunt," he pressed as she made a face at him.

"But I've never used a bow when hunting, before," she protested.

"You're The Huntress," he teased in return. "I'd think it'd make things easier on you." She sighed, giving in. It was a lot lighter than her old spear. Garth helped her put on the equipment, while Sayer and Raby took out the rest of the things they'd need today, having it all ready to go very quickly.

"It feels strange," she commented, then smiled as she donned her backpack and picked up her bow stave and quiver, fastening the quiver onto her belt, positioned toward the back. "I'll go on ahead toward that large stream and see what's actually around here," she stated, "That way you can give the girls a few pointers, since their parents never took them out hunting, before." He gave her a nod of understanding.

"We'll catch up to you soon," Garth promised, then held up his tracker unit. "I'll find you." She smiled and nodded.

"Leave something for us," Raby demanded, laughing lightly as Sayer giggled.

"I'll do my best," Ryes replied, grinning, then turned and plunged on through the bushes behind her, scarcely turning more than a few leaves. The drone followed as quickly in her wake, making no sound.

"Mom just up and disappeared!" Sayer declared, astounded. Garth chuckled at this, giving her a nod of his head.

"She would've been even quieter about it, last year. She's out of practice."

"How're we ever going to begin to do that?" Raby demanded, feeling horribly outclassed. She thought she'd been watching her, but it was just like Sayer said, as if she suddenly vanished. She didn't remember anyone from the Moondance tribe who could do that.

"Rowan started her out hunting when she was five, so she's had a small head start. Give yourselves a chance. All it takes is slowing down and learning to listen and see what's around you. You focus in on the world around you," he assured them, having already locked up the rover and settled his backpack upon his back. The girls looked uncertain, so he waited until they looked ready to leave, with their backpacks on and bows in hand.

"Your first lesson starts right now. Sit down on the ground and don't move for about five minutes, then tell me what's around us. And that gold twitter in the tree next to us doesn't count," Garth told them, pointing up to the bird. Its song filled the small clearing. He sat down immediately, so they'd know he was serious about it. Sayer and Raby looked to each other, then shrugged and complied, as best they could. Sayer realized it was hard to sit and do nothing, for what seemed an endless span of time. What was she supposed to notice when nothing was around them?

Mitt had told her that there was a small herd of tuskers, which seemed to favor this area. She'd noted them several times as she passed by overhead in the last few weeks. Ryes thought it'd be a perfect way to start a hunt. She hadn't tasted fresh tusker in far too long! In just a few minutes, she picked up their tracks and spoor. They looked fairly fresh, in the last two to three hours at the most. It was just figuring out where they did most of their foraging. She trailed them, trotting at an easy pace, with the drone quietly following over her head. Unexpectedly, she realized something large was following her, as if stalking her.

"Something's tracking me," she breathed for the drone. She wasn't sure if she was supposed to make comments, but thought it would explain things for her friends better. She wound her trail more creatively, to get a clear look at what it could be; Hailys being filled with quite a few dangerous predators. And with the tuskers, there'd be other hunters. She withheld opening up Empath, since she did feel this was more of a challenge; that any of her friends might face, if they ventured into Hailys. She had to do this hunt on their level!

She climbed up parts of collapsed buildings and crossed a span of plant-covered beams to the top of another building, then dropped down into a small draw at its base and strung her bow as she watched her backtrack. The drone was hanging near her shoulder now. In a few minutes, a large dark-brown animal emerged, sniffing at her trail along the beam. It looked like a marl, but she never heard of one this color, nor living In the lowlands. Its jaws were huge, with large, tearing fangs hanging down from its mouth. She shivered as she realized it caught her fresh scent upon the wind and looked right at her.

"A forest marl?" she questioned, as she jumped back to the shelter of a nearby slab of stone, scrambling to the top, as it pounced down to where she had been. She fired her heaviest bow shaft as it shifted to come after her, the shaft embedding itself deeply in its side, bringing out a scream of rage from its gaping mouth. It clawed at the shaft, then turned back for her, truly enraged. Ryes dropped the bow and pulled out her pistol, shooting it neatly between the eyes as it leapt for her higher perch, even if it was twelve feet high.

It dropped to the forest floor, still twitching and huffing, as the last of its life leaked away. Ryes holstered the weapon, disgusted with herself for having to resort to use it instead. It seemed so inelegant a weapon and way too noisy. She sat down, trying to deal with her blinding headache and intense pain in her side; trying to separate herself from the animal below her, dying. She resisted the urge to swat at the hovering drone and finally picked up her bow from where it'd fallen; taking a few minutes to get more comfortable with its draw. She wasn't as fast and sure with it, as she'd been with her old clunky spear. She thought if she'd brought her spear along, she would've never resorted to the pistol. She went back to her higher perch, in case of any other marls were in the area. Garth appeared shortly, just as the last of the creature's death throes were fading. His face was a mask of panic with his own pistol in hand. She smiled down at him, giving a shrug of her shoulders.

"I need more practice with this thing," she told him calmly as she held the bow aloft, while he looked at the dead animal on the ground before him in shock. "I'm not fast enough with it, yet."

"But, you're all right?" he asked, finally smiling as he holstered his weapon. It was a huge predator and she was so petite! It worried him that she faced it alone.

"Oh yeah, not a scratch," she assured him, jumping down carefully as Raby and Sayer finally caught up to him. "I wish you would've let me bring my spear out today," she complained, pouting.

"You look as white as a ghost," he scolded her, noting the pain deep in her eyes as he stepped closer.

"Still have to learn how to separate myself the dying, again," she replied in a low voice. "I'll be fine." He saw her shivering a little, so stepped over and took her into his arms; ignoring the drone.

"We could just leave you here," he suggested, as he hugged her tightly.

"Hey, this is uncomfortable with all this stuff," she insisted, pushing back to face him. "I told you long ago that I'll learn how to deal with this heightened Empath Talent I have, otherwise I'll never

127

be able to defend myself. We may not need to hunt now, but this is the best way I can think of to face this off and deal with it. Remember that Vision?" she told him, knowing the girls had no idea what they were talking about. Garth finally let out a sigh and gave her a nod of his head, understanding.

"Well, it'll make a nice rug," he told her, as he saw both Sayer and Raby looked afraid to touch the carcass before them. Ryes smiled and gave him a nod of her head.

"How about a couple of coats for next winter?" she added, brushing her fingers through the thick, soft fur. He huffed a laugh, then took out his beltknife, signing their older daughters to attend what he was doing. Ryes stood up and listened to the forest about them, leaving her bow strung. Something out there was moving stealthily, just within her perceptions, but not distinctly enough to be identified. After having to kill the marl, she didn't want to open up her Empath fully to pin it down. At least she finally figured out which direction the tuskers lay, then bent to help Garth with the hide.

"Look at his paws!" Raby declared, astonished, "But we don't need to use hides anymore. Why are we taking his?" she questioned, sickened as the two people she'd grown to love and respect as her parents, quickly skinned the beast, rinsing the hide and themselves off in the nearby stream.

"When you kill something, you dishonor it by not finding something of value from its existence. We can't eat his meat, so we take his hide. Life is sacred and should never be taken for granted," Ryes explained, having finished , rolled it and tied it to the back of Garth's pack. It was larger than his backpack! She grabbed some leaves and crushed them in her hands, rubbing them all over Garth, the hide, and then herself.

"Why did you do that?" Sayer asked, as Ryes grabbed a fresh handful of leaves and started rubbing them down, too.

"These are alcis leaves and they help hide our scent," she replied, chuckling in a low voice as they squealed and squirmed, being ticklish, making it a game.

"What did you hear?" Garth asked, worried, when she finished. Something was out there; he realized he felt it too.

"It's not his mate. Something far more stealthy. I don't think it's hunting us, just following out of some reason of its own. It might only want our leftovers," she conjectured. Then gathered up her bow, ready to keep going. "Let's stick together for a while," she suggested, leading them onwards. He gave her a nod of agreement.

The girls knew nothing about how to walk quietly in a forest. Ryes gave them pointers in a low voice, but just ended up compensating, as best she could for the racket. Garth had improved, but still needed a few reminders too. He'd sat in that office too long, she realized! At least she still got out with either Brenda, or Wynne, to gather plants, seeds and fruits fairly frequently and rode Honey every few days. She realized the drone was at least as quiet as she.

Eventually, they crested a hill near a stony creek and she signed them to silence.

"They're lying under the hanging leaves, under those trees, just across the creek, right in front of us," she barely breathed, glad the breeze was blowing toward them. Sayer squinted in her effort to see what they were hunting, then saw a nose quivering in the shadows.

"Let us shoot first, then as they break, pick your targets and fire," Garth told them, ready, "Be ready to run if they come at us." He and Ryes slowly got to their knees, loosing their first arrows quickly. There was an explosion from out of the underbrush as the large herd of tuskers broke cover, squealing as they rushed down the stream's stony course, seeking shelter further downstream. The girls each brought down another one as Sayer and Raby tried to make their first kills, in their whole lives.

"I got one!" Raby declared. Garth put a second arrow into it granting it a quicker death.

One of the big males rushed at them, in spite of the arrows being fired directly at it. Ryes pulled both girls behind her and stood to the ready. Before it reached them, Garth managed to drop his bow and bring out his pistol and shoot it, point blank. He'd narrowly missed getting his arm slashed by the animal's heavy tusks, as it fell, still fighting to his last breath. Both girls peeked around Ryes, uncertain about hunting all over again; recognizing it was a bloody fight, at times. Garth saw Ryes was pale and shaking, now that the danger was over, sitting back down on the top of their hill, as he put his pistol away.

"Are you all right, Mom?" Sayer asked, never having seen her this way. Her arm was ice cold, when she put a hand on it!

"I'll be fine," she breathed out. "You'd better go make sure they're dead," she reminded them, knowing two still needed a killing stroke.

"Sayer, stay with your mother and stay alert; Raby come with me," Garth ordered, frowning at Ryes' condition.

"I'll be down to help in a minute," Ryes promised with a tight smile, trying to smile bravely for him. He gave her a nod.

"What's really wrong?" Sayer pressed, her eyes full of worry, once the others were gone and only her drone hovering overhead.

"I can feel an animal's death. Before my Talents fully awoke, I was able to get through it, because I needed the meat to feed my grandfather, aunt and younger cousins. Now that they're fully awake, I'm having a harder time readjusting. But, I'm going to have to learn to deal with it all over again. That's the other reason I refused to let Garth back out of this hunting trip. I need this gruesome practice," she explained. Shock was in Sayer's golden eyes as she tried to grasp what she was saying.

"But what use is it to feel an animal's death?" she asked. Ryes smiled tightly at this, giving her a nod of her head.

"When we were on our journey to Winterhaven, I `felt' there were fish nearby, so used this to find water in a parched part of the land. And I used it to convince a great viper to not bite your father, when his spear was out of my reach and my beltknife was far too small to deal with such a great serpent. It has its uses, just not too often now. I'm feeling a little better, so let's go lend a hand," she said, uncurling and standing up. Her stomach was still queasy, but was otherwise all right. She extended her Healing Talent to ease her body. Sayer took her hand, smiling. She noted it was still cool, but better.

"What are we going to do with," Sayer began, then saw Ryes had already lifted the body of the big tusker and floated it down, next to the stream and the other bodies.

"Let's go," she suggested.

"There're so many things you can do, Mom," she sighed. "I thought it'd be nice if I had a Talent too, but I don't want one, if it's like this one," she admitted. Ryes laughed at this, nodding her head in agreement.

"I wish someone had given me a choice too," she agreed, as they approached the others.

"It might be better if you went back to get the rover," Garth suggested. There were seven tuskers lying next to the stream, six had their glands and guts already removed, and were now being bled, as he bent to the last, biggest one, now that it was here. "We have too many to just carry them back."

"Ugh! These things stink," Raby complained. "I know the meat taste's great, but this is disgusting." She was busy trying to wash her hands off in the creek, her clothes still spattered with fresh blood and gore.

"Maybe I'd better," she agreed. "Next time I'll take you out to learn how to snare birds," she told Raby, seeing she was truly unhappy with today's outing. And it was only approaching lunch time! "It'll be far less smelly, but still work when we have to pluck all the feathers," she teased. Raby laughed at this, seeming to get her jest.

"Be careful," Garth warned her. She gave him a nod of her head at this. It seemed they lost their slinker, but that didn't mean she couldn't run into it on the way back! She took her bearings from the sunlight slanting in through the trees, then trotted off toward the rover, taking a different course back, something more direct.

"Sayer, help me bury these entrails," Garth suggested, seeing Raby was still upset over helping to gut the animals, as she was trying to rinse off her pants and tunic now. Sayer crinkled up her nose in disgust, but took the portable shovel he held out to her and started digging a hole near his. It stank, but she thought Raby was overreacting.

Ryes realized her slinker was back. She'd made sure to avoid the area of her earlier kill, hoping to not attract its notice, but to no avail. It remained unseen, but followed her winding trail with ease. She used all the woodland tricks she picked up through the years, but it wasn't fooled, nor showed itself to her. This denoted intelligence, which only caused her to feel nervous. She finally decided to make a straight dash for their vehicle, in hopes of getting far enough ahead of it, to prevent any tragedies.

After a few minutes, she caught a glimpse of the black hood through the trees ahead. Just as she saw it, there was a distinct rustle in the brush behind her, when she thought her slinker was beside her! She turned, pistol out and ready as another of the great marl predators leapt out at her, swiping with its massive paw. The weapon was wrenched from her grip as she jumped back, trying to find something she could scramble up quickly, to get out of its reach, her hand bleeding from the deep scratches. The dark marl lunged for her as she dodged, trying to put a tree between them, it struck the tree, tearing its bark instead of her head. It was FAST! She slipped on a patch of loose leaves and fell hard as she backed away, just as it took another swipe. She rolled, trying to get away, when the leaves near her exploded upwards, as another great shape rose up, right next to her, hissing loudly and menacingly.

Ryes gasped as she realized it was the great viper she freed from Doran's valley, what seemed so long ago. There couldn't be two of them, as this creature pulled at her from within. He knew her, as she knew him! She suddenly realized who her slinker had been! The dark marl hissed, backing up from the viper as he stood his ground, hissing in return.

Ryes saw the pistol was out of reach, gleaming dully from beneath a fall of leaves, on the other side of the clearing. Her bow had been dropped when it took its first swipe at her. She didn't know if the viper could truly hold it off for long, then she realized there was only one thing she could do. She closed her eyes and reached down within herself and she swept her attacker up into the air, terrifying the animal. Then she cast it far from them, searching within its mind for a trigger to get it to run away and leave her, Garth and the girls in peace. She found out it was a she and she had a great fear of fire, so she made her believe there was a forest fire between them and her, sending her running off through the dense forest of Hailys. Still, she didn't relax. Why was the serpent here?

"Why?" she questioned him, as he bobbed and swayed, seeing his enemy departing quickly. He lowered himself to the ground once again, as he turned to her.

"Am to serve," he replied. In his mind, she saw he was happiest when he served a woman of strong Talent.

"I thank you for your service. But I must go now to my mate."

"You hunt," he stated. There were many emotions coloring his thoughts with this one simple statement. She refused to be drawn in and kept her replies simple.

"We need the meat, but the mate to that one tried to hunt me, so I had to kill him. Did you find your mate?" she asked, trying to distract it from thoughts of blood. Her hand was still bleeding from the scratches. She took out a handkerchief to wrap it, even if the blood seeped through the cloth. It still helped put pressure on the wounds.

"Found mates, many mates," he told her, very happy with himself.

"Good! I must go now," she told him. "I give you my thanks again." She got to her feet and retrieved both the pistol and bow. She saw him watching her, but he didn't move to follow. When she finally got back to the rover, she breathed a sigh of relief. She glanced at the time and knew Garth would be worried, so she gunned the engine loudly, to let him know where she was, and took the best track she could find, back to where she'd left them, the drone followed overhead. She saw the look of pure relief on Garth's face, as she pulled up beside the creek. She put it to standby and jumped out, smiling and happy they were fine.

"What happened?" he demanded as he saw her hand. She'd done a quick healing, needing more of her attention on trying to maneuver the rover through the forest.

"Found the other clawed one, who was the mate to the one I killed earlier, and our slinker," she told him, smiling, feeling more centered again. "I keep forgetting I have Talents I can use, when I'm outmatched," she admitted. He crushed her in his arms, his heart beating strongly as he wondered how close she'd cut it this time?

"You need to practice more with your Talents, so you won't forget them in the future," he told her, "All our Talents should be practicing more regularly."

"The slinker saved me and it turned out to be the serpent from Doran's valley. He said he only wanted to serve me. If he's turned up here, do you think he'll eventually turn up at Winterhaven?" she asked worried, as he pulled back from her to meet her eyes with surprise in his own.

"We'll have to think on that. It's too dangerous a pet to have slinking around," he said, agreeing.

"A serpent?" Raby asked, recalling the animal they skinned earlier this morning. "A serpent stopped one of those?"

"He's a truly huge viper," Ryes told her with a huff of a laugh, "and it looks like he's grown since I saw him last. He looks almost sixteen feet long, now. Let's get loaded up, get this gear off of me, and head for home. I'm sure they'll send out one of the choppers, if we delay much longer," she suggested. Garth released her, giving her a nod in agreement.

"Heck of a day off," he told her, grinning. She laughed, shaking her head at this in amazement.

"Only we could have so much fun on a day off," she agreed. The girls joined them in their mirth, as they all turned to load up the gleanings from their day's hunt. They were all more than ready to head home to the comforts of Winterhaven!

    "We're home," Ryes said as she entered their quarters. They had expanded their small room to include the far larger one which had been next to their room, so now they had a spacious common room and the girl's room on the far side. The girls had a door which opened up into the central room, with their old, smaller room serving as a bedroom for her and Garth on the opposite side. The cubs' small cribs were now in Sayer and Raby's larger bedroom. It was "almost" roomy enough.
    "So soon?" Ryun asked, looking up from her needlework. Rebin smiled too, but noting the dried blood on Ryes' hand.
    "Yeah, it was almost more fun than I could stand for one day," she admitted. "Were they too much trouble?" she asked, nodding toward their bedroom door. The cubs must be taking a nap.
    "Five is definitely a handful," Ryun admitted, smiling. "Ethan and Rowan asked if we would mind sitting in for them for a while."
    "It was no bother. They're all such happy babies," Rebin assured her. Garth came in with Sayer and Raby close on his heels.
    "Mom wins," Sayer whispered to Raby. Garth chuckled at this. "I'm for a quick shower," she stated more loudly. Raby nodded her head as they headed toward their room.
    "Won't they wake them?" Ryun asked, worried. It seemed like they'd barely gotten them to lay down.
    "They've been our adopted daughters since before the cubs were born. They're my best helpers, so I'm not worried," Ryes assured her, smiling. She felt like a shower too, but realized hers would have to wait until the girls were back.
    "Was the hunt good?" Rebin asked, gathering her things and standing up.
    "Not as much as I would've liked, but we bagged seven tuskers, with two of them being of good size. So, fresh tusker tomorrow for dinner at least," she told her, smiling proudly.
    "Seven? And you thought it should've been better?" Rebin was astounded by her standards! No wonder everyone called her "The Huntress!"
    "Well, I'm a bit out of practice. Garth wouldn't let me go out hunting when I was pregnant last year," she admitted, handing Garth her backpack as he went to their room to gather their soaps and change of clothes. He decided to wait his shower, so they could shower together.
    "And she's got to get more used to using the bow and arrows," Sayer put in as she and Raby were ready to head for the showers. "Be right back, Mom," she told her, grinning mischievously.
    "Alright," she replied, waving them out the door.

"See you at dinner soon," Ryun said, smiling as she showed them to the door drape. Ryes returned her smile, giving her a nod and hug. Then she hugged Rebin, too.

"Think we'll actually make it on time, today," she agreed. "Thank you, so very much."

"It was no trouble at all," both women assured her, then left. Ryes sighed as she went to check on the cubs first. Seeing they were fine, she went to her own room, surprised Garth was waiting for her. She thought he'd have gone ahead and gotten his shower, too.

"It IS our day off," he scolded as he saw the surprise in her eyes. She laughed as he put his arms around her.

"It sure is!" she agreed, kissing him as her heart was bursting with happiness. Within their hearts they were one...

Return to Base

"Captain on Deck!" a voice announced as Captain Lindell Walker rounded the bend in the boarding tunnel to arrive at the welcoming open hatch to his ship, The Aries' Wrath. All of his personal equipment and effects had been loaded on the ship yesterday, so his aide had set up his quarters to have them ready for his use today. His aide, Ensign David Snyder, now carried his overnight satchel, as he followed two paces back as dictated by military custom.

"Permission to come aboard?" Walker requested as Kaminski stood ready to greet him with the OOD. The OOD checked the credentials he presented with his palm scanner, then gave him a crisp salute, as did the MAA and his assistant. Walker returned it and gave them a nod.

"Permission granted. Welcome aboard the Aries' Wrath, Captain Walker. The men are assembled and ready for your review, Sir," Commander James Kaminski reported, saluting smartly as Walker returned his salute, then boarded the ship for the first time. There was the sound of an actual whistle being blown for the proper protocol, instead of a recording which was so common now. That pleased him.

Walker had a reputation for daring and from what James heard through scuttlebutt, it usually landed him in trouble with the admirals. Still, Naval Command gave him this newly-commissioned, experimental starship to command, with a secret mission for her maiden voyage. He'd heard a variety of things about his new captain, but reserved judgement until he'd seen him in action. He followed him into the shuttle bay.

Walker gave some small acknowledgements to his new command staff, telling them in a low voice he'd conduct introductions and provide full disclosure soon, then proceeded straight to review the rank and file, as they stood awaiting inspection. Some of the command staff seemed a little miffed, as he'd slighted them. Kaminski gave a small hand sign to let them know he knew, then followed after Walker, ready to assist. Walker's aide went to stand near the podium, appearing ready to assist if signaled.

They held the muster in the main shuttle bay, which had the room to accommodate the whole crew at one time with no crowding. This ship didn't have a large amphitheater as some of the older, fancier fleet ships. They needed the room for their special armor, power systems and weapons which were more central to its mission. She wasn't built for comfort. The shuttle craft had been moved off the ship for this event, but were in a nearby hangar and ready to be reloaded.

Walker went through the whole room of seamen, marines and officers doing a thorough inspection to be sure they met his standards. From the whole room of over three hundred and seventy men and women, there were no imperfections noted and showed Kaminski's attention to detail. At times he'd glare, at times he'd nod his head, but never once smiled. In the end, he found himself satisfied with the crew fleet picked for his command. And this inspection alone told him how tight a ship the First ran things.

"Very well, at ease," Walker ordered, standing next to the platform at the front.

"At ease," Kaminski relayed the order in a booming voice and the rank and file assembled in the hall shifted to an "at ease" stance, awaiting further orders. Captain Walker took the podium. Kaminski on the right and his aide stood to the left side, leaving him on the small, raised platform by himself.

"We stand now at a crux in which the fate of all Earth and her colonies lie in our hands. The human race is fighting for its very existence and we are the answer," he stated. His gaze swept the room and noted he had everyone's attention.

"I'm sure some of you have already noted your external communications have been blocked. At this time, all our objective are considered top secret classified, which is why we now have highly restricted communications outside this ship." He noted some of the crew appeared uncomfortable with this news and his stare.

"Our first mission objective is to prove to Fleet that we finally have the best battleship and firepower to take on the Darkens, toe to toe. We are going to prove, by our numbers alone, that we can decimate all they send against us faster than any ship in Fleet to date. Our second mission objective is to reach out and recruit what firepower still exists in the outer colonies; to use to break the back of the Darkens forces upon our return. And our final mission objective is to raise what help we can from some potential alien allies. They may be the unexpected lynch-pin to help us win this war. I expect each and every one of you to give your best at every minute of each day. We will win Earth's freedom from destruction!" He waved his fist in the air, as if ready to strike the Darkens and eliminate them with it alone.

There was applause at the end with enough energy to make it feel as if he had finally reached this battle-hardened crew. He had Kaminski dismiss them; turning now to get acquainted with his new quarters. He would be meeting and briefing his command staff within the hour, as he laid out in his mind the orders he wanted to make sure were passed down and followed.

The Aries' Wrath will be leading a task force of twelve experimental ships which will be running the Darken's blockade. The Darkens had gotten too clever in finding the vulnerable points on their standard fleet ships and took them out too quickly now. These twelve ships were each unique with not one like any other, in any way. They also had the best of cutting edge weaponry and ship armor developed in the last two decades. Aries' Wrath herself had part of her ship plating modified from a new alloy developed the last few months from a sample of metal included in a probe message satellite sent out from Beda IV. It was lightweight, durable and tough. It'd proved exciting and the applications were still being explored.

Fleet Intel had given them a window for punching through the lines and as a further precaution, a distraction of no less than twelve other attacks were to be made against the Darken fleet. Some were going to be small skirmishes, but others would be full out offensives – to take out as many Darken ships as possible. Most of these ships were fully automated; remotely commanded to lessen the loss of lives.

They'd be underway in another twelve hours. In a way, this would be the crucible to determine the best designs to incorporate into future ships. Walker had watched this particular ship's construction closely, having had a hand in some of her innovations like the overlay on the front of the ship of the new alloy. She HAD to be the one to break through the Darken's blockade, and prove they could seriously take them on, once and for all time. He couldn't face another failure!

"Ryes!" She heard her grandfather call out as she was rushing down the hall, heading for her office and the small sanctuary it'd give her. She sighed as she stopped, wondering who in Winterhaven hadn't seen the copy of the recording from the scans from yesterday's hunt? But Rowan, she knew with no doubt, would be upset with her. She hadn't had time to ask Neil why he didn't edit it! It would've saved her a lot of scoldings this morning.

"Yes, grandfather?" she asked, turning to see his angry face, bracing herself within again. Ethan was behind him, appearing upset too. She winced internally, but wasn't surprised.

"We saw it," he stated, "It was on the Winterhaven morning news, on the vid. Why didn't you tell me you felt your prey's death so strongly?" he demanded.

"Why don't we go to my office?" she suggested diplomatically, "It's closer than Ethan's or your craft center office." Both men gave her a nod in agreement, seeing discussing something like this out in the hallways wasn't the best idea. As they turned toward her office, she saw Mitt approaching too. But, Mitt realized she'd already been accosted by the elders, who didn't look happy.

"I need to talk with you later today," she informed Ryes, stopping briefly. She got Ryes' nod in response, then continued down the hallway heading toward her brother's office. Larissa appeared surprised as Ryes came back to the office, but immediately saw the elders on her heels and understood. She gave Ryes a nod as a sign to let her know she'd make sure they'd be undisturbed. Ryes smiled and gave her a nod, having found Larissa wonderfully useful as her assistant. Ethan appointed her, in spite of her protests at the time, so she now had to use the inner office, which she didn't mind.

"Yes?" she asked as innocently as possible, after they went into her office, closing the door as the elders settled into chairs at her small conference table. She stepped over and took one of the open chairs.

"You once told me you could feel an animal's death, but I didn't know it was so personal," Rowan finally got out around his conflicting emotions. She sighed as she nodded her head.

"Why do you insist upon hunting, if it causes you so much pain?" Ethan added, his brows knit with concern.

"I have to inure myself to the pain and find a way to still function around it, or find a way to channel it, so it doesn't impact my sense of the world around me so strongly. I know of one instance where I may have to actually have to use my Talents to defend myself. Maren and I had a shared Vision again. From what little we saw, I feel I need to desensitize myself, once more. Hunting is the only way I know I can do this, while still providing something positive to both the community here, as well as not trying to be outright cruel and heartless."

"What do you mean, you and Maren had another shared Vision?" Rowan demanded, puzzled as this was the first he'd heard of it.

"We had our first almost a year ago in Hailys. We saw Garth wasn't going to be here for the cubs' birth, but had hoped he'd only be out hunting, or something. I was relieved it wasn't because he'd journeyed on ahead of me," she explained. Ethan appeared puzzled while Rowan nodded his head in understanding.

"Like the way Jana has journeyed on ahead of me," he explained to Ethan. His eyes brightened, as he gave him a nod of enlightenment. "Show us both of these Visions of yours," he ordered, turning back to his granddaughter.

"If you truly insist," she replied, unsurprised by his insistence. They both looked determined and she was too tired to refuse them; having had bad dreams all night long. So she closed her eyes and reached her hands across the table to them in invitation. After they established their rapport, she opened up the first Vision she'd ever had in her life to them fully. Their shock of the clarity of the Vision put a small smile upon her lips. Next she showed them their second Vision, the night they returned from Matlowe.

"The first was EXACTLY?" Rowan pressed, still in the inner link.

"Yes, it was. In fact, between realizing it and because of Bethy's added presence soon afterwards, I finally managed to stop fighting Maren. Gareth was born shortly thereafter," she told him, showing them her memories of those few moments and her joy at meeting her first son sang through their joined minds. It warmed all their hearts.

"Does Garth know about this second Vision?" Ethan asked, his curiosity clearly felt.

"Yes. He says we're not allowed to go out without an armed escort from now on. We don't recognize the area and I only worry we're risking the lives of the men and women escorting us. Whatever Maren's fighting, it's very dangerous. Dotti's wearing a holster, but her pistol's gone. So, did she try to use it? How many are involved in the attack? We've no idea," she related, still deeply worried about the whole thing. "I don't know if I'll be in a position of having to actually kill someone, to save those I love and care about."

"Do you actually have to do the killing for your training, or just be nearby?" Ethan questioned, seeming to have an idea of his own now. It could be important training for her; for now and in the far future, like fighting the Snagospin.

"Being near might do the trick," she admitted, recalling the many times on the trail when the others killed and she'd felt it too. As they caught small wisps of these recollections, their horror renewed.

"That strongly?" Rowan pressed, at a loss for her dilemma.

"Yes," she reluctantly replied, embarrassed, "and I didn't even have my Empath Talent called up. It's like it's always on and running in the background."

"Why not try to be near when the birds are slaughtered for cooking?" Ethan suggested, "It'd give you the exposure, at least." His heart when out to her, not envying her such a gruesome task.

"I'll try," she agreed, feeling this was a good idea and would serve her purposes.

"Dotti's pregnant in your Vision," Rowan started and suddenly felt a strong reaction from both Ethan and Ryes. "Is she pregnant now?" he instantly demanded, feeling unfairly left out.

"Yes she is and Maren's the father. We combined our Talents to help her conceive their daughter," she confessed, knowing he deserved to know before their formal announcement. Then she opened up the memory of him coming to her, so torn up inside about it, and what they actually did to pull it off. With the shared joy between Dotti and Maren at their success filling their senses as she gently released them, letting the link dissolve.

"They ARE deeply connected," Rowan finally said aloud, having let his anger go, through it all. "I can see why they've spoken true-mate vows." He realized he'd need to be ready to help Maren fend off Tanns and Tennan's tempers, when it did come to announcing the pending birth.

"Yes, they are," Ryes agreed, smiling warmly at the memory. Ethan let out a long sigh.

"Thank you, my dear, for granting me a glimpse into paradise," he said; his voice soft and his eyes looking far away, deep into his own soul. It was the way he once felt about a lovely lady named Shelley. She too had long blonde tresses and knew her own mind.

"You're welcome," she replied, seeing he probably didn't hear her. "I truly must go see to my cubs, now," she said, standing up. "Sorry about the headaches, but Larissa has some pain killers," she added in apology, heading quickly for the door, realizing she should have used her Healing Talent on them first, as she hesitated by the door.

"We're getting used to them by now," Ethan teased, coming back to the present. "We'll talk some more later," he promised. She smiled for both of them, seeing their smiles in return, then ran out the door, leaving it open for them.

"It brought back too many memories," Rowan admitted, his eyes misted with unshed tears, while his lips were stretched with a huge smile. "I hope Ryes will be able to heal Dotti and herself. I don't think Garth, nor Maren, would be the same without them. And I can see why she thinks she might have to fight back using her Talent. She'd do anything to protect her younger cousin, even kill, if needed."

"I believe you're correct in your assumption," Ethan agreed, feeling a sense of helplessness to remedy the situation. "Considering it's almost lunch, should we head for the mess hall?" he asked, a smile once more alighting his eyes.

"Yes, we should. And I want to ask Raya if Metta's taken his `quick course' in English. I wonder how long before he'll realize it's the only way to truly understand us, here in Winterhaven?" Both men chuckled at this as they stood and left the room. Larissa watched them with puzzled eyes. She hated it when she could only catch small snatches of interesting conversations. She'd have to ask Ryes about it later. She was more a good friend than a boss now.

"Ryes, I know you're mad at me," Shadd began as Ryes was sitting and feeing her cubs. Her friend sighed, as she met her eyes, appearing troubled.

"No, I'm not mad, only at a loss at how you did it. I would've thought you might've told Torr beforehand, at least. He did understand, saying it was your choice, but I saw how it tore at him inside. And I truly don't understand Tobin. He's still so little and needs you," she replied, quickly looking down at Gareth, as he lay in her arms. "I don't understand that part the most."

"Of course you wouldn't understand. You've taken true-mate vows with Garth! But, if you hadn't, would you still want only him with you day after day? Wouldn't you like someone new in your life? Someone who can bring new happiness to your days? Even one of the humans? You deserve it!" she insisted, trying to sound convincing as she grinned; a strange light danced in her eyes.

"I don't think..." she started then shook her head with a smile.

"The only reason I left them both was because I didn't want to give Torr any excuses to see me. That's why I left him our quarters, too, instead of making him move out to find new ones," she cut in, explaining with a touch of rebellion in her bright eyes. She knew this was going to be hard, but she valued the friendship they shared and wanted to know she had Ryes' support, at least.

"Even if we hadn't taken the vows, I'd only want Garth with me. I still can't get enough of him!" Ryes assured her, smiling in spite of herself with light in her eyes. "Weren't you the one who was warning me about Mason, when Mitt was interested in him? That he was one to go from woman to woman? What'll you do when he gets tired of you?"

"Then I'll find someone new, too," she quickly snapped back, seeing her friend was concerned for her welfare still, it was clear in her wonderful green eyes. "Maybe by the time I come into my next season, I'll be ready for Torr again?" she conjectured, liking that idea now that she voiced it. "Tobin had turned out well and healthy."

"Now you're sounding like the way Teris used to sound – just for breeding purposes," Ryes teased in return smiling, yet within she felt herself reviling such usage. Shadd wasn't thinking of Torr's feelings at all!

"There's still a lot of time yet, before that happens and who knows what we'll all be doing by then," she offered. It did sound like something Teris once used when talking to Mitt about mating choices. It upset Mitt so much that she threw herself at Minn, who was far older than she. It was one of the things which puzzled Mason, who had free mated with Mitt before she settled with his half-brother, Minn. Mitt wouldn't have her first season until later this year and she knew Mason was trying to find a way to take her back from him. She wasn't sure if she wanted to share him with Mitt!

"That's true," Ryes voiced in agreement. "So, what do you think of our very own Founder's Day? Want to be in on our planning committee?" she pressed, trying to change the subject. She knew she had to talk with Torr about this and find a way to help him let go and move past his grieving.

"It's a great idea! How about if we get Ardis and Raya in on it, too?" Shadd suggested. Ryes gave her a nod of agreement of her idea.

"Sabin's drawing up a list of candidates; why not drop by his office and talk with him about it?" Ryes prompted, hoping this might get her back into something more normal again.

"I think I will. Aren't they a lot to keep track of?" she suddenly asked, indicating her now burping Gareth, with two more left to feed and the remaining two fighting, even if they were still babies.

She couldn't imagine being stuck with so many cubs! Tobin had been
a chore, all by himself!

"I've gotten used to them," she assured her, smiling. She put
Gareth down on the floor with his siblings, picking up Jann next to get
her away from the others, since she was fond of latching onto her
siblings' ears.

"It seems like a lot of work," Shadd replied, glad to be free of
crying cubs! "Well, I'd best go see Sabin. He usually takes an early
lunch and should be back by now," she said, standing up with a warm
smile. She was relieved Ryes wasn't mad at her and seemed to
understand her reasons overall. "See you later!"

"You bet," Ryes returned, still smiling, yet glad she was
leaving. Shadd stood and sauntered out the door, letting the drape
fall into place behind her, as she quickly headed down the hallway.

"How can she do that to Torr and Tobin?" Sayer whispered,
coming out of her bedroom, now that Shadd was gone. They didn't
hear anyone in the hall outside, but it was wise to speak in lower
tones when in their main room since their door was usually open. She
gently got Shaysa to let go of Rhin's arm, giving her a soft toy to hold
instead. She was learning to do that from Jann and now loved to lock
onto anything she could reach! Rhin's crying quieted, as he realized
he'd been rescued.

"I don't know," Ryes replied with a heavy sigh, "I don't
understand it, truly. Even without our true-mate vows, I could never
treat Garth in such a way, much less all these adorable cubs of ours!
Including you and Raby! How can she just turn her back on Tobin?"

"I hope I'll find someone whom I love enough to take true-
mate vows," Sayer breathed, wishing it in her heart. Ryes chuckled at
this, shaking her head.

"Just make sure it's truly the right man! Even if you have to
bug Raya, or me, to be very sure," she warned. "True-mate vows
should never be spoken lightly!"

"No, they shouldn't," Garth agreed, stepping into their main
room; letting the drape fall behind him. "I thought you'd be here,
busy," he teased his wife with a grin. Ryes smiled, her eyes lighting
up at seeing him, unexpectedly.

"What's up?" she asked, since he normally spent every free
minute during the day with Sabin and the other men.

"Just wanted to spend some time with my family," he assured
her, coming across the room to give her a kiss, then Sayer a kiss on

her cheek. "And it took me a while to get over how close you cut it, yesterday, when those jungle marls attacked you. Don't wear your luck too thin," he warned, as he sat on the floor and picked up Rhin, holding him up in the air and making faces at him. Rhin was giggling and drooling in return, happiness in his face. Ryes smiled, giving him a nod of her head.

"I'll remember I have a few useful Talents and can use them at will, more often," she assured him. His eyes met hers, seeing she meant it. He hoped so, and realized he needed to thank Ethan for his pushing Ryes to use her Talents to defend herself. Ethan's foresight was still more clear than his own. Then, there was a knock on their doorframe, surprising Sayer and Ryes.

"Oh, I had our lunch delivered today. If you can't occasionally exercise a little decadent authority every now and again, what's the point of being in charge?" Garth asked, chuckling, as he put Rhin down on the floor, again. Ryes and Sayer laughed at this as he got up to help bring the cart inside, giving Sana his thanks for the favor.

"Garth, come quick!" Ryes shouted, as she saw he was in a conference room with Torr, Sabin and Maren. She wondered where they'd disappeared off to, so realized she could use her Empath to find him. His eyes met hers, but instead of staying to explain things, she dashed back out the door, running down the corridor, heading outside.

"What was that all about?" Sabin questioned, as the four of them stood up. Garth looked puzzled, but realized if she didn't feel as if there were time to explain it herself, it had to be something important. The rest realized this too, at the same time, and rushed for the door. There were a few others in the hall, running toward the main hallway. They trotted behind, noting there was excitement, not panic on the faces around them. Following the crowd, they ended up outside where Dr. Cruthers was directing Neil and Anders about handling a large, badly-battered cylinder which was resting in a cradle. They were near the Star Quest's bulk and nearby sat the outer casing of the drone, itself. It, too, looked the worst for wear, but apparently had been somewhere and landed here at Winterhaven, safe and sound.

"What is it?" Torr asked Ryes, as they found her standing nearby, watching the others work with the cylinder.

"The inner core of the drone Ethan sent out, after everyone off the Star Quest had been revived. It was to let others know they were alive. And, it came back! He's going to see if there's a response to his earlier message, or if it merely returned due to some programming glitch," she explained, smiling happily.

"Where was this drone supposed to have gone?" Garth questioned, this being the first time he'd ever heard about this device. "Aren't you afraid the Snagospin might trace this back to them here on Tayna? If an attack fell now, we'd be helpless to stop them!" he demanded. His fears and frustrations built up and he knew he needed answers. He suddenly strode up to Ethan, to find out if he'd taken precautions to ensure this thing hadn't been traced! Ethan looked up to see Garth at his side, appearing upset. He smiled at him as he nodded his head in acknowledgment.

"We'll have access to the data storage, very soon," he assured him, thinking this wasn't what he was concerned about in this moment.

"Can we be sure the Snagospin didn't follow it back here?" he demanded a little gruffly, as Ryes following him, stepped up beside Garth. She sighed, but kept her silence, having faith in Ethan's strategies. He explained the steps he'd taken to her long ago when he launched it; to hopefully avoid them being targeted because of this messenger.

"We have no way of truly knowing. The computer on the Star Quest is still feeding information directly into our AI here at Winterhaven, so if it was followed, we'll have a few minutes of warning. But I would think, if there was an attack pending, it would've fallen some hours ago, long before it reached Tayna's surface. I believe the most the Snagospin would've seen was a derelict starship, which was hopelessly scrapped and incapable of flight, and would've figured that the drone was merely a plea for assistance. They'd have a far better return in awaiting any ships sent out to `rescue' us, than in wasting their energies here," he replied in a low voice, meeting his friend's eyes. Garth finally gave him a nod of agreement, appearing to relax a little. Then looked over to the Star Quest's blackened, torn bulk and realized the ship held far more value in being a decoy for any snooping enemies, as they built their own starships. Perhaps the outer shell could be taken apart last? The two repaired and modified shuttles were almost ready to launch, after all, but safe inside their hangar.

"You've more time and wisdom than I, Ethan. I apologize for my outburst," he replied. Ethan chuckled merrily at this, giving him a nod of his head.

"You're worried about the lives of everyone here. I can well understand. I explained to Ryes last year, when we launched the drone, that I only used locational names, not stellar coordinates. They'd have to know where the Beda system lay, and that Amitell Research Station ten thirty-three referred to what we now call Winterhaven. The drone has a primitive tesseract system built into it, which I programmed in several jumps, which could lead anyone following off on a number of tangents. Still there's always the possibility that it could've been tracked, which is why I had it land out near the Star Quest and only had the core brought here," he explained as he watched Neil and Anders working on the device.

"It's intact, Dr. Cruthers, and there's a new seal on it, which I've never seen before," Neil reported, having opened the access panel. "She's been somewhere and came back to us." Ethan quickly stepped over to his side to have a look at this seal.

"Sixth Fleet, Mander's Outpost?" he questioned with a frown. "It looks genuine. All right, remove the data cartridge and anything they put inside. Get me a copy of its contents, as soon as you possibly can," he ordered, straightening up.

"Is there a problem?" Ryes asked, wondering at the look in his eyes. He seemed unsettled.

"In my day, the sixth fleet was stationed outside of the Sol system. And I've never heard of `Mander's Outpost' before. I can only speculate that there may have been quite a few changes in the last eighty years. I don't even know if this drone even made it to Earth. Maybe it only stopped by a busy colony? I hope Earth, herself, still exists."

"But Garth's supposed to save the Earth," Monty insisted, overhearing their conversation. Ethan looked at him with wonder in his eyes for several long moments, then smiled and gave him a nod of his head.

"So we've been told by a woman with great foresight, who even foresaw we humans living here," he agreed with a low chuckle. His eyes met Garth's, seeing his inner struggle with this new burden still weighing his heart. "Don't worry, if you're supposed to save good ol' Dirt, she'll still be there to save," he assured him, smiling. "Let's go back in to see what messages she's carrying, as soon as Neil can get them decoded." Garth gave him a smile and nod of his head, then followed the good doctor back into Winterhaven.

"You didn't happen to name any of your colony worlds, Dirt, did you?" Ryes questioned, smiling merrily as she caught up to Ethan's side. He chuckled at this, shaking his head in denial.

    "No. One was quite more than enough," he assured her. She laughed lightly at this, but he frowned, hoping she hadn't seen something in the two names, they hadn't.

Messages

"Garth?" He heard Rein call out as she entered his open office door, seeing he was working on his computer, catching up on his messages while waiting for Neil to signal that he finished downloading the messages from Earth. He wanted to know if there was anything real for them to make plans around for a true future. Somehow there had to be answers to give him some direction! He jerked his head up and focused upon her radiant face.

"Do you have some news today, Aunt Rein?" he asked, trying to not sound too hopeful and sure he failed. She nodded her head as her lips sketched a broad smile.

"We've finally broken through all the crystal's locks! And we have the secret segment recorded, so we have an independent copy we don't have to unlock their ways," she told him; her excitement was easy to see.

"Excellent!" he replied, grinning as he stood up, "You cannot know how truly grateful I am for all the work you've poured into this project." She laughed and swept into a graceful bow before him, then straightened up and sighed.

"I wanted to be the first to honor you, Prince Garth of House Ladearis of Tayna and Kahmarr," she teased in a mix of lightheartedness and seriousness. He stopped and had a puzzled look with an uncertain smile now. "Prince Callas of House Ladearis of Kahmarr declared you his heir. You are now the leader of all starmen, across all our worlds. There were holos, videos, documents and many other items of interest, which will still take more time to understand. We even think there're pieces of computer programming, which we have the AI working upon unravelling in what Neil calls an isolated, protected mode." Garth was thoughtful for a few moments then smiled and gave her a nod, and then a small bow in return.

"That's something unexpected and I'm sure Ryes will tease me endlessly about for some time," he said with a laugh. "Let me get out a few messages and let's go see what this great ancestor of ours left for us to use." She nodded, having expected it as she swept her skirt aside to perch upon one of the chairs in his office. Excitement still coursed through her whole being. Jett had heard the whole thing from her desk and was just as excited.

"So now that we're all here, let's see what Prince Callas has to say, Oh Great One," Ryes teased. She'd been practically squirming in her seat while they'd waited for Ethan and Rowan to arrive. They were finally tracked down and urged to leave Neil and Dotti to finish the data retrieval off the probe. Light laughter sounded from most of the others in the room at her ribbing. Around the table where the large crystal reader now sat in a large conference room in Winterhaven were Garth, Ryes, Sabin, Ardis, Rein, Torr, Maren, Ted, Bethy, Mitt, Axel, Monty, Rowan and Ethan; all eager to start the rest of the main holo message left for Garth by the Kahmarr Prince. Once they settled and the lights dimmed, Garth started the machine exactly as Rein instructed, getting her nod of approval.

"Hello Garth," the man in the chair said right off, "Please forgive me as I did know your correct name, but knew for some of the people who would be seeing the small first segment of this recording, it was not wise to reveal how powerful a Visionary my wife actually is; let them believe what they will believe. My proper name and title are, Crown Prince Callas su Akindin of House Ladearis. Interesting to note, my youngest, full-blooded sister, Isyiah of House Ladearis, was vacationing with me here upon Tayna and married in her own time and passed down the family name to her daughters in turn. She is not a Forester and will never surrender the family name. Your mother is one of her descendants, Marla is of House Ladearis, so you can rightfully claim the family name." There was a moment of stunned silence in the room, as Prince Callas paused, as if to give them a chance to absorb what he just said.

"You truly are the heir of the royal throne, Garth," Maren breathed, breaking it, "and your mother, sisters and Gann all carry a house name, too!" Garth, who was looking into Ryes' merry, teasing green eyes, looked at Maren and gave him a nod of agreement.

"So it seems," he replied, finally smiling and relaxing a little.

"I'm Mitt of House Ladearis!" Mitt breathed out with a laugh, "I have a last name and am royal!" She appeared highly amused and shocked at the same time. Ryes gave her a nod of her head with a happy smile.

"Our family blood and the blood of the others here with me will run deep in Matlowe Village, so many of you will also be related to me to some degree," he continued with a broad smile. "I know this is a heavy responsibility to lay upon all of you, but you will succeed in breaking the Snagospin forces and discover what truly lies behind their drive of conquest. Your strong Talents will be the best foil for their evil plans. Garth, you, your family and friends can end their pillage of the systems for all time. You will be in time to save your current ally, Earth, from total destruction. It will not be an easy fight and you will have factions upon Earth, herself, working against you, but you will triumph. The humans there with you in Winterhaven will be some of your best defenders, even against Earth. They are true citizens of Tayna and dedicated supporters. More humans will come to your aid and support you fully, too. Alas, the Kahmarr we all knew and cherished is gone. This you will discover for yourself. Of our allies of old, I will say nothing, as you will find your own among them in time"

"You can count on me," Monty breathed, not realizing he'd said it aloud, which got the others to chuckling in the room.

"Thank you, Monty," Garth said, giving him a nod of his head. He blushed, but nodded in response.

"This being said, I do bequeath all of my titles, duties and honors to you, Crown Prince Garth of House Ladearis upon Tayna and of Kahmarr, and charge you to uphold the Laws for the good of all starmen, upon all the worlds we call home. I have included all documents which support the validity of the titles you carry and what lands which are a part of your domain for you to use to support your claims at future dates. Print them out at need. I have hidden the Royal Seal I have had made for you in a special place, which your wife will discover at the proper time."

Ryes squeezed his hand, as he heard her soft giggle. Garth realized that the whole time this recorded holo image was speaking, he was looking right at him, as if meeting his eyes across time, as he passed down this information. It surprised him how strong a Talent this wife of his actually held! How did she know them all so well, from so long ago? He'd picked his seat at random! And he could guess that Sabin had to be one of her descendants, too. It gave him a chill up his back, but he held on and paid attention. This was too important for them all! He wanted Winterhaven to have a strong, peace-filled future, so all their children could grow up in a world with only normal childhood cares to concern them.

The rest of the recording was filled with images and original layouts from all the destroyed cities upon Tayna and pointing out what they might still be able to salvage with the time involved and natural elements to assist to clearing out the poisons the Snagospin used to kill off the city inhabitants. There was also a long, drawn out discussion about strategies for using starships against the Snagospin and star maps, which he said they will use in the not too distant future. This had his, Sabin, Axel, Rowan and Ethan's sharp attention, as they were fully absorbed in this discussion. Possibilities danced in their heads; as if they had the ships to take out to battle right now.

"And finally, we have included some upgrades for your numerator, which you call an AI computer. It will help it to develop into a better machine, which can be replicated and used in other places, where you will need its intelligent assistance for all your efforts. It was a type of numerator we had never created before, but these changes will make it the best of what we had on Kahmarr and what your friends had on Earth. It will understand what we have given it and go from there," he assured them with a smile. Ryes raised an eyebrow in surprise, but kept silent.

"This has been a lot of information to process for you, Garth, and your family and friends, but you will be able to use it to create a new future for all starmen and your allies. I wish I could be there with you to advise and assist, but must merely count on your strengths, intelligence and good heart to succeed in my stead. I feel I have picked the right man to carry our cause into the future. You all have my blessings and thanks," Prince Callas said, then stood and saluted them, turning as if to meet each of their eyes in this small gesture. After a few moments the image faded out and they let go their collective breaths.

"Wow," breathed Monty, amazed by the whole thing all over again. He and Rein had finally watched it first thing in the morning to be sure it was ready for the rest to watch, but not the whole thing and somehow seeing it fully played out, had a bigger impact. Rein nodded her head in agreement.

"We have a lot of work ahead of us and only two small shuttles available to get it all done," Axel stated with a chuckle. "From the way he's been talking, we're going to have a whole fleet at our beck and call." Mitt laughed lightly at this, nodding her head in agreement.

"I guess we can build all our starships by hand?" she suggested, grinning from ear to ear.

"Or dig them up out of Hailys," Ryes threw her way. The look of surprise on her face and the others in the room got her to laughing.

"What a great idea," Ardis declared, slamming her fist down on the table. "There has to be something left in their starport!"

"Or the parts we can use to create new ones," Axel agreed, nodding his head. "There were also the remains which we thought might have been a space station on Shaysa, which might be something we could salvage, too. And with Ryes' new Talent, we should be able to go forward with making our own starships."

"What new Talent?" Garth and several others asked, wonder in their eyes. Mitt and Ryes were laughing merrily, having forgotten about it already.

"I was going to tell you," Ryes started, spreading her open hands and blushing as she tried to stop laughing. "I was thinking of calling it Molecular Manipulator Talent. That makes another new Talent, and I don't know how many I may actually have now," she informed the others around the table. Maren shook his head as if he didn't believe how amazing she was becoming.

There was a sudden loud knock on the door, startling everyone. Monty was instantly on his feet to unlock it and see who it was, with Torr right beside him. It turned out to be Neil and Dotti with happy smiles upon their faces.

"We have the news from Earth decoded," Neil announced, once they were allowed into the room and the door secured again. He held aloft the chip for all to see. "It was a smart piece of work, but between the both of us, we got it." Dotti nodded her head in agreement then shifted around to go sit next to Maren. He gave her a proud kiss, then put a possessive arm around her shoulders for a few moments. She laughed and blushed, but gave the others a nod of her head.

"It turned out to be an amazing puzzle. I think you would have to be a human to figure it out," she agreed.

"Please show us what you've found," Garth invited, turning off the crystal viewer and activating the small comp console on the table. Neil nodded and put the chip into the slot, setting it up for its run, then taking a seat next to Rein, across from Garth near the head of the table.

"What did we miss from the crystal?" Dotti asked, as Neil settled into his chair. Mitt blushed as she gave her a nod.

"Garth is now Crown Prince Garth of Tayna and Kahmarr," she said. Torr laughed and shook his head.

"But still my cousin," he minded them with surety in his eyes.

"Most definitely, Torr! Still your cousin! Our fathers were littermates!" he assured him, laughing. "There was a lot of information on the crystal about the Snagospin and how to fight them, with most of it I still don't understand," Garth admitted. There was more laughter and agreement from around the room.

"That goes for all of us," Ryes assured him, her green eyes afire with excitement, questions and plans. "We'll have to go over it a few times to be sure."

"Prince Callas said he picked the right man for the job, Garth. Have faith in that assertion and know you'll find a way to understand. Added to that, you'll have the full support of everyone in this room," Ethan stated with assurance, gesturing to include everyone around the table. "I agree with him, you'll succeed." Garth took in a deep breath, then let it out slowly and gave him a nod of agreement.

"It's a lot to take in," he finally said, "but I'll do my best."

"No one could ask more," Rowan agreed, looking very excited.

"It looks like we have some work ahead of all of us, if we're going to take on the Snagospin," Ted teased him, grinning. "We're here for you, Garth."

"I appreciate the support from all of you, but let's take a look now at what Earth has sent in response," he suggested, mostly as a distraction to get the focus in the room off of himself. Ryes nodded in agreement as Neil reached over and activated the recording. They all settled back again as an officer appeared on the wall at the end of the table. A two-dimensional image instead of the three-dimensional holo Prince Callas employed. The difference was noted around the room with smiles and light chuckles.

"I'm Captain Marcus French, and am currently stationed at Mander's Outpost, which now lies within the Sol system's inner planetary defenses. We received the probe launched by Dr. Ethan Cruthers on behalf of the survivors of the Star Quest. First, may I offer my congratulations on your survival against incredible odds; it was a miracle which I'm sure you all appreciate. The data collected from off the Star Quest at the time of the attack, which Dr. Cruthers included, was very helpful in establishing the information we lacked about this attack method of the Darkens. But, let me say first of all that Earth still exists!"

"Thank God!" Axel said in a low voice. Mitt gave him a nod.

There was a cheer that went up through the room at this news. Laughter filled with tears of relief was expressed by all their humans present. Bethy grabbed Dotti for a moment with a joy-filled hug. Neil had paused the message to give everyone a chance to recover. He wiped at this own eyes, while his heart bounded with happiness. The starmen there were very happy for them all, understanding the emotional impact of knowing their original home still existed. Once they settled down, he took off the pause at Garth's nod.

"But I will follow that up in saying the Darkens have laid siege to the Sol system. We're still able to hold the inner system, but from Jupiter outward the colonies have fallen and the Darkens have eaten any survivors of their attacks. No prisoners are ever taken for exchange, so we don't take any prisoners, either. They've never responded to our requests to conduct peace talks, so we've stopped asking and go on with the business of war. We've studied their physiology and found their normal range of living tolerances is a match to our own, which Command has felt is the reason they are so hot to grab our colony worlds. They breed so fast, they must've run out of room on their own worlds. They're very insect-like, even if they're warm-blooded, and will swarm. We're hoping to use this against them if we can get them in number when we have numbers on our own side to take them on," he further explained. He stepped forward a step, as if to speak more personally to the camera. Everyone in the room was holding their collective breaths.

"We need any allies you can gather out there among the stars. We're sending out a task force of twelve experimental ships to break through the blockade and fetch what can be gathered among our colonies, first. We've given them orders to gather at Tayna. We can hope that by the time they arrive, you'll have what you can gather from your alien allies. If nothing else a fresh supply of foods and sundries will help, too. We've given the task force certain codes to use to communicate with Inner System Command, to allow us to coordinate our forces for any offensives that we can use to rout the Darkens for all time. We need you to join our fight, as soon as possible!"

"As for the survivors who previously held military positions, we have such personnel now listed as retired, since we have no idea the long-term effects of being in stasis had on their minds and bodies. But they can be called back into active duty by the task force, if they can serve and are needed. If they are reactivated, they need only serve one Earth standard year and then will be formally retired from all military obligations, unless they choose to re-up and sign new contracts for service. The civilians can choose to enlist if they meet our current criteria for military duty. We have no current openings, nor established standards if any of the indigenous peoples from Tayna, who may choose to join our military, but we will leave such options open for the starship captains to make their own decisions on that matter."

"I'm including some files that will detail what we call history, and for you would be news, to help everyone catch up on what you slept through in the intervening years. Also included here you will find a few personal messages from the families we could contact before the probe was sent back your way, for their kin on Tayna. Any further questions that are not encompassed by the included materials can be addressed to the task force captains. Do not send back this probe as we don't want it to be a common sight for the Darkens to further ponder." With this, the officer stepped back and gave them a formal salute, then the image faded out.

"Whew, that was a smelly load," Ted commented in a low voice. Bethy chucked and gave him a nod as Ethan's eyes were filled with questions.

"You have copied the rest of the included materials, Neil?" he pressed. Neil gave him a nod, as Garth was frowning.

"They mean to take over our former military people as their own, again?" he questioned. "I would've thought they released them from any further service. They're part of Winterhaven now, not theirs to command."

"Who in this room was in their military before?" Sabin asked, not sure now.

"Just Monty and I," Neil assured him, understanding. Sabin gave him a nod.

"We'll have to negotiate your service positions to remain here with us to the end of your terms, with these captains, if they choose to reactive your service," Garth told them.

"I was wondering, if we should they reactivate us, what if they expect us to act against Winterhaven? It's not something I'd ever do, no matter what they say otherwise," Monty asked, his brow furrowed.

"Good question," Dotti said, wondering about it, herself.

"Captain French said it would rest with their ship captains," Ethan suggested. "But if they give orders that endanger innocents, I believe you can refuse the order. They can take you before a military court and you'd have to prove your case to them," he added. The look of pure relief upon both Neil's and Monty's faces was obvious to everyone in the room.

"Good thing we live far from Earth," Neil commented with a smile.

"Glad I never joined," Axel stated with a huff of a laugh and smile. Neil gave him a nod of agreement. Monty groaned and did a face-palm, then looked up at Garth.

"Can we forego wearing uniforms if they reactivate us to work here, Sir?" he requested. This sparked a round of merry laughter around the table. Garth finally sobered after a few moments and gave him a nod.

"Yes, you can, Monty. As your Base Commander I order you and all our other former Earth military members to leave off wearing any uniforms other than our own Winterhaven ones, unless they have excellent reasons for ordering it otherwise," he stated. Neil and Monty nodded their understanding, and appreciation of this small favor he granted them.

"We'll see what can be worked out," Ryes assured the men, then turned back to her own husband. "That's a great idea! We should have our own uniform. Nothing formal, just something to use when we need it." Ardis laughed as she tugged upon her T-shirt with the phoenix emblazoned upon it.

"This one does for me," she stated proudly. Ryes smiled, giving her a nod.

"You're right. We do have one already," she agreed.

"And now for the news for which some of our people are anxiously waiting to hear," Garth announced. There was laughter in response; the starmen knew their humans had been fretting over this report all day. The tension running through the humans gathered in the dining room was almost visible in the air!

"First off, Earth still exists!" He paused as a cheer went up through the room. He smiled, then continued when everyone quieted down once more. "The Sol system has been laid to siege with no ships being able to make it through the blockade successfully, yet. There's a group of twelve experimental ships that will be enroute to Tayna by now. They hope they'll be able to slip through the blockade. They hope some of Earth's outer colonies might still be struggling to survive by maintaining a low profile. They've come to call the people we know as the Snagospin, the Darkens, but they're the same people who attacked Tayna hundreds of years ago and wiped out Kahmarr. The images of their ships and the beings, themselves, are identical."

There was restlessness in the room as the adults realized the reach of such a people. To first destroy Kahmarr and her allies, then to decimate Earth's fleet, isolating the humans to their solar system of origin. It was a nightmare!

"On another note, those who were formerly enlisted in the Earth military forces are now retired, but can be reactivated. The documents accompanying the message state you will serve as active duty for a period not to exceed one Earth year if the captains of the task force being sent out from Earth reaches us, and choose to do so. We are hoping if reactivated, you can serve out your year here in Winterhaven." This was met with more than a few disapproving looks from the humans and starmen. No one approved of such arrogance as to still own a person years after they'd normally be beyond their service years.

"There are also a few personal messages, for those who still have family members they could locate, in the time span they allotted, before sending the drone out on its return journey. The task force should've launched by now. We won't know of their success, or lack of it, for some months, as they weren't planning on taking a direct route to Tayna. They need to swing by and check on some of their other colonies, first. If they can break through the blockade," he warned them. "I believe we should have a few moments of silence, to pray for their success. Dr. Cruthers will have the messages available for pickup, after dinner."

Garth then turned off the mic and bowed his head, hoping their ancient gods would grant them this small bit of good luck; that the humans would make it through to them, at least. Others about the room also bowed their heads in either prayer, or introspection. After a few minutes, he stepped down from the platform, seeing the solemn looks in most everyone's faces. Even the starmen understood this was no light venture, and offered their support to the humans they'd come to accept and value greatly. Regular conversations started up in lower tones around the room, as dinner was being served.

"There was more you could've told them," Neil stated in a low voice, having taken a seat opposite Ryes. Brenda looked at him surprised as she sat down next to him. Ryes nodded her head in agreement.

"Not until we've gone through that material on the memory rod a few more times, first. Then we'll give them a larger picture of what happened in the past, what's happening now, and what we're planning on doing about it," Garth asserted, before Ethan could speak up. Sana looked puzzled, as well as several others seated around them.

"What?" Justin demanded, needing to know, worried about Earth.

"That if they can't drum up some support from out here, pretty quickly, the perimeter will fall and the inner system planets will be easy prey for the Snagospin. They eat people instead of taking prisoners," Ethan told them all, in a soft voice. "Somehow, we have to get whatever older colonies out here, which still exist, and what remains of Earth's colonies, united, to break the Snagospin and drive them back to their own worlds." He saw Brenda's face go pale at this news, as well as the astonishment in Sana and Minn's eyes.

"WE HAVE TO DO THIS?" Sana demanded, amazed as she tried to grasp the scope of such expectations.

"I have to do this," Garth replied, "I'm hoping to understand the information Prince Callas left for us to use for this end." Ryes saw the terrible burden he now bore in his heart and knew this was why he was suddenly turning up around her, every chance he got. He didn't know if he'd survive such a battle.

"Well, I'm here to help," she reminded him, throwing her arms about him. "I may not be that `Talent of One' they were looking for, but I do have Talents and power, which you'll need," she reminded him. There was a flash of fear in his eyes as he realized she was right. And that Visionary from the past had said he was supposed to use all their Talents in this fight, against this dark enemy. He sighed as he put his arm around her, briefly hugging her back.

"I'd rather you didn't, but I don't think I'll have much of a choice," he replied.

"We'll be fine," she assured him, smiling. She saw Mitt noted his reluctance, too. "At any rate, we can't do anything, until we get our shuttles up and operational, and then see if that task force reaches us. Until then, let's focus upon Tayna concerns. We still have the Caravaner's Spring Gather to attend next week. We have yet to determine how many we're allowing to go and what kind of lottery we're setting up to determine who," she teased. "Of course, Sabin and I think that those who win the lottery for this gather, should be held back from the lottery for the Great Spring Gather, in a couple of months. Then they'll be allowed into that one, after all the other slots are filled. Right, Sabin?" she asked, diverting the conversation to something they could handle for now. Garth let go of her to take the platter Sabin was passing him. He finally quirked a smile, seeing what Ryes was doing, and that she was handling it better than him.

"That's right," Sabin agreed, smiling as he shook his head. He saw the look in Justin's eyes, as he was thinking upon the conversation he just heard. He realized he never knew the kinds of things they could end up discussing at mealtimes, when they were all together! Maren saw it too and chuckled.

"We never learn how to stop talking shop," he teased Justin, smiling. He met his eyes, seeing his understanding. This was to be kept only among this close-knit group, of which he'd just been admitted. It was an eye-opening experience. Sana laughed, nodding her head in agreement.

"You'd never believe how hard it is to not correct someone who's out trying to spread a rumor, when you know the truth of the matter, and it hasn't been let out, officially, yet," she admitted to him. He laughed at this, giving her a nod of his head. It amazed him, even so.

"Yup, anything and everything can happen when this rowdy bunch is together," Ryes pipped in, smiling. "Matlowe was probably as quiet as a tomb and deadly dull, when we took off last year." Mitt laughed merrily at this, nodding her head.

"I think that's the real reason Kovin and Teris decided to track you. And there was no way I was going to be left behind," she assured her.

"It was pretty quiet when you left," Rowan agreed, chuckling. "I still miss the Yuri's voice, though."

"I'll drive you over to it in the morning, if you really want to see it, again," Ryes offered, grinning mischievously, then handed Jann a biscuit; having finished feeding the little ones. "I haven't tried to teach the girls how to fish, yet."

"Now that's a good idea!" Maren declared, "I haven't been fishing since late last fall. But, I'm not sure about tomorrow. Ptan's due very soon."

"Fishing?" Raby protested, "Do I have to?" she asked, appearing distressed with the notion. She hated having to clean and gut the smelly things, and knew it'd be expected of her!

"You don't have to go," Garth assured her, chuckling with the others at the look on her face. She wasn't an outdoors kind of person. He wondered if she'd ever been happy when she was a simple, plains dweller?

"Thanks, Dad!" she replied, instantly relieved and grateful.

"But, I want to go," Sayer protested. "I love fishing! I used to fish every chance my brother and mother would let me, when I lived with the Moondance Tribe."

"And I love fishing, too," Justin spoke up, hoping he could be included in this outing. Ryes laughed, nodding her head.

"Alright. After Ptan has her baby, we'll take a day to go out fishing and playing in the river. Do you know how to swim?" she suddenly asked Justin.

"Yes, I do," he replied, smiling assurance.

"I know how to swim!" Lixi piped up, grinning. Ryes laughed, nodding her head at this.

"Yes, you sure do, Lixi." Sela looked surprised at hearing this, almost as if being told her daughter had grown wings.

"We should have Phil and Kovin throw in an indoor swimming pool, so we can teach all the children how to swim, and be able to enjoy swimming, even in the winter," Brenda suggested, smiling. Neil nodded his head, laughing.

"Oh, what a great idea!" Ryes agreed, looking to Sabin. He held up his hands before him to forestall her.

"You're telling them. I don't think they can take too much more from me!" he protested, grinning. This brought out laughter from those around them, in full agreement.

Gone Fishin'

"Why do you always braid all your hair when we go out? You usually only wear a couple of small braids when we're home," Sayer asked, as they travelled down the Caravaner's road, heading toward the Yuri.

Garth was driving and noted the road gave him little trouble and he saw it was wider now, too. Kovin and Phil had a crew out for the last two weeks, providing an enduring, deeper, smoother foundation for the road surface, then covered it with crushed rock then paved it on top; making it a solid, smooth road which was wide enough to accommodate three large rovers, side-by-side. It make a huge difference! They planned to rebuild the road up to where it entered the plains tribes' territory, all the way through to Matlowe. But for now, they only refinished what immediately lay near Winterhaven; since they accessed this road to get to their main water intake equipment. Garth knew Darman and the rest of the caravaners would be delightfully surprised when they returned in the fall. They'd kept the project a secret from them the whole winter.

"So my hair won't get snagged as much by the bushes and trees, when we're outdoors," Ryes replied. Sayer's eyes reflected her immediate understanding.

"Could you braid mine too?" she requested. Ryes laughed, giving her a nod of her head in agreement, and then noted Garth looked as if he wanted to pull over.

"Keep going, Garth. Wynne and I have a good spot already picked out, just a little more upriver," she suddenly directed, wanting to stop him before he pulled off for the river.

"And exactly what do you ladies do when you come out here to `gather plants'?" he asked, smiling as he kept driving.

"Truly, that's what we're doing," she assured him, smiling impishly. He noted her smile and chuckled.

"Sure," he agreed, knowing she'd know that he was teasing her. She started laughing merrily, but pointed out a break in the trees ahead.

"Through there," she directed, "Our path should be pretty obvious. It's a great place to stop for lunch." There was laughter from the others in the back as everyone realized the path was well worn already.

"Honestly, we only stop here every now and then," she protested. This only got them to laugh louder. Garth slowed and carefully navigated the turn, then stopped the vehicle in a large clearing which fronted a shaded, inviting, expansive, sandy beach, right up to the water's edge. He realized there was enough room here to set up several large homes and live in some comfort. It might be a future consideration for family getaways.

"Now, this is a nice spot!" Rowan agreed as he stepped out of the vehicle, amazed. "It'd be a great place to camp overnight."

"Yes, it would," Garth concurred, feeling the lazy peacefulness of this place reaching him, even with all he still on his mind! "We'll give it a try once the cubs get a bit older." Ryes gave him a nod of her head, having already planned upon that, too. They'd left them at home today with Sabin and Ardis' cubs, under the care of some of their trusted cub-sitters, who worked today under Katas' and Raby's supervision.

"Let's grab our gear," Minn suggested, as Mitt gave him a nod of agreement. Garth joined them as Ryes kicked off her sandals, leaving them next to the vehicle and ran down to the water's edge; Sayer right behind her.

"It's too cold for swimming," Justin warned, holding Fane as he enjoyed the gentle caress of the wind, playing over the water.

"That's what Wynne often tells me," Ryes quipped back, "but, I wore my swimsuit, anyway." She pulled off her jeans and folded them, but left on her T-shirt and waded out into the rushing, cold water. "It is a bit nippy, but very refreshing," she told him, and turned to swim out from the shore toward a heap of boulders, about twenty feet out. As she approached, she extended her Empath awareness so she'd know exactly what was out here, today. The one time she surprised a family of small, furred fishers, trying to catch their meal and they took an exception to her trespass. Singly, it would've been no problem, but a whole family group enraged was perilous! Luckily, nothing dangerous lurked today, so she locked it back down.

"Where's she going?" Garth asked, annoyed his wife appeared to be pulling little stunts, already. Sayer had stayed on the beach, standing next to her jeans, as if trying to make up her mind.

"It looks like to those rocks," Maren observed, smiling, understanding Garth too well.

"Ryes!" Garth called, as she climbed up on the rocks. She waved to him with a smile, and then turned to gaze down into the water, intently. After a few seconds, she dove off the rocks and disappeared beneath the waves. She appeared a few moments later, swimming toward the beach, once more.

"Got that container ready?" she asked, as she walked back to them. Dangling from one hand was a large, thrashing fish. Garth noted a tightness around her mouth and quickly moved to set it out for her, ready to receive her catch.

"I forgot to ask you how you fished," he teased her, smiling and relaxing now that he understood. "When we were on the road you used to use a line and hook."

"No, this is the way she prefers to fish," Rowan assured him, stepping over to get a look at what she caught. "Ah, a silversides and a big one," he added, "She used to fish off our dock, back home. Plenty of fish there in the shallows."

"That's right," she agreed with her grandfather, giving him a smile and nod of thanks. "I knew you didn't want me out swimming in the water when I was pregnant, Garth, so used the hook and line more out of frustration. Do we have an extra container I could take out there with me? It'd make it easier to just fill it," she asked. Minn laughed as he handed a big one over. "Thanks," she told him, the light dancing in her eyes.

"You're not going out there alone," Garth ordered, more than half serious now. She gave him a playful pout at this.

"I'm going along," Sayer said, having stripped down to her T-shirt and undergarment. She promised herself that next time she'd wear a swimsuit, too.

"You know how to swim?" Ryes asked, wanting to be sure as she turned to face her daughter. She smiled and nodded her head in agreement.

"Learned when I was little," she boasted proudly. Ryes smiled and her eyes merry as she signaled her to turn around and deftly braided her hair for her, tying it off with a small cord Maren handed her. She gave him a smile of thanks.

"I'm going, too," Maren told them, giving Garth a nod to let him know he'd keep an eye on her. He'd already let Dotti know, who agreed he was the best one to make sure Ryes would stay safe.

"I'm not going. I'm not a good enough swimmer to keep myself out of trouble, yet," Ardis stated, having one of the human's fishing poles in hand, ready to give it a try, their way. "This thing looks complicated," she commented. Sabin laughed as he gave her a hug.

"We'll figure it out," he assured her.

"The water's too cold," Sana called back, protesting, testing it with her foot. Justin laughed, nodding his head in agreement; glad she wasn't as wild as Ryes. Garth had his hands full, at times! She took back Fane, so he could go help Minn get out their large, portable grill from the rover.

"I guess I have to go," Monty said. He was serving guard duty for her, today. "But I'll need to keep the pistol dry," he stated, looking around for something that might serve to that end.

"Here," Mitt said, handing him a sealable plastic container. It was one of the ones Ryes liked to use for her plant collecting. It looked air tight. He took it gratefully, giving her a nod of his head, putting the weapon inside and checking the seal.

"Thanks," he said, then started to strip down to his T-shirt and underwear, feeling a little self-conscious about it. His legs were totally white, as he didn't get out much to get a suntan.

"You don't have to," Garth decided seeing his determination in spite of his obvious reluctance. He placed a hand upon Monty's shoulder. "You can keep an eye on her from here and Maren will keep an eye on her from there." Monty paused, unsure, but realized Garth was their commander after all.

"If you say so, Sir," he replied, trying not to look too relieved, as he pulled back up his jeans and fastened them, once again. Sabin chuckled as he took up his fishing pole and dug for that packet of oily herbs Ryes recommended, instead of using wigglers.

"Let's grab some chairs and get to fishing," he told Ardis. She laughed at this and snagged a couple of lightweight folding chairs, heading for a promising spot. Ryes, Sayer and Maren headed back for her rocks. Garth went to help finish the unloading and setting up a cooking area. They settled upon an open area near the two rovers. Minn already had the grill unloaded and moved into position. They still needed to set up the tables and chairs, and unload the rest of their supplies.

Dotti gathered Maren's siblings around her and made sure they each had the planned toy they picked to bring, then got them settled out in a shaded part of the beach, a little away from those who were fishing. She sighed and smiled, as she put a hand for a moment upon her lower stomach, wondering. She tried to imagine what she'd look like? She and Maren were picking a good name for their daughter now, and had yet to settle upon one they both loved. She wanted it something that was from both families and he heartily agreed. Seeing the cubs happy, as they learned to play in the sand, she went over to sit near Ardis, Sana and the others.

"This is cold!" Maren protested, then ran into the water on her heels. Ryes laughed and gave him a nod.

"You've been cooped up inside too much," she scolded, but saw Sayer was feeling the cold, too. "Keep moving and you'll feel it less," she advised, towing the container along as she swam. She kept a close eye on them as she mounted the rocks, then saw Mitt swimming out to join them.

"You're probably right," he replied, through the tightness in his jaw. If she could do this, then he could do it! They reached the rocks, very quickly. As he climbed out of the water, he noted the warm breeze was ice cold. The water now felt warmer! He began to extend his healing to help restore his body to the proper temperature, then did the same for Sayer.

"Stay in the sun," Ryes advised both him and Sayer. Mitt arrived and climbed up to join them. She appeared to wonder about the other two.

"Can't take it?" she asked. Ryes shook her head, biting back her laughter.

"Guess not," Sayer replied, as she huddled in the sunlight, glad of Maren's light, warming touch.

"Okay, so how do you see the fish?" Maren asked, wanting to start diving back into the water. He knew a little physical activity would help him fend off the cold better, and fishing was what they were here for today.

"Sit still and watch the shadows as they slip by under the water," she invited them, gesturing below.

"Come on, on the trail you were using your Talent," Mitt scolded with a teasing smile. Ryes smiled back, shaking her head.

"There's so many fish here, I don't need to. It'd be a waste of effort. Look, there goes a big one now," she pointed. She wasn't going to remind her that with her Talent fully awakened and in use, she'd feel their deaths more acutely. It was bad enough with it as a background sense. Maren saw the fish and dove after it. After a few moments, he surfaced with his claws embedded in a slightly smaller fish.

"It got away," he explained as he threw the one he caught up into the waiting container, appearing disgusted with himself. Ryes laughed lightly and clasped him on the shoulder, giving him a nod.

"They're quick. They're used to being hunted," she reminded him. He gave her a nod.

"There it is," Sayer said, then dove in, too. She surfaced with the fish, barely holding onto to it. Maren laughed as he helped her get it into the container. "Come on, there's a lot of fish down here!" she declared, excited. Ryes and Mitt laughed as they dove into the water too. In a very short time, the four of them filled the container and Ryes realized she needed a break, as she had reached her limit on dealing with their suffering.

"Are you all right?" Mitt asked as she saw her sitting on the rocks, panting, trying to control the heaving in her stomach. Maren extended his Talent for her, seeing she was too focused upon the pain, to do this for herself. In a few moments she calmed down as she could let it go.

"Thanks, Maren, I'm much better now," she told him, her voice still sounding a little strained to Mitt's ears, as she stood once more.

"Show me. What is it like to feel something die?" she demanded. Ryes was shocked as she met her eyes, wondering where this came from?

"You truly don't want to know," she replied.

"Yes, I do. I need to understand how deeply this touches you, so I can know how to help you," she pressed. "Here, sit down and relax. Then I want you to show me."

"Me, too," Maren pressed, seeing Mitt was right about this approach, "but I need to know what it's like for myself, since I'm a Healer. I know at some point I'll have to deal with death, so I need to know it as intimately as you, cousin." For a few seconds Ryes' eyes had a caged look, but then she sighed, giving in.

"All right. I'll show the both of you. Sayer, why don't you go ahead and take that container back to your Dad," she suggested as she sat down, wanting her out of this, but then she saw a frown cross her young face, as she met her eyes.

"No, I want to see it, too," she insisted.

"You don't need to," she assured her. "Give yourself some time to grow up a bit more, first."

"Haven't you told me that death is just another part of life?" she pressed, her face serious. "I'm not a cub!"

"Yes it is a part of the dance of life. Creatures die so that others may live, as some plants die to become the mulch to feed the next year's seedlings," she agreed with a heavy sigh. "But this is a lot to take on at your age," she scolded, knowing Garth wouldn't approve at all.

"She needs to learn this at some time. It's best while it's the three of us, as we can all help her through it," Mitt reasoned, feeling Ryes was being unfair. "It's not like Sayer's a young cub! She's twelve years old, after all!" Maren nodded his head in agreement. Ryes sighed, then sat back and considered it.

"I'm old enough!" she retorted, worried now.

"Garth won't approve," she replied. Mitt nodded her head to this, understanding.

"So what! You're her mother and have more say," she quipped back.

"It seems like her cousin and aunt have more say, today," she teased in return, smiling, once more. "All right, Sayer can see it too. I need you to sit down next to me, close your eyes and relax, imp," she told her, seeing her happiness at winning this struggle.

"Thanks Mitt and Maren," she told them, then quickly moved to comply with Ryes' instructions. Maren and Mitt grinned to each other as they each got as comfortable as possible, closing their eyes too.

"Ah this is so nice to relax and get away," Justin commented, realizing this was his first chance to actually get out of Winterhaven, from even before when it was just humans; since he arrived on this world! He didn't realize how much he missed the outdoors and doing things like sitting and fishing. This place was nirvana! A far better spot than where his grandfather took him, back on Royal. He wondered how the world of his birth fared?

"It's been well over a year since I last went fishing," Sana said, recalling the day. "I snuck out with Sabin and his friends, leaving Fane with our older sister for the day. It seemed so long ago! And the fishing places in Matlowe were nothing like this spot!" Sabin chuckled at the memory.

"Sela almost had a fit when we didn't get home until just about dark. It was a good thing we'd caught a few fish to show her we truly were out doing something!" he related, still chuckling. Sana nodded her head in agreement.

"Maren just caught another one," Minn observed, having only caught one, so far. "Maybe they had the right idea, after all? But, I don't want to have to deal with the chilly water! It's been almost an hour and I think they've almost filled their box," he related with a chuckle.

"It's too cold to go fishing like that! I'm waiting for the summer warmth to try it," Ardis commented, with a sigh. "And I hope I can learn to swim better by then." Sabin nodded his head in agreement.

"I made sure to teach Ryes how to swim, from almost the day we moved out beside the river. I didn't want her to drown, too. She learned it fairly fast, it was as if she knew what to do, instinctively," Rowan told them, just realizing he had a nibble on his line. He saw Sayer and Ryes dumping more fish into their container, then diving once again. He started to play his line, seeing if he was still as good at this, as he used to be.

"Jana drowned and I didn't want to lose another member of my family in such a way. I also taught Maren and Tennan, but Tanns hasn't let me teach the younger ones, yet."

"We'll teach them," Dotti assured him, smiling. She watched the kids playing in the sand; having a lot of fun. He shook his head at this.

"Let Maren or Ryes do that. I don't want you getting hurt accidently," he scolded. Shock was in her eyes as she turned to look at him. Did he know? She knew Maren hadn't told him, yet! Rowan glanced over, seeing her surprise, then smiled. "Ryes and Ethan told me, after a fashion. It wasn't on purpose, just that she was showing us that Vision she and Maren had, when they got back from Matlowe," he explained.

"Oh," she replied. "I haven't even seen this Vision, yet," she protested. "It seems everyone else has."

"That's about the way it goes around here," Ardis assured her. "Just corner Ryes, if you're up to a headache, or get Maren to show you through Raya. They don't mean to keep things to themselves, but it sometimes works out that way."

"You truly don't need to see it," Garth assured her. "Yes, you're in it and your pregnancy's obvious, but there's little else we can figure out about it, so far. You'd only end up worrying about nothing. It may never happen." Dotti realized every instinct was screaming from within that whatever it was, it would happen! It was only a part of her human nature to want to know!

"If you say so," she said, appearing to give in and relax. She'd talk to Ryes about it, later. She could easily tolerate another headache. "How come Mitt and Maren never get headaches from Ryes?" she suddenly thought to ask. She saw Rowan finally netting his fish, looking proud since it was a big one.

"They're too much alike," Sabin quipped with a laugh. "That's the only reason I can think of. The first time we tried to find Maren's Talent, they gave me such a blinding headache!" He still recalled that one, too well. Ardis nodded with a laugh, at the memory of that day.

"Mitt has a strong Talent, too, so can commune with the two of them easily," Minn stated, sighing.

"Maybe she has more than one?" Garth asked, wondering about it, himself. He started to realize he had no troubles communing with them, either. Could he have a Talent which never awoke, or is so subtle that he's never noticed it?

"I wouldn't doubt it," Minn agreed with a nod, as he thought upon it.

"What're they doing?" Rowan asked Garth and Sabin, pointing out to the rocks, after having put his fish into the container. Their container appeared to be full of fish now. And the whole group was sitting close together and it looked like they were starting to close their eyes. He had a suspicion and wanted it confirmed. They had to be up to something and using Ryes' Talents!

"Probably getting into trouble. It looks like Ryes is going to show them something. I can't believe she's letting Sayer participate," Garth sighed out, standing up.

"I'll go check on them," Sabin offered, wondering what they were up to now? He started removing his boots and jeans.

"I'll go with you. There's got to be a way to curb this impulsiveness those three possess, in such great quantities. I should've known better than to let them all go out there alone." Garth handed his fishing rod to Rowan as he kicked off his sandals and pulled off his jeans. He and Sabin walked around, so as to avoid stepping on any fish hooks, or entangling any fishing lines, and waded out into the cold water.

"This better be worth all this," Sabin muttered, trying not to let his teeth chatter. Garth huffed his agreement. They climbed out of the water and noted the four of them didn't hear them. So, they sat down and extended themselves into the inner commune, wanting to know what they were up to, this time.

Ryes, Maren and Mitt first had to acquaint Sayer with their inner commune. Her mind and spirit seemed to fit right in with their own. Sayer thrilled to this contact, bringing joy to the other three as they recalled their first joinings, only a year ago. When they were all comfortable once more, Ryes reached down for Empath and like phantom voyagers, she opened up the world around them to how she saw it, when she had this aspect of her Talents called into usage. The stirrings of life around them were many, with movement, color and grace. She reached down to the fish, gliding through the water, as if it were, indeed, her natural element. She could feel the excitement of the others as they jumped from one creature to another, experiencing what they did, hearing what they thought. She wasn't ready to seek out death, so stayed with the flow of life. Suddenly, Garth and Sabin joined into their foray. What they were seeing and feeling amazed and surprised both men, so they held back their scolding for now.

Maren and Mitt urged Ryes on, seeing she paused as the men joined them. She shifted and found the fishers in their little den on the opposite shore. Two were sleeping, two out hunting, swimming through the water looking for some tasty, bottom-dwelling crawlers. The remaining three were involved in a mating, up on the beach, on the shore near the den. The two males were taking turns with the female.

Ryes drifted upward. They touched the thoughts of the birds nearby, drifting on the warm thermals above, looking for suitable prey. The movement of effortless flight and the view from above was breathtaking and they lingered there for several long moments. Then the hunting bird spotted a scatter-chase on the ground and dove. They felt him extend his talons and strike swiftly, grasping the furred animal and beating strongly with his wings to regain the safety of the sky, once more. They felt the death of the scatter-chase; glad it'd been fast, but also knowing the hunter needed this meat for his nestlings. Ryes veered away from this, ready now to let it go, but Maren and Mitt pushed her to go deeper.

She remembered when she had first briefly brushed the very essence of Tayna, herself. What they wanted was that awareness and she hesitated, unsure if Sayer was ready for such an experience. Sabin now added his will to theirs, as did Sayer. Garth held back, unsure. She finally released her fears and delved down, seeking that awareness, once more, holding onto them tightly, if it was too much. She brushed the spirit of their world, and then it was as if they exploded out into a world consciousness. They could feel the greater movements of life, as well as the small ones, if they chose to look at any of them closer. There was the life pulse of a whole world, taken as their own, as they tried to encompass all that was being unfolded before them.

Ryes suddenly reached out further, instead of deeper, taking them outward to feel how the planets and stars, themselves, seemed to pulse with their own awareness; of a life of their own. Then they could feel the smaller pulses of life upon the other worlds around them. There was a strong pool upon the moon of a world close to Tayna, which puzzled them. There was more order here, as if structured on a purpose. Ryes pulled them back to Tayna and they could feel the cities and villages, great and small, each with that same sense of order and structure. It was as if they hovered in the darkness of space over their own world and marveled at its beauty. Finally, feeling the limits of her power, she pulled them back slowly. Until finally, they were only six beings sitting on a pile of rocks, situated in the swift moving waters of the Yuri. They opened their eyes and each had broad smiles for one another.

"There was life and order on that moon!" Maren stated, still amazed. "We have to check it closer. I never knew…" He breathed, unable to put the experience into words. It was all amazing!

"I didn't know you could do that, Mom!" Sayer declared, finding her voice, once more.

"Neither did I," Ryes replied. She didn't think she even had the energy to reach the shore now. "I've felt Tayna, before, but never extending out so far beyond her. I never thought to try. We'll explore that moon more later, Maren."

"That's why you can feel it when something dies," Sayer said, realizing what Talent truly meant, for the first time in her short life. It was wonderful, terrible, and a lot of responsibility!

"So, for getting to sit and feel a fish dying, you get to be a part of Tayna, herself. I don't think it's a bad trade-off," Mitt told her, seeing she looked pale and shaky. "Are you going to be all right?" she added, knowing they probably pushed her too much. Ryes nodded her head as Garth wrapped his arms about her.

"I think you've all spent enough time out here, come on," he ordered. They returned to the water, with Maren pulling the full container of fish and Garth helping Ryes fight the current, she had no trouble with earlier.

"What were they doing?" Rowan asked once they reached the beach, again.

"Joy riding on the wings of a hunting bird," Sabin replied with a wonder-filled smile. He let out a long sigh.

"But at least we already filled our container," Maren boasted, showing it to the others, Ryes put her jeans back on; Sayer got dressed, too.

"Good, then you can all start cleaning them," Rowan ordered, smiling and wishing he'd seen it, too.

"Ah, yuck," Mitt commented, but went to get some chairs, so they could get the job done more comfortably.

"A grand tour of the world and housework, too," Ryes replied with a smile, as she sat down on the chair Mitt provided and reached for her first fish, her beltknife ready. She truly felt more ready for a nap, than anything else.

"I had no idea," Garth commented in a low voice to Sabin, as they dried themselves off and dressed, once more.

"It seemed to scare her a little, too. I wonder if Prince Callas was right about using her against the Snagospin? She could be the only real hope we have, after all. If she can feel Tayna, herself, and become a part in the dance of the planets and stars, then the Talents of those Snagospin should be easy for her to reach out to and control," he replied.

"I don't know about easy, but it looks possible," his friend agreed, "I love it when she shows us what it's like to fly as the birds do." Garth shaded his eyes and saw the tiny specks far up in the sky, which he knew were the hunters, upon whose wings they'd ridden.

"It's the way flying should be," Sabin agreed with a laugh. "She looks ready to pass out now. I bet she'll be asleep before we pull back out onto the road."

"Let's stay for lunch, as we already planned," Garth decided. "She can nap in the rover, if it's too much for her. I'll have Maren keep an eye on her, just in case."

"Sounds like a good plan," Sabin agreed with a nod. Ardis had noted their low-voiced conversation, but pretended she hadn't heard. She wanted to see what they'd seen and thought to ask Ryes to show her later.

"I forgot about her overextending herself," Garth commented.

"I forgot about it, too. Well, we can tell Ethan that we have our secret weapon to use against the Snagospin, at least. We only have to get her out there, closer to them."

"And figure out what she can do, once we do," Garth agreed, giving him a nod of his head.

On the Road

"Sorry I'm late," Ryes said as she slipped into the big conference room. Garth gave her a nod of understanding. She had fresh baby food still smeared on her T-shirt and probably hadn't noticed it, yet.

"About time," Mitt agreed with a laugh. "We need your input!" She pointed to her own shirt at where the baby food was on Ryes' shirt and then pointed to her. Ryes was puzzled for a moment, then looked down at herself and shook her head with a rueful smile upon her face. She took a chair between Mitt and Ardis.

"Thanks," she whispered. She took out a wipe packet from her pocket, but Mitt gently put her hand over hers and gave her a shake of her head.

"Use your Talent. You need the practice, even on small things. It'll help you focus," she advised in a low voice. "Axel has me practicing on finite parts now, so I know the machines and the way they actually function much better. And I'm going to be training you in that too, when we get a few days," she informed her with a merry grin lighting up her eyes. She saw the light dawn in Ryes' eyes as she gave her a small nod of her head and put the still-sealed packet away. She looked up at Garth, who'd been waiting on them and smiled.

"So, what did I miss?" she asked him while she opened up her Manipulator Talent and tried to pull off the particles of food from her shirt, then added the Molecular Talent to make sure she only affected the food particles and didn't take chunks of material off of her shirt, too. Carefully she dumped the resulting tiny ball of food down the food disposal chute in the coffee bar area of the conference room. Once Garth had seen this, he gave her a nod while the rest of the room cheered for her. She blushed a dark gold now. Then upon an impish impulse stood up and took a small bow to the room with a big grin and happy light in her eyes.

"Yes, you do need the practice," Sabin agreed, laughing as she sat down.

"Even the finite things might be important, someday," Ethan added, chuckling merrily. She gave him a nod of understanding.

"We've decided with all the equipment we're taking, we'll need three large rovers, one small rover, one large chopper with a smaller chopper for support," Ardis told her, giving Ryes a thumbs up gesture. Ryes gave her a nod and smile.

"So what are the plans on the shelters and how many are we allowing to go out?" she asked, opening up her minicomp and set it on the table in front of her.

"Here, sent you the file," Ardis offered with a chuckle. Ryes nodded and did a quick inventory scan, then frowned.

"Are you counting on hunting out there?" she asked, wondering. "I never did go over what boundaries Darman would have for us, for things like hunting," she minded them.

"We'll have the smaller chopper to take out for hunting forays, if needed," Garth advised her, giving her a nod. "We'll have the lottery draws for those who're going, other than the necessary, key personnel."

"And those who win for this round, will have to go last when the drawing open up for the Great Spring Gather," Sabin stated.

"That's what I was thinking before and it still sounds fair," Ryes agreed, "And if we truly need to get something from Winterhaven, or evacuate someone, we can use the bigger chopper to make a run."

"That's the idea," Maren assured her, nodding as he smiled. "For my part, I'm dividing my staff in half and only three can go and four will stay. So, I'm having a separate drawing."

"Ryes, I need you to take all of us out to the site, so we can get a feel for the area," Garth pressed, before she got distracted by other matters. She sat back with a light laugh, but gave her husband a nod of her head while laughter still danced in her emerald green eyes.

"This is going to be interesting," Ardis commented with a wide grin, "and it's been a long time since I last got to see Tayna your way!"

"Me, too," Torr commented with a laugh, glad of Garth's idea.

"Then you all know what to do," Ryes said, giving Torr and Ardis a nod of her head. She closed her eyes. She heard some shifting of chairs, as she called up her Talents and extended her hands. She distantly felt both hands gripped solidly, as well as others latching onto her arms, too. She smiled as she opened up her Mind

Voice, with Raya adding her own Talent to form up the commune. Once they were all settled in, she fully opened up Empath and noted that Maren added her own pool of power, surprising her, while she gave him her highest approval. It'd be a day of practice for them both!

"Make sure the place you have in mind as the site, is actually the site," Garth advised quickly as she was reaching for the world view Tayna normally grants her.

"As you wish, O Great One," she teased, then once they had the open connection to Tayna, she reached for Darman, but only touched him peripherally to get a measure of his mood and a feel for how busy he actually was today. He was used to this contact from her, as she occasionally checked in on him and Rinna to be sure they were all right. He seemed very busy and involved with a large trade. She back away and sought Rinna, who was also busy, but not as much as Darman.

Rinna immediately told Nalin, who was helping her, that she was taking a short break and urged her to finish making the broth she was working on. She was a little flustered, but Rinna put a hand upon her shoulder and gave her a nod to let her know she had faith in her abilities. Then Rinna sat down on a nearby chair and closed her eyes, ready to see what Ryes needed. This wasn't the time of day she usually contacted them. Raya gently enfolded her into their meld.

"Grandmother Rinna!" Ryes and Mitt both practically shouted as she joined them with lots of love and warmth in their sending. Their energy almost knocked her out of the link, but both she and Raya managed to hold steady, making them instantly contrite.

"My girls," she returned with lots of love of her own sent in return, along with plenty of humor. The others gathered around them in the link were also sharing their humor and love for her and one another.

"What do you need?" she asked, after a few moments, feeling this visit was something important.

"We need to make sure of the site for the Caravaner's Spring Gather," Sabin told her. "Ryes' way, of course," he added. Her humor filled the link again as she agreed.

"It's the best way," Rinna assured them, then calmed herself as she tried to clearly picture the campsite. Ryes opened up more of her world view and sought the site directly. After a few moments she thought she found it. It appeared to be a shallow, natural bowl valley, rimmed with abundant trees and two main ways in. A wide, deep stream crossed it on one side, running swiftly with clear pure water.

After checking it through Ryes' Talent, Rinna agreed that it was their campsite.

Then suddenly, Darman and a caravaner they hadn't met before named Tova joined them. Tova was visiting with some of their Southern caravaners. Darman saw what they were doing and highly approved, while Tova was almost reeling at the power running freely in this commune. Raya welcomed Tova and enfolded her freely into their joining.

"That's where we'll have the vans parked," he told them with Rinna's agreement clearly added to his mental voice. They could see already there were seven vans camped in that area. "And that is where we'll set up some stalls for our own exchanges of goods," he showed them, and they could see some older, permanent stalls all ready for use.

"And this will be where we'll have our central tents set up," Rinna added, showing them where clearly, as well as the largest firepit Ryes had ever seen.

"We were thinking of letting all of you set up your part of the campsite next to the stream, near the main road," Darman added, trying to indicate the area. Ryes got the idea and pulled back out a little, so they could get an idea of the space by looking at it from above.

"Perfect! We're planning on bringing three large rovers, a small one and two choppers," Garth supplied, after the others got over the way Ryes could change the perspective on an impulse.

"We're looking forward to seeing you all soon!" Rinna supplied with Darman's agreement. There was soon an outpouring of love and small comments from both sides for a few moments before Raya and Ryes gently released all three of caravaners from the meld.

"Let's take one more look at our best route," Garth insisted. Humor colored Ryes' mental tones, as she recalled their problems with getting home last year.

"I won't let anyone keep us from getting there, or back again," she assured him.

"Wasn't there a bridge we needed to cross on the way?" Torr asked, recalling seeing one on the map.

"Can it hold the rovers?" Ethan questioned, while Kovin took sharp notice. "But they can cross shallow creeks without a bridge," he added and Axel agreed.

"Let's go check it out more closely," Ryes suggested, finding the road and following it back along their route to Winterhaven. Soon the bridge stood before them, as it crossed a small river, which was too deep for the rovers. Ryes pulled them in closer to look it over.

"This looks like old, original Taynan and probably over three hundred years old," Kovin declared with Mitt's full agreement. They all caught small wisps of memory about the bridges they found in Hailys from the both of them and it sparked the others' curiosity.

"Come on, show us," Raya invited, wondering. They both seemed a little embarrassed, but finally Kovin opened up to show them the bridges they'd seen when traversing Hailys. The one which still supported part of a fallen building truly impressed them all.

"That was amazing! I wish we'd taken more time when walking through Hailys, when we were there to go see them," Ardis said, surprised at the adventure they survived before they joined them. This contact made it all more personal, as shivers had run up her back at their recollections.

"We were glad we finally found you," Mitt supplied.

"Let's look more closely at this bridge, then," Ethan suggested, silently urging Ryes to extend her Talents to do a thorough examination of the structure.

Ryes opened up her Inner Sight with Earth Shaper and Mitt opened her Inner Sight too, to aid in the evaluation. It was overall very solid, but there were some issues which appeared to be due to time and erosion. So Mitt tapped into more of Ryes' Talents and between the two of them brought it back up to what it had been when new and accounting for the change in the river's course. Then Ryes, with Kovin's urging, used some of the stone, sand and other materials near the bridge and built it and the road up to it wider and stronger. They could now run two huge rovers on it, side by side with lots of space. And now there was railing on each side with a safe footpath, as Ethan thought was important to have.

"I think we have a bridge," Garth stated, his pride coming through the link clearly. They all clearly appreciated the cooperative effort used to form it and the team work of everyone involved.

"And later, Phil and I need Ryes and Mitt to help build another one, across the Yuri," Kovin added, utterly amazed. Humor was clearly expressed by all.

"I think I've had enough bridge practice for today," Ryes told everyone.

"How do you feel?" Mitt pressed, as Ryes was bringing them all back to Winterhaven, once more; lightly checking the rest of the road on the way – to be sure. There were some small problems, which they fixed, and It seemed to weave through, or around some villages, too. It was shaping up to be an interesting trip ahead of them. She made sure every inch could accommodate their largest rovers. These efforts deeply satisfied her as she was also making the road better for everyone.

"A little winded, but electrified," she answered before bringing them fully back to themselves and slowly dissolving the link. Raya let go of the commune at the same time, glad of the practice she'd had today, too. She loved these larger forays! Maren quickly helped Ryes balance her body temperature back to normal, then let go of her arm.

"Thank you all, and especially Ryes," Garth said, more than satisfied now. "I think we now have some solid plans in place."

"Ahhhh…. We forgot to ask about hunting," Ryes laughed out, shaking her head in amusement. This got the rest to laugh with her.

"Here they come," Rowan commented as several timid people slowly approached the campsite they just finished setting up.

It was their third night out on the road, headed in for the Caravaner's Spring Gather. Tonight they had both helicopters with them; they'd just joined them, flying out of Winterhaven earlier today. Now, before sunset, they set things up for the coming night and all the farmers and villagers from the nearby village they were just outside of, were coming out to see who, or what was camping here. Their Winterhaven banner must have appeared foreign to them all.

"Hello, how can we help you?" Leon asked, standing ready to greet their visitors. They now had it down to an organized operation for greeting the locals. They found one of the humans was best at the start so as not to surprise anyone later, when they were noticed.

"Who are you? And what are you?" a tall elder asked. Leon chuckled at this, giving him a nod of his head. Garth and Sabin stepped up to join him.

"My name is Leon of House Rhona, I'm a human and am a traveler passing through," Leon told him, smiling.

"We're from a village named Winterhaven," Garth said, striding up next to Leon and putting a companionable hand upon his shoulder for a moment. Leon nodded agreement. "We're passing through to the Caravaner's Spring Gather and will not be staying any more than the night."

"We have dinner started. Would you like to come and share a meal with us?" Sabin invited as the others were now crowded in a bunch before them, on the road.

"We also have two Healers if anyone needs to be treated," Garth offered, "We offer their services in exchange for spending the night here, near your village." His simple offer stirred some excitement among the people gathering behind the elder; and two ran off, he was sure, to spread the word, or fetch someone in need of treatment.

"My name is Toud and am head elder of Gian Run Village," he said as he offered his hand, palm up to Garth. "We are happy to meet you, and yes you may camp here for the night." Garth smiled and nodded and crossed his palm with his own.

"My name's Garth. Please come over by our fire and let's talk," he invited. The elder gave him a nod as the others with him followed behind Garth and Elder Toud. Sabin and Leon greeted the locals and nodded their heads in approval; giving them all smiles. Finally, there were two young men supporting a very pregnant woman between. Leon was fairly alarmed, then shifted inward to let Maren and Ryes know, so they could be prepared.

"Bring her this way," Sabin invited, as Monty stepped up to take Leon's place. He gave Sabin a nod of assurance. The woman groaned, so Sabin simply scooped her up in his arms, surprising the younger men. "Follow me," he advised them as he went straight to where he knew Maren would be found.

"The cubs are late and we are worried," the lighter-haired man told Sabin. He gave him a nod, but didn't pause.

"Maren!" he called out and saw he'd been about to head to the bigger campfire, but turned and saw what Sabin bore.

"Ryes," he called in turn, then gestured Sabin to the extra shelter they put up as a treatment area. Sabin quickly entered it and set her down upon the raised bed within. Ryes came trotting from over at the main fire, having been warned by Leon, and was closely upon Maren's heels.

"The cubs are late and she's had a hard time with these ones," the lighter-haired man told them. The woman was moaning and now sweating profusely.

"Please wait outside and let Maren Heal her," Ryes insisted, as she gently ushered the young men back out. Sabin stepped out, too.

"Maren's the best Healer ever born," he assured them with a smile.

"A man who can Heal strongly?" the darker-haired youth questioned. Sabin just gave him a nod of his head in reply. Ryes laughed at hearing this, shaking her head, then let the inner drape drop into place, to give them some privacy.

"This may take a little time. Let's go over to the main fire and have a cup of tea," he urged, getting them to leave so Maren and Ryes could work in peace.

They seemed to come reluctantly, and once they got to the fire, took up the mugs of tea offered and sat down to wait. They didn't get into the discussions going on around them, but seemed to be focused upon their own inner fears for the woman they brought in for help.

"Who is she?" Dotti asked them, as she held Rowis on her lap. She sat next to them and heard what Sabin told Garth in a low voice in English.

"Our mother, Aleea," the darker-haired youth explained, seeming to just note there were others sitting near them. "I'm named Aplan and this is my brother, Attis. We heard you have a Healer and only pray to Korenda that he can save her. We've done all we can to make her comfortable, but it's not enough."

"Maren's the strongest Healer that I've ever met," Dotti assured him, placing a hand upon his knee, as she met his eyes. "He'll do everything he possibly can for Aleea. My name's Dotti and this is his youngest sister, Rowis," she introduced them.

"My brother is the biggest, bestest Healer," Rowis added, all smiles for them. Attis chuckled to see the determined spirit in this child's eyes. He gave her a nod, as he gave the strange blonde-haired woman a nod. She was a new people to his eyes, but still pleasant to look upon.

"We will hope," he told them, then lifted the cup of tea and took a sip. He closed his eyes for a moment in prayer and pleasure. Their tea alone was exceptional! He hoped their man-Healer would be so, too!

"Where did you get this tea?" he heard Aplan ask with surprise in his voice. Dotti laughed lightly at hearing it.

"It's one of Raya's new blends, which she and Wynne created," she told him with a smile. "It's my new favorite, too."

"It's amazing! Do you have some we can buy?" he pressed, after he gulped down the last of his mug. Dotti turned and signaled to Raya, who was nearby. She caught her hand sign and excused herself to step over.

"Aplan wants to know if you have any of your new tea blend for sale?" Dotti explained, gesturing to the excited young man a seat away. Attis still was looking back to the pathway between the shelters, as if hoping for some word about his mother, soon. Raya frowned slightly, then smiled.

"I have a little set aside for trading," she told him, "but I had wanted to sell it to some of our caravaner friends."

"I have caravaner coins," he insisted, excited, "please?" She gave him a nod.

"I'll go get a container for you," she said, then stood and left, laughing lightly as she shook her head in wonder. A few minutes later she returned with a glass jar in her hands. As she arrived and they were agreeing on a price for it, Ryes appeared, stepping up to them with a big smile upon her face.

"You have a new, little sister," she told them. They jumped to their feet, ready to run back to see, but she held out her hands to stay them. "There's another cub waiting to be born, yet. It won't be long, but I'll come to get you when Aleea's ready to show them off to everyone else." She had made this announcement to all those gathered near the big fire. There was a cheer and laughter that arose from the villagers, so she guessed she was a beloved neighbor, or family member. Relief and happiness ran through the crowd now, which gave Ryes a big feeling of relief, too.

"I must go back to help, Maren," she excused herself as she turned and trotted quickly back to the treatment shelter, her large, red braid bouncing behind her.

"How're you feeling?" Maren asked Ryes, as they helped to bid the villagers a goodnight, finally after several hours of healing and repairing things. Ryes grinned, then a yawn snuck out, which she quickly stifled behind her hand.

"Actually, fine. Last year I would've been floored, but now, I'm not tired at all," she admitted, "other than being normally sleepy."

"Me, too," he admitted, as he started yawning, too. They both laughed at this, as they headed over to get some leftover dinner and mugs of tea. They saw Toud and three other Gian Run elders were still there discussing The Laws with Garth, Sabin, Rowan and Ethan over at the bigger fire. They retreated to the smaller one and the food still being kept warm. Raya joined them, all smiles, with her daughter on her hip.

"I think this was our busiest stop," she said, as she grabbed a bowl of pleip stew for herself. Kaye kept trying to grab her spoon as she sat down with her on her lap. Ryes grabbed an extra spoon and offered it to her baby, and Kaye grabbed it in delight; immediately putting in into her mouth.

"Thanks," Raya said as she finally got a spoonful of food into her own mouth. Ryes nodded and laughed.

"So like Jann," she admitted, knowing her own cubs were sound asleep at last. She and Maren took seats next to her, with their own bowls in hand.

"Our two are quite a handful," Kovin said, as he sat down next to his wife. He took Kaye so she could eat in peace. "I finally got Kaspa to sleep," he told her with a smile, as he kissed her lightly on her forehead. Raya sighed and gave him a nod. He then looked over at Ryes, "I can't imagine trying to manage five!" She laughed at this nodding her head.

"It does take a lot of energy!" she replied, still chuckling. "And they do keep myself, Garth and the girls busy most of the time."

"And a lot of helpers," Maren added with a laugh. Dotti came out of their shelter and sat down next to him, trailed by Tars, who sat next to Dotti after getting two fresh mugs of tea. She handed one to Dotti, which surprised her and she gave her, her thanks.

"This is a truly good concoction, Raya," Ryes said with a heartfelt sigh. She laughed and nodded her head.

"I think Wynne named this one, `Dancing on the Tongue,'" she said. "We've started giving them each funny, unique names. As long as we have a good working recipe for each blend, we're happy," she admitted.

"Dancing on the Tongue," Maren said, then smiled as he took another sip from his cup. "I like it!" He stood and put his empty bowl and spoon into the portable dish cleaner. He sat back down next to

Dotti and put an arm around her, while he hung onto his mug with the other hand. "Let's finish our tea then head off to bed," he suggested to her as Tars jumped up and sat down on his other side and hugged him tightly. He laughed as he carefully draped his other arm around her, hugging her, too.

"That is a plan," Dotti agreed, as she now took a longer pull from her mug to hurry. He laughed as he let her and Tars go to finish his mug, too. Tars fetched hers from the table she sat it upon for a few moments. She tried to gulp hers down quickly, which got the adults to laughing, again.

"You don't have to rush," Dotti told her, smiling. "We'll be fine."

"I can't wait for my bedtime story," she told her, grinning. The human custom of telling fanciful tales to the children before putting them to bed had caught on in Winterhaven and now all the parents were doing it as a way to bond with their children more closely. It proved to be a fun custom.

"I have an old one from Matlowe," Maren teased her, tickling her tummy, "just for you." She sprayed the last of her tea out as she laughed, which only got her to laugh harder. Dotti gave her a cloth to use to wipe off, but she was laughing at their antics, too.

"He can be ornery, sometimes," Ryes warned, laughing.

"It's hard to tell who the cubs are and who the adults are," Rowan commented with a chuckle, as he stepped over to join them, getting a mug of tea for himself.

"A pair of caravan vans have arrived and decided to join us for the rest of the night. They were all practically asleep and hadn't realized how late it actually was," Sabin said, as he, too, got a mug of tea. Missa and Nottin trailed after him and Sabin gestured for them to help themselves of their food and tea. Another six travelers followed and they soon had a small, grateful gathering by their fire with the two children soon dropping off after eating. Missa and Nottin then left to take care of their windracer teams, while the others just rested by the fire. In the meantime the Winterhaveners put up two shelters for them to use tonight.

As they returned, Missa practically ran into Rebin, who had just emerged from the showers and was headed to her shelter. He had his arms around her to help steady her, or himself... he wasn't quite sure, being that tired. But, by the bright smokeless lights they used, her dark brown eyes were enchanting.

"My apologies," he told her, as he gently let her go. She giggled and blushed as she let him go, too.

"I wasn't looking. I'm sorry," she admitted, looking up into his tired, but bright gold eyes. "Are you one of the caravaners?" she added, wondering.

"Yes, I am. I'm a trader," he told her, "and you? You come from this mythical Winterhaven?" She nodded her head.

"I'm living there now and am never going back to Matlowe Village," she vowed. "I do a variety of things there, but love teaching the cubs and working in the kitchen the best." He nodded and smiled.

"Perhaps, once we reach the gather site, we can have a little time to talk. I apologize, as I'm too tired to go on, tonight," he admitted, feeling ready to just fall over on the spot. She smiled and gave him a nod of agreement.

"I'm looking forward to it," she replied, then helped him to the extra shelters they just erected for the caravaners to use. Somehow, her heart was dancing, even if she didn't even know his name.

"I think we finally got a start of an understanding of The Laws in Gian Run Village," Garth told Ryes, as they finally settled for the night. He'd checked the watches to be sure there was adequate coverage before finally coming to bed. Ryes chuckled in a low voice.

"One village at a time," she teased him, then gave him a kiss. "But it's progress, at least."

"That makes five so far," he agreed, smiling into the darkness, "Tayna first and then we'll see about other worlds." He then wrapped his arms about her and gave her a proper kiss. She melded with him into it, giving back of her own heart. Then she pulled back a little.

"We'll make it," she assured him, "I know it!"

"I'll believe with you, then," he whispered.

"Smart man," she teased him, as they finally turned more serious about their free-mating.

Arrival

Come on Axel, Mitt, we're almost there," Ryes protested over the radio. She wanted to time this so they'd all arrive at once. She'd slowed down until they were down to a measly fifteen miles per hour! It was like creeping along as a baby crawling!

"Give us another five minutes, O' Impatient One," Axel teased back, as Mitt's laughter could be heard, too.

"No problem here," Leon returned with a laugh, "I was having a time keeping up with her, up until now."

"She does have a lead foot," she heard Shawn put in, with laughter backing him up from their third rover. Monty, driving the small rover, was just laughing as his response.

"I do not. I just like to get where I'm going," she replied, huffing as she handed the mic back to Garth, blushing, while her eyes were flashing with humor. He was laughing.

"Stand by, everyone. We'll stop here and wait. We're waiting for you, Axel and Mitt," Garth said, then hung up the mic. "Just because you can drive well, even on this road, doesn't mean you have to go at top speed," he scolded his wife. She braked the vehicle, in obedience to his order and sighed.

"It's not like we're going to be late," Rowan voiced, sitting on the other side of Garth. He'd been enjoying this road trip immensely. It'd given him a chance to meet and get to know people he never imagined exited before. Even if he didn't agree with everything they said, or did, it still enriched his world view of Tayna.

"All right," she surrendered, as she ran her hands up and down on the steering wheel's rim. She took up her canteen, pulled off the cap and got a drink of water, then looked back to see how the rest of her passengers were doing. Everyone seemed in good spirits, considering they'd been on the road for almost four days solid! "How's everyone doing?" she asked, having spun her seat about.

"We're fine," Dotti assured her, smiling. Maren added in his nod, as his youngest sister smiled happily. She gave them a nod, then swiveled back to the front again.

"We need to do something about this road," Ryes added in comment, after capping her canteen.

"One crisis at a time, my dear," Dr. Cruthers reminded her, from behind her seat. "We'll take care of Winterhaven first." She smiled at that, knowing he was right, even if she wanted to unleash her Talents and take care of a few things right now, herself. They were a mile from the camp site. She was using Darman's communicator as a homing beacon, as well as the markings on the maps she had up on her overhead display. It was just on the other side of these trees!

"Okay, we're about one minute out," Axel told them. Ryes started the rover creeping forward again, glad they were almost here. Darman wanted to show them off to the rest of his people in grand style. With the rovers pulling in and the choppers overhead, it'd be an amazing sight. She only hoped they wouldn't give anyone heart attacks with all the excitement. It'd be like Darman to keep it quiet, until they arrived and had scared everyone into a panicked flight! Suddenly, the coppers were low, over their heads, so Ryes gunned the engine and pulled out at her more normal speed.

"Slow down, you don't want to run anyone over by accident," Garth cautioned. She gave him a sideways glance and grinned.

"I have Empath and Manipulator," she reminded him. He sighed in surrender.

After using her Talents to redirect some trees, to keep from crunching branches which had overgrown the road, they emerged from the thick forest into a wide bowl of a meadow, fronting a broad stream. There were almost two hundred vans sitting down near the stream, with their cook fires, fresh laundry hung out to dry, and children running and playing nearby. People stopped in their tracks, as others ran back to their vans in panic. Ryes slowed and pulled up onto the grassy verge, facing her vehicle outward, yet leaving plenty of space between them and the vans, as they planned upon earlier, when she parked. The other two rovers pulled up beside her, with the small one parking behind them; while the choppers sat down before them. It gave them free access to the stream for their own needs, too.

"We're here," she stated merrily, powering down the vehicle and doing her systems' check.

"Ah, there's Darman and Rinna. It looks like he's laughing. Does he think we'd forget?" Rowan asked, chuckling.

"No. I'm betting he didn't warn anyone and wanted our arrival to be a surprise," Ryes replied. "He can be such a prankster at times."

"It must be a good one at that. Look, there's Paul and Steve," Maren pointed out, now standing next to their seats. The doors opened and people started pouring out of the vehicles and choppers, glad to have finally arrived. "Hurry up, Ryes," he urged.

"I can only do this so fast," she responded. "Go ahead, I'll be along."

"Let's stretch our legs, grandson," Rowan urged, opening his door and climbed out, lightly using the inset steps. It felt good to be able to do so! He trotted ahead, heading for his old friends. Ryes chuckled at this as she finished and locked down the vehicle, doing it "by the numbers" as Neil taught her. She felt it was more important when they were so far from home. The rest of the passengers unloaded out the back doors.

"Ready?" Garth asked her. She finally smiled and nodded, as she joined him on the lower level, in the back of the rover and gave him a quick kiss. She stepped down and out of the vehicle, then he started handing out their cubs. She barely managed to hold the three he handed her, then as soon as he emerged with the last two, she handed back Gareth. He could more easily support three, than she could now.

"They're starting to get too big for this, we need to find their stroller," she warned, both amazed and worried. He laughed his agreement as Maren, Dotti and Dr. Cruthers now joined them.

"Then you're just going to have to start floating them in the air," Dotti teased; "I can just see that. It's got to be the quickest way to round up a bunch of unruly kids, when they don't want to come in to wash up for dinner!" She sounded a little envious of her abilities.

"Now that's a good idea!" Garth agreed, laughing with the others as Ryes blushed. It was true that she hadn't thought of it, but it did hold promise in the future.

"Wouldn't it be flaunting my abilities?" she questioned with her brows furrowed.

"No, my dear, it would be utilizing them in an appropriate manner. After all, with five children you're outnumbered and it only evens the odds," Ethan assured her, grinning merrily. "And I believe you said you could use the practice." She nodded in surprise, and smiled.

Ethan took out his pipe and started filling it with tobacco. The air was so sweet and fresh in this meadow. He realized all he wanted to do was walk around and explore it a little; and not get enmeshed in the local politics right away.

"Let's greet our hosts, first," Garth suggested, then lead them over to Darman and the rest of his followers. Darman finally got his raucous mirth calmed.

"You're a little early. I didn't expect you for another two, or three days. It's a good thing I had the windracers corralled on the other side of our encampment this year, or it'd take us days to find them!" he scolded, chuckling.

"Oh, Mom could've found them all in a few minutes, Grandfather Darman," Sayer declared, assured. Ryes blushed at this, as Garth rolled his eyes. He forgot to have a talk with Raby and Sayer about what they could, and could not, say to others about their mother's abilities. Whereas Darman and Rinna knew them, the other caravan elders didn't and he saw their sharp interest now. He could only blame himself.

"Yes, she probably could," Darman agreed, seeing Garth unhappy with the child's bold statement. Their eyes met and Garth knew Darman understood and would support him in fielding any questions.

"Ryes, Little Ryes?" an ancient elder questioned, stepping forward, before any other questions were raised. He saw his opportunity to disrupt the others. She looked at him puzzled, trying to place him, as he did feel familiar to her.

"Yes," she replied as the rest chuckled. He stepped over to cradle her face in his hands. The look on his face was pure delight as his eyes took in every feature of her face, as if to be sure. She was the toddler he treasured, now grown!

"I knew it had to be you! I saw years ago, that you'd arrive here in such a fashion. I'm happy to see you came through," he told her. Then laughed at the puzzlement in her eyes as her tiny cubs were squirming, one having grabbed his tunic sleeve. "You wouldn't remember me, I'm Dastin, Darman's father," he explained, letting her go and gently disengaging his sleeve from Jann's grasp. "You were all of two years old when I last saw you."

"I'm happy I didn't disappoint you," she replied, her green eyes merry now. Darman laughed heartily at this, nodding his head in agreement.

"My father is a Visionary, but not as strong a one as Sabin. He tried to tell me, as he first held you in his arms so many years ago, that he saw many wondrous things. One was that you'd come to see him here riding in a great metal monster. I just remembered that one, as he said it," Darman explained, still smiling. He suddenly recalled the other things he said about the strong Visions he had, as he held tiny Ryes. He told him then that he thought she had to be a Booster, at least. Considering how many times Maren made comments about how grateful he was to be able to tap Ryes' "pool of power" when he most needed it, he realized his father had been correct. Ryes had to be a Booster, too, along with her other wondrous Talents!

"How's the trading this year?" Rowan asked, knowing it was still early, but knew Darman would have a good feel for it, already. And it would divert them from Ryes for a moment. They were traders and making money was one of their important focuses.

"It's been good," he replied with a chuckle. "Let's retire to our central fire and we'll hold more formal introductions," he offered as Rinna relieved Garth of Shyla, smiling in pride as if she were her grandmother in truth. Most of the rest of the Winterhaveners gathered around them now, all ready to meet their hosts.

"We know how the caravaners were first begun," Garth told Darman in English as they walked together. He looked surprised at this, then nodded his head.

"Then the underground structure in Matlowe has proved useful?" he asked, staying to the English. His father and the other elders were looking at them curiously, trying to guess what they were discussing. It seemed these strange people and the starmen, who just arrived, understood what they said, as well as Rinna, who smiled mischievously.

"I brought a copy of the original holo, but wasn't sure if you wanted to view it alone first, or how many you wanted to see it right away. I've kept the full version to our main staff, with an edited one now ready for everyone in Winterhaven to see."

"Do I get the full copy, or the edited one?" he pressed, wanting to know.

"The full copy, of course; you're part of Winterhaven now. There's still more information on the memory rod it came off of, but we're just starting to understand it, so I don't know it all, myself, yet,"

Garth admitted, smiling. Darman smiled at this, nodding his head in relief.

"Darman, you're being rude," Dastin scolded, finally speaking up. "What language are you using? I've never heard it before. I want to understand what you're talking about so freely."

"This language comes from my own homeworld," Ethan spoke up in his friend's defense, smiling merrily. "We've come to speak a blend of both our English and your Dolbith in Winterhaven, and do forget ourselves at times."

"That's true," Rinna agreed promptly, "we do forget."

"You're not from Tayna?" another elder questioned, amazed and unbelieving.

"No, I and my people are not from Tayna; we come from worlds far away," Ethan assured him.

"Then what were you discussing?" Dastin pressed, still irritated, but appearing to believe his claim, unlike the others.

"Just some newer gossip out of Winterhaven," Darman replied as smoothly as possible. "We've decided to make it our main winter encampment and the new above ground apartments are finally going up. I only wanted to know if they'll have our section finished, by the time we arrive back there for the winter. Matlowe seems too slow and backwards now," he asserted. Garth nodded his head to this, smiling and in full agreement.

"I was only assuring him they'll be ready in time," he advised Dastin. He gave him a nod in response, but still seemed unhappy with his son, knowing a lie when he spoke it.

They walked into the center of the main campsite, seeing a larger, central fire burning, with ancient logs and flat stones ringed around it for sitting. There was a kind of cleared area to the one side, as well as room around the fire, itself, for dancing, or a speaker to be able to freely walk around the fire and tell his, or her, tale. This being further north than Winterhaven, they would still need the campfires at night. But this time of day, the fire was low, just being maintained. Darman took the center seat, gesturing the Winterhaven visitors to take the seats set aside to his left. Since there weren't enough seats, the men decided to stand, leaving Rowan, Ethan, Metta and the women and cubs, the seats. The pandemonium settled down after a few moments.

Garth recognized Dara sitting among the other visitors, on the seats on their other side, which surprised him. There was another elder, who sat beside Dara and who looked at Garth speculatively. He wondered why, and who he was, but wasn't going to ask Raya about it in this moment. Once the rest of the caravaners settled down to their seats, with the cubs gathered onto their laps, or sat within the grassy circles, near the great fire, Darman stood to perform his official duties.

"We are welcoming some very special guests to this year's Spring Gather," he began, in a voice which Garth thought carried through the whole clearing. "Some of you already know Rowan from Matlowe Village and his granddaughter, Ryes, many of you do not. In this last year Ryes and Garth, her new husband and true-mate, have relocated to a place named Winterhaven. Since establishing themselves in Winterhaven, they've brought people of vision out of Matlowe, called the remains of a starship out of the sky and rescued the humans, who were still aboard. The humans were the original people who built Winterhaven long ago. Dr. Ethan Cruthers is their elder and a great man of vision, himself. We've established Winterhaven as our winter encampment, instead of Matlowe, yet maintain our Marketplace shops in Matlowe."

This last got laughter from the other caravaners, being they were traders by profession. When he announced she and Garth were true-mates, Ryes noted quite a few people gasped out at this, recalling as Maren told her before, that it wasn't a common practice among starmen. There were two elder strangers, who sat to their far right, with the own attendants, who seem greatly interested in them as a group, and in her and Garth in particular. She wondered who they were? Neither dressed like the others, nor in the fashions favored by the caravaners; one looked like a plainsman, but he wasn't dressed simply, as they usually were wont. As she was puzzling it out, Rinna was suddenly beside her, handing back Shyla.

"Someone needs changing," she teased in a low voice, smiling as Ryes took her, grinning in return.

"Do you think they'll be upset if I go take care of them? I think two others need one, too," she whispered in a low voice. Sayer nodded in agreement.

"No one minds cubs and their needs. Go ahead," she urged. She knew Darman would well understand, having helped managed these little ones before. Ryes took Shyla as Rinna took the remaining two from Garth and Sayer helped by taking Rhin, then the women excused themselves to a grassy area well behind the seats. There was light laughter from the crowd as people realized the reason for their desertion. The cubs were fussing loudly now, so Darman waited on what he wanted to say until they cleared out.

"Cubs do have their own priorities," Darman stated, excusing them. There was more laughter from the gathering at this and he let them go on for a few moments, then held up his hands to gather in their attention, once more.

"Garth is the leader of Winterhaven and with myself, Rowan and Ethan, have set forth a great plan which will, in the end, encompass all of Tayna. I asked them to come out in their great machines, so you could all appreciate a part of the scope of our collective vision. Next year, we hope to have some new vans built for our own use, along the lines of the designs of the humans, and what we've learned from our ancestors, who fled Hailys' destruction so long ago."

They could clearly hear his speech and Ryes smiled, shaking her head. Since they were out of direct sight of the others, she floated all her cubs in the air just above the ground for a few moments. Sayer was giggling at the sight, highly amused, while Rinna smiled and nodded her head in approval. Ryes spread out a groundsheet she brought with her and then a blanket, from out of her backpack - glad she snagged it before leaving the rover. Then placed the cubs on the blanket and she started the process of changing and cleaning them, glad Rinna and Sayer were helping her, in spite of her Talents.

"They've all really been pretty good about this trip," she said in a low voice, smiling as she unbuttoned her shirt and started nursing Shyla, once she had all the diapers changed.

"Is Garth going to let you drive back?" she questioned, teasing. She'd ridden with Ryes before!

"I don't think so," she said with a chuckle, "He'll probably take the wheel for most of the trip back. You should've heard the way they were complaining along the way, about how I was going too fast."

"I think they sometimes have cause, but then we each do things to the best of our abilities. I think your Talents would warn you if there was any great danger ahead of you, even on the road," she replied. Ardis joined them with Tobin in her arms, smiling gratefully as she sat down. Raby and Katas had come out with her, each holding one of her cubs and quickly settled onto the edges of the blanket.

"This seems like a never-ending chore," Ardis stated as she started checking her three; glad of the blanket all spread out, already.

"Why are you taking care of Tobin? I thought I saw Shadd was here," Rinna asked, looking at the young women sharply. Ardis and Ryes' eyes met for a moment, then Ryes gave her a nod.

"Shadd left Torr and Tobin," Ryes informed her in a low voice. "It's her choice, but it's been hard to get used to for all of us."

"Tobin's finally settled with me, but it's like he keeps looking up at me, trying to figure out why I have him, instead of his mommy; especially if he notices she's around, like today," Ardis related with a sigh. "Adris and Dale don't mind him being with them, but they're a little older and I have to keep a close eye upon them, to make sure they don't accidently hurt Tobin."

"I thought she would. Shadd seemed to me to be one who'd need time to play around, before settling down with one man. I was like that in my youth, but I never left any of my cubs behind. They were still my cubs, no matter who fathered them!" she related with a sigh, disturbed by this callous desertion.

"She said she didn't want to give Torr any excuses to stop by to visit her," Ryes told them as she frowned. "She's taken up with Mason for the time being."

"Give her time and understanding. She'll settle down in a few years. I only hope she doesn't do this with any other cubs she has, in the meantime," she said, in encouragement and dread. She extended her hands to Ryes. "Here, let me burp her," she offered, smiling. Ryes handed Shyla over with a smile, then picked up Gareth, as he was the next noisiest, and put him to one of her other breasts.

"They eat a lot and are growing like weeds," she commented, smiling down at her brood. Sayer, Raby and Katas were helping with crowd control, keeping the cubs on the blanket as they tried to crawl away, in explorer mode. She loved both her little and older cubs, so much.

"Do you feed them any real foods, yet?" Rinna asked. Both younger women nodded their heads.

"If we don't, we'd never get any sleep," Ardis admitted, smiling. "How much longer do you think they'll go on with these speeches?" she asked, hearing Rowan addressing the crowd now.

"We'll probably have all the cubs settled and napping by the time they're finished," Rinna admitted with a heavy sigh. "Men seem to value their loud words, far too much. If you ask me, it's the ones they speak in low voices, which carry more weight." The older two women laughed lightly at this, as Raya and Brenda joined them, nodding their heads in agreement.

"I think all our little ones have finally figured out that we've stopped moving for a while," Raya whispered, sitting down to join them with a bright smile, as she laid both her cubs on the blanket to check them over, first. Brenda nodded accord as she sat, too.

"Looks like It," Rinna agreed, directing Shaysa back in from the edge of the blanket, then Adris, too. They were all, very active and healthy babies. "So, what did you discover below Matlowe?" she pressed, meeting Ryes' eyes.

"A great library, which we're still copying and transferring to Winterhaven. It might actually take years for us to figure out what they left behind, and they only have one and a half floors of the ten for the library space filled. There's working power equipment and readers, so we have something of our ancestors, which is functioning and we can study. We have a team there now, compiling and analyzing everything and should have a better idea of what's truly there, by the time you arrive for the winter," Ryes explained, keeping her voice low.

"But, what did Garth mean when he told Darman about his now knowing the origins of the caravaners? You know our own tales," she stated forthright, frowning. Ryes took in a deep breath, glancing to the other women and girls around her first, then met Rinna's eyes once more.

"Originally, the caravans were formed to provide a way to link the remaining villages and cities on this continent and the other larger continents, across the oceans. They were Foresters, who were to bring out the established laws and enforce the peace among the peoples, and create trade agreements to help cement all of Tayna together, through the aftermath of the crisis where Hailys and the other great cities of Tayna were destroyed," she told her in a low voice, so it shouldn't carry. "I know the old legends, but they only hold a small shading of the actual truth."

"Oh, my," she replied, shock in her eyes.

"The one who started it was a real Prince and heir to the throne of Kahmarr. He was the leader who established the laws, the caravans and the great trading fleets. He wanted access to intelligence from across Tayna, and to salvage as much as he could of his civilization for future generations. He held his seat of power in Matlowe and that may be the other reason three major caravan roads intersect there, as well as why the Great Chief of the Caravaners always winters there. It's not just the nice weather, nor available empty housing, but because it was the place where strategies were planned, which used to affect all of Tayna." Rinna and the others sat quietly, caring for the small infants, for several long moments, as they all thought on what Ryes had said.

"I know you always tell the truth, or as much of it as you're allowed," Rinna stated in a low, tight voice. "I'll wait to see what Garth decides to tell Darman, before breathing out any of this. It seems we're picking up where our ancestors left off, only shifting the location to Winterhaven."

"He has a full copy of the holo the Prince left behind for us. He didn't have Neil edit anything out; wanting Darman to see the whole thing for himself. I saw it for the first time two weeks ago and it's amazing when you think on all that he said, and left unsaid. I think that because the caravans were originally formed by the Prince, he felt all of you should know the whole story."

"Then what of this edited version he has for Winterhaven?" she pressed. "Don't the people there deserve to know the whole story, too?"

"There's a part where the Prince names Garth as the one who will reunite the colony worlds to save the Earth. His wife and true-mate was a strong Visionary and foresaw us finding and opening the library. Garth doesn't want the people of Winterhaven to get obsessed with these goals, feeling that we'll first work on what we're doing here on Tayna, before reaching out to what lies beyond. Smaller goals are far easier to face and deal with, than ones which seem impossible. The Snagospin, or Darkens as the humans have come to call them, are the ones who attacked Tayna and destroyed Kahmarr, and they're the ones Garth's fated to take on. He doesn't sleep as well as he used to," she admitted to this small bunch of listeners. "I don't have to tell you that this isn't general knowledge and is to be kept quiet," she added, seeing the weight of what she told them in their eyes. There were nods as each of them realized the importance of keeping this knowledge quiet.

"What about you and the cubs?" Rinna asked, worried now. Ryes smiled oddly at this and shrugged her shoulders.

"We're going to need every Talent we have to fight these monsters. That means I'll be in the thick of it, too. I just wish I knew what to do, to take out those Snagospin Talents, so they can't direct their forces against us as effectively," she admitted.

"You'll figure it out," Brenda told her, grasping her shoulder in comfort. "I know you will." Ryes smiled for her, but her mind was still full of doubts. Garth wasn't the only one going without sleep lately.

"Are you women finished with the cubs?" Kort asked, stepping back to the women, gathered on the large blanket. "They're almost ready to have all of you up front, to be officially presented," he told them. He'd heard a little of what Ryes was saying, and while it surprised him, he too knew this wasn't something to gossip about. He'd wait until official announcements came out, but for now it gave him something to think upon.

"I still have to finish with Jann, and then feed Rhin," Ryes protested. "You try caring for and feeding five at one time," she scolded. There was laughter from the others; understanding her distress only too well. Kort smiled, gave her a nod of his head, then went back front to pass on the message. Rinna laughed lightly at this, as she gave her a nod.

"I'll go help delay things," she offered, getting up and leaving them there.

"Affairs of State. It's nice to know that sometimes great leaders have to wait upon the needs of their tiniest followers," Brenda breathed out with a laugh. Ardis and Raya laughed with her as Ryes nodded her head.

"I hope it gives them some perspective," she replied, smiling as she burped Jann, almost ready for her other son.

"Mom, are you going to leave the cubs with us, when you go out to fight the Snagsgospills?" Raby asked in a low voice, her eyes wide.

"Snagospin," she corrected her with a light laugh and smiled. "I'm hoping they'll be grown by the time I have to go out to fight them, but I'd be honored if you and Sayer could make sure they're safe while I'm gone."

"We can do that, Mom," Sayer promised, giving her a nod of her head, then wrinkled up her nose as if she smelled something foul. "Let's call them Snags, it's so much easier to say," she added as a suggestion.

"Now that's a great idea," Ardis quickly concurred with a laugh. The others laughed in agreement, too. Ryes gave her a nod, as she grinned.

Enlightening

"We'll set up our shelters near our vehicles," Garth ordered in English, having gotten an affirmative from Darman on the placement of their campsite. It was a generous size, considering the size of their party and vehicles. "Keep all vehicles secured while we're here. We're only going to offer rides to a select few, starting tomorrow. Either, Sabin, or myself will accompany them on the rides. Although, I've agreed to have Mitt take up Darman and his father in another hour, to search for some of their straggling vans."

"How about allowing people into our shelters, Sir?" Monty questioned, wondering.

"Only if you already know them, or feel very comfortable with that person. You can always double check with either Ryes, or Raya, if you need to be sure. If there's something you want to discuss and don't want it overheard, stick to English. Other than that, just enjoy yourselves," Garth told them, smiling. "We'll cover any important issues at dinner and breakfast mealtimes, so be prompt. Ryes and Sabin will have the duty assignment schedule posted outside the dining tent, as soon as it's set up. I expect all of you to be on your best manners. We have caravaners here from many faraway locations on Tayna. Since we don't know the differences in the way they conduct themselves, we expect you to be open to changes. But if confronted with a questionable situation, get help and don't drop your guard."

Everyone saw Darman's nod of approval and understood that while they were among friends they'd spent the winter with at home, there were many strangers present, who were not friends.

"Everyone, let's get our campsite set up and comfortable! Ware the cubs!" he added, then clapped his hands. The crowd started to disperse, but Ryes let out a loud whistle, which surprised many, and got their attention.

"And I need to see Paul, Wyatt, Steve and Eric," Ryes called out, before the group broke up, to get busy with the setup procedures. The four humans wove through the crowd, puzzled looks upon their faces, as they stepped forward.

"That's it, let's get busy," Sabin stated, grinning. He took Adris and Dale, leaving Ardis with Tobin. Tobin had tried to reach for Shadd, but she turned away from him and walked off. Ardis frowned at Shadd's back, and turned to reassure the infant he was still much loved, as he started to cry. Ryes already had Sayer and Raby each holding a cub, then was surprised as Garth took the remaining three from her arms.

"I'll watch them for a while," he offered with a smile. "Come on, girls," he said, urging their two older daughters to follow him. He thought, once he got the smaller ones settled in a play area, he could let the two older ones get some free time with their friends here in the encampment.

"What do you need, boss lady?" Paul asked, teasing as he winked at Ryes. She smiled, rolling her eyes at this, then laughed; it was a game they played. She urged them to get closer, now. Once they did, she scanned each of their faces, so glad they looked well.

"It's so good to see you all still safe and looking happy! But, first let me give you news from Earth," she started, staying to the English. Their faces went from joking fun to serious curiosity, in an instant.

"What news?" Wyatt pressed; the hope and fear showing on his suntanned face.

"Let's sit down," she decided, heading for a nearby log, sitting by the stream. The men followed her with questions in their eyes. She sat upon the stout branch that curved out and they sat upon the main trunk.

"How bad is it?" Eric asked, worried-looking, too.

"First off, Earth still exists. She's hard pressed, as the murderers who attacked Tayna centuries ago, have now laid siege to the Sol system. They have an almost impenetrable blockade set up encompassing the solar system. We're still scratching our heads, wondering how our lowly little probe got through twice," she told them. There was relief in their eyes, as they were glad to know their homeworld still existed.

"Secondly, by now they've already launched a task force to reach out to the colonies. They need an accounting of who still exists and how much firepower they can draw up from them. They're going to come to Tayna last, so it may be some time before we actually see anyone, if they do get through the blockade."

"They're coming all the way out here? Why?" Paul questioned with a frown.

"Probably to check on what available resources we have here that they can use. If they don't get help soon, the perimeter will fall and with it, the inner worlds, including Earth, will perish. We're doing everything we can to think of ways to help them gather allies and break the people we call the Snagospin, and they the Darkens, away from all of us and drive them back to their own worlds. If we can make the Snagospin stay there, we will. We don't want to think of genocide, but we don't know how far we'll have to go to enforce the peace. And they've freely killed plenty of people through time, so we'll see what it comes down to, when we confront them, ourselves."

"But, what can we actually do? We don't have any starships, nor armies," Eric pressed, wondering and amazed at the expectations and her calm acceptance of the circumstances.

"We have Talents," Ryes told him. "And from what we found beneath Matlowe's Village Square, the only way to defeat the Snags is to use our strongest Talents against their Talents. That's the only way we'll win."

"Does that means you'll have to go to battle, yourself?" Wyatt asked, knowing she was very Talented.

"Yes, it does. And believe me, it gives Garth little comfort," she told him, seeing shock in all their eyes. "I also have some personal messages for both Paul and Steve. Apparently, there's still some family of yours on Earth, who managed to get messages to the Sixth Fleet, before they sent the probe back."

"You mean, after eighty years, there's still someone who might remember who we are?" Paul asked, incredulous.

"Guess so," she replied, handing over the chips Neil made for them, with a smile. "I'll take your reports later, or give them to Dr. Cruthers. I'm a little tired after driving for four days and need a nap right now," she told them, getting smiles in understanding.

"If you'd been the only one driving, it wouldn't have taken so long," Paul teased, knowing how she drove any rover from personal experience. Eric laughed and nodded his head in agreement.

"Too true," she quipped back, standing up with a yawn. "So, if there's anything pressing, talk to either Dr. Cruthers, or Sabin. Later!" She left quickly, hoping they'd take their questions to Ethan.

The only thing she wanted right now was a nap, and she didn't care where.

"Oh, Ryes, Garth needs you," Neil told her, finding her at last. She sighed, but gave him a nod of her head.

"Thanks, Neil, I'm heading that way," she promised, groaning within. She knew he wasn't used to handling all five at once! As she wove her way through the shelter raising going on in their encampment, she finally found him with the two strange elders she spotted earlier. She stepped forward with a smile, realizing they had to be important people.

"Ryes, I'd like you to meet Dara, who's the Great Chief of the plainsmen, although he says he recalls you well, from when you were little," Garth introduced her. She realized she did know him, even if it'd been a very long time and gave him a nod. "And Kyma, the Great Chief of the mountain tribes." She stepped forward to give Dara a hug, then found Kyma hugging her too, which got her to laughing.

"I was concerned about the infant girl Senah sent off, thinking she'd die with Garth and Sabin," Kyma told her, then gestured to their cubs on the blanket, inside their play enclosure under the shade of a massive tree. "But I see she's found her rightful place. Will you be seeking out her father at the Great Spring Gather?" he asked, his brown eyes looking intense.

"I'd never thought about it. Garth told me he was a plainsman. I'd think he should know his little daughter is safe and healthy, but I don't know what I'd do if he wanted her for himself," she admitted. "She and Shaysa are almost like twins, and as you can see, they're usually close together. I'm not ready to give her up, either. I feel she belongs with us and is a full member of our family. This isn't like adopting a pet. She's out daughter and we love her!"

"But with so many, it would lighten your burden," Dara pressed, watching her face closely now, seeing a fire in her fascinating green eyes. He remembered her eyes clearly from when she was young.

"She's never been a burden to me. My own mother died when I was very young and I'd never turn my back on her," she stated firmly, meeting both elders' eyes in turn. Dara started chuckling, nodding his head in approval.

"She was granted as a gift to Garth. I can see how much she's loved and if her father presses for her return, I'll remind him he wasn't in Menna's Hold for her birth and whom her mother granted her to, was her own affair, not his," Dara assured her, needing to be sure of her feelings in this case. Five did look like a lot to handle, but she already proved she placed their care over affairs of state. Kyma smiled and nodded his head in agreement.

"What did you name her, if her twin was already Shaysa?" Kyma asked, curious. She smiled grandly at this, looking to her infants with pride.

"Shyla," she replied. She picked up both girl cubs and showed them to the elders. "It's hard to think they come from two mothers, looking the way they do. This is Shyla and this is Shaysa," she told them, indicating each of the cubs in turn.

"They do look alike," Kyma agreed, with a chuckle and wonder in his eyes. "We'll talk with you later tonight," he promised. "It looks like they're ready to lie down for their naps." Both cubs were sleepy-eyed and looked as if drooping now.

"Yes, they are," she agreed with a nod of her head. They said their good-byes, then she climbed into the enclosure and sat down on the blanket with them, glad they weren't going to try taking Shyla from her. After they left, Garth joined her, looking relieved.

"I was worried there for a moment; envisioning having to send you and the cubs back by chopper, immediately," he told her, as she was settling down all the cubs.

"I'd never give her up," Ryes assured him, smiling, glad he felt the same way. "She's our daughter," she stated, "And right now, I think I'm ready to nap with the cubs," she admitted.

"You go ahead and lie down. I'll keep an eye on things," he promised. She brought out little blankets for each of the cubs, covering them with them and plenty of kisses for each child; then she lay upon the blanket with them and dropped off, in spite of the camp going up around them. Garth smiled as he shifted over and kissed her and went and fetched a light blanket to cover her, too.

"Just got word, they've arrived and are all safe and sound," Jim told the others gathered in the dining hall for lunch. It appeared busy, but was about half empty right now. There were some cheers and other positive shouts. He smiled and gave the room a nod of his head. Bethy looked up to him and gave him a big smile.

"Small blessings, but good ones," she stated, her eyes merry. She'd been talking with Larisa in a low voice and Larisa appeared happy with his news, too.

"It's too quiet with all of them gone," she protested. Anders laughed as he was passing their table, headed to get his tray.

"So, does that mean you're going out to the bigger spring gather?" he asked, as he stopped to chat.

"Of course, I am. We don't get much excitement here," Larisa assured him, nodding her head. "Strange though, I don't miss my wire, since Maren removed all of them when we were first revived." Anders mouth dropped open as he realized what she said, while Bethy and Jim were laughing.

"I don't miss the constant ads, the weird warnings, IM interruptions, the political crud, newscasts, and everyone knowing exactly where you are every minute of the day, even strangers you might've seen in passing," Bethy put in, nodding her head, once she caught her breath. "And I think I love raising our kids without the constant electronic leash." Jim squeezed her shoulder and smiled.

"I forgot all about that. The wires were handy for getting messages out fast, but honestly, I never realized how controlling they were before, until now. I forgot how free we actually are without them!" Jim stated with assurance. "We can't instantly share vids, but I rather like having my head being my own. Our kids don't need that!"

"The atmosphere of general anger and discontent is gone," Bethy added in, surprise in her eyes at that realization.

"Yeah, and we can hear our own thoughts," Anders laughed out as he pulled his red bangs out of his eyes. "I can walk alone down an empty corridor and not feel lonely, nor threatened. There're a lot of things about being immersed in a big civilization I don't miss and I never thought I could love being so provincial," he laughed out.

"Me either," Phil agreed, having come out with his tray and hearing their conversation. "It's like we've hit the reset button on our own segment of civilization and can build it and decide what we want to keep, or cast aside, all ourselves. I like reading a book, which I can hold in my hands. And I love being a founding father."

"And you're actually getting to design our own little city, as we build it a piece at a time," Larisa added, giving him a nod as he sat down next to the ladies. He smiled grandly, granting her a shallow bow in return.

"Years of studying architectural modeling and drafting, and getting my degrees are finally paying off," Phil admitted, blushing slightly at being noticed. "And Kovin's grasped everything so quickly, almost like he was born an architectural engineer," he laughed.

"That's what I've found so amazing," Bethy admitted with a nod to him. "Wasn't he just a hunter before? And how we've all fallen into our own elements here in Winterhaven; as if we were born to be here and together." She looked amused and amazed. The others laughed, with many nodding their heads.

"I'll go with Ryes' favorite god, Aletagga, for that one," Larisa laughed.

"Oh, I almost forgot," Jim said, then stood up. "Computer, please relay this message I'm about to announce to everyone not present here," he requested and clapped loudly to get everyone's attention.

"Affirmative," it responded. Then the screens shifted to show Jim standing beside his table.

"Winterhaveners, I have an announcement sent directly from Garth, our Base Commander," he began in a loud voice. "We retrieved a holo from a special crystal stored in the vaults beneath Matlowe Village and have it decoded. There will be a showing of this holo in the Village Circle today at three thirty this afternoon. It is required attendance by everyone with the exception of the control room watch, who can watch it remotely. Garth felt it was important that everyone here see it, as it pertains to us directly. So be aware and be ready to attend. Thank you," he ended, "Computer, end transmission."

"Affirmative," it responded.

Jim noted that everyone had stopped at his announcement and they were collectively staring at him, some amazed. He smiled, gave a nod at the others in the room, then sat down.

"What was that about?" Bethany questioned her husband, her brows furrowed with concern.

"Nothing too dire and you'll see it soon enough," he assured her, then gave her a quick hug.

"Now you have things more exciting again," Larisa commented with a laugh.

"What could be so important?" Phil asked, but Jim just gave him a shake of his head.

"You've actually seen this already, but the rest will have to wait," he assured him. Phil had a surprised look for a moment, then gave him a nod, diving back into his lunch, while Anders went to get his food; his mind was awhirl with possibilities now, recalling that vault.

"Everyone, just grab a seat," Jim urged from the stage as residents started to arrive in the theater, now named the Village Circle. It took a good half hour to get everyone settled down; especially Karr. Once she and all the cubs were as ready as possible, Jim took the podium again.

"What you're about to see came from a deep vault below Matlowe Village. Surprisingly, even if this is over three hundred years old, it was meant for us here in Winterhaven and had been foreseen that we'd be the ones to find it and save the library Prince Callas of Kahmarr left as a treasure for all of Tayna," he started, being direct about it now. He had everyone's attention riveted upon him, as they awaited further revelations; some wanted to ask questions, but no one was taking the lead right off.

"How can you be sure?" Nicos finally asked as doubts and questions danced in his eyes. "Is it really for all of us, starmen and humans?"

"Yes, it's for all of us here in Winterhaven; starmen and humans," Jim affirmed, while Torr gave a nod of his head in support. "He even names Winterhaven outright, in a second part, which we're still studying. And he mentions Garth's human allies in Winterhaven as being strong supporters; it's for all of us here," he assured them. He saw the surprise in quite a few faces before him. So he gave them a nod, damped down the lights, signaled the podium to sink below the stage and stepped back as he activated the holo to play; having expanded the image so it could be clearly seen by all in the huge room. They would soon learn their new roles. He quietly stepped off the stage, noting people in the higher back seats moving down to the front, now.

There was a wash of light and static, then the center of the stage began to glow and a large image was projected, much like the holos of the humans. The people sat practically holding their breaths. The image suddenly grew distinct and an elder stood before them, who looked almost exactly like Maren. He was a little taller, a little heavier, but the resemblance was remarkable. He looked at them and smiled warmly, then sat down in a tall chair. His hair was silver and his face seamed, but even if he appeared aged, he moved with more ease than many a younger man. His dress seemed simple, but the fabric appeared rich and his bearing was of a man who was used to commanding respect. And here he did command respect.

"Please, take a seat. I have much to cover and hope you are not in any pressing hurry," he said. Even his voice sounded like Maren's, but his accent was strange, although not hard to understand. He had everyone's intent attention; even the cubs were fascinated with the holo image.

"Word came in earlier," Sonta told Ellen as she came up out of the library, heading for a nearby shelter to take a break and grab a snack. She stopped with a puzzled look in her blue eyes as she focused upon him, then smiled.

"What word, please tell me, dear Sonta?" she asked teasing, pulling her long platinum-blonde hair back behind her ear again.

Sonta and his wife, Shimi, had insisted she and Poinsettia stay with them in a spare room which had belonged to their sons long ago. Since their sons were now grown and living with wives of their own, they gladly accepted the invitation, until new quarters of their own could be built. And Sonta had sworn they'd be safe with him, as he'd tear apart his nephew, Korman, if he came anywhere near them. He was of a size to Korman and somehow they trusted him and his word and felt very safe in their home. Still, they did carry their activators with them at all times, to be sure.

"The Winterhaven party, including my father, reached the Caravaner's Spring Gather site yesterday safely. It just came through on the message machine they left us. I was going to check it earlier today, but there was that fuss starting up with the new Easterners, who arrived this morning," he told her with a smile.

"At least they got there safely," she replied, appearing relieved. "I wonder about the Easterners, though. I would've thought more would merely head further west where there's more abundant open land to grow crops and create their own new village." He gave her a nod of his head, more serious now. Even if she was a human, he thought of this young woman more as if she were one of his daughters. He knew Shimi felt the same about her, too.

"Taroom and the others who're already established here have been a great help, but he also thinks we should continue to urge most of them to travel up the northern road and onward to the west coast towns. I think he makes a great young elder, much like Garth has become," he related a bit bemused. "To see open wisdom in such younger men is a great blessing." She chuckled at this, nodding her head.

Then they both paused as a strange noise filled the air, seeming to come from outside the village, but rapidly approaching. Ellen seemed to identify it first, from long exposure and smiled confidently.

"Ah, a rover," she said, then started to get excited. Not that she didn't love the peace and relative quite in Matlowe Village, but every now and then she craved something new.

Those villagers, who weren't off in the gardens, hunting, or out at the animal pens, emerged from their homes to see what was coming. The small knot of new stragglers out of the east quickly came out of empty homes they'd been told to use, so they could recover their strength before continuing on the road. They appeared alarmed, but when the saw the rest of the villagers merely curious and happy, they relaxed a bit. Presently, the smaller rover entered the Village and came to a halt near the Elder's platform. Nicos and Keels emerged to happy greetings from the villagers.

Sonta and Ellen were quickly by their sides, while Setta, Taroom and Siah emerged from the vault with happy smiles upon their faces. Heart-filled hugs were exchanged, with Sonta finally looking at Keels up and down and chuckling in astonishment.

"You've gotten taller and broader," he commented, smiling broadly. Keels' brown eyes sparkled with humor.

As he was about to reply, a challenge cry shattered the afternoon's peace. Everyone froze for a moment, then as the second one sounded, Nicos and Keels ran toward the cries. The rest, including many of the other villagers and easterners followed. A scream of rage and despair rent the air, too.

Sonta expected Keels to want to join in and voice a cry of his own, but instead he grabbed both contestants and pulled them apart by the back of their tunics, then lifted them into the air. The startled men were twisting and trying to break free, while Nicos helped Kaytas back to her feet. She appeared shaken, but accepted the assistance readily. She gave him a nod of thanks as he stepped back from her, now that she seemed all right.

"Choose, Kaytas, who do you want to have as your mate, if either of them?" Keels asked in a loud voice, as he shook both men again. Jain calmed down and seemed to realize what was happening while Nali struggled for a moment more, not quite comprehending his situation. Nicos stood by with a hand to his stunner – just in case.

"I get to choose?" Kaytas questioned, not quite sure she heard him correctly. There were questions and wonder dancing in her eyes.

"Okay, it's the Winterhaven way of doing things, but in Winterhaven, the women choose whom they mate; we don't leave it up to a pointless fight where everyone can end up unhappy with the results," Nicos explained.

"And the men are fine with this in Winterhaven?" Sonta questioned as Nali also calmed down, realizing his situation at last. Keels set both men upon their feet but still held them firm. Sonta noted he didn't have his claws extended and while actually seemed very firm, he was calm himself. The Winterhaveners were laughing at this and nodding their heads.

"Aside from Ryes tossing someone into the air, the women in Winterhaven are a strong united front and if you want a chance to mate with anyone, you have to let the woman you want in your life know that you love and appreciate her well before her season comes on," Keels told the crowd with a broad smile of pride. "And Sela has decided I'm still worth keeping," he added, getting another laugh from Ellen, Setta and Nicos. Kaytas smiled at this, her eyes dancing with humor, but also assuredness. She stepped up to be closer to both men, as if inspecting them now.

"I've been with both of you, but now that it's finally my chance for a cub of my own, I need to know if either of you would truly stay with me and help provide for and care for the cub we could have?" It appeared Siah wanted to speak up in defense of her brother, but instantly subsided as she realized this commitment had to come from him, and him alone.

"You know I would, Kaytas. I love you with all my heart!" Nali spoke up quickly as he met her eyes squarely.

"I love you, truly, Kaytas and will be there by your side, always!" Jain declared, also meeting her eyes as she looked to him. Kaytas sighed, trying to decide.

"Who's been there for you up to now? Whom do you trust?" Setta asked, wondering. "Go with whom you want," she advised with a smile. Kaytas looked at this human woman and gave her a broad smile and nod of her head. She turned back to Keels and her two suitors.

"I'm choosing Nali, as we've been very close and he's been helping me with even everyday chores and hunting. I trust him more," she stated with assurance and her head held high. Keels smiled as he let him go. Nali turned first to Keels and gave him a respect-filled bow, then turned to his lady and took her into his arms.

"I love you so much and we're going to make the best cub ever," he promised while Kaytas laughed merrily.

"We'd better. I never took the last time and want one now," she assured him. "I love you so much too, Nali!" They kissed and then walked off to the Yuri path and New Matlowe. There was a collective sigh of relief.

"We're both peacekeepers in Winterhaven and even if we're not of Matlowe Village, we couldn't ignore our calling," Nicos offered the now-gathered elders. Sonta was beaming with pride. Farra and the other elders were smiling now.

"You've both handled it very well and I cannot thank you enough. Jain, if you need someone to talk to, we're here for you," he offered as Keels released him, watching his reactions closely. He noted Nicos did, too.

"We need to follow this here, as in Winterhaven," Aril stated with a huff, then a smile lighting up his whole face. "It'd save lives and everyone's sanity."

"Thank you for bringing back my better mind. It's the best way," Jain agreed, still looking sad overall. Keels laughed and clasped him on the shoulder in comfort. He noted Korman standing a ways back from the other villagers, appearing to have witnessed the whole event. He looked unhappy with the outcome and turned back for his own home. Keels was glad he hadn't tried to head off toward the Yuri after Kaytas, but then recalled she was one of his daughters and he'd never been known to try to take any of his own daughters.

"So, why the visit?" Ellen asked, curious now the excitement had died down and the crowd was breaking up. Siah and Joce had stepped over and were comforting Jain.

"To show our people and any of the villagers who want to see, a part of the message left on that big crystal we retrieved," Keels explained with a laugh, having forgotten. "It's on orders from Garth and you'll see why."

"I have seen some of it," Sonta stated, "but would love to see the complete message."

"We'll have to wait for nightfall to see it well, though," Nicos added, "but I think you'll be amazed." He gave them a nod of his head. "And we have some supplies and special equipment for the team here, too."

"Let's go get the rover unpacked, then," Setta urged, as she turned back to the waiting vehicle, a big smile across her face, lighting up her bright eyes.

Viewings

"Sorry, we have the shelter filled to capacity right now. You'll have to catch the next showing later this evening," Leon advised as another pair of caravaners, who arrived too late for the first viewing. It'd been a restricted group for the initial one, controlled by Darman, himself. And he'd conducted the groups as they arrived to the shelter himself, so Leon knew these two hadn't been meant for this first showing.

"But, Darman said," the woman insisted, appearing unhappy with his denial of entry into their campsite.

"Everyone will see it," he replied, cutting off her throwing the tantrum he knew was coming next; she seemed like Karr. "You'll get your chance, but the shelter's already filled. We'd rather you be comfortable while watching it, instead of squeezed in, crowded and uncomfortable," he quickly added, being as diplomatic and firm as possible. Rowan stepped over to see what was wrong and lend a hand.

"Good afternoon," he greeted, not recognizing this pair of caravaners. "Is there something you need?" he asked, being direct. The pair took a step back and gave him a bow together.

"Elder Rowan," the man breathed, "we were only here to see the hallow that was being displayed today. Chief Darman allowed us to be included."

"And this creature will not let us pass," the woman added and then saw the spark of anger in the elder's eyes and immediately regretted her words.

"Leon of House Rhona, is from a people known as humans, and is a fine gentleman. He's doing as Garth requested. There'll be another showing of the holo in about three hours, I believe," he responded as civilly as possible. He took in a breath to help calm down.

"Then we'll return later," the woman offered, giving Leon a small bow, too, before turning back to their own camp.

"They even have houses!" Leon heard the man comment as they walked away, which got him to chuckling.

"Thank you, Rowan," he said in a low voice, "I'm sure they'll get used to us soon." Rowan chuckled as he gripped his shoulder in assurance.

"They will, give them some time," he agreed with a smile, giving his shoulder a light squeeze, then letting him go.

"I can see where Ryes gets her quick temper," he added in comment, laughing lightly. Rowan blushed, but nodded his head.

"And her stubbornness," he told him, chuckling now. "They're family traits. You'll see them in Maren, too," he pointed out, as Leon joined him in laughter, nodding his head in agreement. "If anyone gives you any trouble, use the headset. You're not alone here," he advised, sobering. They each had a headset, which Neil had brought out, as well as a portable base station to enable their use out here for quick communications and a way to contact home. Leon gave him a nod.

"I didn't think they'd truly be a problem," he replied, wondering about it.

"They're from one of the southern groups and that bunch can be a bit touchy with we northerners. They still don't even refer to Darman as their Great Chief, as they should. I've heard of their attitude for decades, so it's not you, it's them," he explained, "it surprised me they gave me honor."

"Then we'll have to find a way to kill them with kindness, each time they're rude. They really have no idea what humans are like, after all," he reasoned with a smile. Rowan smiled at this and nodded.

"We can only try," he agreed, surprised at the suggestion. He gave him a nod, then returned to helping organize the rest of the camp. He approached Garth and Sabin as they were discussing something nearby.

"Perhaps we should establish a perimeter around our camp; something physical," he suggested as they gave him their attention.

"We're thinking the same thing," Garth replied, "it's figuring what to use." He saw a group of cubs running through the camp, not having come through their main established entry. He didn't recognize any of them.

"Ryes repaired a bridge using the materials lying near it, before. Why not have her build a wall around our encampment tonight, when most of them will be sleeping, then take it down when we're ready to leave," Rowan suggested, "Then they will think we have some mysterious Talents among us. For all they know the humans did it." Both men saw the merit in his idea and smiled grandly.

"And she can use some of the sand on the sides of the stream banks to form clear panes, so we can see what's happening outside, too," Sabin suggested, chuckling at the idea.

"Those widows will go both ways, but still better than people wildly running though the camp," Garth said, agreeing "I'll talk with Ryes as soon as she's finished with the caravaners' viewing of Prince Callas' holo. And we'll plan ahead for the Great Spring Gather, so we don't have to rely upon her spending her Talents in such a frivolous manner."

"But she can use the practice," Rowan teased him, laughing. A light appeared in his eyes at this reminder.

"Yes, she can," he agreed, chuckling and giving him a nod of agreement.

"So Prince Callas names Garth outright as the one to save us all," Rinna commented with a heavy sigh when it was all done. She met Ryes' eyes as she frowned, "And you, Sweetling, have to go out to fight them, too!" She quickly stood and wrapped her arms about Ryes, suddenly crying her heart out. Ryes thought it was like what they usually went through when the vans were about to leave in the early spring. She hugged her back, fiercely, her own tears starting to spill now. But instead of giving into sorrow, she opened up to her grandmother from within and shared with her all her own love and as much courage as she could draw up from within. After a few moments of a deep inner sharing for them both, Rinna was finally able to let her go, and wiped at her eyes, as did Ryes. They both laughed, understanding each other so deeply now.

"I'll do my best to take out those nasty Snags," she assured her. "I don't want them near Tayna ever again!"

"First you're going to need a few starships," Darman reminded them, laughing. "This might not happen for some years to come." Ryes shook her head at this, as she wiped off the rest of her tears with the side of her hand.

"No, we got other messages from Earth, herself. They're not going to last much longer. We have to find a way to save her soon, before the Snags destroy her. There's a task force headed out here to get some allies. But, I'd rather go out to meet the enemy in my own starship, than as a passenger on one of the human ones," she admitted with a sigh. Dastin stepped forward and took one of her hands between his own.

"You will meet them on your own ground, soon enough," he promised, meeting her green eyes with his golden ones twinkling. She smiled in spite of herself. Somehow she believed him, and gave him a nod of appreciation.

"Thank you, great-grandfather," she replied as humor lit her own eyes now. He laughed merrily at this, nodding his head.

"My great-granddaughter of my heart," he affirmed, then wrapped his arms about her in a warm hug. Ryes closed her eyes, then extended her Healing Talent and did a full restore of his body while he held her. When he let her go, he looked at her puzzled. "What did you do, child?" he gently asked, wonder in his eyes. He could breathe with ease, which hadn't been possible in too many years!

"I was practicing and it was only what you needed," she said, smiling and blushing now. Darman stepped closer with questions in his eyes.

"Rinna and I will be by later tonight to see you, granddaughter," he promised, unwilling to voice anything further, now that the other caravan elders gathered closer to hear what was being said. Ryes stepped over and gave him a real hug.

"I'll be waiting for you both," she whispered into his ear. He finally smiled for her as she let him go.

"Are there any questions about what Prince Callas had to say to all of us?" she asked of the gathering behind her dear family.

"Where did you say you found this message?" one of the elders asked, curious about the source; still in some shock over the whole thing.

"In a hidden vault below the Circle in Matlowe Village," she responded, giving her a nod of understanding.

"If it was hidden, how did you find it?" another elder asked, trying to get her to spin out the tale for all of them to pick it apart. She laughed merrily, shaking her head at this. She gestured towards the chairs, for them to go back to their seats.

"You wouldn't believe my story, so I bought along a recording of the day it happened. There isn't any sound, but at least you can see it," she said as she queued the video to play, once everyone was seated again. "We found it originally from a data scan several months before and had gone purposefully to uncover it and its secrets on this particular day."

She heard their exclamations as the Village Circle itself rose up into the air and then gracefully folded itself out of the way. She'd carefully edited the segments where she stopped the fire and the door from crushing others, so it appeared as if the explosion propelled the door skyward, then the people under where it was going to land, ran away before it impacted. She'd learned a few useful things from Neil, through time.

When it finished, the talking suddenly got loud again. Everyone had questions to ask. It took Darman a few moments to calm everyone down enough so they could ask them one at a time. They managed to finally get everyone focused and most of the answers they were looking for taken care of, and then finally on their way back outside. By the time they were done, Ryes realized she needed a drink of water, as she was fast losing her voice.

Darman, Rinna and Dastin were still with her once the rest departed. Rinna handed her a bottle of water, seeing her need. She gave her a smile of thanks as she quenched her thirst for a few moments.

"You do know for the next group that you're only to play the first part of the holo, they don't need to see what follows. The view of the Snagospin itself will bring plenty of nightmares alone. They don't need the rest until later," Darman advised, once she could give him her full attention, again. She gave him a nod in understanding.

"And that goes for anyone else here in the camp?" she asked to make sure. He gave her a nod. "Including Kyma and Dara?" she pressed, to be sure. He paused at this one, then looked to think better of it for them.

"If you can give them a private viewing, they must see the whole holo," he added, now sure on this score. She smiled, her eyes lighting up.

"We're playing the full one for the rest of our own people tonight, so they can join us then, if they're not too busy. In a few moments we'll have the next round of caravaners," she affirmed, "with the shorter version." He gave her a nod.

"Now truly, it had to be you doing something about that vault door," Rinna insisted, scoffing and annoyed. Ryes laughed and nodded her head.

"I thought I'd edited it better than that," she admitted, spreading her hands helplessly. This got a short laugh out of Rinna, as she gave her a nod.

"I know you better than that! So, when do you want us to come back?" she pressed, needing to know now.

"How about while we're running the holo for the Winterhaveners? I don't intend to be in this shelter then, as people get upset that I'm going to have to go out to do battle. In my mind it's no different if it's me, or Garth, even if it appears it will be both of us. If it's something that has to be done, it has to be done."

"It's only harder with you, Sweetling," Darman said, stepping closer to cup her face in his hand. "And all those wonderful cubs you're going to have to leave behind." This got her tears to start up again, as she gave him a nod. He gave her a light kiss on her forehead, as he used to do when she was a cub. She smiled as he let her go and she wiped her eyes, once again.

"See you later tonight," he promised. Dastin then stepped closer to her and likewise gave her a kiss on her forehead, which made her smile even more.

"Thank you for the great gift you've given me," he said, in a low voice, his eyes merry and clear.

"You're so very welcome," she assured him, as Rinna stepped over and kissed her ear, as she was wont to do at times. Ryes laughed as she bid them a good-bye until later in the evening. She slipped out the one mem chip from the holo player and put in another one, to be sure there'd be no errors, as she tucked the full version one into its case in her belly pouch.

"What a beautiful morning!" Darman declared as he showed up early at the Winterhaven camp. He'd walked the perimeter, checking on the clever wall that had appeared overnight around it. There was a locked door meant to accommodate the rovers and the wall was at least two feet thick and sixteen feet tall with thick glass windows of various shapes worked into it in a decorative manner, as well as small holes for breezes to come through. The windows by their main entrance were shaped as a great fire-bird with panes colored in reds, white and yellows, rising out of flame-colored rocks at the base; they were shaped so cleverly he had to lightly touch one to be sure it wasn't a piece of lava. He highly approved and understood its necessity, and knew who had to have created it – with no doubt. This was something he was going to tell them to leave in place for future use.

He was immediately allowed inside and directed to the dining shelter. There he found all the people he wanted to see in one place. Ryes was juggling between trying to get a few mouthfuls of food herself, while trying to feed her cubs. Garth seemed to be in a deep discussion with Sabin, Ethan and Neil and oblivious to Ryes' need for a little help. He stepped over, sat on a spare chair and took over feeding the cubs for her, so she could eat too.

"Thank you, grandfather," she breathed out in relief, letting him take over for a while, appreciating the help, then dived into her own breakfast, trying to finish it before the day's events took over. He chuckled, noticing her haste.

"Slow down Sweetling, and breathe," he mildly scolded with a chuckle. Garth turned and noted his presence for the first time and smiled with a chagrinned look on his face.

"I forgot I was supposed to be helping her this morning," he admitted, as he blushed. He gestured to take over feeding the cubs, but Darman shook his head, enjoying both Garth's discomfiture and spending some time with the little ones. He hadn't seen the cubs in months, but they still knew him and seemed happy he was back. And they'd grown so much! Ryes chuckled at the stand-off. Maren stepped over at this moment and saw what she saw and laughed too.

"Ryes, can I borrow you for a little while this morning?" he requested, calming and giving her a more serious look. Her own smiled faded from her lips, but her inner humor still shone brightly from her eyes.

"What do you need?" she asked, curious. He sat down across from her, giving her a nod as he grabbed a clean mug and poured himself some honeyed tea from the pitcher on the table.

"First off, for you to finish your breakfast. I had mine almost an hour ago," he admitted with a huff of a laugh. "Rowis woke me up early to see the new wall that magically appeared this morning." He chuckled as he sipped his tea. Ethan laughed and gave them both a nod.

"After everyone else saw that holo last night, it might seem a minor piece of magic, I'm sure," he commented.

"It seems quite this morning," Sabin observed, as Ardis gave him a nod. She was finishing up feeding her own two sons and Tobin.

"I think everyone that can is sleeping in today and enjoying a morning without traveling on the road," Ryes replied with a big smile as she finished her morning bowl of mixed grains.

"That's it! Everyone's more relaxed, even after last night's news. Did you show the whole message back at home?" Ardis thought to ask Garth as he was now trying to help Darman with the cubs' care. He turned and gave her a shake of his head, while Jann made a try to grab at his ear, since it was close for a moment. He smiled as he leaned away from her grasping hands.

"Not yet. Since enough of the elders here had seen it, I thought our people here should too, in case we're asked a lot of questions. Like the other caravaners here, they only saw the first segment. We'll show them the rest when we get back home, so I can be there to field their questions, personally."

"That sounds fair," she commented, giving him a nod and a smile of understanding.

"I'm done," Ryes said, looking Maren directly in the eyes. He gave her a nod, then smiled.

"Kyma asked me last night to show some of our healing techniques to his Healer, Aina. And since you could use the practice, I'm including you in our training classes," he informed her.

"We have some Healers who can use some fresh perspective," Darman offered, finished with feeding the infants and letting Garth now take over cleaning them up, once again. "Do you have a runner," he started to ask, as Ryes chuckled.

"I have Mind Voice and can let Grandmother Rinna know to pass on the word," she offered, smiling brightly. He gave her a nod of thanks. She nodded back and closed her eyes. She opened them shortly and said, "She says she'll send them over to our camp. I'll let Mason know to expect them." Which she quickly contacted him directly to do so; which surprised Mason, not having expected it. But he grasped it right away and agreed to keep an eye out for them.

"Where are we meeting, since it's going to be a larger group?" Maren asked as he chuckled; giving his cousin a nod at her swift handling of the situation, as she focused her eyes upon him again. She did save a lot of time, to be sure.

"We could use the area around our smaller fire," she suggested, "since the big shelter is still being used to show that holo to the rest of the caravaners." He gave her a nod, liking her idea. "It'll be away from the crowds and quieter."

"That sounds good," Sabin agreed. "I'll have Security keep the area clear for you," he offered, filling in for Torr, while Torr was still back in Winterhaven keeping order there, while they were gone. Maren sketched him a salute with his now-empty mug, gave Ryes a nod, knowing she still had to get her cubs settled, and got up and headed outside.

Mitt stepped in and looked around, as if she were looking for someone. Ryes waved her over and she gave her a nod.

"I'm all ready to go," she told Sabin and Garth, as she stepped up to the table. "Hello Darman, do you know if Kyma's up yet?" Ryes noted her tone was far more respectful when addressing the Great Chief of the Caravaners, but she managed to keep from chuckling. He smiled merrily as he and Ethan had been quietly discussing something, then looked up to her.

"He and Dara should be finished with breakfast by now," he promised. "Give them a few more minutes, Mitt."

"And I'm ready now," Garth stated, as he picked up Jann and Rhin. "Where are the girls?" He just realized neither Sayer, nor Raby were anywhere to be seen.

"I let them sleep in," Ryes told him, as he frowned. "They're just getting out of the showers, now. I've been keeping track," she teased him. He finally chuckled and relaxed.

"And will still need to get their breakfast," he added, understanding now. She went and put her bowl and mug, as well as Maren's empty one into the opening of their portable cleaning machine. Metta stepped into the dining shelter and approached Garth, as he waited for Ryes.

"Future savior of all starmen and humans, and father of more cubs than you can appear to handle," he observed with a laugh. "Good morning, Garth," he greeted him. Garth laughed heartily as Darman was handing him Gareth to carry too. The three squirming cubs in his arms were almost too much for even him, now. He smiled as he gave Metta a nod of agreement. Darman was laughing now and nodding his agreement.

"I believe we all will have our own parts in the coming conflicts, too," Ethan said, appearing thoughtful. He was seeking a way in his heart to lay aside the future for a few moments, so he could enjoy the present a bit more.

"Very true," Metta agreed, his humor unabated. "I'll grab some breakfast then go assist with showing that recording. Very clever editing Ryes, by the way, of vault door handling." He hoped to get the reasons for doing it out of her this morning. She blushed and shook her head.

"I want to downplay her Talents and all she can do," Garth spoke up quickly. "There are many others here whom I'm not sure how much to trust."

"And do I get to see the real recording?" Kyma asked from the shelter doorway. His expression was tentative. Ryes huffed a laugh and gave him a nod as she was now holding Shyla and Shaysa.

"You are trusted," she assured him with a big smile. "I just didn't think to bring it along with us, so perhaps for the Great Spring Gather, we'll have a private viewing?" she asked, looking to Daman then Kyma, both men now were smiling and giving her a nod. "I promise to make the time just for you two and a few others, for a special viewing and be there to answer any questions."

"Why didn't she include you, Metta?" Darman asked, curious. He huffed out a hearty laugh, giving him a big smile and nod.

"Because I was there and saw it all," he bragged, then went to see what tempting treats were set out this morning. He'd grown fond of many of the foods they served at mealtimes. Ethan nodded in agreement, as did Rowan.

"It was an event-filled visit," Rowan assured the others with a merry smile. Some of the other Winterhaveners in the shelter were laughing agreement.

"Gluing Korman to the wall is still my favorite," Shadd assured everyone with a laugh. "That was landmark!" Ryes was now blushing, as she was putting her younger children into their stroller, which had been finally found and retrieved.

"It was my second favorite part," Sabin agreed with a merry laugh.

"Now I have to see it!" Darman declared, laughing. "Ryes, you did this?"

"It wasn't my best moment," she admitted, as she finished getting the cubs strapped in and ready. All five were talking loudly in their own baby language, trying to be a part of the discussion, too. This got the people nearby laughing. And Ardis' two sons were making their own comments; talking back.

"Mitt, are you ready?" Kyma asked, now grinning broadly.

"I am! I was only gathering everyone else who's coming along this morning," she assured him, seeing he was excited about flying now.

"I'm not getting as much time as I'd like with my cubs!" Ryes quietly protested as she, Ardis, Raya and Brenda were playing with their children in the shelter set aside as their care center in the camp. The screened windows provided lots of light and fresh air, yet it was overall enclosed and protective and set up with all the things they'd need for child care.

"The session with the Healers is important," Brenda started, "but then, your cubs are even more so. I don't envy you the choices you've been given." She didn't mention the coming war outlined in the holo last night. Somehow, she believed it was actually coming.

"Give the Healers a little bit of your time, then slip back here and spend as much as the rest of the day you can with your little ones," Raya encouraged with Ardis giving her a nod of agreement.

"Grandma Rinna will understand," Ardis added. Ryes gave them a nod, as she cuddled Jann for a few moments, reluctant to leave. She was waiting for Raby and Sayer to show up. She promised them the afternoon out on their own, if they stuck together, and if they cub-sat for her this morning. Dotti showed up with Maren's sisters and brother. The younger cubs went for the toys right off while the women chuckled in delight. Tars hung back with the mothers, trying to appear grown up.

"You have all of them?" Brenda commented, "Has Wynne taken over Tanns' time, again?" Dotti nodded while she sat down with them on the chairs by the door.

"Come on, Tars, get comfortable," she invited with a smile. "She and Wynne are in seventh heaven trading plant secrets and recipes for medicines and all kinds of things. They're the best medicine for each other right now," she said, shaking her head as Rowis handed Shaysa Jann's rattle. Rowis grinned mischievously and Dotti knew she did it on purpose; and smiled.

"So, what do you think of our little wall?" Ryes asked with a grin. She laughed, as did the others.

"You made it pretty," Tars assured her with a laugh. "Whoosh, it was there like magic!" She threw her arms up in the air as she laughed some more.

"I wanted to keep all of us safe. Even if we're among a lot of friends and extended family, I wanted to give us time to get to know the rest, first," she explained.

"It's a good idea," Ardis commented, "And we needed it. So, what do you ladies think of the proposed farms near Winterhaven?" she questioned, wanting to know their minds, now that they were away from the men.

"I love the idea," Raya spoke up quickly, a big smile upon her face. "It'll give the windracers more room and a chance for us to see if we can raise our own animals for food – away from the main building." Ryes nodded her head in agreement and smiled, too.

"No more mucking out the bird pens for me!" she laughed, while the rest started laughing with her.

"You still do that?" Brenda asked, amazed.

"Yes, I still take a turn at it. After all, how can I ask someone to do the task if I'm not doing my share?" she replied as she gave her a nod. "It's not my favorite, but is easier now that I can use my Talents." More laughter followed this admission.

"It makes sense, but you're helping to run Winterhaven and I know that's not a job I'd want to take on," Dotti commented with a big smile. "There're simply some jobs that take different skill sets than I realize I have," she admitted with a merry laugh.

"Who's going to want to work on a farm?" Tars asked, her brow furrowed as she wondered. Sayer arrived and sat down next to Ryes and she appeared surprised.

"We have a farm?" she asked, questions dancing in her eyes. Ryes laughed and nodded her head, her eyes merry.

"Oh, that's why we had a study of farms in our class last week!" she exclaimed, seeing the connection now. "Are we going to have classes out there to learn how to raise animals?" Dotti laughed and nodded at this in answer.

"Yes," she assured the young girls. "We'll have a teaching farm, as well as a few real farms where people will live and work."

"My favorite vid was the one of people chasing chickens," Tars responded with a laugh. This got Ryes, Ardis and Raya almost doubled over in laughter. Ryes wiped the tears from her eyes with the side of her hand and gave her a nod.

"We remember that one," she assured her. Then there was a shadow at the shelter doorway and Maren was standing there with a curious look on his face; having missed the conversation.

"Time?" Ryes asked, her eyes still filled with humor.

"Time," he assured her. She gave him a nod, then passed Jann to Sayer, giving them both a quick kiss, and stood up.

"I'll be back later," she told her, as Raby and Katas arrived to assist. She gave both the older girls a kiss too, as she left. Then she took Maren's hand as they walked back to their smaller fire, a smile still playing upon her lips.

"What was that about?" he finally asked, as it had gotten to him. She laughed, then gave him a nod of her head.

"Chasing chickens," she teased, as they came around the last shelter and approached the others sitting there waiting. He thought for a few seconds, then burst out laughing as he remembered it, too. He shook his head at her, as she smirked. He knew she timed that on purpose...

Healing Lessons

"Let's sit and get comfortable," Maren invited as he and Ryes joined the small knot of six Healers who'd joined them this morning in their camp. They had everyone rearranged the camp chairs under a huge, shady tree near the fire, so to keep the sun off of them for this session. As they sat down, introductions were begun by Ryes, who wanted to get to know the people they'd been working with now.

"I'm Ryes from Winterhaven," she said, starting things and keeping it simple. There were smiles and light laughter in response.

"And mother of five cubs," one of the women responded. "How do you manage so many?" Ryes laughed merrily and shook her head.

"Sometimes, I don't know how I manage them, myself. I have help from my older daughters and some friends and family, but they do spend most of the day with me in my office," she replied, her eyes merry. "I even have small beds in there for them to use when they're sleepy." Raya walked over to join them with a warm smile upon her face.

"I thought I'd help you with your session today," she offered, "That'll free up Ryes to concentrate on the Healing." Maren smiled and gave her a nod in response.

"Your help is very appreciated," he agreed, "thanks, Raya!" Ryes smiled and gave her a nod, too. Raya went and brought over another chair and they spent a few moments rearranging to get everyone settled again.

"Are you a healer, too?" a young man asked, curious, as Raya sat down and was comfortable now. She shook her head and laughed lightly.

"I have Mind Voice and am going to be the one to hold the meld together today, so all of you can concentrate upon Healing," she assured him. "My name's Raya and am originally from the Moondance Tribe," she added in introduction.

"We have Mind Voice-gifted people we could've used," one of the other women started, but Ryes, Maren and Raya all shook their heads in denial.

"I know Ryes and can filter things so you all don't end up with headaches," Raya assured them, smiling with mischief in her eyes. Maren laughed and nodded his head while Ryes blushed.

"You do often have that effect," Maren agreed, teasing her. She shook her head and swatted at him playfully.

"My name is Aina and I'm from Hagg Craig Hold and am Kyma's Healer. How's Sernn doing? I strove to heal him with every shred of my Talent, but couldn't truly do much for him," she admitted with her hands open and spread, still showing how deeply this disturbed her. Maren's smile faded as he gave her a nod of his head in understanding.

"It was a deep healing," he told her, meeting her amber eyes with his brown eyes directly. "Raya, could you please call Mitt over? Ask her if we could borrow Sernn to show everyone what we ended up doing for him," he requested. She gave him a nod and quickly extended his request to Mitt. She gave her an affirmative and then went to track down her son.

"They'll be here soon," she informed him.

"I'm Tova, one of the caravaner's out of the South," she said in an odd accent. "Could you please show us what you tried to do to heal Sernn, Aina?" she requested, wondering if she was just incompetent?

"Let's see, so we have a comparison," Maren invited, sure Tova's attitude of superiority was behind the request. She'd snubbed him earlier for his apparent youth, which had galled him a bit, being used being treated better at home. "Raya, if you could please?"

She gave him a nod and closed her eyes, then extended her hands. Ryes grasped one readily enough, then Aina took her other one, closing her eyes and extending out her other hand, too. Tova grasped Maren's hand, while his other one clasped one of Ryes' hands. Soon everyone was ready to begin. Raya helped Aina open up her memories of that day when she was trying her best to deal with the wrongness she found in Senah's son. They all soon saw the depth of his maladies were not trivial, nor easily dispatched. They felt her heartache and all seemed in harmony with her experiences. This deep sharing helped to set the opening tone of this small gathering.

Mitt and Sernn stepped over to the small group and stood for a moment, uncertain. Ryes heard them and opened her eyes, then gave Mitt a nod to step over to her. Mitt smiled broadly and gave her a nod.

"We need to hold onto your Aunt Ryes' arm, close our eyes and then let them draw us into the meld," she instructed her son. She went and grabbed two chairs, then lead him over to Ryes' side. He gave her a nod, sat down and was suddenly eager to see what this was all about and did as she'd instructed. Once she "caught" them, Ryes gently handed them over to Raya so she could include both Mitt and Sernn into the meld.

"Sernn's here for you, Maren," Mitt stated, feeling the other minds around her, but knowing Raya and Ryes would hold the true control. Sernn's embarrassment and excitement caused a ripple of amusement among the others.

"Aunt Ryes, why did you need me?" he finally braved to ask, as he knew her and Maren the best. Her amusement was plain, as was her warmth, as she encouraged him. He reveled in it for a few moments, feeling more at ease now.

"The Healers would like to see what Maren, Tennan and I have done for you, to heal your body and keep you from dying," she requested. "May we allow them to truly see you from within?"

"It's to help them learn from the Healing we did for you," Maren added in explanation. He felt his mother's approval of it, too.

"Yes, you may," he finally agreed, bracing himself within. Raya enfolded him in a protective warmth, while Ryes channeled her Healing into Sernn's body, once Maren directed her to do so and Raya also bridged the others in to see it all.

Everyone had their own Healing Talents active as they delved into his being. Maren and Ryes filtered and directed their attention so as not to cause him any undue harm in this close examination. All could see that Sernn has been truly restored and repaired and was at full health. His healing had been complete all the way down to the cellular components Ryes and Maren called DNA, within his cells. It was impressive. Aina was in utter shock. She "knew" this child and knew he was the same boy she tried to save, and here he was fully healthy with no trace of the curse his birth mother gifted him with when he was born! The others saw her knowledge and recognition and realized this was an amazing truth.

After they'd all seen his new truth, Maren thanked him and told Mitt to go and let Sernn return to what he'd been doing before. She was amused and had gained a perspective from Aina and the others of how much a miracle Sernn's healing had truly been. She blessed Maren and Ryes in her heart as they withdrew from the meld and opened their eyes on the world once again.

"There, that wasn't too bad," she teased her son, as they stood and grabbed their chairs to return them to their places near the fire. He laughed as he swatted at her hand. As soon as they put down the chairs, he wrapped his arms about her in a fierce hug.

"I love you, mom," he told her, as he buried his head into her chest. His mind was in a jumble, but his heart was full of love for her and the rest of their big family. The shadows of the memories of what he had before had threatened to engulf him, but she anchored him to this time and place, making those dark times fade again. Mitt hugged him back tightly, tears in her eyes now as she truly understood.

"We were meant to be together," she told him, smiling. "I found you, brought you home and love you ever so very much." After a few moments, he pulled back, smiling up at her, then kissed her cheek and laughed as he nodded his head.

"You are my true mother and I think you're right. We're meant to be family! Can I go finish helping putting up our booths? We're almost done and ready to sell some things we made," he told her. "Grandfather Darman was going to give me some pointers on being a trader!" She laughed and nodded her head, letting him go.

"Sure, and don't get into too much trouble afterwards," Mitt advised with a laugh. He nodded, then ran off with a laugh. She sighed. She was tempted to rejoin the meld to see what else they were up to, but decided she'd better finish helping with checking the rovers. She'd just finished the choppers, making sure they were ready for more flights later this afternoon. And she could always get Ryes to share it with her later.

Maren and Ryes showed the others their memories of Sernn's healing and the depth of Maren's extension of Talent he had to tap in order to bring it about.

"Ryes, you have Healing Talent, I can feel it. Why didn't you do more to help?" Tova asked, wondering. She felt her easy humor clearly through the link.

"My cubs were delivered soon afterwards," she admitted to her. "All I could do at the time was boost Maren and Tennan with my pool of power."

"What pool of power?" Nottin questioned. He'd come from the Southern paths with Tova and wasn't sure how to believe these two. The Healing had been dramatic, as he found Aina's memories of her attempt true, and then seeing the same child now fully healthy was amazing.

"Let's first review the techniques I used to effect the Healing," Maren diverted him with Raya's help. Aina, Tova, Nottin, Teenah, Kilsey, and Luba closely followed the process as Maren shared it, then they all fell into a detailed discussion about it and asked him endless questions. Ryes hung back, paying attention, but other than the occasional support, stayed out of the discussion. There was still so much she was still learning about healing, that she didn't want to miss a moment of what was being discussed. Sometimes it wasn't always what was being asked, but how it was being phrased. Then, she felt a nudge at her shoulder, so she pulled back a little and opened her eyes.

"Sorry to interrupt, but we there was an accident and one of the cubs is hurt," Kort told her. She gave him a nod.

"Put her into Maren's arms," she suggested, seeing he was holding the howling child as she clutched his tunic, holding her arm close to her body. She could clearly see the blood and exposed bone. She showed this image immediately to Maren and the others; letting them know what she suggested Kort to do. Then as he fully called up his Talent, she opened up her pool of power. She felt the shock of the others joined with them, while Raya was merely amused, taping it freely herself.

Kort knelt down and placed the girl onto Maren's lap, while comforting her as best he could. She squirmed, but then as his Healing aura opened up, she was placed into a gentle sleep. Kort stayed to carefully hold her in place – just in case. Ryes gave him a nod, then closed her eyes, once again.

While the others watched, Maren delicately mended her arm, tapping Ryes' Manipulator to put the bones back into alignment, restored her body's balance and then cured a budding infection, as well as removed a parasite she apparently picked up not too long ago. He strengthened her immune system to resist the parasite in the future as well as a few other diseases he could help her resist, having known them well by now. Then he was finished and gently lifted her sleep. He opened his eyes and smiled down at her in his lap.

"You'll want to get a bath and change, but are free to go now. Just stay out of the trees until you're bigger," he urged, as she giggled and Kort laughed. She squirmed, so Kort let her leave, then turned back to Maren and gave him a nod.

"Is there anything you might need?" he asked, still feeling compelled as he did know better by now.

"Only to let anyone who needs treatment to come over so we can do this as a team," he requested. Then Maren let go of Ryes' hand and grabbed his wrist, closed his eyes as he did a quick check on Kort, seeing he was still in good health, as he tweaked a few of his resistances he'd given him a few months ago. Kort laughed when he let him go once again, knowing what it was about. He stood up and gave Maren a nod as he took Ryes' hand, again.

"I'll go spread the word," he promised, smiling as he headed out of the Winterhaven camp.

"What were those adjustments you were doing?" Aina questioned, puzzled.

"I was strengthening his immune system to be aware of certain proteins that some of the contagions here on Tayna carry, so his body will know them and destroy them before he can be truly harmed," Maren explained, realizing they might not know about this type of Healing. "Preventative measures help save lives and our energy later."

"What an excellent idea!" Nottin stated, excited with the concept. "Teach us, Oh Young Wise One," he teased, but was truly serious about learning this new aspect of his Talent. Ryes' humor sparked at this as she added in her support, too. They could start the demonstrations on their own bodies.

"Do you so freely invite them for Healing all the time?" Kilsey asked as they finally dissolved the meld and could open their own eyes again. Maren laughed and gave her a nod.

"Why would I not? Their need existed and I'm a Healer," he replied; a bit puzzled by the odd look in her eyes.

"What do you gain of it?" Luba started to ask, when a woman rushed over to them with a basket in her hands.

"You healed my daughter and this is but a small token, but you have my thanks," she told Maren. She laughed as she threw her arms around him, then left the basket in his lap and hurried out, smiling.

"I'm not here to make money, but to give to others what I can of my Talents," he stated, flat out. Ryes laughed lightly and nodded agreement. "And sometimes people will give me small things in gratitude, but that's not what drives me to use my Talents to help others," he assured them. He looked into the basked, smiled, then handed it to Raya. She looked into it and laughed; giving him a nod of her head, looking very pleased.

"I'll put these to good use," she assured him. "Bubblenuts for dessert tonight!"

"Grandmother Rinna probably told on you, Maren," Ryes teased with a laugh.

"Ryes, your `pool of power' is aptly named! I don't feel exhausted at all, even after helping to heal half the people camped here now," Aina assured her with a smile lighting up her face.

"How many Talents do you have besides Booster and Healing?" Tova questioned, curiosity dancing in her eyes. Ryes shook her head, remaining mute.

"And Manipulator and Mind Voice," Nottin supplied with a laugh as he stood up. He lent a hand to Tova, so she could stand with ease. "I can't believe how both you and Maren can open your eyes and hold other discussions without breaking the meld, nor letting your Talents diffuse away. How do you do that?" he pressed, wonder still ranging within his mind; still astounded at today's healing session.

"Practice," Ryes supplied with a laugh. "Lots of practice!" she assured him as she stood up, too. Maren stretched then got to his feet.

"It was hard to learn for all of our Talents, but we felt it was too important not to take on the task," he added in support. Raya nodded her agreement.

"It was hard to learn," she added with a smile, "but we've all gotten pretty good at it, now."

"I'm going to have to work on that," Nottin assured him with a laugh.

"Me took" Teenah supplied, grinning merrily. "Raya, how did a plainswoman come to live among Matlowe Villagers?" he asked. She laughed merrily.

"They found me and saved me, and I've found my true place in Winterhaven. If I want to see my tribe, I can either fly out to see my mother and aunts, or they can come to see me. I've a wonderful husband and an occupation that makes me very happy, as well as two healthy, happy cubs to raise. Why would I ever go back? I've outgrown the Plains," she assured him with a huge grin. He blushed and gave her a nod, understanding most of what she was saying.

"Not everyone can freely fly across Tayna," Luba agreed, a tinge envious now. "Do you know how to fly the flying machines?" Raya nodded and laughed.

"Ryes and Garth made sure everyone knew how to operate all the different machines – just in case of need. I love flying, but love baking and cooking even more," she bragged. "I'm going to put these to use, please excuse me," she said as she stepped away from the small group, glad she'd been there to help, but even more so to extend more of her Mind Voice skills. She noted she'd surprised Tova, who did have Mind Voice too, with her abilities and power level, which was all her own and separate from Ryes' sharing of power. She was proud of how far she'd come from being a simple plainswoman. She wore her Winterhaven phoenix with pride!

"Great Chief," Aina breathed out as he returned late in the evening to their small encampment within the gather. She stood up as she had a lot on her mind and needed to let him know more of what she'd found out about the Winterhaveners. She knew he wanted to know all that could be learned of them.

"Cousin!" he greeted her, smiling as he and her brother, Antes, stepped over to their center fire. "What keeps you up so late tonight?" he asked directly, noting Antes' irritation with her taking his time and attention. "Antes, go on to bed. I'll be off to my own, soon," he assured him, not wanting him constantly at his elbow.

"But," he started, as he put his spear into the holding barrel near the fire. Kyma shook his head. He seemed to get the idea, but glared at his sister before turning for his own tent.

"He's never grown up," Kyma breathed in a low voice as he signaled Aina to come with him to his tent and chairs around the small fire outside of it. "What can I do for you, Great Healer?" he asked as he sat down and loosened his tunic, taking off his tabard. She laughed lightly, shaking her head.

"I'm not even half the Healer young Maren is, in truth," she admitted as she sat down next to him. He pulled off one of his boots and paused to look at her with questions in his eyes.

"What?" he asked, puzzled, not sure he heard her right. She was the strongest Healer he'd ever met! She laughed and nodded her head.

"I spoke truly," she assured him, "I've spent most of the afternoon and evening trying to understand all I experienced during this morning's Healing class. It was amazing and his Healing abilities are unthinkably strong and focused in a way I've never seen, ever in my life. Then his cousin, Ryes, who has Healing, but is even more amazing as a Booster. Old Kann was a Booster, but for all his Talent, he was nowhere as powerful as Ryes! Between the two of them and Maren's sister they fully healed Sernn, who was born with the Curse of Senah."

Kyma looked at her and the way the firelight gleamed in her eyes. This was something that was moving her deeply. He wanted to get to the bottom of it, but it was late in the evening and everyone would be settling down to sleep. Still he couldn't leave her in such a state. She meant too much to him.

"Why not get some sleep and tomorrow morning we can go over to the Winterhaven camp and I can see it all for myself?" he asked, wondering if she would back away from such a possible confrontation? Instead of looking unsure, or panicked, she smiled and sighed in relief, happy with his suggestion.

"Yes, you must see the both of them in action!" she told him, laughing out in happiness. "We must find a way to make sure Ryes is protected. I don't know what other Talents she has, but the one alone is an amazing treasure for us all." She stood up, appearing relieved now. "Goodnight, dear Kyma," she said, then kissed him on his head and left for her tent, her burdens lifted. He sat for a few moments thinking of all she said and the way she said it. He liked what he saw in the young mother and the way she was willing to fight for her adopted daughter, but this was something deeper. If it was as Aina insisted, he did need to get to know these people far better. It could be a great boon for his people. Yes, their ideas were scaring some of the people here at the gather, but he felt like a night-wing drawn to their new flame. He only hoped he wouldn't be destroyed in the end.

The next morning Kyma and Aina found out Ryes and Maren had flown over to a nearby village to help with a difficult birth at Rinna's request. Disappointed, but determined, Aina then sought out Raya, in hope of securing her help with getting Kyma to fully understand what she experienced yesterday. Raya was just putting her two cubs down for a nap and saw them outside her shelter, waiting.

"Aina, how can I help you?" she asked, feeling her relief at finding her at last. She smiled as she saw the joy bloom in her eyes.

"With Ryes and Maren out this morning, I wanted to ask if you could show my chief what we experienced yesterday during the Healing lessons? Maren's highly-skilled Talent and Ryes' pool of power are something I've been trying to explain to him since last evening," she requested, meeting her eyes. Raya gave her a nod as Kovin stepped out of their shelter and saw their guests. He recognized Kyma on sight and gave him a small bow. Kyma smiled and returned it, liking these people more all the time. There was never derision in their offers of respect.

"I'd be glad to show you, as I'm sure Ryes would want him to understand it too," she offered, smiling.

"I'll go round up some chairs," Kovin volunteered, smiling. Raya gave him a bright smile and nod, glad of his offer. He returned shortly with four chairs, which didn't seem to surprise his wife. She laughed as they all set them up, after Kyma marveled at their simple construction and ease of use for a few moments, while Kovin had to resist chuckling; understanding his fascination. They all sat down and joined hands and closed their eyes.

Raya shared with them the memories of the day before with Aina adding in her deeper understanding of the skills used for the healings performed. The presence of Ryes' pool of power as she Boosted everyone at once without a trace of being tired, still amazed Aina and startled both Kyma and Kovin. Raya had known of her abilities for some months now and was not surprised at all.

"That must be why Garth keeps such a close eye upon his wife! She's priceless!" Kyma commented at the end of the sharing.

"That's not why," Raya assured him with humor coloring her mental voice. She showed them the deep passion and inner connection they shared, having seen it many times before. "He'd never willingly risk her against those Snagospin Talents, but will have little choice as he sees she might be our best weapon against them," she related. She gently released them, opening her eyes to see the understanding upon their faces, as she wanted.

"He does this only to protect all civilized life, no matter what world it lies upon, from our enemies of old," Kyma said, feeling changed by this knowledge. Yes, he'd seen the unedited copy of the holo, but hadn't appreciated what they truly risked in this venture, and it had been foreseen, far back in the hazy past. "I don't envy him this destiny. I don't know if I could do such a thing, if I had to risk someone to whom I was that close," he admitted.

"It hasn't been easy for either of them, but for now, they try to think small and do what they can for Winterhaven and Tayna. The time for the battles is still in the future, and they're trying to make as many preparations as they can for it now," Raya told them, knowing Garth needed Kyma's support and this was a good way for him to understand that all of Tayna might be involved.

"I'll talk with him later today," Kyma said, then stood up and bid them a good day. Kovin gave his wife a quick kiss, having seen her reasoning, then left to walk with Kyma and talk with him a few minutes.

"They're so close. Now I know why Darman announced to everyone from the start that they were true-mates. He wanted all the men to know that she was spoken for and out of reach in a way they couldn't mistake. He knows about all this?" Aina asked, wondering.

"Yes," Raya assured her, smiling merrily. "He spent last winter with us and we've gotten to all know each other well. Anyway, we have an injunction in Winterhaven against challenges. We women have decided that it's our choice whom we mate with, and the men know better than to protest. So, it wouldn't have done the men here any good to even try to challenge Garth for Ryes," she related, happily. "I hope that one day it would be the standard for all of Tayna!" Aina looked at her strangely, then smiled as she thought on it.

"It sounds like heaven," she told her, smiling. It was the way it should be, she thought! She realized, she needed to know more about these people. Raya laughed and nodded her head in agreement, catching the drift of her surface thoughts and happy their ideas were taking root in new places. There was hope for Tayna.

On the Wings of an Empath

The large vehicle demonstrations were now daily, twice a day. For just being mainly the caravaners, there were a lot of elders to explain things to and demonstrate how these marvelous machines worked. After a while, it became a tedious chore. The encampment grew to almost four thousand people, with two ship captains and some of their crews attending from out of the western ocean. Sabin and most of the other Winterhaveners were almost sick of it all, but they were still vigilant, and took pains to keep everything secure in case of mischief, or theft.

Their booths, selling a few simple products to use in homes, did an astoundingly brisk business each and every day. Simple mops, buckets and brooms and various other brushes went fast. It seemed they appreciated the well-made products. Ardis was not surprised. The bows and arrows were also a hit, once they were demonstrated. The crossbows and compound bows were the most popular items at that booth. Garth ended up gifting Dara a crossbow, so he could have the latest and greatest hunting device, which almost sparked a family feud as Darman was jealous until he was also gifted a fine crossbow, too. Ryes just laughed and nodded her understanding.

Garth spent most of his time meeting with the elders to help strengthen his authority and feeling them out over establishing The Laws. Rinna and Darman were still expressing distress over Ryes having to go out to battle the Snagospin Talents. And Dastin and Metta took full control of the holo display shelter to help others in understanding what they were seeing and why. The message from the recorded holo had a deep impact upon the caravaners as a people. Garth saw a change in them, even if he'd only gotten to know a small group the last few months of the winter. It gave them a sense of worth and purpose beyond simply making money in their trading ventures. They knew, once again, they were the peacekeepers of Tayna and they had to guide others upon this whole world to find a better way to live. The new sense of responsibility made them all walk a little taller.

The ship captains wouldn't have believed any of the recording, except for the presence of the machines. Both were practically itching to get their hands on their own radio devices, too! One, Captain Tees, invited Dr. Cruthers to assign one of his human explorers to voyage with him on The Sandweaver for a year; so to get an idea of what life was like among the islands and the far western continents of Tayna. Ethan agreed with him, but offered to have a team of two ready by next year's spring gather. He assured them that once they had up the weather and communications satellites, they should be able to outfit the ships with transmitters, to know when and where the larger storms would lie. This delighted both captains to no end!

Kyma was deeply interested in both the choppers and the radio equipment. He tried to go up with Axel and Mitt every chance he got. He'd heard the way the Menna Holders described the great flying machine, which had found them deep in the mountains, and had been curious about it ever since. It's why he attended this smaller gather, because Dara had messaged him back that Garth and Sabin were supposed to attend this gather and he personally wanted to meet them. He found not only had they survived the ice storm, but had well prospered since, too. Through time, he'd become not just welcomed by the Winterhaveners, but treated as one of their extensive family. This delighted him as he knew he and his elders would need to review their own laws and practices to see how to better fit into the new Tayna being shaped with its ties to the far past. He was determined that he and his people were not going to be left behind!

"Ryes, I really hate to bother you," Ethan began, seeing she was just putting the cubs down for the night, "but, I need your assistance with an important matter." She looked up to see him and Captain Tees standing in her shelter's doorway. Ethan did appear apologetic.

"Give me just a few minutes," she requested with a smile, then turned back to the cubs as she saw him give her a nod and thumbs up sign. Sayer and Raby were spending the night with a friend she trusted, so she had the young ones all to herself, which she'd been enjoying immensely. Once her younger children were sound asleep, she emerged from their shelter to see the two men seated next to their small fire. Maren stepped over, his eyes full of curiosity, sitting down to join them. He wanted to talk with Ryes for a few moments, but could wait.

"How can I help you?" she asked, sitting down. They'd been out here a week and partied every night. Now she wanted a little quiet time, without the dancing and crowds. And her cubs gave her the perfect excuse, but she knew she couldn't deny Ethan her help. He asked her so rarely!

"We're trying to set up the meeting place for next year, for the team I'm assigning to The Sandweaver. Captain Tees won't be here for the Caravaner's Spring Gather, so we'll have to fly them out to the ship," he told her, "And there's some discrepancy between his maps and our maps. We need to be sure we're talking about the same place. Garth once told me that you could probably locate any point upon Tayna, through one of your Talents. Could you please do this for me?" he requested. He knew he was pushing it, with Garth wanting the knowledge of what Ryes could do being kept discreet, but this was important; not a flight of fancy. She met his eyes, understanding his need.

"On the rocks, in the Yuri," Maren breathed, realizing what he wanted. She nodded her head, seeing it for herself.

"All right," she agreed, then saw her grandfather and Darman approaching. She knew that they and Ethan were usually together in Winterhaven, most times, and never were to be found far apart. Kyma appeared, seeming to be following in their wake.

"What are you agreeing to?" Rowan asked, as he sat down next to the small, comfortable fire. There was still a little nip in the air here at night.

"To view Tayna, as only Ryes can," Maren told him, smiling. "They're having a dispute over some map coordinates." Darman looked surprised, but nodded his head as he realized this wasn't trivial. Tayna was still a large world, no matter how fast their choppers could fly! He took a chair too. Kyma appeared curious about what they were discussing and sat down to see if he could be included.

"You do realize, child, you're not leaving us out of this," Darman warned her, smiling. She nodded her head, having guessed it already.

"All right. Please close your eyes and relax. Everyone join hands and hold on tight, really tight," she teased. She forced herself to relax and closed her eyes, ready as she could be. She established their inner commune, surprising Captain Tees, as he'd never touched another mind directly before. Once she got everyone calmed down and relaxed, she had first Captain Tees bring up his mental image of where he wanted to meet Dr. Cruthers' team, then had Ethan project where he thought it lay upon his map. There was a wide difference between them it seemed.

She called forth her Empath and delved down into the life around them, large and small, then she delved deeper, going down into the very heart of Tayna, herself. There was the great pulse of life of their very world, herself, and she rode this for a few moments, letting each of them know that Tayna had a life of her own and each of them were a part of it. Then she pulled back, as she and Maren thrilled to opening up to the dance of the cosmos. The nearby worlds beckoned, but she pulled away from them. Her interest was in Tayna.

They drifted over their world, clearly seeing the life infusing it. She found the coastline being debated, tracing it as the last light of the sunset was caressing it with its reddish-golden light. She found the signs of ordered life, and located the town of Yventia and the dock where the Sandweaver sat, awaiting her captain. It took him a moment to recognize her, not used to seeing her this way. They swooped in low, gently touching those aboard, making sure all was well. Peace reined as she pulled them back, then fixed this place in her mind, overlaying the map she recalled Ethan projecting and finding its location. This delighted both Ethan and Captain Tees.

Now that this was done, Ethan pressed for her to turn outwards, once more. He wanted to see what actually lay near Tayna, as only she could see it. There was deep humor from Darman and Maren, as Rowan, Kyma and Tees were still awash in the wonder. She gave in and pulled back from Tayna to feel the life pulse of the planets and stars. She lightly touched the spirit of Monrush, at first unsure of her welcome here, but soon understood she was a child of this star and belonged. There were other stars beckoning from afar, but she felt best if she remained close to Tayna. They did a slow check on the planets within Monrush's system, not so much as to see what lay upon them, but to get a general feel if there were any Snagospin ships nearby. Not finding any, relief was shared among them all freely. Still she paused for a few moments, just to take it all in. It was freedom in a very true sense!

The wonder of the cosmos danced before their very souls, teasing them to become a part of the dance. After a few long moments, Ryes finally pulled back, returning to the gather site, gently touching the people and animals around them to help connect them again with this world, then letting them once more back into themselves, letting the link dissolve gently. They opened their eyes, not believing what they'd seen and felt.

"This Talent of yours in unbelievable!" Tees remarked, still astounded; trying to find a way to grasp that for an instant, he'd been a part of the great sun, itself!

"You've given me the greatest gift I could've never imagined," Kyma declared, laughing and ducking his head in a bow in her direction. "Thank you!" She blushed and gave him a bow in return.

"I don't believe I'll have any problems finding that location on my map, now," Ethan assured her, chuckling. He saw she looked tired and could well understand.

"I could never appreciate what Garth meant, when he said he'd found our weapon against the Snagospin Talents, until now," Darman stated.

"But I still don't know how to fight them," Ryes replied, "And how would I ever get the practice?" she added, smiling. "Thankfully it's not a pressing issue right now, with no Snags nearby."

"No, it's not important at this time," Rowan agreed. "We'll leave you to rest. Maren could you please keep an eye on her, until Garth returns?" he requested in English. Maren gave him a nod of his head, not mentioning that Leon was sitting nearby, armed and watching out for her, too. The older men got up to leave and she heard Darman warning Tees and Kyma about headaches after experiencing direct contact with Ryes' Talent, as they left.

"Why does he want you to stay with me?" she asked, puzzled. She was a little cold, but otherwise all right. Maren laughed at hearing her uncertainty, as she was bringing back up her body temperature to normal, again.

"You're becoming hot property around here," he told her in English. "There've been polite inquiries as to whether or not your and Garth's true-mate vows are real, and in case you didn't notice, you've now got at least two bodyguards around all the time. I think Darman's worried that someone will risk damning his soul for all eternity to kidnap you and breed you the next time you come into season," he told her, smiling as he saw the shocked surprise in her eyes, her mouth hanging open as she tried to wrap her mind around such a concept. After several moments of struggling to understand, she smiled with a hard light in her eyes. It gave Maren a chill.

"You could always put it out that I could make any man sterile with my Healing Talent, so it wouldn't do them any good. Not to mention no one could hold me for long. If I can hold Korman in the air, I wonder if I can support myself for a long enough period of time to get out of reach? Like flying myself home?" she asked, wondering. This was not the time, nor place to experiment, she realized. Maren gave her a nod of his head, wondering about it too.

"I hope you'll never have to find out," he told her with a shake of his head. "Now I wonder what the Great Spring Gather's going to be like? At least Captain Tees and his people won't be attending it, so the stories of that Empath flight won't go too far. I'm sure Darman's warning him and Kyma right now to keep the whole thing a secret. I hope they will. And I'm sure Rowan's scolding Ethan in English, at the same time too." He chuckled as he imagined it.

"So, have you, Dotti and the cubs been having fun?" she asked, wanting to change the subject. It was astounding to believe anyone could think like that - that she was no more than a possession to be used at will! It touched her deeply in a way which seared her soul. NEVER, she thought.

"I think we're partied out; even my siblings have had enough and want to get back to school! Sabin's talking about sending back the large chopper and one of the rovers tomorrow. Anyone who wants to, is going to be allowed to go. We're closing down our booths as we've sold all the stuff we brought out to sell, and then some of the things we never imagined we could sell. I think Kerry and Axel have had about as much fun as they can stand, and are going, too," he told her, grinning. He realized she looked like she was still mad. It must bite deep for her to see other men would look upon her as no more than an animal - to be bought and traded! She'd never expected it of the caravaners!

"Well, that's good. Are you and Dotti going to stay, or leave tomorrow?" she asked, seeing his amusement and knowing from where it stemmed. She let her anger go, feeling drained by the whole experience.

"Dotti and my siblings are going back by chopper, but I'm staying. I'm sticking it out with you and the others. If anything major happens back in Winterhaven, I can either have Mitt fly me back, or they can put the person in one of the suspension tubes in the clinic area. With things shaping up the way they've been, I've finally realized I can relax a little and not hang around the clinic all twenty-five hours of the day." She smiled at this, glad to see the change in him. He needed some time for himself!

"With pending events, I can well understand," she assured him. "What did you think of the reaction to the two weddings yesterday?" she questioned.

"That we simple, isolated villagers have a far more worldly view, than those who tramp Tayna's roadways all their lives," he replied with a light dancing in his brown eyes. Mitt came into the firelight, sitting down next to them, smiling.

"I agree. I couldn't believe the attitude! I never saw it in the caravaners, who came to winter with us in Winterhaven," she stated, too astonished to laugh at the whole situation.

"At least Justin and Sana, and Gleds and Sadie all seemed too happy to notice it. And Darman acted as proud as if he'd been the grandfather of both of the brides," Ryes commented, her eyes merry once more.

"I'm sure that set a few of those superstitious creeps back," Mitt concurred with a wicked laugh. "They never expected that their Great Chief to openly support the marriages, much less conduct them."

"Are they going back with Axel, tomorrow?" Ryes suddenly asked, concerned.

"They're riding in the rover, but yes, both couples are heading back to Winterhaven tomorrow," Maren assured her, seeing her relief, "Why?"

"I don't want their happiness spoiled by fools," she told him with a sigh and a smile, glad they'd soon be home and away from such an atmosphere. The other two gave her a nod of their heads, understanding.

"I think Metta's partied out now. He's heading back with Axel. But we've had to move Riss in with Sernn, `cause Ryun and Rebin are having fun and can't get enough from their choices of men, here," Mitt chuckled out, as she told them in a highly amused manner. "We're ruining the Village!"

"Hmmm," Ryes commented with a smile in her eyes at this, "I'm sure Matlowe's way too slow a lifestyle for them, now. It's too bad Arann died in that fire, trying to save Tara and her cubs. He would've been perfect for Ryun." The memories of Tara's laughter filled her mind for a moment, softening her smile.

"But she's settled down with Aril, who I thought I heard was a brother to a man who died tragically," Mitt stated. Ryes chuckled at this nodding her head.

"I heard he's Arann's brother," she affirmed with a nod. Then several people approached them out of the dark. Stepping into the firelight was Ryun and Rebin with two men, the other three didn't know. This put all of them on the alert, as well as Leon, in spite of who was with them.

"Maren, I have to ask you for a big favor," Ryun stated, sitting down next to him. Her face was beaming; filled with happiness. Maren smiled warmly at the woman he'd known all his life, yet barely knew; guessing what it could entail.

"Let me guess, you want me to accelerate your cycle so to begin your season now?" he asked grinning as he looked to her face.

"Yes," she replied breathlessly, her face blossoming into a beautiful smile. He gave her a nod of his head, then closed his eyes and placed a hand lightly upon her stomach. He reached down within her and saw she'd be starting her season in just a couple of weeks, anyway. It was a simple matter to accelerate it a little until she was now ready for mating. He opened his eyes, withdrew his hand and gave her a nod again.

"You weren't too far off from having it naturally, so it wasn't much effort at all," he told her, "Enjoy yourself." She blushed as she jumped up and grabbed her partner's hand, ready to rush off on the instant.

"Wait a moment," Ryes said, standing up, realizing she was derelict in her duties, "I want to make it perfectly clear that everyone understands we do not tolerate any challenges, so if anyone is so bold as to try to issue one here, it'll be handled. The women of Winterhaven decide whom they mate, or don't - not the men!" This got smiles from the two women's faces, while doubt clouded the men's. It was an unheard of standard. But the man with Ryun suddenly smiled as he looked down at her. He realized it wasn't a concern, as she'd already picked him.

"Thanks, Ryes!" Ryun told her, then the couple turned and headed back to the shelter she shared with Rebin.

"It's the way it should be," Rebin agreed as she sat down next to Maren. "I don't know if you could work a miracle here, or not. I'd understand if it lies outside of your abilities, but I wanted to ask if you could help me have one more season?" she requested, "Please, Maren?" There was a look in her eyes which touched his heart. He smiled for her.

"Let me see what I can do," he offered. She gave him a nod of her head, as the man with her crouched down next to them, looking anxious for her. There was caring in his eyes and Ryes knew that it wouldn't matter to him if Maren could do this, or not. Maren closed his eyes again and touched her stomach lightly. There was damage here, and not just from giving birth. He suspected Riss' father might've been the same as his own from this. He curbed his anger, knowing it did him little good, as he concentrated upon the repair process. Suddenly, he felt a flood of energy as he realized Ryes had joined him, extending her Healing Talent and power to help him. Together, they worked quickly to heal her whole body, as they had for their own elders, then he accelerated her cycle so her season would be at the optimum time for mating. They withdrew, letting the linkage dissolve.

"How does that feel?" he teased as he removed his hand. She smiled strangely, puzzled.

"I haven't felt like this in years!" she declared, throwing her arms about him and giving him a kiss. She released him to stand and wrap her arms about Ryes, kissing her too. "I can't thank you both enough!" Her joy was bright in her eyes.

"My name's Missa and I thank you, too," the man said, standing up and offering his hand to Maren first, then Ryes. They each crossed his palm with their own, smiling. This one seemed another good choice.

"It was no trouble," Maren assured him, giving him a nod of his head. The happy couple quickly rushed off. His smile melted quickly down into a glower. The storm clouds gathered in his eyes, as he struggled with his anger.

"Let it go, Maren," Ryes ordered, knowing what was in his heart. She saw Leon relax, now that the strangers were gone.

"He had to be the one to have done that to her!" he practically growled out, surprising Mitt. Ryes lightly touched his shoulder, realizing she was almost gun shy after their last Vision, then stood and began to give his shoulders a massage, trying to get him to relax. His muscles were tight and in knots, so she applied some of her Healing Talent as she tried to work his stained muscles. He didn't object but she didn't know if it was due to her ministrations helping him, or he was too focused upon his ire.

"It was in the past. He's getting old and weak. I don't think he'll be able to get to anyone, anymore," she tried to assure him. He pulled away, standing up and facing her, still angry.

"He can still be cruel. He's stronger than most women and I'm sure WILL continue maiming anyone he can. The men of Matlowe are not used to standing against Korman!"

"What do you want us to do? Cage him and put him on display? It wouldn't truly satisfy what you think, you need," she scolded, meeting his eyes. "Give it up, Maren. It's not worth the cost of your soul." He squeezed his eyes shut as he realized what Ryes was saying; knowing she was right. Mitt was there at his shoulder nodding her agreement.

"Maren, you only hurt yourself with this anger. You deserve so much more! Let it go," she pleaded, hoping to reach him, too.

"I'll try," he whispered in a husky voice. "I think it's time for bed." He gave both Ryes and Mitt a kiss, then headed back to Dotti, forgetting his promise to Rowan to stay with his cousin. He knew he needed Dotti to get through this and leave it behind again.

"He's still as fixated upon his father, as much as his father's upon you," Mitt observed, as Ryes sat down again. She did too. "I'll stay with you," she offered, smiling.

"No, you don't have to," she assured her. But, Mitt shifted her chair closer, with a serious look in her eyes.

"I truly wanted to talk with you about something," she said, speaking in a lower voice, hoping it didn't carry to Leon, right now.

"What's the matter?" Ryes asked, worried now as she met her eyes.

"I was talking with Garth after our fishing trip, and he was wondering if I didn't have a second, dormant Talent, or one so subtle I wasn't aware of it," she began, suddenly feeling nervous. "It'd explain a lot, like how I'm always able to drop in with you and Maren, no matter what you're doing at the time." Ryes met her eyes, suddenly feeling it could be the answer. Dotti and Bethy could also tap in, but they used her own Talent when they did it. Mitt's contact was usually much stronger and she hadn't tapped into her Talent in a long time!

"He might be right! Do you want me to check?" she asked, wondering if she had the energy for it tonight. It'd been a very busy evening, so far!

"You'd better!" she replied with a merry laugh, "It's been driving me nuts since last week!"

"All right. Just relax and we'll see," Ryes told her, closing her eyes and readying herself. She'd never thought to check on the others, who she lived around every day! She felt Mitt's easy contact, so called up her Catalyst Talent and delved into Mitt's being, as she'd done once before. She realized as soon as she called up her Catalyst abilities that it was screaming to her that Mitt did, indeed, have a second Talent. It was only a matter of finding it now.

Mitt tried to remain calm, sensing the sudden excitement in Ryes, and felt she could guess what it meant. But it was so hard to be still, when she began her deep probing. Something very deep inside protested this intrusion and only wanted her gone. But Mitt held back, denying her natural reaction. She needed this opened up within her - now. She suddenly recalled what Raya had looked like as she huddled in the corner of the kitchen and she vowed this wasn't going to happen to her! But this in-depth probing was almost torture!

Ryes finally found Mitt's second Talent. It was already seeping out, as it diffused into Mitt's aura. But she sensed it was almost ready to fully open soon. She circled it warily seeing it pulse with power, drawing her. It wasn't as strong as her Inner Sight Talent, but knew it wasn't weak either! She felt Mitt was barely tolerating this, so she quickly extended herself, releasing the pent up energy fully and immediately backing away, letting it fill Mitt's being.

"Fight it, Mitt. Make it yours!" she encouraged her, assuring her at the same time that she was still here for her. But in the end, this was still Mitt's fight, and from their experience from the last one, she knew it too.

Mitt realized she was engulfed in a new torrent of power. She knew she wasn't going to let anything rule her, most especially her own Talents! Her inner core of steel rose up and she fought the wild torrent until it obeyed her will. Ryes' presence helped to anchor her through the contest and she turned to her from within, sending her, her gratitude and joy. They both opened their eyes at the same time, smiling.

"You did it!" Ryes rejoiced, "and Garth was right, you do have a second Talent," she added, wondering if he had a Talent too?

"He sure was, but it feels strange. What kind of Talent is it? It isn't like my Inner Sight," Mitt stated, puzzled.

"Let me check," Ryes requested. She gave her a nod of her head, so she closed her eyes and called up Catalyst again. After a few moments, she withdrew, her eyes mirroring shock, then she smiled knowingly.

"I should've guessed; you have Mind Voice," she scolded, grinning. "It's an old Talent which used to be very common on Kahmarr. Perhaps Raya could give you some pointers," she suggested. Mitt gave out a yell then jumped up and grabbed Ryes, pulling her to her feet. She danced with her around the fire, merrily. Leon grinned at the unexpected mirth, then saw two men approaching the campfire, coming to the alert on the instant. But it turned out to be his leader and Sabin. He gave him a nod as they passed, getting a nod and thanks in return from Garth.

"If you wanted to party, there's still dancing going on back at the central fire," Garth teased. His sister turned, then threw herself at him, covering him with kisses as he laughed.

"I have another Talent! You were right! I've got to go tell Minn!" she declared, then turned back to give Ryes kisses too, as she laughed happily for her. She ran off, heading back for her own shelter to spread the news.

"Rowan told me what you did for Captain Tees and Ethan. If it had been anyone but Ethan, I would've never allowed it," Garth scolded. "I thought he said Maren was going to be with you?" he questioned, not seeing him around.

"He was, until just a few minutes ago. I sent him off to bed," she told him. Garth looked down at her, puzzled. So she smiled and admitted, "All right, I got into an argument with him and gave him a headache. He left because he realized he needed Dotti's counseling and love, and I think forgot all about staying with me. I'll apologize to him tomorrow, when he's feeling better. Mitt stayed with me, at least." Garth sighed and nodded his head to Sabin, who then turned to leave. Sabin thought to have a quick talk with Maren, before he went to bed.

"You're cold," Garth scolded, wrapping his arms about her. She rested her head against his chest and sighed. She started to bring back her Healing Talent to warm herself back to normal, once more. She was trying to remember to do that, so as not to worry the others around her.

"I think I'm at my limit for tonight. After taking Ethan and the elders out on a flight over Tayna, I helped Maren repair and heal Rebin. That's what set him off. He realized his father was probably the one to inflict the damage. He wasn't happy with what I told him, but he knows that I'm right. Then after all that, I helped Mitt find her second Talent," she told him, in a low voice, then looked up to meet his honey-colored eyes. By the firelight, they held a strange glow, giving her a shiver up her spine.

"Let's go to bed," he suggested, smiling. He could finally relax, now that he was with her. He'd been hearing about all kinds of offers raised for Ryes, but kept assuring everyone that not only was she not for sale, but was his true-mate. He realized he'd never give her over to any other man's keeping, even if they hadn't been true-mates!

"What's the matter?" she questioned, realizing an inner fire was burning within him tonight. It reminded her of what he was like when Korman challenged him in Hailys, what seemed so long ago.

"Nothing now," he assured her as he scooped her up in his arms and went into their shelter, sealing the doorway behind them.

"This seems very familiar," she teased him, then his lips passionately sought hers, as he carried her to their bed.

New Talents

"Ryes! Come quick!" Kort demanded, panic on his face and in his eyes. He was breathing hard from running and finally found her. She was talking with Maren as she nursed her cubs, just outside her own shelter. They looked up, surprised to see the desperation upon his face.

"What's the matter?" Maren asked, standing up.

"Nalin," he panted out, "She's sitting in a corner screaming. She can't tell us what's wrong, but Nahees thinks it's a Talent awakening in her."

"Sayer!" Ryes called out. She and Raby appeared from within their shelter, surprise was written in their eyes at the tone of her voice. Seeing Kort and the way he was, they knew there was a problem. "It's an emergency," she explained as she handed over Shyla to Raby. "They're finished for the most part, with only Gareth left to feed." She quickly buttoned up her shirt and found her sandals. "I'll be back soon," she promised, then she and Maren rushed off, following Kort back to his van. Leon waved them through their checkpoint as they ran full out, hoping they could reach her in time. Monty joined them, ready to help watch out for Ryes.

There was an uneasy, large crowd gathered outside his van, with everyone appearing tense. Darman comforting the distress, as well as he could. The relief in his eyes at seeing them, pulled at Ryes' heart. He looked desperate! Ryes recognized two of the Talents who'd been in on their Healing session last week, giving them a nod of her head as she caught her breath. Another two men she didn't know practically ran out of the van appearing mad and panicked at the same time. Nahees appeared in the doorway in their wake appearing panicked, then she saw Ryes and Maren were ready to go inside, and relief lit up her eyes.

"Thank you," she breathed as she went back in and gave them room to join her. As Ryes stepped up to go in, there was pain-filled screaming coming from within. She gave Nahees a nod as she rushed inside; Maren quickly on her heels. Monty stayed outside, but alert to the strangers around him. Darman gave him a nod of understanding.

"NO! NO!" They heard Nalin screaming at the top of her voice. They found her crouched in a corner, like an injured animal. Both Ryes and Maren were quickly upon their knees, next to her with their eyes closed as they fully extended their Talents to the stricken child. But the wild, coursing energy running loose within Nalin almost immediately knocked Maren back out. His stubborn streak awoke and he fought his way to the inner essence they knew as Nalin.

"Nalin, you must fight this and make your Talent obey you!" Ryes sent through, letting her know they were here to support her. Nalin was Sayer's age, but was such a quiet child, she feared for her in this battle. There was so much power here. Could she make it bend to her will? She kept these dire fears from her thoughts, as she wanted to try to empower this precious child.

"Her Talent's as strong as mine, but this is very different," Maren sent to Ryes, then let Nalin know he was here for her, too. "Fight Nalin!" he urged, "Think of it as making a bothersome boy leave you alone." Her terror was clear in their linkage, he wondered if she could hear them at all, through it?

"What do I do?" she whimpered out, suddenly realizing she could "speak" back to these two people, whom she trusted and loved. They'd know what she needed to do!

"What do you do when you little nephew's bothering you?" Maren returned, "Put this Talent of yours in its place! It's supposed to obey you, but you have to make it listen! You're its boss!"

"Feel free to slap it down and tell it to mind you," Ryes prompted, humor in her tone as she realized Maren's approach was right. With their encouragement, Nalin turned and did just that, thinking of it as a bothersome little nephew she could slap down, without getting into trouble. She conquered her Talent, bending it to her will very quickly.

"What kind of Talent do I have?" she asked, after she triumphed, feeling more herself again. She was still breathing hard, but was calming down as she realized she was safe now. Her Talent was under her own control.

"Can you feel it?" Maren asked, surprise in his mental tone, "Something with water." He felt it largely through Ryes' Catalyst Talent, and amazed she hadn't beat him to it.

"A Water Shaper!" Ryes declared, realizing it too. "It's an older Talent and I would think, very rare. You can shape water by your will alone," she explained, happy with this outcome. At least Nalin was still sane, whole and in control now!

"What do you mean?" Nalin pressed, not understanding.

"Try to keep the rain off of you, the next time it rains. You could also try practicing making shapes out of the waters of the creek, but you should be careful. Your Talent's strong and you wouldn't want to accidently cause a flood, a drought, or kill off all the fish because you're playing with the water they need to live in and breathe. I'll talk with your sister, Kort and Darman about it," Ryes promised. They let the link dissolve, opening their eyes with smiles of relief all around. Maren helped Nalin to her feet as Ryes stood and turned to face two caravaners she'd known since she was very small.

"Nalin's a Water Shaper," she told Nahees and Kort with a smile. "She's very strong. Just try not to let her get carried away with it, so as to cause a flood, or drought," she warned them. There were tears of joy as the three of them were grabbed and hugged, kissed and fussed over by them both. Darman was relieved it came out well, stepping up to them as they emerged from the van.

"Gurri tried to help her, but said he wasn't strong enough," Darman explained, indicating a starman standing beside him.

"Her Talent's very strong," Maren admitted. "It almost knocked me out of the link, but I'm too stubborn." Gurri looked at the two of them, curiosity in his eyes.

"What's your Talent?" he demanded, practically sneering down at him, as if he felt they were beneath him for an unknown reason. He eyes were narrowed as he looked them up and down.

"Healing," Maren returned, not sure what to think of his rude question. Ryes remained silent, just nodding agreement with Maren. She knew Garth didn't want her to discuss what she could do, much less how many Talents she seemed to have. She saw Monty looking at her puzzled for a moment, then his eyes reflected his understanding, as he nodded his head as well. Darman chuckled and stepped forward before Gurri took her silence as an insult.

"Come, come," he said, "it's almost lunch time. You can all discuss your Talents after we eat," he urged. There were six Talents of the caravaners gathered around them and the anger seemed to almost hang in the air over them. This odd behavior puzzled Ryes. She realized she didn't know any of these people, so thought they might be out of the south, by their mode of dress.

"What's your Talent?" Gurri demanded, meeting Ryes' eyes. She shrugged and turned away, as if he wasn't important.

"There're other times to discuss something like this," Maren countered, seeing the sudden anger around them. He couldn't understand what their problem was? Ryes had the right to not say anything, after all. "Let's go get something to eat," he suggested.

"Gurri, that sounds good to me," Tova urged, stepping over to his side. He turned to her, not wanting to back down, but seeing in her eyes that she wasn't granting him a choice in the matter. "We should drink to the child's rescue," she reminded him with a smile. Rinna showed up with several other women and he immediately backed down, and turned to give Tova a nod of his head. They moved over to the central fire and the food being served there. Rinna gave Tova a nod of approval. She turned to follow her husband and the rest of his friends fell in behind her.

"Are all your Talents like these ones?" Ryes asked Darman in a low voice after they ate a light meal. "I never knew people could be so touchy about Talents and treat others in such a horrible manner."

"Actually, very few," he chuckled as he gestured to the others standing behind him. "There're others who have kinder hearts and stronger Talents, with good sense to back them." One of the men stepped forward and offered her his hand, palm up, claws retracted. She crossed his palm with her own, meeting his eyes. Yes, this one looked as if he had a clear conscience. She felt him bringing his Talent up, wanting to speak with her privately within. She responded, wondering what he wanted.

"I apologize for your unjust treatment here," he offered her.

"Thank you, but I truly didn't understand why they'd be so upset because I didn't want to tell them aloud about my Talents. My husband bid me quite on the subject," she replied.

"They're even more petty than their abilities," he sent with humor, "Don't worry about Nalin's training. I'll see to it, myself," he assured her. He opened himself up to her, so she could see his heart and mind. She responded in kind, feeling it was his due. Then they both released the linkage, gently.

"You're very powerful," he told her aloud. "My name's Shams and you can be sure that Nalin will be trained to use her Talent in an honorable fashion."

"Thank you, I appreciate your assurances. My name's Ryes," she replied, smiling, "Nice to finally meet you, grandson of Darman and Rinna." He chuckled at this. Then she stepped back, as Garth stepped over to her side. She could almost feel the tension in his body as he did. She glanced up to him, puzzled. She hadn't known when he arrived on the scene, but was glad to see him here, now. The other caravan elders had also appeared, as well as Mitt, and Dastin, who were now standing near her, too. She smiled.

"With this surprise blossoming of a new Talent, perhaps you could use your Catalyst abilities to check all the other caravaner children here – to be sure they'll have no problems later?" Garth suggested, looking down at his wife as he playfully tugged on one of her red braids. She shook her head and laughed lightly at his display.

"Ryes, I believe Garth's correct in that we do require your services as a Catalyst. Our Catalyst is currently on another continent, helping out over there. Could I ask you to check our older cubs, to see if any others might have a Talent ready to bloom?" Darman asked, smiling to see the jealously in Garth's eyes. She looked to him and smiled warmly.

"Of course, Grandfather, I'll be happy to help," she offered, "just have them come by our main fire circle and I'll do the best I can. I'd better get back. Got some little ones to check on," she reminded him. He chuckled at this, giving her a nod of his head.

"I'll start sending them over, soon," he warned her. She nodded her head to this, gave Garth a quick kiss, then trotted back for their encampment with Monty on her heels. Maren stood looking at this Shams, wondering what he said to Ryes while they merely crossed palms. It seemed to take longer than the gesture warranted. He decided to get it directly out of his cousin, so turned for their shelters, with Mitt following, too.

Ryes returned to her shelter and saw Sayer, Raby and Katas with all eight of her and Ardis' cubs sleeping on the blanket, on the ground inside an outdoors cub pen.

"They wore each other out," Raby commented, smiling. "Is everything all right?" she added, having worried about the nature of the emergency. Quite a few people had run off after she did, to help out.

"Nalin will be fine. It turned out her Talent awoke and she's a Water Shaper. Now, I'm going to have to check everyone, to see if they have a Talent, or not. And I'm starting with the three of you," she warned them, smiling; having made up her mind on her way back.

"I don't have a Talent," Sayer assured her, shaking her head at such a notion, "I'm sure I would've felt something by now."

"Ryes said my second Talent was just about to awaken, when she found it last night," Mitt scolded, with a frown. "I didn't know I had a second one, either."

"Mitt, could you get Sernn? I want to check him, too," Ryes urged. She sat down and closed her eyes. "All right, first I want to check you, Raby," she said, reaching out her hand.

Raby reluctantly put her hand in Ryes' and closed her eyes, as she'd seen Maren and Mitt do, whenever they were in commune with her. There was a wash of charged emotions then a presence which she knew was Ryes. She opened herself up to her, feeling her love for her directly, for the first time in her life. Tears were in her eyes as happiness rang through her heart. Ryes very gently delved into Raby's being, finding no core of power within. Still it was such wonderful time with their two minds and hearts joined in happiness. She gently released her. Katas grabbed her hand next, wanting to see if she could possibly have a real Talent of her own. Ryes greeted her with joy, feeling her hopeful anticipation.

"So, do you have one?" Mitt asked Raby. She had such a joyful smile, which lit up her eyes.

"No," she sighed out, "but, Mom truly loves me," she replied smiling, knowing nothing could ever diminish that love. Mitt laughed in agreement, nodding her head.

"Yes, she does love and care for you," she agreed, recalling she knew Ryes loved her, too. She forgot that so many others said they loved you, but you could never know for sure, unless you could link up in an inner commune. With Ryes, her brother and Maren, there was no doubt in her mind of their love for her. "I'd better go find Sernn," she said, trotting off.

"What's going on?" Ardis asked, seeing Ryes and Katas sitting, holding hands with their eyes closed.

"Ryes needs to check everyone for a Talent, now," Sayer told her. Katas opened her eyes, smiling with happiness.

"Sayer, you're next," she told her, then saw Ardis standing nearby. "I don't have a Talent, either, but now I know how much you truly do love me, Mom," she said. Ardis knelt and wrapped her arms about her adopted daughter, laughing. Sayer took the chair on the other side of Ryes and closed her eyes, taking her hand as she smiled.

"Of course I love you!" she assured her, smiling as she kissed her. "How could you ever think differently?"

"It's just nice to truly know it," she replied, kissing her back.

"Why don't you two girls go ahead and take a break from the micro monsters, and I'll take over for a while?" she suggested. "I'll tell Sayer she just has to catch up to you."

"Thanks, Aunt Ardis," Raby said.

"Thanks, Mom," Katas added. The two of them first went into Ryes and Garth's shelter to get Raby's belt pouch, then hurried to her own, for Katas'. Ardis sighed as she sat watching Ryes and Sayer. Maren joined her, sitting down on the blanket, which overflowed the enclosure's space.

"I'm sure Sabin will tell you about it later, but it's been an interesting day," he commented, doing a quick, health check on all the infants before him, with his eyes open.

"What?" she demanded, frowning as she wondered what had happened now?

"Nalin's Talent awoke. The caravaner Talents Darman had couldn't help her. Between Ryes and I, we managed to reach her and got her goaded into controlling her Talent. Oh, my. Sayer!" he said, then reached over, calling up his Talent fully. Sayer had a Talent and Ryes found it.

"Fight it, Sayer! Show it who's boss!" Ryes told her, feeling Maren drop in on them, too.

"Geeze, Sayer, you could take this Talent with one arm tied behind your back," Maren teased her, encouraging her. She was uncertain, then seemed to realize they were right. She turned her will upon this wash of power within and wrestled it until she could make it obey her will.

"I have a Talent!" she declared to the both of them, very pleased with herself.

"Yes you do," both Maren and Ryes sent in agreement, at the same time. Humor colored their inner commune, then Ryes dissolved the link.

"I have a Talent!" she declared to Ardis. Mitt joined them with Sernn, hearing her and laughed with her in joy.

"Good for you! What Talent do you have?" she asked.

"Mind Voice," Ryes said, her eyes now open as she smiled. "I'll ask Raya if she'd mind helping with her training. Raya tells me I'm too strong, when I try to use my Mind Voice Talent."

"I never considered you too strong," Maren protested. "Sayer, when you need to practice, use your mother, myself, or Sabin. We wouldn't want you to hurt anyone else, accidently," he warned. She nodded her head sagely.

"Hey! What about me?" Mitt demanded, smiling, "I think I'm perfectly capable of handling it, too."

"All right. You can practice with your Aunt Mitt, too," he added. "You have no idea what you're getting yourself into. I remember the first few days after Raya's Talent awoke!"

"Your turn, Sernn," Ryes urged, knowing better than to interfere with any argument Mitt and Maren were having. Sernn stepped over to her, reluctantly. "Come on, you know I don't bite," she teased, a warm smile lighting up her green eyes.

"I know, Aunt Ryes, but what if I don't have one?" he questioned.

"Then you'll be the way you're meant to be," she replied, smiling gently, "No matter how it comes out. You are the sum of your heart, mind and soul; a Talent's only an added gift." He knelt down beside her and closed his eyes. Mitt couldn't resist, so she joined them and soon saw Ryes' search turned up nothing. Mitt poured her love and caring out for Sernn, and found him responding in kind. Ryes left them time for each other, understanding both their needs. Mitt was still struggling to learn her new skills, so this was also practice for her at the same time.

"While your Catalyst Talent is awakened, why not check on your own cubs?" Maren pressed, so only the two of them heard him, as he'd taken her hand to chat privately. He was good at taping her Mind Voice. He felt her shock at his suggestion and smiled to himself. "I don't mean to activate any Talents they might have, I mean just to sense whether or not they have any," he pressed. Mitt and Sernn dropped out of the link, sensing they were discussing something between them.

"You're right. That way I'll know to be alert for when they're older," she finally agreed. She opened her eyes, keeping her Talent fully awakened and looked at the cubs on the blanket before her. There were spheres of power in each and every single one of them, even Ardis' two, and Torr's son! She was shocked.

"See, Rhin's?" Maren prompted, "There's a diffusion throughout his being, but the core Talent is still intact. He's going to be a handful when that awakes," Maren commented. She realized he was right. What they tapped was only a mere leakage of his true Talent! Ryes closed her eyes, once more.

"Garth's never going to believe this! All our cubs and Sabin's and Torr's? I wonder if your daughter will be born with your Talent, too?"

"Maybe this is what happens with strong Talents? That they're passed down to the children, becoming more diffuse through time. From seeing your cubs and now knowing Mitt has two strong Talents, perhaps you'd best check Garth, himself? For all your cubs to carry Talent, he must carry one, too," he asserted. He wondered about his daughter now. Could she carry a Talent, as well?

"Maren, you're not just a Healer," Ryes suddenly told him, excited. "You do have Visionary and Booster, too! I can see they're already awake. I haven't truly 'looked' at you with my Catalyst Talent active, since I awakened your Healing. No wonder we keep having those Visions!" she teased.

"Me? A Booster?" he asked, feeling it as Ryes fed what she felt directly to him. He was amazed. The Visionary he more than half expected. "Could that be why I'm such a strong Healer?"

"No. That's a deep power all in itself. Your Booster power is weaker than your Healing Talent. But it may be why you can help teach and direct other Healers, like you did for Aina," she suggested.

"You'd better get ready. Darman will be sending the cubs over for you to check out, soon," he suddenly warned, wanting time to think on all this. He had three Talents! It was amazing and he suddenly didn't know if he felt like shouting it out, or just mulling it over quietly. He now wished Dotti hadn't gone back home early this morning.

By the end of the day, Ryes found herself stumbling back to her shelter. All afternoon and evening, she had her Catalyst Talent up and checked what seemed to be an endless number of teenaged cubs and young adults. From all these people, she found a dozen new Talents. Most were Empaths and Healers, but one was actually a Visionary. Shams, and the other Talents Darman trusted, were there to take possession of the new Talents, to get them started upon their training. As she slowly made her way to her own shelter, a pair of strong arms wrapped around her, helping to steady her feet. She was starting to shiver from the cold of over-doing things and appreciated the warmth, until she realized it was Shams.

"I'll manage, thank you," she assured him in a low voice. She tried to pull away from him, but almost fell as she stumbled. He steadied her again.

"It's no trouble," he asserted with a smile. He worried about her with a chill in her limbs. It wasn't that cold outside tonight! In a few minutes they arrived back at her small fire. She sat down near it, trying to warm her hands. "What's with your chill? Are you coming down with something?" he asked, as he sat in a chair beside her. She puzzled him, being so very powerful, yet so very gentle with others. He had no qualms trusting her with the younger cubs today.

"It only happens when I overdo things," she replied, smiling. "I have a Healing Talent, nowhere as strong as my cousin's, but I'd know it if I were coming down with an illness," she assured him, realizing she was too tired to call it up effectively to return her body to normal right now. Shams saw one of the humans sitting upon a rock, with his back to one of the strange tents they used, across from them. She paid him no attention as she poured out two mugs of hot tea, from a pot near the fire. "I don't know how this will taste. Who knows how long it's been sitting here," she said, offering him one of the mugs.

"Thank you," he replied, taking it from her hand. "Darman says he's known you, almost all your life. He's my grandfather and he told me that if you hadn't found Garth, he would've pushed for you to accept me." Ryes' eyes met his as she blushed. She remembered it had been Darman's plan.

"You'd make a good second choice," she finally commented with a smile, then sipped her tea as she thought on it. He wasn't bad, but he just wasn't Garth! Shams chuckled at this, nodding his head. He knew they'd taken true-mate vows, so knew he had no chance now, but it satisfied his ego to think she might've chosen him, if chances had worked out differently. He sipped his tea, realizing, for a pot that had been sitting about, it was surprisingly good.

"This is good!" he told her, wondering what it would've tasted like fresh?

"Maren loves my tea, too," she remarked, smiling. "But, it's much better when it's newly made."

"Speaking of Maren, where is he?" Garth asked, striding up behind them. They looked just a little too cozy to his eyes. Then he saw the exhaustion in Ryes' eyes and he realized she was practically asleep in her chair. She smiled at seeing him, happiness in her eyes for him. He sighed and relaxed.

"Since Dotti's gone on home, he's in with the cubs, sleeping I'm sure. He was helping me today and I think I wore him out," she explained as Garth poured himself some tea and sat in a chair on the other side of his wife. He smiled.

"You're not supposed to abuse him, you know," he teased as she chuckled in response.

"I know. But, he keeps thinking he can hold out as long as I can! Sayer was trying to stay up to tell you she has a Talent, too. It took hours to get her calmed down. Raya spent some time with her, earlier, to get her acquainted with the do's and don'ts," she told him.

"She's a Mind Voice?" he questioned, impressed. Ryes nodded her head. "How did it go today?"

"We found one Visionary, seven Healers and four Empaths," Shams informed him, proud of these discoveries. It was interesting that children he expected to hold Talents didn't, yet ones he never suspected, did. Nalin had been the biggest surprise of all, today! An ancient Talent, practically unheard of anywhere in the world.

"And I found that Maren has three Talents, not just the one," Ryes piped in, grinning.

"Ah, multi-talented, just like you," he replied. "Sounds like you were both busy today. Anything else?"

"I'd give it at least a few days before we see Ryun, or Rebin. I forgot to tell you that Maren helped things along, so they could come into season and mate, while we're here. Who would've known?" she asked, "Raya left some food and a pot of tea outside their shelter."

"Well, Rebin's last son, Riss, is a Visionary. If you found so many Talents among the children today, maybe she'll have another Visionary?" he teased, sipping his tea.

"We've tried breeding for Talents for years; it just doesn't work," Shams stated with a heavy sigh. "None of the cubs I fathered seem to have any Talent, at all. Of course, they're far too young to tell, but it's frustrating."

"It's not too young to tell," Ryes assured him, smiling. "I could tell if they carry Talent, without awakening it. The only one of our cubs we KNEW had Talent from the minute he was born was Rhin."

"You can tell?" he asked, wanting to be certain.

"Yes, I can," she replied, meeting his eyes. He bowed his head to her, then stood up.

"I'd better get back to my van. I'll see you tomorrow, Ryes," he promised with a smile. She gave him a nod of her head as he handed back the mug, then turned and quickly left.

"So, how many of our cubs carry Talent?" Garth asked, fighting his jealously, once more. Something about Shams got to him!

"All of them," she replied, smiling brightly, "as well as Sabin and Ardis' cubs, and little Tobin, too. Raya's son doesn't have any, but her daughter does." She leaned forward to put down hers and Shams' mugs when Garth leaned over to nuzzle her neck. It sent chills up her spine in pure delight.

"All of our cubs?" he pressed, still not quite believing it.

"Yes, all of them. We're truly going to have our hands full when they get older. By the way, Maren thinks that if all of our cubs have Talent, and Mitt has two Talents, then you probably have a Talent, too. So, we're just going to have to delve within to see," she teased as she jumped out of her chair to sit in his lap. He wrapped his arms about her with a laugh, spilling the last of his tea. He set the mug down on the ground.

"Later. You look far too tired tonight and I know tomorrow's going to be even worse," he told her, not sure if he wanted to know it now. She gave him a long kiss, then smiled into his eyes.

"Oh, I'll show you that I may be tired in some ways, but not others," she teased, then laughed as he stood, scooping her up in his arms.

"I'll hold you to that one!" he assured her, then waved to Quinn before carrying his wife inside.

Shams watched them from the shadows, making sure the human on guard didn't see him. He felt a little jealous of Garth, still. So, all their cubs held Talent? He wondered if his grandfather knew of it, or not? He'd have to talk with him about it tomorrow.

Garth awoke, feeling very different this morning. He lay upon their bed, with Ryes still asleep beside him, thinking about last night. Somehow the whole world felt different. Then he saw Maren's face at their door slit, looking in to see if they were up yet, and smiled for him.

"With the way you two were going at it last night, it's a wonder that anyone gets any sleep around here," he teased in a low voice.

"Ryes found my Talents last night, right in the middle of our free-mating. I've never felt anything so intense before - ever!" he admitted, blushing.

"What timing! As the humans would say it, 'kinky,'" he returned with a grin.

"Oh yeah, definitely kinky," he agreed.

"So, what are your Talents?" Maren pressed, wondering.

"Would you believe Flame Shaper? And she said there was also a weak Empath Talent." He sighed, still trying to feel comfortable with the thought of having Talents of his own!

"Sounds interesting. Just be careful when you start playing around with matches," he advised, wondering how strong Garth's Talent was? And why were all these old forgotten ones coming out, now?

"She should be up soon, so go ahead and hit the showers. I'll listen for the horde awakening," he assured him. Maren nodded his head, having already sent Sayer and Raby out to do the same.

"See you at breakfast," he told him, then left, sealing the door slit once more, letting him have a few more moments of privacy.

Garth lay and thought on what Maren said. He'd need time to practice his Talents. He didn't want to get caught off-guard, when he might need them sometime. Ryes operated more on an instinctive level with her Talents, but there were times when she would consciously try to practice and direct them, to hone them. With planning and building Winterhaven, they'd been too busy for her to get in as much practice as she probably needed. The only one who actually was getting regular practice was Maren! When they got back, he'd make sure they scheduled in weekly practice times, so they could all hone their skills. It was what was best for everyone and Winterhaven itself!

Consequences

"Why are you looking so grumpy this morning, Gurri?" Luia asked as he finally emerged from his van to join them at breakfast. She grinned at the sour look he cast her way. "Truly, what's the problem?" she pressed, using Mind Voice. She felt a painful barb attack as he shut her out, so relented. She'd felt his minor attacks before, but this one was meant in earnest. She warned her brother, Lall, to be careful when using his Talent.

"I know you're bored, but I'm telling you to leave it be," Tova lightly scolded her husband. Their son Thon ran over to her, seeing his father's ill mood.

"Mom, can I go play?" he begged, as he tugged on her hand to catch her attention for a moment. She smiled down at him and gave him a nod.

"Only for a little while," she told him, as a joyous smile lit up his face. His face was so like Gurri's but she saw happiness there instead of a bitter dislike for the world around him, like his father. "I want you back by lunch." He nodded and ran off.

"You spoil him," Gurri sourly commented as he grabbed a cup of still-warm tea. Tova ignored him, having had that argument with him before. She saw he was hoarding a bad mood like a precious treasure.

"So, what're we doing today? Darman, Rinna and Cassin are keeping us on a tight leash this year," Aminda commented as he put his breakfast bowl into the wash bucket. He didn't want to say it, but he was bored too.

"Did you hear them calling us weak, yesterday? Just because we couldn't reach that girl to get her to control her Talent!" Aminda prompted, sneering with disgust.

"That prissy, little, goodie Catalyst was truly annoying me. When I asked her what her Talent was, she just snubbed me; it still makes me mad," he growled out, clearly irritated. "I want to put her in her place in front of everyone. So she rides in a big fancy machine instead of a van. She needs to be shown who's more important here. This is our gather, not hers!"

"Gurri, leave her be," Nottin tried to warn him as he sat down next to Kiah, his wife. He saw Tova shake her head as she met his eyes. Gurri glared at him next, so he subsided, taking the hint that she had probably warned him off last evening.

"She's not someone you want to take on," Tova finally voiced, but Gurri made a move as if to slap her and she flinched, stepping back, her ire plain in her eyes as theirs met. She saw his naked fury, but he was the first to break eye contact.

"You set it up and we'll take her down together," Aminda assured him with a nod. Gurri returned his nod, then turned to get his breakfast.

"Watch them," Maren said in a low voice, in English, warning Ryes as they passed a small knot of the southern caravaners. They easily stood out by the odd and colorful clothes they wore. Leon appeared surprised, but then noted the looks cast their way by them. Ryes was already alert; not understanding why Gurri was so belligerent and seemed focused upon her for his ire. Still, they arrived at Darman and Rinna's van and some relative safety. Monty appeared relieved. They'd been invited to lunch today as a small thank you for helping open up the Talents of the caravaner cubs yesterday.

"Come along," Darman invited them all to an open air kitchen, set up near his own van. Rinna greeted Ryes and Maren with kisses. Nalin came running up, trailed by Nahees, Aravan and Nils. She quickly wrapped her arms around Maren, giving him a kiss on his cheek, while she laughed, then let him go to kiss Ryes, too.

"Thank you for saving me!" she told them, as she let Ryes go amid laughter from the gathering. She grabbed a cup of water off a nearby table, which she held up to show them. "See what I can do?" she invited, then closed her eyes and a small finger of water hesitantly rose up from the still surface to dance lazily about for a few moments. Ryes' eyes lit up in merriment as she felt a tug within, from what she just recognized as her own Water Shaper Talent. She knew she needed to practice with it now too! She and the other caravaners around them clapped their hands for her triumph. She opened her eyes, grinning from ear to ear with pride.

"You're starting out wonderfully!" Ryes assured her, giving her a quick hug and sloshing the water.

"You've got a long road ahead of you, Nalin, but I'm sure you'll make it, with people like Maren and Ryes to teach you," Rinna told her, smiling grandly. Nahees pulled Nalin back to allow the other new Talents to come up and give Ryes and Maren their thanks too.

This went on for a while, as everyone was so happy with their newfound skills. Then Rinna got Ryes to sit and she was given a plate heaped with her favorite foods. She sat between Maren and Monty, with Leon standing nearby. The rest were fed next and everyone dug in with sounds of delight. Garth and Sabin turned up soon thereafter and were given plates, as well and seated next to Darman and the elders. Other caravaners were now sitting around them on the grass, enjoying lunch. As they all ate in peace, a conversation started up of various Talents from the past, the different people had known. Ryes listened, enjoying the friendly banter as people talked around her; overall, these were the people she'd grown up around.

"I wish I'd known your mother," Rinna sighed out after several long minutes, looking at Ryes. "Rowan says you look just like her and she was supposed to have many Talents."

"She does look just like her mother," Maren asserted, having just swallowed the last of his stew.

"How would you know?" Tova questioned, having joined them, as everyone ate. She had her cousin, Victa, feeding and watching Thon, while she came over to see what her husband was plotting. Gurri and three of the other southern Talents were here, listening and looking for their chance; she could almost feel it in the air! "I heard she was killed when Ryes was a cub."

"We've met her spirit and spoken with her," he assured her, smiling as both Garth and Ryes were nodding in agreement.

"Her spirit?" Tova's voice sounding shocked. They were so calm in their truth, but it seemed an incredible tale. She looked like she didn't believe it.

"She watched over Garth while I fought Doran, then later she asked if we could remove her body from Matlowe and bury her with Ronn and the rest of my siblings," Ryes told her. "I thought Darman's group would've spread that story by now, since they made me repeat it several times in Winterhaven's Village Circle, for everyone." Kort chuckled and nodded agreement.

"She must've been very strong," Gurri stated, speaking up with scorn, doubting the tale. He sneered at her with hate in his eyes.

"She was supposed to have been," Sabin replied, his eyes narrowing as he noted this man's focus upon Ryes. They'd had enough of situations like that in the past, and he didn't want the headaches he figured might be coming. He noted Darman was ignoring Gurri, as if hoping he'd do something that might provoke Ryes. He wondered if this was his way of getting her help with the headaches Gurri was causing him? It was possible.

Gurri saw the way the men protected this one woman. She was the one, he was sure, who was said to be a strong Talent, but he didn't know how strong, yet. This not knowing was like a splinter in his finger, and he wouldn't be satisfied until he plucked it out. The surface thoughts of most of the non-caravaners were obscure, as if they knew how to fend off a Mind Voice Talent. The two strange other-men, who looked to protect the woman, were easier to read, but nothing of note passed in their surface thoughts. Suddenly, he was blocked out - cold. His eyes met the emerald green eyes of the woman's, and knew it came from her, and she appeared mad about his delving.

"That's a bit rude," she scolded, as she put her cup down, meeting Gurri's brown eyes. Garth looked puzzled, but didn't question it; he noted the tension in both Sabin and Maren. He still had so much to learn about using his newly hatched abilities!

"What's the point of having a Talent, if one doesn't use it?" Gurri returned, sounding a bit snappish after being blocked out so quickly. He hadn't even had time to retaliate against her move. And it felt like an impenetrable wall, which he couldn't force his way through, nor around! How?

"For a specific purpose, is one thing, like if a person were a real danger to everyone around you, but out of idle curiosity, it's nothing more than a lack of manners," she returned. Tova laughed lightly at this, giving the younger woman a nod of her head in understanding. She knew her mate was too aggressive with his Talent.

"You speak the truth, especially among friends," she readily agreed, "Gurri, let it go. This is a fight you can't possibly win," she urged, seeing a determined set in his eyes. She wanted to warn him of Ryes' power and abilities, but then realized she was tired of having to bow and scrape to get him out of the problems he caused. He had an ego that was rarely sated. She let it go with only her warning, as she'd done last night before bed. If he didn't know her well enough to listen, then nothing more she could say would dissuade him.

"I think we need to have a more direct discussion about this, which only those of us who can, will participate," he suggested, with narrowed eyes and a menacing grin. He didn't think this little miss could handle their united minds, no matter how strong her mother had been.

"That's a good idea," Sabin agreed, speaking up. He glanced to Garth as his friend gave him a nod of his head in concurrence. Garth wasn't ready to reveal his own Talents yet to all gathered here. He'd tell Darman and Rinna later, in a more private setting. And he wanted some practice – to get to know his Talents – before participating in a confrontation, which he saw was coming now.

"Shouldn't we do something to stop this?" Rinna asked Darman in a low, tight voice, deeply concerned this was happening at all, and in the middle of their own encampment. They all stood up. "Ryes is family!"

"No, it'll be all right," Dastin assured her, stepping forward to be a part of it. He patted her shoulder in comfort. "I'll help her out." Rinna appeared surprised, not expecting his assistance.

"They've needed to be put in their places for some time, even killing people in the past," Darman told her in a low voice. "Garth consented, so I'll have faith in Ryes too. And she can use the practice." This surprised Rinna anew; he was letting it happen on purpose!

"Practice?" she demanded in a low, hoarse whisper, shocked.

"Alien Talents," he reminded her in a low voice. He saw the understanding in her eyes, as her mouth was still a thin, disapproving line. Cassin heard their exchanged and wondered; did they mean the Snagospin?

The rest of the caravaners pulled back; most were deeply disturbed over this coming confrontation and were talking about it in low voices. Even the ones, who didn't know her, knew Ryes always addressed their leaders as her grandparents and had been the hero yesterday when saving Nalin and finding their other, new Talents. This contest didn't settle well with the caravaners. But, Monty did hear a few making bets on the outcome. He didn't hear many good things said about these southerners.

The children were ushered away, in case of any violence. Four more of the southern Talents appeared and joined Gurri's small group, making it eight in total now. Tova and Nottin made sure they were far from their friends; not wanting to be considered a part of the challenge, now standing near Cassin, who was their leader, Rinna and Darman. This seemed to irritate Gurri further, as he appeared to think they'd join him. He glared at them, his anger showing clearly. And he knew his uncle Cassin never joined him in any confrontation. He considered him weak.

"You're not helping Gurri?" Cassin quested in a low voice, curious. Before, they'd be a part of the team, looking forward to the inner battle.

"I know better than to ever go against them," Nottin told him, Tova and Rinna in response. Tova nodded her head in agreement, while interest played in Cassin's honey-colored eyes. His nephew caused him enough headaches with their leaders, so if Tova stayed out of it, he wanted to see what would happen now. He usually counted on her levelheadedness to keep a reign on Gurri, so this could go very bad – for everyone.

"Gurri wouldn't listen when I tried to warn him, and you'd think he'd see I'm staying away for a reason," she replied, with a sigh, having ignored his anger. She might have to deal with the repercussions of that later, if he survived.

"At least you tried," Rinna assured her, clasping her upper arm in comfort. Tova nodded her head, but didn't appear comforted. She didn't shift, nor pull away from her, which Rinna took as a good sign, as she dropped her hand.

The Talents, who were sitting, got up and sat down away from the non-Talent caravaners, in a wide circle on the grass. The warm afternoon sun slanted down through the trees, giving occasional bright flashes of light through the leaves, making it a deceptively nice day. On the Winterhaven side was Ryes, Maren, Dastin and Sabin. On the southerner's side were Gurri, Kiah, Eyad, Aminda, Luia, Lall, Galine and Hind, all of whom appeared highly confident. Nalin wanted to join in, but Darman held her back; wanting to protect her from whatever might end up being unleashed here.

"You need some training, first," Garth minded the child, smiling to help take the sting out of it. She nodded her head, like she understood it a little. Kort took her hand and lead her away – just in case. Mitt and Kyma appeared in the clearing, watching them get settled and starting to close their eyes.

"What's going on?" Mitt demanded of her brother.

"A contest of wills, among Talents," Darman told her, before he could. Her face displayed surprise, then Mitt rushed over to sit wedged between Maren and Ryes, quickly closing her eyes as she did, weaving her hands into both of theirs.

"Mitt!" Rinna called out, not wanting her hurt in this challenge. She'd recalled dire things about his particular band of Talents, from before.

"She'll be all right. She's been through quite a number of inner forays with Maren and Ryes in the last year, and yesterday Ryes found and awoke her second Talent. So, we can't exclude her," Garth assured Rinna. He sat back down to wait, lifting up his cup for a refill. A serving woman quickly complied. "Since this may be a while, let's all get more comfortable," he suggested. Kyma laughed at this, fetching a cup of his own as he sat down too. Darman and the others weren't as free about the matter, but did see it was pointless to worry about something that was fully out of their hands. Shams arrived to see the two sides formed up and had questions in his eyes.

"What?" he asked his grandfather directly.

"A contest of wills," he offered, gesturing for him to sit and wait it out with them. He shook his head, suddenly curious about it. He started to step over to join in when Rinna grabbed his arm, shaking her head, as he looked at her with protest in his eyes.

"You weren't here at the start, so let them finish. If they need help, then be ready to help," she suggested.

"They're underhanded and have been known to kill," he started, but she shook her head; her eyes were filled with this knowledge already. He saw the silent order in them and gave her a nod of acceptance. He knew better than to cross Rinna! He turned and sat down next to Garth, but his eyes were upon Ryes. Garth noted it and realized he was a little irritated by it, but let it go as he was more worried about his wife now.

Their minds were falling into the link which Ryes forged. Each side first formed its own commune, but no hands were held to help make a solid connection between the two groups, themselves. Ryes, Sabin, Maren and Dastin joined their hands, knowing this was going to be a true contest, then unexpectedly, Mitt dropped in.

"Mitt?" Maren demanded, not sure if he recognized her now, with this rush of power flowing from her presence, realizing she had Mind Voice, too.

"It's me, Maren," she assured him, delighted with surprising him. "You can't keep Ryes all to yourself, anymore," she teased.

"Tell that to Garth," he quipped back, amused.

"What's your new Talent, Mitt?" Sabin asked, having forgotten about it, after everything that happened last evening.

"I've added Mind Voice to my Inner Sight now," she informed him. She'd been practicing with it this morning with Raya. There was amusement from Dastin at seeing what she shared with them, with so much to learn ahead of her. She caught a wisp of that in the link and was curious.

"And what kind of Talents do you carry, Little Ryes, other than being a Booster, Healing and Mind Voice?" he pressed, needing to know with this contest before them all.

"I can Time Walk, have Empath and can stop things, which in the old days was called Manipulator. I'm also a Catalyst, which is why Kort came to get me, when Nalin needed help," she explained. He took this all in, thoughtful. He saw Gurri had no idea where his childish little game was going to land them. He could clearly feel the strength of her Booster Talent supporting them effortlessly, too. It made him giddy with the power at his call now, but remained focused upon the battle ahead.

"We're facing off eight of them?" Mitt asked, wondering if she understood this correctly.

"Yes, and they haven't a chance," Sabin assured her, "even without you in the mix, Mitt."

"Gurri's needed this for a long time now. You're correct, Ryes, he is rude and believes he's above everyone, even the Great Chief of the Caravaners. Do what you must, but don't kill him," Dastin advised. This last shocked her. She had no intension of killing anyone, nor allowing anyone to be killed!

"They'd take it that far? They would try to kill us?" Maren questioned, clearly sickened.

"Yes, they would and have in the past," he replied, confident now the people he was with would never allow it to happen. The way such an idea surprised them told him it'd never been a part of their plans. "He's even left several Talents witless with some kind of mind attack he's quite proud of," he assured them, "Their minds are at the level of young cubs for the rest of their lives."

"That's not going to happen here," Sabin stated, girding himself within; as ready as he could be.

"So, something like facing off Doran. It feels like they think they're ready for us," Ryes sent, now that she knew the stakes, she knew how to approach this situation. She knew she had the stable support of her team; even if Dastin was unknown, she still felt his strong support.

Gurri saw they were waiting for them to begin, as if it were a sunny outing for pleasure. He'd set up the field within resembling one of his old favorites; they were standing upon the center of the Bridge of Trust, which in truth spanned across a narrow straight between the island of Fettin and the mainland. It was a wide, sturdy bridge from ancient times, with the perpetual dark mist about them, which came from the soot generated by both large cities on each end of the bridge. Such a setting seemed to surprise the others, as they saw it now.

"A dream setting? Like when my mother showed me Hailys?" Ryes sent to her own team, alone, pausing. She'd already been blocking out their attempts at snooping, with Mitt watching that closely, learning it.

"Let's choose our own," Sabin urged, excited with the idea. Ryes thought for a moment. Not Matlowe, not Winterhaven, maybe Hailys? The others caught her thoughts and agreed with her last choice.

"Not as it is now, but as it was," Mitt pressed. Ryes agreed, delighted, and formed it up in her mind, placing it with the bustling crowds moving around them, as they stood on the walkway, next to the broad street. The sun was shining and the occasional shuttle flew past, down a track behind them. This shocked the southern Talents, as they had no reference of such a place in their lives, ever. Dastin was amazed too, but stayed steady, as he tried to study this memory of hers, while keeping a wary eye upon Gurri. It was very detailed! His own team seemed comfortable in this strange setting, as if they knew it well, too.

This impossible vision used for their side of the battle field further angered Gurri, which made it easier to open with a vicious strike, which he planned ahead to catch them off-guard. It was a thrust of their joined minds meant to disorientate the others. The projected image was a volley of great spears being hurtled at the other team.

Ryes fumbled for a moment, as if not sure if it was a physical or internal attack, flashing back to Doran's attacks from before when she had hurled real weapons at her, she'd pulled up Manipulator to block it, but they passed right through. Dastin took over holding up their side of the battleground for her, to give her freedom to deal with the spears, suddenly understanding why she would use Manipulator for defense. Pain was felt by everyone, as if they were physical weapons, cutting them all deeply, until Ryes realized how and deflected it, as if it were no more than pebbles being tossed against the door of her rover, sending its energy away from them all and letting it dissipate, so it wouldn't harm anyone. Maren extended his

Healing aura to ease the pain, surprised it worked. He decided to keep his Talent fully active in the link now.

It seemed Gurri paused for a few moments, waiting for her counterstroke. It never came. She sensed he was puzzled by this. They waited patiently. Ryes felt doing a counterattack now, would give them a way to judge their true strengths, and either change their tactics, or quit the fight at the start, so they waited. She needed to understand these people!

"They're not striking back?" Eyad stated, as puzzled as the rest in the link with him.

"Do they know how?" Kiah asked, wondering, too.

"That place they're standing in, I've never seen the like of it. What city is it? There are machines similar to the ones they use. Could this be where they come from?" Lall asked, curious.

"Don't let them distract you!" Gurri ordered, holding the meld in a tight rein. He noted ghostly crowds of people now walking past them. His battle arena was being subsumed by hers. Their sunlight was burning away the choking fog!

"I should've brought a deck of cards," Mitt teased, letting them clearly hear it and her humor. This goaded him to use their strike once more, using the same spears of pain. But this time it was rendered harmless immediately by Mitt, as she'd seen what Ryes had done before. This lit a deep anger in Gurri, Eyad and Hind, who were unused to humor being projected their way. This was a fight, not an entertainment!

"They're laughing at us?" Eyad stated incensed, his feelings of being insulted goading them again. He realized their battle arena was slowly being overtaken the other, but didn't distract Gurri by pointing it out. Still, oddly dressed people from various races were walking past him now, all in a great hurry, and paying them no heed. It was unnerving!

Dastin practically chortled noting the other team was seeing their arena around them now, as he slowly powered it from Ryes' Booster Talent and carefully shaped it to better clarity from her memories of ancient Hailys. These were true memories and he wanted to know more, but this was not the time. He'd love to travel to see it with her, now. Time Walker, indeed!

"Let's use this. It's a true physical attack, and if the illusion before confused her," Galine suggested as she visualized what she was planning for Gurri and her team. She got their approval and backing, so she opened up her Empath Talent fully and put out a strong luring call to all the varmints in the area, with glee.

Suddenly, they were being swarmed by small animals, who were viciously biting them. Ryes opened her eyes – startled to see a dozen squeakers attacking her and biting her arms and legs! She saw all of them under attack by dozens of different small animals. And even the caravaners nearby were being attacked. This angered her; for someone to casually use the animals and have no care for neither them, nor others nearby. Her charged emotions caused her to fumble with their inner link, but Sabin and Mitt helped her stay connected and took it over, managing it for her. Apologetic to her team and frustrated, she opened up her own Empath Talent and cleared the area around her team; giving the little ones the fear of fire and watching them scamper off. She then blocked the other Empath from reaching out to the animals again. She told Mitt her brother now had Empath, which surprised her, yet didn't. She mentally gave her a nod.

"Garth!" Mitt yelled, unhappy to just see him sitting – surprised by this unexpected attack upon everyone in the area, as they were all on their feet and jumping and swiping at the rabid animals. People were screaming in terror while being attacked. "Use your Talent to help out!" And she sent him what Ryes had done to clear their own immediate problem. She felt him fumbling, then saw through Ryes' eyes that he was closing his eyes to concentrate and open up his own Empath.

Garth fumbled with his Talent within his mind, but then saw he could reach out to the small ones – now directionless overall but still under the previous geas – and applied the thought of fire and flee to them. He realized Fire Shaper was active now, too, but didn't want to harm the animals, so struggled to quiet that Talent, as it thirsted to actually toast them all to ashes! The rest of the animals ran off with the fear in their eyes. Ryes closed her eyes, as Maren extended his Healing to again help the others to recover.

The caravaners, who'd been waiting for the outcome, backed away further from the contestants for their own safety. Shams looked to have expected it. The panic calmed down with the fast departure of the animals. Garth opened his eyes once more and now looked relieved.

"You have Talent, Garth?" Darman asked in a low voice, amazed now. He gave him a small nod of his head in response with a chagrinned smile upon his lips.

"Ryes found my Talents last night, too," he admitted. "I was going to tell you, when we got a quiet moment." He gave him a nod

of understanding in response and smiled. Somehow it seemed to fit
very well, and he could understand if it was new to him, he still
needed to get to know his Talent, first. He wondered how many now,
but held his peace until the outcome of this face-off was settled.
Kyma had heard and was surprised, but then gave him a nod of
understanding too.

Galine was fully frustrated! Ryes' Empath Talent had
overpowered her own – far too quickly. She wanted them all to suffer
and panic, but it seemed no more than a minor distraction! And she
opened her eyes and still remained in full contact with the others!
How had she done that? While the battleground background remained
constant throughout! This amazed and angered the rest, still needing
answers to this enigma named Ryes.

Gurri slashed at them, using a sword made of bright mental
and emotional energy. Ryes conjured a bright spear and shield to
use, recalling the shield from some of the old human books. And the
spear was her own, favored, weapon. It was far easier to rebuff his
sword using the shield, and using her spear to make him back up.
She started thrusting her spear at him, which now put him on the
defensive. The hatred in his eyes puzzled her, but she got him away
from them for now, feeling a moment's relief. This battle was far
unlike any other she'd been in, but was learning. The others on her
team were using their Talents and tapping hers and using them freely,
and were supporting her whole-heartedly.

"Here, use this," Aminda offered, having an idea of a tactic
they hadn't used in a long time. "It's a Healer's Talent reversed.
Instead of soothing pain, it forces pain upon their bodies. They'll soon
be rolling around on the ground and helpless against any further
attacks." He felt Gurri's delight and approval and together they
formed it and rained it down upon the others with the mental force of
a gale storm, with the support of their group.

A hail of bubbles filled with pain and anguish was rained down
upon the Winterhaven team and the nearby caravaners. They were
all engulfed in agony, feeling as if their bodies were being torn apart.
Mitt opened her eyes and saw they were all writhing with pain, but
stubbornly held on to each other's hands. And the other caravaners
were also in pain, some rolling on the ground. She saw the distress
on the faces of Garth, Rinna and the others. She closed her eyes as
that solicited another kind of pain within, which added to her own
agony.

Ryes and the rest saw it though her eyes as she concentrated,
trying to block the attack out, but blocking it didn't work. It slipped
by, as if coated with a fine oil. Then Maren figured it out and was
protecting them using both his own and her Healing Talents. He

extended the Healing to them all, giving them relief and the attack's power dissipated. Their team quickly recovered with the Healing auras they projected now fully active, as she left that in Maren's more than capable hands. Nottin, Tova and the other Healers present quickly soothed the rest in the area. Ryes thought the southerners had no idea what real pain and anguish truly felt like, as that attack faded away. It'd been effective for an instant, but they did find its key.

"I could've taken the point on this one," Sabin sent, making sure their opponents heard him, taunting them. "We don't even need you here, Ryes!"

"That's the truth," Maren agreed, while Dastin and Mitt added in their mirth, deliberately provoking them.

Gurri gathered Mind Voice strength from his followers, who had it, and formed up a huge net, with great approval from all. They cast it together at the others, almost gleeful about the attack! Dastin recognized it instantly and called up his own Talent fully using Ryes' Booster, to help fight its effects.

Ryes tried to use her shield to protect them from it, but it melted it and suddenly, the Winterhaven team was engulfed in the net. All their senses were distorted, even their physical ones! They instantly had no frames of reference and were now feeling sick from the vertigo they were experiencing. They tried to hang onto each other, but couldn't even find themselves! Maren tried to extend Healing to ease their symptoms, but he couldn't fully connect with his Talent, now. He couldn't find it, nor himself, in this chaos. Ryes was struggling to find the right Talent, or combination of Talents to overcome it and was failing. She felt lost and was on the verge of tears.

"Ignore it," Dastin stressed, trying to warn the others, seeing they were helpless in this moment. Then, his Talent fueled by her deep Booster Talent awoke fully and the city of memories was replaced by a city of the future, he was actually seeing now. Sabin's own Visionary Talent linked in with his bringing clarity to this future Vision. Instead of comforting the others, or bringing them anchorage, it only seemed to add to their confusion. But not Sabin, who knew this place, he then drew in a deep breath, calmed and opened his eyes.

He was looking at his lap at first, and the rest of the effects of the distorted reality faded from his mind and he was fully himself, once again. He looked over at Dastin, who then smiled and gave him a nod, but kept his eyes closed. He looked at Maren, who held his other hand and saw him finally find his own anchor. He too smiled at this, once again himself. He extended his Healing and removed the feeling of reeling sickness from everyone. Sabin closed his eyes, amused at what lay about them within, now. Ryes and Mitt then found their own centers, once again, and the last of the effects of the distorted reality were gone.

Now they stood in the middle of a huge city that was busy and filled will all kinds of people, standing next to the Phoenix fountain, with the bright Windrose Stone shining over their heads. There was a sheltering dome protecting the city, but still the sun shone brightly through it. As if the Windrose Stone were here in truth, they were all strengthened by its presence. It was the home they were hoping to establish someday. It was theirs!

The southern caravaners saw they had too quickly overcome their Mind Distortion attack. Their ability to open their eyes to see true reality had been totally unknown in other contests. This galled all of them and frustrated Gurri.

"The city's changed and grown," Kiah noted, somehow liking this one more, as it was now all around them, even if it didn't seem any less busy. She recognized the great firebird from the symbol worked into the wall around their encampment. Gurri practically growled, but was still determined to take them all down somehow.

"Come on, we can find a way to flatten them, yet," he insisted. Gurri and the rest cast a different-looking weapon, which they hurled at them in retaliation. It looked like a huge hammer that was supposed to flatten them, while they were supposed to be still under the effects of the distortion attack. Ryes extended her shield to protect them and the hammer suddenly burst when it contact it, shattering into wild energy, which fell back upon Gurri and his team. They screamed in agony for a few moments until they figured out how to dissipate it, themselves.

"Exactly, what is the reason for all this, to begin with?" Ryes sent clearly, as if shouting, so all could "hear" her, as they were recovering. "You haven't proved to me that you're anything more than a rude, spoiled bully. I shudder to think that people like you will have a hand in training Nalin. She deserves far better than this!"

"Nalin's a caravaner! What do you truly know of the Caravaner's Way?" Kiah demanded in return, feeling insulted. This made her angry. Who did this stranger think she was?

"What Tara taught me from the time I was a baby," Ryes replied, from the heart. "She called me her Wild Child because I loved the forest, more than anything else. I'd never dishonor her memory, nor the things she taught me, to stoop down to the level of such pettiness, as Gurri seems so proud to display. With her, Rinna,

Darman and Rowan, I've learned much of the world and know the difference between what's right, and what's wrong. Being blessed with a Talent only makes it more imperative to treat others in a fair manner. Those people who have Talents, and most especially those who don't, need my help and protection. It's my responsibility to serve when needed, not abuse others because I feel like it, and know I can."

The tension was almost visible in the southern link, then Kiah backing out of it suddenly, after hearing what Ryes said. She hadn't warned her team – just left. This shocked Gurri and the rest. Still, they adjusted for her dissertation, and didn't lose their resolve.

"Who are you?" Gurri sent, anger still coloring his mental voice, as if he were shouting at her now.

"Only myself," Ryes returned steadily, not letting any emotion color that simple statement of truth.

"You're nothing and deserve to die!" he retorted, furious.

"Others have tried," she taunted him, finally realizing he truly angered her. She couldn't let him do all this to any other Talents – especially Nalin - ever.

The loss of his teammate only goaded Gurri on, having to use his most powerful stroke. He gathered all the power of the others remaining on his side and used it as a burning blast to kill this annoying woman and any of the rest that he could reach, and be done with it. The Winterhaveners saw from their side, not a spear, nor hammer as before, but a huge ball of black energy being formed up, then it was sent streaking toward them. This one looked deadly, as if a dark star meant to engulf them. They all saw its intent was to outright kill everyone in the area, not just themselves. Ryes got an idea and calmed herself, then absorbed the energy of the blast fully by herself, transforming it with her Molecular Talent and finally making it part of her own pool. Sabin, Dastin and the rest highly approved, and it amused them to see her learning uses for her newest Talent.

"Now it's my turn," Ryes stated with ice in her mental voice. Gurri sneered disdainfully at her, she hadn't made any moves again they, yet. What could she truly do? She was only another weakling with some flashy tricks.

Ryes calmly reach over and pulled their own link apart and dissolved it, using Empath to sever the bonds. Then with Manipulator, she physically knocked them down flattening them, as if hit by a strong wind. Because Gurri and the rest meant to kill her and the other people, she reached within Gurri, seeking his core, as her friends were watching her back. He struggled against her, fighting her with everything he had left of his own Talent, trying for a lethal strike with every passing second. Sabin and Mitt helped deflect the force of the attacks, seeing what she was after. And they held their own side intact while she worked. It was like trying to walk normally thought a blizzard filled with imagined pain, but Ryes finally found the core and burned out his Talent forever. The cessation of his attacks was almost deafening.

"He would've died quickly if he'd tried to take on Doran, who used more physical attacks," Ryes commented to them all. She then turned and burned out the Talents of the others, who were still gathered on the grass, who'd helped with that last attack too, because they willingly supported him in his effort to kill them all. Ryes released her own link in a far gentler manner, and they each opened their eyes to see their opponents with hands to their heads, as if they had terrible headaches. Gurri was weeping openly, as if he were a young cub, once more, curled into a call on the ground.

"You do tend to do that to others," Sabin commented, smiling. His own headache wasn't too bad. Either he was getting used to the power of her inner communes, or was falling in tune more with her and Maren. He knew Mitt never suffered the headaches, even before she had her own Talents! Maren helped him and Dastin, by relieving their headaches quickly.

"I can't figure out how to prevent it," she sighed out, nodding her head. Garth stepped over and offered her and Mitt a hand up. She saw Kiah and Tova urgently speaking with Darman, Rinna and another caravaner leader, with Darman nodding his head in response and speaking to them both in a low voice. Rinna looked reproving, but held her peace for now. Shams followed Garth, but stayed back, seeing the Winterhaveners appeared all right. It was the southerners who seemed to have been hurt, which was a first. Their screaming in agony earlier had raised the hair on the back of his neck.

"That was kind of pointless," Maren commented. "Ryes didn't need us at all."

"Yes, she did need us, and it was educational," Dastin chuckled, as he rose and stepped over to his son's side, to hear what the women were saying. He fully agreed with Ryes, that these people should not have the responsibility of training new Talents, ever again. They were too interested in their own petty selves, which he thought was a pity. Removing their Talents was justice.

"I don't think any of the individuals in the whole group were a match for any one of us," Mitt stated in a low voice. "They didn't have any real power!"

     "No, they didn't and will never have it again," Sabin agreed. "I think you're right, Mitt, but never underestimate their tactics. They meant to kill Ryes and the rest of us outright, with that last attack." Garth's eyes took on a hard edge at this as he surveyed the way the other Talents were staggering to their feet. Almost as if they had been in a true, physical fight. They only lacked bruises.

     "Are you all right?" he asked his wife, taking her into his arms and holding her close. She smiled up at him, nodding her head.

     "Of course I am. It's too bad people like that have Talents, if all they want to do is harm others. I pulled the plug on their Talents forever, so to speak," Ryes replied. "I burned out Gurri's Talent, since he did mean to kill me, and the rest who stayed with him, because they supported him in doing it. I didn't want them doing that to anyone else, who annoyed him in the future."

     "At least you and Maren saved Nalin," he said. "If we hadn't been here, Nalin might not have lived," he told her, then released her as he saw Darman approaching them, with Rinna and the others following behind him.

     "Everyone is fine?" he questioned, smiling. He got nods and yeses from the Winterhaven group. He saw the caravaner Talents, who were in this contest, holding their heads in pain. "You do have that effect upon others, Ryes," he added in comment. Ryes blushed as she nodded her head in agreement.

     "I still can't help doing it," she admitted while those who knew her chuckled.

     "Is this what the other woman meant the other day?" Tova asked, wondering, "She had to filter it for us?" Ryes nodded her head in affirmation, then looked to Darman again.

     "I did take away their Talents. Gurri meant to kill with his Talent and the others openly supported him," she told them straight away. Darman was not surprised as he gave her a nod of approval. Tova's eyes held shock at hearing it, as did Kiah's.

     "It might've been the best solution, in truth," Darman finally voiced, meeting her eyes with a deep understanding and love for her in his own.

     "I'd almost say that they deserved the headaches," she replied, then blushed, "but I'm not inclined to cruelty. Do you want Maren, or I to relieve their headaches?" she offered.

     "I'll take care of them," Tova insisted, as Cassin gave her a nod of approval. She stepped over to her friends. Nottin joined her to help ease their pain; knowing their hearts' pain at losing their Talents would not be so easy to cure.

"Now I have an idea of what to do to the Snagospin Talents," Ryes commented, giving a nod of her head to the once-Talented. "We can band together as an anchor when combined, and I can burn out their Talents for all time." Sabin huffed a laugh and nodded, while Garth smiled in agreement.

"Now, to get you to the stars to take them out. I don't want them to come calling here to wreck more havoc upon Tayna, again," Darman stated, also nodding in agreement. The turn this conversation had taken had Cassin shocked. He'd never thought they'd be the ones to actually face off the murdering enemy of the far past. This was far more important than just showing off who was stronger!

"If I can help it, they'll never tear up Tayna, ever again," Ryes vowed, ideas were dancing in her green eyes, now. Her mind was also filled with the truth of the Vision they saw during the fight. Winterhaven, as she'd hoped in her heart, to evolve into in the future.

Home

"Ryes?" she heard a voice hail her as she'd just finished breakfast. She turned to see Captain Tees and what might be another ship's captain she hadn't been introduced to before, standing just inside their dining tent. She noted the longing look towards the service area, so gave them a nod as she stepped over.

"How can I help you?" she asked, smiling.

"We were hoping to get a ride home on your great flying machine," Tees requested, being direct. "You've shown me a greater slice of Tayna than I ever knew of before and with it taking over two weeks to walk home, we were hoping to make a trade for a ride." She gave him a nod, understanding weeks of walking, herself.

"The roads are not as safe as they used to be. If you're travelling with a caravan, the bandits stay far away, but otherwise can be a true problem," the second captain stated, his yellowish eyes meeting her own as he spoke. She saw his truth, giving him a nod too.

"First off, please help yourselves to some breakfast while I go see if Mitt's willing to take you out, and then see how many people you have and how much stuff," she invited, gesturing towards the nearby food.

"Ah, thank you," Tees stammered out, giving her a nod of his head. "We skipped breakfast as we were packing for the journey home with the dawn. There are eight of us in total and several bags of our belongings and trade goods," he added. She chuckled, then made sure they each got a good plate of food, then left them chatting with Ethan and Rowan. She found Mitt just finishing up her check on the chopper.

"Mitt, do you feel up to a bit of a run today?" she asked. Mitt's eyes lit up as she turned to face her, having just buttoned the compartment back up.

"Where're you going?" she asked, knowing Ryes was usually too busy to play tourist anymore. Ryes smiled, her eyes lighting up in humor.

"Captain Tees has requested us to take him out to his ship. There are eight of them and their things. Having only been there by Empath, I'd like to actually see what an ocean is like, too," she responded, going with her heart. Mitt gave her a nod.

"Let's see if we can fit them and their stuff all in. This baby can easily accommodate them, but is not to the capacity of the one we already sent home."

"It's good enough," Ryes replied, giving her a hug.

"I'd like to see the ocean, too!" Mitt agreed, as they released each other, laughing.

"I'll let Garth know, make sure the horde's looked after and start getting things rounded up." Mitt gave her a nod, leaving such details in her capable hands.

It took almost an hour to get everyone gathered and healed, as many were suffering from various maladies and injuries, both old and new. Maren gladly made sure everyone was in top health, before boarding the chopper. And Kyma showed up, wanting to see the ocean with his own eyes, too. So, it ended up a very full chopper with a pilot and eleven passengers, since Maren was not going to let Ryes go without him. Captain Tees had given Ryes a stunning necklace made of a polished silver-white metal, with orange-red gems, set into a large pendant depending from the chain of the same metal, in exchange for the ride. She was dazzled and amazed and would have turned it down except for Mitt's insistence, via Mind Voice, that she keep it, or it'd be insulting him.

Finally, after almost six of hours of flying at top speed, they arrived. Not wanting to panic the town's people any more than they already had with their flying over it, Mitt set the chopper down on the beach near the piers, well away from the obvious tide mark. Their passengers had been highly excited by the flight and all they saw when viewing the land from the air. Everyone piled out and Mitt and Kyma opened up the compartments and helped them gather back their supplies. Both captains stepped over and offered their palms to the Winterhaveners, having delighted smiles on their faces.

"It was an amazing trip to fly over the land so swiftly!" Captain Sunne declared, after the three had crossed his palm with their own. Mitt gave him a light laugh and a nod.

"I can't wait for the star ship shuttles to be finished," she bragged. "Now that will be even faster!" The men around her laughed, many shaking their heads, unable to imagine faster than today's journey. Kyma warmly clasped her shoulder.

"I can't wait, either," he assured her with a laugh, this being the first he'd heard of them.

"Visitors," Maren noted in a low voice, having seen several townspeople headed their way, some bearing swords and pikes in their hands.

"I will reassure them," Tees offered, as he stepped off in their direction. Ryes gave Maren a nod and rushed up to walk beside him, giving him a nod and smile as he noted her now with him.

"Better together," she assured him. Kyma and Maren joined them, too. She laughed lightly and had a big smile on her face as they approached the townsfolk.

"What is that?" a leader of the men demanded, appearing unsure. He recognized the captain at least and noted the other sailors were busy carrying bags towards the docks. Sailors from off the ships noted it too and rushed out to lend a hand, looking a little fearful of the machine.

"A flying machine. We were generously given a much faster ride home, today," Captain Tees told him, smiling reassurance. "We started out the morning at the Caravaner Gather place." It was only past sunrise here, now.

"I'm Ryes of House Li and am from Winterhaven. We wanted to make sure Captains Tees and Sunne made it back to their ships safely," she stated, still smiling. "We'll be leaving as soon as everything is secure on their ships." He gave her a nod and signaled his men to stand down, but none of them had appeared to brandish their arms aggressively.

"And I am Kyma, Chief of Hagg Craig Hold," he introduced himself. "I'm here to see the ocean and watch after these cubs," he offered with a nod. He got a nod in return and saw questions in their eyes.

"I am Raftin, Chief Elder of Yventia. May I take a closer look at this air machine of yours?" he asked, questions dancing in his eyes now. She grinned and nodded her head.

"First off," Maren interrupted, "does anyone need a Healer here today?" There was genuine surprise on many of the faces before them and quite a few smiles blossomed upon their lips at this question.

"Yes, if you can?" one woman stated, pushing her way through the crowd. He smiled and gave her a nod.

"Please bring anyone needing Healing here to the beach and I and my cousin will be happy to help," he offered. There were tears in her eyes as she gave him a bow, then turned and ran back into town, shouting as she went.

"He's the best Healer, I've ever met," Tees added, giving them a nod of understanding. Then he turned to Maren, "I do have a couple more crewmen who could use your help, too?"

"Bring them," Maren agreed with a nod and smile. Tees quickly headed off towards his own ship, waving to Sunne.

"Let's set up some shade and a place where you can work your Talent," Ryes suggested, eyeing the beach sand around them. She could form up a small pavilion from it and give them some comfort, too. She closed her eyes and shaped up a large, graceful pavilion using a concert of her Talents to make it look both pleasing and be sturdy enough to withstand time, as much as possible. She opened her eyes to see that the sunlight, as it ran through the glass columns, appeared as if they were made of rainbows. The roof was artfully peeked, darkened and provided plenty of shade, and appeared large enough to hold at least thirty people. The sides were filled with openings, which were gracefully arched to allow gentle breezes to flow through. She smiled, then noted the shock on the faces around her.

"All we need are some chairs," Maren laughed, as he draped an arm over her shoulders.

"I'll go find some," one of the townspeople volunteered, his eyes still filled with wonder. Kyma laughed and nodded as he hurried off. Maren and Kyma escorted her over to her new creation.

"You have to be careful about doing things like this in front of people we don't know," Kyma breathed out in a low voice. They were strangers here. But it looked wondrous! Now he knew how the wall around their encampment had come into being, but this seemed more than simple Earth Shaper!

"I will," she replied. "Only healing and helping for the rest of the day," Ryes promised, still feeling proud of what she just brought into being.

"Act exhausted, at least," Maren teased her with a laugh, not believing her for a moment. He saw she had formed up built-in benches along the inside walls – also made of the glass from the sand about them. He steered her over to one and urged her to sit.

"Here they come," Kyma warned, still smiling, but it was a tight smile. Maren looked over and saw what must be most of the town's inhabitants coming out to see the wonders here today. He smiled and nodded his head in agreement.

Ryes turned her head to the ocean. The ocean was breathtaking! The sounds of the waves, the warmth of the sun, and the motion of the water, all interlaced with a gentle breeze were calling to her, almost akin to the forest's call. She had to have a chance to explore it, too! They might not make it back to the gather site for a while...

"Torr, you wanted to be informed when the rover came into sight," Dodi said, speaking up over the intercom, piped directly to his office. "Well, it's in sight."

"I'll be right there," he replied, smiling to himself. About time, he thought! The big chopper had safely returned late in the morning and he worried about the rover. He knew they'd stayed together each night, for safety away from home, even if the chopper could've easily made it home much more quickly. He rushed down the corridor to the control room. Dodi was on watch right now and smiled her greeting, as he entered the room.

"There it is," she indicated one of the screens showing the view from one of the cameras on the Star Quest.

"Just barely in view," he commented with a smile. "You've got good eyes, and it's ours, all right." He stood for a few moments studying it, then shook his head. "There's sure a big difference when Ryes isn't driving! Took them almost four days coming back." Dodi laughed at this, nodding her head.

"She does drive very fast, but still seems careful," she agreed. Torr chuckled at this, nodding his head in agreement.

"That's the truth," he said, then stood back with a sigh.

"How's Tobin been doing? I haven't seen him with you, around here, for a while," she asked, looking up. There was an echo of pain in the depths of his eyes and she immediately regretted asking. "That's all right, if you don't want to talk about it," she assured him, then turned back to the screens before her.

"He's fine. Ardis has him with her, still out at the gather site. I think she was planning on flying back, instead of using one of the rovers," he explained, smiling tightly. It wasn't that he minded her question, it's that he was still having a hard time dealing with what

Ryes showed him of her brief meeting with Shadd. How could she believe that she could do all this to the both of them, then think she could just jump back into their lives, whenever she felt like it?

"So, he'll be back in a few days," she breathed in response. "You're so good with him, Torr. It's too bad Shadd couldn't stick it out with you. She's the one who's losing out."

"That she is," he agreed with a heavy sigh. "I'm going back to my office for now. If you need anything, let me know." He turned to leave when Dodi leaned back in her chair, to apologize for upsetting him so much, and the wheel beneath her gave, instantly spilling the chair onto the floor. He was immediately beside her, helping her back up while she blushed a dark gold.

"Are you all right?" he demanded, as she rubbed the back of her head. She'd been stunned for a few moments.

"Fine. I know better than to do that in these chairs. Sorry to worry you." She tried to gain her feet, then found herself lifted up in Torr's strong arms.

"Let's get Tennan to look at you, first," he offered with a smile. "Computer, please alert whoever's standby for the control room to assume duty," he requested, looking to its console.

"Affirmative," it responded.

"I can get myself there," she protested, but it seemed he wasn't listening. A few seconds later, Max came running into the room, looking panicked.

"What's the problem?" he asked panting, suddenly puzzled, as he saw Dodi in Torr's arms.

"Just a small mishap. I'm taking Dodi to the clinic, if you don't mind watching the shop for a little while?" he asked. Max saw the chair on the floor and gave him a nod of his head in understanding. "The rover is finally in view but looks still a half hour out," he informed him. "Just keep an eye on it."

"Not a problem," he replied, smiling as he righted the chair and sat down carefully upon it. He knew these chairs could be a problem, at times. Maybe he could get Phil and Minn to help design some new ones? He typed in a quick message, to remind himself to ask Minn about it later, when he returned. Torr and Dodi left the room.

"Honestly, it's not that bad," Dodi insisted, smiling as Torr carried her down the hallway.

"I want to be sure," he stated, looking down at her.

"I want to apologize if my questions earlier got you upset. I'm only worried about you and Tobin. I don't know if you noticed it, but you've practically stopped smiling, and I've missed your smiles," she explained, blushing as she did it. Torr looked down at her a moment, giving her a nod.

"I didn't mind the questions. I'm getting through this, I think. Ryes showed me something several days ago, which has me rethinking my whole relationship with Shadd," he replied, his heart still heavy. "I hadn't realized I've stopped smiling."

"Well, you have," Cliff teased as they stepped into the clinic reception area. "What can I do for the two of you?" he asked with a smile, noting the way he was carrying Dodi.

"Dodi fell, so I'd like Tennan to do a quick check to make sure she's all right," he stated, "If she's available."

"I'm sure she has time for her," he replied as he typed in a message for Tennan and made entries onto Dodi's record. "What happened?" he asked, needing to know for the report.

"Overbalanced one of the chairs in the control room and hit her head upon the floor," Torr told him.

"It was only a small accident. I'm sure I'm fine," she assured them.

"We'll let Tennan make sure, first. Go ahead to treatment room B," he directed. Torr gave him a nod, carried her there, then set her down upon the exam table. Tennan stepped into the room, shortly thereafter, smiling coolly.

"Just let me wash up and I'll check you over," she informed them, stepping over to the sink and washing her hands. Torr nodded his head, but Dodi looked puzzled. She smiled as she shrugged her shoulders. "Let's get a look at you." Tennan gently placed a hand atop her head, and one upon her shoulder, closing her eyes. After a few moments, she opened them with a smile.

"Is she all right?" Torr asked, needing to know.

"She is now," Tennan assured him, giving Dodi a nod of her head and a smile. "Now you two can run off and have some fun." She walked out, leaving them alone. Dodi blushed at this as Torr chuckled.

"We will," he assured her as she left them alone. "See, you did need the check," he told Dodi. He put his hands out to help her down from the table, when she slipped down to the floor. He caught her and they were both laughing as they ended up almost nose to nose. Suddenly, Dodi started kissing Torr, her eyes closed as her heart pounded. It surprised him for a moment, then found himself returning her kiss, with far more passion than he intended. When their lips finally parted, she smiled up into his eyes.

"Sorry, I guess I'm just a little klutzy, today," she apologized with a bigger smile alighting her eyes. "But that was a very nice kiss."

"Did you mean it?" he questioned, needing to know. His blood was still pounding in his veins. He hadn't felt this way in what seemed a very, long time.

"Not slipping, but the kiss, yes I meant it, Torr. I've wanted to see what it's like to kiss you, for a very long time," she admitted.

"Since it's almost dinner time, and the end of your watch, why don't we talk about this over dinner?" he suggested.

"That would be perfect," she agreed, still smiling; not believing her good fortune!

"Great, then let me make sure nothing else is happening around here, and then we'll see where this goes," he promised, smiling. She saw it was more like one of his old smiles, lighting up his eyes the way she first fell in love with him. Dodi gave him a nod of her head and they left the clinic area, with their arms around each other.

"WE'RE FINALLY HOME!" Mitt announced as she touched down upon the helipad outside of Winterhaven, proper. She saw there were smiles as all her passengers started unfastening their restraints. She started her shutdown systems' check as Garth opened the rear door and helped people out of the back. To Raby and Sayer, he handed each of them a cub, then took two of them as Ryes dropped down with their last infant in her arms. Maren smiled as he was right behind her, taking one of the cubs from Garth's arms.

"Now I know why you never go anywhere without a crowd! With so many little ones to carry, you need the extra arms," he teased his cousin, as she grinned and rolled her eyes skyward.

"Let me have her while you go say hello to someone who's missed you, I'm sure as much as you've missed her," she urged in response, seeing Dotti trotting toward them, a bright smile upon her face. Maren saw her too, and smiled happily, handing back Shaysa as he ran toward his wife, having missed her terribly. Garth chuckled at this display.

"Give us a few days and everything should be back to normal, around here," he promised his wife, happy now that they were home.

"I couldn't get over the way you behaved around Shams," she commented as they started walking slowly toward the main doors. "He could never equal you!" she assured him in a low voice. He grunted at this as he saw the warm smile in her eyes.

"I've never had a problem like that, before. I don't know why I kept acting like that," he admitted, now feeling embarrassed. She sighed, as she nodded her head, glad they were finally home.

She saw they now had the windows and doors up in most of the new apartments. And the doors looked fantastic with the intricate carvings on them. It appeared they were progressing with the construction, very fast! She bet herself that Kovin and Phil were trying to get it finished, before any more changes could be added! Next would be the school complex. They decided to centralize everything in one complex, for now. With the elementary classes in one building, the secondary classes in another and the adult education going on in the third. There was a nursery planned, so the smaller cubs could be cared for, while their mothers and fathers were attending, or teaching classes. She knew the cubs weren't looking forward to this, as then they'd have to attend class on a regular basis. Now, it was a task to merely get everyone rounded up at the appropriate time!

"With all the fun of that gather, I wonder what the Great Spring Gather's going to be like?" Minn questioned as he, Mitt and Sernn caught up to them.

"I'm betting noisier, with more headaches," Maren put in; the rest having caught up to him and Dotti. Ryes crinkled up her nose at this, betting he was correct.

"We'll just have to see; at least it's two months away; right before summer," she stated, as they reached the outer doors. "And we mostly know what to expect for next time. I think our archery booth did a brisk business, for a first time product. I wonder how well it'll do at the larger gather?"

Torr was there to meet them inside, smiling grandly. She saw the pain in his eyes was finally gone, and glad Mason and Shadd were taking the longer way home, on one of the rovers. He laughed as he heard her question.

"We're still hunters, we'll probably make a `killing,'" he teased, giving her a hug, then his cousin too. Garth laughed, happy to finally have the Torr they knew best, back.

"Now, if we could get enough materials to make plenty of radios, we'd even sell more off of those than anything else," Garth commented.

"Then we'll have to build a regular radio station," Dotti teased, smiling. Suddenly, Ryes and Garth both turned around to look at her, ideas dancing behind their eyes. "I was just kidding," she assured them, but Maren laughed at this.

"That doesn't mean it's not a great idea," he told her, hugging her to his side. "We'll just have to figure out which bandwidths the Snags will ignore."

Garth gave them both a nod, suddenly thoughtful about the matter. They felt their lesser use of on-world communications wouldn't be worth the interest of the Snagospin, but if they were to become "louder," then it could become a true concern. Just how much was enough, and when was it too much? There was only one way to find out, and they weren't ready to try it, yet.

"Where's Sabin and Ardis?" Torr questioned his cousin, wondering.

"Taking the slower way home on the rovers," Garth told him. "Don't worry, Tobin's just fine. And Ardis has decided to keep him as far away from Shadd, as she possibly can. She doesn't want him confused."

"Torr, I have to tell you, your son carries a Talent. I didn't want to accidently awaken it in him, so I don't know exactly which Talent, or Talents, he carries," Ryes told him. His eyes bulged in surprise, not sure what to think of such a thing. "I'm now going to have to check everyone in Winterhaven, to see if there're any more Talents." Garth nodded his head at this, seeing his cousin's shock.

"We'll start tomorrow, after we've all gotten some rest," he stated, realizing he only wanted to stretch out on the bed in their own room! In spite of Mitt doing most of the piloting, he was exhausted. The others around him chuckled to see the look on his face.

"Tomorrow will be soon enough for a lot of things," Maren asserted, glad to be home, too.

"It sure will be," Ryes agreed with a happy sigh, smiling as they walked back into Winterhaven, proper. "Right now, I've got cubs to bathe, change and feed." There was plenty of laughter in agreement.

They were home...

The End of Book Four

And a small treat... a peek at book 5 of the

Adventures of Ryes and Garth

Rescue!

Prelude
Two Hearts Under the Stars

The stars wheeled overhead as Ardis and Sabin sat near the Phoenix fountain. The lights reflecting through the water of the underground pool up thought the glass-like panels that surrounded the fountain on two of the eight sides, making it seem a more magical tonight for Ardis, as they sat on a bench near the fountain. She smiled as her eyes met Sabin's.

"I can't believe it! Two Talents?" she breathed out, still stunned. "You're an amazing man, my dear husband!" Sabin grinned in pride as he shifted closer to her side and wrapped an arm around her waist, pulling her closer to him.

"It surprised me, to be truthful," he admitted, embarrassed. "I'm still trying to wrap my mind around it." She nestled into the warmth of his embrace, then reached up and began a long, passionate kiss. It wasn't often when they could get a few moments of escape like they had tonight! Katas and the cubs were staying at Ryes and Garth's overnight.

"And both our sons having Talent, too! They're going to be a true handful when they're grown," Sabin admitted with a sigh, once their lips parted.

"I'm hoping all our cubs will be Talented," Ardis said, her eyes dancing by the moons' light. She realized she was clutching at his tunic top, almost as if she was afraid to let go of him now.

"Ardis, Love, you may not have Talent, but are extremely talented in your own way. Don't ever forget that! What is truly bothering you tonight?" he teased, knowing the answer and understanding why she'd insisted they come out here late tonight.

"You know," she breathed, trying to find her smile once more as she looked into his warm, wonderful eyes. "You left for a couple of weeks to return an evil man to his chief and then ended up gone for months! And when you did make it back home, you were barely able to do anything with that broken leg. I shudder to think what this trip into what our Sleepers call, `The Dark,' will do to you, or if you'll truly make it back home!" The women they'd rescued out of the frozen tombs of Doran's valley were still leaning and adjusting back to what living again actually meant. Their lives had actually started hundreds of years ago and the changes left many uncertain.

Sabin sighed as he held her tightly in his arms, trying to figure out a good way to reassure her. Then inspiration hit and he opened up to her from within with his Mind Voice Talent, as he still struggled to learn how.

"Let me show you, truly show you, a few things," he teased her, suddenly feeling she was unwilling to be this intimate with him. She saw he was puzzled by it, as she didn't understand it either. Finally, she relaxed and opened up to him, from within her heart, ready. He then showed her what both he and Dastin saw during the battle of the Talents with the southerners, the great city that Winterhaven is now destined to be; and he was now fully confident it would happen! They both marveled at the huge buildings, crowds of people, the shuttles riding on rails overhead and the bright light that came off the Windrose Stone, which wasn't mounted above them as yet. But it was their Phoenix fountain.

"There's a dome overhead?" Ardis noted, wondering why it was there. "Do our descendants become that unused to wonderful things like rain or snow?"

"I've no idea, but I've come to believe that we will both be very active in making sure Winterhaven evolves into a great city that might actually rival Hailys, in its own time. So while I might be out in `The Dark,' my heart will be here with you at home," he assured her. He let the memory go of this wondrous Vision. "I never knew I could have a shared Vision that way, either," he admitted a bit chagrinned; understanding Ryes and Maren's shared Visions better now. He felt her warm-hearted humor.

"With Ryes powering things up, I can imagine a great many things can happen. She's gotten stronger and has more Talents to call upon, but somehow I don't think she knows yet how to cover her own back. I don't fully trust our Sleepers, either. They used to plot to take over Winterhaven, but I believe that's died away now. Is there anything I can do to help her, since you and Garth aren't going to be here for a few days?"

"Why not learn how to tap into her Talents and learn how to use them, too? I know Bethy will grab onto her and pull up her Mind

Voice and other Talents, and Ryes lets her. She'd let you, too, you know," he asserted. He felt her humor again.

"So I can see how you're doing up there? That's an idea!" she returned, merrily. "She loves and trusts me and will let me do it, too! And I'll help watch after her."

"You two aren't going to let us get too far anymore," he replied, teasing and giving her an upwelling of his deep love for her.

"After all the trouble we had figuring out you guys were the ones for us, no way," she assured him. She returned her own deep love for him. Sabin then laughed as he opened his eyes, keeping his Talent up, and scooped her up in his arms.

"You are going to see exactly how much I love and care about you, my dear lady," he sent, as he stood up and headed back to their home. He'd be up in The Dark in just a few days now, and could watch the stars all he wanted to then.

www.ingramcontent.com/pod-product-compliance
Lightning Source LLC
Chambersburg PA
CBHW050858130726

47900CB00013B/340